"HOUSTON, THIS IS *PHOENIX*.
WE'VE GOT AN IN-FLIGHT EMERGENCY."

"*Phoenix*, we copy. What is your status?"

Cochran turned and watched Post tap out commands for the GPC to locate the problem. The engine status light was flashing red.

"Houston, we've shut down number one engine," Cochran said. "We're ready for an abort decision."

"*Phoenix*, you're in the gray zone. The decision is yours."

"Switching escape system to manual operation," Cochran said, pressing a toggle on one of the side panels. "We will throttle up and abort to orbit."

"Are you sure we can make it?" Post asked.

"This lady has new engines with an extra 50,000 pounds of thrust," Cochran said. Then he nodded to Post. "Take us to the red line!"

JOHN-ALLEN PRICE
THE PURSUIT OF THE PHOENIX

ZEBRA BOOKS
KENSINGTON PUBLISHING CORP.

ZEBRA BOOKS

are published by

Kensington Publishing Corp.
475 Park Avenue South
New York, NY 10016

First printing: April, 1990

Printed in the United States of America

This book is dedicated to the undying courage and indomitable spirit of the following men and women:

Virgil L. (Gus) Grissom
Edward H. White
Roger B. Chaffee
—The Crew of Apollo 1, January 27, 1967—

Vladimir M. Komarov
—The Pilot of Soyuz 1, April 24, 1967—

Georgi T. Dolrovolsky
Vladislav N. Volkov
Viktor I. Patsayev
—The Crew of Soyuz 11, June 30, 1971—

Francis Richard (Dick) Scobee
Michael J. Smith
Gregory B. Jarvis
Judith (J.R.) Resnik
Ellison S. Onizuka
Ronald E. McNair
Sharon Christa Corrigan McAuliffe
—The Crew of Mission 51L, the Challenger,
January 28, 1986—

Let us not remember them as martyrs or victims, but as voyagers and explorers. And we should know that those who have fallen are still voyaging.

Chapter One

The New York Times   MONDAY, FEBRUARY 8, 1991
Department: Domestic
Section: Section One
Headline: AMERICA'S NEWEST SHUTTLE SET FOR
ROLLOUT TOMORROW; FEW OFFICIALS
WILL BE PRESENT
Byline: Lance Pearlman   Special to
The New York Times.

DOWNEY, Calif., Feb. 8— The *Phoenix,* the newest addition to America's shuttle fleet, will be given its first official viewing tomorrow morning. The spaceplane will emerge from the final assembly building at Rockwell's Space Systems Division for its public dedication and christening. A crowd of NASA, military, and aerospace industry officials will gather for the ceremony, but no major politicians or senior administration officials will be present.

Both the Vice-President and NASA's chief administrator, Robert Engleberg, were scheduled to attend but had to cancel their appearances due to what a NASA spokesperson said were "conflicts in their schedules." This shunning is only the latest incident in what has become a long-running controversy over the future of the nation's space program.

SHUTTLE A TARGET FOR CRITICS
From the time the construction of a fifth space shuttle

7

was proposed there has been controversy over the wisdom of the decision. Five years ago, in the wake of the *Challenger* disaster, questions about whether or not a replacement shuttle should be built were swept aside by a national feeling that we had to get "back in the saddle" again. Since then, however, questions have again arisen and critics of the space shuttle program have become more vocal.

The Proxmire Foundation, a liberal watchdog group organized by the late senator, has targeted the new shuttle with three of its "Golden Fleece" awards. The organization Physicians For Social Responsibility has condemned the shuttle for the role it will play in the SDI program. A national association of astronomers has even called for the scrapping of the entire shuttle fleet, declaring manned space flights unmanageable, risky, and dangerous.

On the other end of the spectrum, the right-wing American Space Institute has criticized the *Phoenix* as obsolescent. This organization and similar groups complain that the billions wasted on it could have been better spent on a new spaceplane. Critics inside and outside of NASA point to the *Phoenix* as an example of how the agency has lost its bearings and vision. Instead of being bold, they charge, NASA has fallen back on the safe and conservative.

ASTRONAUTS EAGER FOR THE SHIP

Ironically, the building of the *Phoenix* has been on schedule and within costs. Its assembly has gone more smoothly than those of its earlier sisters, and the astronauts are eager to get ahold of the new ship. Many of them will be in attendance at tomorrow's ceremonies, including the flight crew assigned to take the shuttle on its first mission.

In the astronauts' view, criticisms of the space shuttle are largely unfounded. They point out that all the improvements to the *Phoenix* make it a virtually new

8

spaceplane. Its main engines and orbital maneuvering engines have been modified to increase power and reliability. Its more advanced computers allow for expanded flight operations, and an innovative shuttle escape system has been incorporated into the design. (See related story: Section Two)

NASA officials are optimistic that, after the *Phoenix* has been handed over to them, they will have it ready for its test flight by the middle of the year and declared operational by 1992. In spite of the controversy swirling around it, many people here at Downey await the shuttle's debut tomorrow with great anticipation.

-30-

"Ed, what the hell are you doing here? The crowd's outside."

The voice echoed through the cavernous hangar, its question heard clearly from one to the other. Normally it would have been drowned out by the clamor of workers but today the hangar was nearly empty. Except for the crew of a tow tractor and some security personnel, only one other figure was in the assembly hangar; he spun around when he heard his name called.

"Renewing a relationship," said Edward Cochran, facing his companion. He turned back to the *Phoenix* and ran his fingers across its hard, grey nosecap. "I haven't seen her for at least two weeks."

"Better not let Marcia catch you stroking her like that," advised the companion, who wore the same bright blue flight suit as Cochran. He moved around the tractor and its crew and was standing beside Cochran by the time he had finished his warning. "Even after twenty years and three kids I think she'd be jealous."

"No, she knows better than to get between me and an airplane. Marcia knows I lost my heart to them a long time ago. What's it like out there, Clay?"

"Our guests of honor have just arrived," said Clay Reynolds. "The science fiction writers—Hal Clement,

9

Fred Saberhagen, Nancy Kress, and Chip Delany."

"But no Vice-President, or our illustrious adminis-trator. No one wants to be identified with a billion-dollar mistake, except those who gave us our future. Even some of them want a new, expensive toy and not a proven workhorse. Who loves the lady? It seems like only those who'll fly her."

"I hate to spoil this one-sided admiration society, but if you don't join us in the grandstand, the higher-ups may decide to give your lady over to someone else for her first space flight."

"I hope not," said Cochran, "it would break her heart. Mine too. I'll see you later, honey. Right now it's your coming out party."

Cochran gave the shuttle's reinforced-carbon nosecap one final caress before turning to follow Reynolds. They left the hangar through one of its side doors, and for several minutes the *Phoenix* stood alone except for the tractor crew hitching a tow bar to its nose gear.

And then the hangar's main doors opened. Section by section they slid back from the hangar centerline, allowing the light of a bright, mid-morning sun to flood the interior. A smattering of applause drifted in from the waiting crowd, but mostly the spectators held off, as they had been instructed.

When the main doors finished opening, the tractor crew began towing the shuttle out. The moment its nose emerged from the hangar, an Air Force band struck up a slow, somber rendition of "America." Again, the crowd had been instructed to preserve the dignity of the occasion by remaining silent. This time, however, a few people in the astronaut section of the grandstand started singing, and by the third line of the song it had spread throughout the crowd. The brief rebellion ended as the music died, and the *Phoenix* completed its roll out, its nose positioned in front of a raised platform extending from the grandstand.

"Christ, did you see the way Dickerson was glaring at

10

you?" Reynolds asked in a low whisper. He nodded at the man who had taken the podium and was addressing the crowd. "He knows you're the one responsible for the impromptu chrous."

"I don't care if dickhead knows it or not," said Cochran, irritated, but in a low voice as well. "He can't kick me out of the flight crew, and she deserved something more than a funeral dirge. I remember when the earlier shuttles were rolled out they played the themes to 'Star Trek' or '2001.' Those were happy times, almost celebrations. This feels like a memorial service."

"In a way it is. Listen to what Hal Clement is saying. 'If it were not for tragedy, this event wouldn't be taking place.' We're still living under the shadow of *Challenger*. NASA in general, and this shuttle in particular, have a lot to overcome. As the new shuttle's first commander, you're taking on one hell of a responsibility."

"All my life I've taken responsibilities. This one could be the most important of my life. I accept it fully; it's exactly what I want."

Following Clement, the other writers took the podium and read speeches that described the *Phoenix* as the vehicle to push mankind's frontiers, to bring the world the future they had written about. When the last of them were finished, they were led onto the platform which extended from the grandstand. Both they and the officials presiding over the ceremonies arranged themselves around the nose of the shuttle for the television cameras in the crowd.

Since she was the only woman among the guests of honor, Nancy Kress had been chosen to christen the ship, and now she received that specially wrapped bottle of champagne. NASA officials instructed her to strike the shuttle on its nose module of thruster engines. This was one of the few surfaces on the spaceplane that could be hit without damaging any of its heat tiles.

"I christen thee *Phoenix*. May all who fly on you

11

return safely, and may all your voyages be triumphs," said Nancy Kress, holding the bottle in her right hand and raising it over her head.

She brought it down forcefully against the lower row of thruster nozzles, and it exploded on contact. The bottle had been left out in the open while the ceremonies were being prepared, and the morning sun had caused its contents to heat and expand. The explosion sounded like a rifle shot. Its force ripped open the layers of protective wrapping, allowing a spray of champagne and shards of glass to escape. The blast split open Nancy's hand with a razor-like cleanness; she would need nearly thirty stitches to close the wounds. She had turned her face away the instant she felt the bottle disintegrate in her hand, and her long, curling hair had protected her face and neck from the glass, but many of those standing around her were hit by the shards. Until some of the stunned officials rushed to their aid, all the guests could do was try ineffectively to stop their blood from dribbling over the shuttle's black and white tiles.

The TV cameras had recorded it all, and on the evening news what was shown was neither the speeches made in praise of the *Phoenix* nor the spaceplane's initial roll out. What was shown was the accident. The sensational footage set the tone of the coverage the shuttle would receive. Its unfortunate baptism had marked it. The ordeal had begun.

Time   JULY 11, 1991
Department: Domestic
Section: Nation
Headline: FATAL RETURN
             Shuttle Test Flight Marred by Accident on
             Landing.

Its first launch had gone off with remarkably little trouble, and even in orbit the *Phoenix* had had fewer problems than any of its sister ships. But as it descended

12

through the clear skies over Edwards Air Force Base, a tragedy awaited America's latest shuttle. As usual, on landing a convoy of vehicles rushed out to meet the expensive spaceplane. They would service it, provide it with electrical power, and remove the astronauts. On every other flight these procedures had gone smoothly. This time, however, about an hour after the shuttle had landed, something went fatally wrong.

Two ground technicians, Jeff Clancy and Reid Silverstein, were assigned to service the OMS (Orbital Maneuvering System) engines. The OMS engines are two 6,000-pound thrust rocket motors used to change the spaceplane's orbit while in flight, and are fueled by a mixture of monomethyl hydrazine and nitrogen tetroxide. Hydrazine in particular is a very dangerous chemical and protective clothing and breathing equipment is usually worn by those who work with it, but for some reason the two technicians were not wearing their cumbersome packs. Silverstein was standing on the shuttle's left wing and Clancy was working under its main engines when the accident occurred.

According to normal procedure, hoses were connected to the fueling ports at the base of the tail, and both the OMS and thruster tanks had been pressurized to remove any residual fuel. Apparently the hose to the hydrazine tanks either broke or detached from its coupling. The pressurized cells immediately vented a thick cloud of orange-yellow gas. Because he was so close to the fueling ports, Silverstein was overcome almost at once, while Clancy may never have heard the shouted warnings before he was felled by the same toxic vapor. Both died later at the Edwards base hospital due to severe respiratory failure. Five other workers who were also injured are expected to be released at the end of this week.

Fortunately the shuttle's flight crew, made up of space veterans Commander Edward Cochran, Pilot Clayton Reynolds, and Mission Specialist Rhea Seddon, were not anywhere near the site of the accident. They were at a post-mission press conference describing their otherwise successful flight. When news of the accident reached the conference, NASA officials understandably cut it short. NASA, Air Force, and National Transportation Safety Board teams will investigate the accident. Their preliminary reports are expected within two months.

The *Phoenix* tragedy has cast an additional pall over the manned space program. It comes on the heels of the cancellation, four weeks ago, of *Discovery*'s latest mission because of problems with its main engines. NASA administrator Robert Engleberg is confident that the upcoming launch of the *Atlantis*, with the European Spacelab on board, will put the program back on track. Officials say that in spite of the accident they will keep the *Phoenix* on schedule. Her first operational mission is set to go later this year, when she will launch a telecommunications satellite for Indonesia.

Credits: Written by Richard Duffy. Reported by Ted Hacker/Edwards Air Force Base and Anne T. Jackson/Houston.

Aviation Week   OCTOBER 24, 1991
and Space Technology
Department: Space Technology
Reporter: Jerry Linovitz
Headline: PAM FAILURE LEADS TO SATELLITE LOSS

HOUSTON, Texas—The first satellite to be launched from the *Phoenix* was destroyed, some forty-five minutes after it was deployed, when its Payload Assist Module exploded shortly after ignition.

The McDonnell Douglas Astronautics PAM-A had burned for only twenty-three seconds when it suffered an apparent burnthrough in its solid rocket motor. Both the PAM-A and Indonesia's Hughes-built, Palapa-C satellite were completely destroyed, their spectacular end recorded by the orbiter's long-range cameras. NASA spokesmen report that the debris from the accident will not interfere with other satellites or spaceships. Many fragments are in eccentric orbits and are expected to re-enter the atmosphere soon.

There is no preliminary evidence to suggest that the crew of the *Phoenix* did anything to contribute to the loss. They had properly maneuvered the orbiter into the correct attitude for spin-up and release. The satellite and its PAM were spinning at the right number of revolutions and deployment was picture perfect. NASA spokes-persons report that all telemetry on the accident will be studied; conclusions will be released in several weeks.

In spite of the loss, the orbiter crew will continue with their schedule of experiments, including some SDI-related operations for the Department of Defense. The *Phoenix* is still expected to land back at Cape Canaveral at 8:30 A.M. EST, on October 28. So far, the main consequence of the accident has been the Indonesian government's decision to accept an offer by mainland China to launch their next satellite on the *Long March 2*.

The Titusville Bee   FRIDAY, JANUARY 20, 1992
Headline: SHUTTLE COMMANDER DIES IN PLANE
                 CRASH
Byline: Michael Weeks

TITUSVILLE—Astronaut Thomas Scholl, 39, of Sea-brook, Texas was killed at 9 A.M. today when the World War II vintage plane he was flying crashed near Highway 95.

The county sheriff reports that Scholl had taken off about ten minutes earlier from the Space Center Executive Airport and was apparently engaged in low-altitude aerobatics when he crashed. Eyewitnesses say the plane was inverted when they heard a sharp crack and it nose dived into the ground.

It exploded on impact and started a grass fire which local rescue crews had to put out before they could get to the wreck. NASA personnel and a crash team from

15

Patrick Air Force Base arrived quickly and took control of the accident scene. They flew Scholl's body to the Kennedy Space Center instead of turning him over to the county medical examiner.

The plane, a World War II SNJ-type fighter was co-owned by Scholl and several other astronauts. It was normally based at Seabrook, which is near the Johnson Space Center, but arrived here a month ago when Scholl and one of its other owners were assigned to the crew of an upcoming shuttle flight. SNJ fighters are a familiar sight to Titusville residents, as many such planes attend the Valiant Air Command airshow which is held here every March.

Scholl was to have been the commander of the space shuttle *Phoenix*, which is due to blast-off on a joint French-American mission in early April. The co-owner of Scholl's fighter, Walter Post, is scheduled to be the shuttle's pilot. It is not known if today's tragedy will delay that mission, and NASA's public relations office does not know who will replace Scholl as the shuttle's commander.

-30-

Time   APRIL 3, 1992
Department: Domestic
Section: World
Headline: JINXED SHIP?
            Troubles Plague America's Newest Spaceplane
            on the Eve of Its Most Ambitious Mission Yet.

Whether it is political cartoons labelling it the "Edsel of the Space Age" or critics charging that it should be scrapped, the *Phoenix* finds itself the most controversial of the almost two dozen shuttle flights to have been launched since the *Challenger* disaster. Second-guessed from the moment of its inception, the newest of America's spaceplanes is now rumored to be a jinxed ship heading for disaster.

16

Controversy was raging long before the troubles began, but the new rumors are providing extra fuel. Proxmire Foundation chairman Everet Warner has termed the *Phoenix* the modern day Flying Dutchman, declaring further that "the only sensible thing to do is to ground it before it kills somebody else." The sensationalist tabloids have found what they consider a gold mine in shuttle-related stories, publishing lurid tales about the spacecraft being possessed by space demons, claims that priests have been brought in by NASA to perform exorcism rites, and speculation that the troubles are being caused by Soviet sabotage. NASA spokespersons have found themselves wasting almost as much time denying these outlandish reports as they have spent answering legitimate questions.

While to be sure many of these allegations are groundless, there has been a series of incidents which have given the appearance of serious problems with the three-billion-dollar spaceplane. The most recent incidents include: the destruction of an Indonesian satellite launched from the *Phoenix* (its replacement will be launched by the Chinese the same day this week as the *Phoenix* liftoff); the death of shuttle commander Thomas Scholl in a private plane crash on January 20 of this year, and the removal, one month ago, of mission specialist Lisa Peters from the flight crew when it was discovered she was pregnant.

The shuttle's troubles would have remained a domestic issue were it not for France's participation in the upcoming mission. Three of the seven astronauts in the crew are French, part of their country's own shuttle program called Hermes. With the *Hermes* I set to fly next year, the French National Space Agency wants to have experienced personnel man it and so is paying for most of this mission. This has elicited some congressional criticism, since Arianespace is NASA's chief rival. And in both Congress and the French parliament questions are being raised about the wisdom of using the *Phoenix*. It

17

has been argued that one of the older, more reliable shuttles should have been used on so important a mission.

The criticisms and rumors have in recent days obscured the historic significance of this week's flight. In the past foreign astronauts have tended to be guests on space missions, often with little more than ceremonial duties to perform. This time, the three French astronauts will be working in space to gain experience and to test various pieces of French-designed hardware, among them a manned maneuvering unit (MMU). The French team is led by Paul Vachet, 42, a former test pilot well known in his country for a book of prose and poetry he wrote on flying, called *Velocities*. George Pellerin, 35, an engineer who helped design the French MMU will further test it in space. Renée Simon, 28, has the distinction of being not only the first French woman in space but also one of the youngest astronauts in the history of space flight. She will learn the duties of a mission specialist and perform extravehicular (EVA) walks later.

The Americans in the *Phoenix*'s crew are led by shuttle commander Edward Alger Cochran, 46, a highly experienced astronaut, though he has been criticized within NASA as a maverick. He replaces the late Tom Scholl, and was commander of the first *Phoenix* spaceflight. Walter Post, 39, is the shuttle's pilot and, as a U.S. Navy Lieutenant Commander, is the only military officer in an otherwise civilian crew. Jack Ripley, 34, is a mission specialist experienced in using both the robot arm and the MMU. Julie Harrison, 30, is the most recent addition to the crew. She replaces Lisa Peters and will be the second black woman in space, after Nobel laureate Dr. Ruth Wendelle.

When the *Phoenix* lifts off this week, it is hoped that its diverse crew will be able to ignore the rumors and controversy and perform their historic mission with the cooperation and professionalism that will make both of their nations proud.

Credits: Written by Anne T. Jackson. Reported by Ted Hacker/Cape Canaveral, Mark Joels/Houston and Kerry Smith/Washington.

"Edward, the van is here," said Paul Vachet, when he entered the men's room in the crew preparation building. It was unoccupied except for one of the stalls. And the door to it opened as a loud gurgling filled the room. "Are you having some difficulty?"

"No, I'm just enjoying one last chance to use a real toilet for the next week," said Cochran, zipping up his flight suit as he emerged. "That may sound crude, but wait until you have to sit on the largest cuisinart man ever made."

"Do we go to the launch complex? It seems a little early for us to be leaving."

"It is early and we won't be going to the pad just yet. There's a small ritual we have to perform. We're going to the monument."

At the main entrance to the preparation building Cochran and Vachet found the other five members of their crew. Dressed in the same bright blue flight suits, they also wore the same bilingual mission patches over their right breast pockets. All that separated the French from the Americans were the flags on their upper arms and the CNES patches they wore in place of the usual NASA insignia.

"You ready to go, boss?" asked Walter Post.

"Sure thing, let's get our smiles ready for the cameras," Cochran answered, moving to the front of the blue-uniformed group and pausing for a moment before he nodded to the guards to open the doors.

The shuttle crew walked from the preparation building in a single file, escorted by other NASA personnel and tracked by a phalanx of still and video cameras. To fill in the long, early morning shadows many of the cameramen used spotlights or flash units. The barrage continued even after the crew had boarded the mobile home waiting for them, and they kept up the waving and smiling until it pulled away, taking them on the first leg of their voyage.

"This is Kennedy Launch Control to all stations, we are at T minus two hours, fifty minutes, and counting. We have begun filling the liquid hydrogen tank in the orbiter's external tank. Mission Control, Houston, do you copy?"

"This is Mission Control, we copy. Ray, this is Bill Corrigan. I just came on duty; is George Reiss still there?"

"Yes, he hasn't flown back to Houston yet. He wants to keep an eye on this crew right up to the time they're launched. He doesn't want another incident like that press conference."

"Good, you can have him. Maybe we can relax a little and get some real work done around this place."

"Cool it, he's here," said Ray Fernandez, when an out-of-place shadow walked past his console. He immediately changed subjects as the shadow stopped and turned toward him. "Houston, the filling of the liquid oxygen tank is proceeding normally. We began it exactly on schedule. This is Kennedy Launch Control, out."

"Who was that?" asked George Reiss, looming over the console. "It sounded like Corrigan."

"It was, we have our FIDO on duty. He wanted to know if you were staying here or flying back?"

"I'll stay here at least for today. I want to see this mission get off the pad without further incident. Where's the crew now? Have they reached the launch complex?"

"No, they're going to the monument first. They should be there by now."

"Cochran. I'll bet he's responsible for this," Reiss grumbled. "You keep me posted on it. If they're late to the pad I'll cite him for a schedule violation."

*　　*　　*

The American half of the crew grew somber the moment the van pulled away from the preparation building. For a time the French astronauts were still charged with the excitement of the photo encounter, especially when they saw cameras from their nation's TV networks. Soon, however, they too had grown silent for the ride down Cape Road past the launch facilities for the Titan, Delta, and other unmanned rockets, past the two massive complexes for the shuttle missions, until they were almost at the boundary between the Kennedy Space Center and the Canaveral National Seashore. Here, on a spit of land running into the Atlantic Ocean, stood the monument.

There were ten bronze statues in all, each larger than life-size. In front of them was a granite obelisk which bore a simple legend: "The Cost of The Final Frontier." The mobile home stopped in the small parking lot beside the memorial and the astronauts filed out to collect around the memorial's centerpiece. Three of the ten statues were sitting in sculptured seats familiar to anyone who had seen the interior of an Apollo capsule. Virgil Grissom was in the center seat, crewmates Edward White and Roger Chaffee were on either side of him. Behind the crew of *Apollo 1* stood part of *Challenger*'s last crew, its pilot and commander, with the rest strung out in an arc pointing to the sea.

"They seem so lonely out here," observed one of the French astronauts, Georges Pellerin. "Do many people visit this site?"

"Yes, when there isn't a launch on," said Post. "Only a mile or two down the road is a national park. NASA allows the public in on almost every day except a launch day."

"When I remember the fight that went on to get them here," said Cochran, wistfully. "And the fight over the statues themselves—we even had senators getting in on it. And all the kids wanted to do was honor those who had fallen with the money they had collected. At times I

21

wonder if it would've been better to have this memorial in front of the Huntsville offices. To let the damn bureaucrats know not only the cost of the final frontier, but of their own bungling and buck passing."

"I understand your sentiments," said Vachet. "But this is where they belong, my friend. Those who died to give us the future deserve to see it."

"We had religious groups condemning the size of these statues," Ripley bitterly recalled. "They said we were making false Gods out of our martyrs. Then there were the asshole politicians who didn't like this inscription. They said it criticized our space effort."

"But it merely states a fact. And states it very eloquently." Vachet backed up and took a long look at the front of the obelisk. "To rephrase a line from the greatest statesman of our century, 'never before has so much been advanced by the sacrifice of so few.' Whenever mankind tests new waters, pushes back the frontiers that confine him, tragedies will occur. We must remember at those times that we gain nothing by being timid. We must mourn our loss, and then continue. That is the essence of our kind."

"A Frenchman who quotes Churchill," Cochran noted. "You're very different from most of your countrymen."

"At times I am made to feel too different," said Vachet, turning away from the obelisk and moving toward the line of statues. "I'm certain I would not have been picked to command my nation's first spacecraft were it not for my public notoriety."

"Yeah, they were afraid of all the letters to the editor you'd be writing if you didn't get what you deserved," said Ripley.

"Gentlemen, I think it's time for us to leave," Cochran advised, glancing at his wristwatch. "We wouldn't want to be late and give Reiss an ulcer."

"A minute, just a minute, my friend," said Vachet. "I would like to appreciate what the artist has done here.

He's created a rather 'active' sculpture."

Vachet walked down the arc of statues, which were posed in increasingly dramatic stances. Those of the *Apollo 1* crew and the men standing behind them had only sedate, knowing smiles on their faces and barely a hand raised in gesture. The rest of the *Challenger* crew were more animated. Their faces turned upward instead of looking across the marshlands to the shuttle launch complexes, their expressions were almost joyous, and they waved, pointed to, and cheered an imaginary space launch. The last figure in the arc was Christa McAuliffe, her face turned back to her crewmates, her outstretched hand pointing along the flight path most of the shuttle missions would use to leave the cape.

"So, he used the schoolteacher to point our way to the future," Vachet observed, a faint smile, like those of the *Apollo 1* crew, on his own face. "Christa McAuliffe represents the rest of humanity, the average citizen. I admire what the artist did. He must be French."

"She was a Chinese-American and this was her first public sculpture," said Cochran. "Now it really is time to leave. Our jinxed ship awaits us. Let's take the lady home."

"This is Kennedy Launch Control, we are at T minus two hours and counting," reported Fernandez, glancing from the event clock in the launch center to a television monitor at the next console. "The astronauts have entered the white room in the crew access arm. They will be boarding the orbiter shortly."

"They finally got there, did they?" Reiss questioned, though he didn't need or want an answer. "Maybe now there won't be any more surprises. Cochran and the others treat that memorial as if it were some kind of damned shrine."

*   *   *

23

The crew access arm was attached to the left side of the *Phoenix*. The first to enter its tiny compartment, and the first to board the shuttle, were Cochran and Post. After the ingress-egress team helped them through the hatch on the middle deck level, they climbed to the flight deck and crawled into the two pilot seats. Once their restraint belts were fastened, they started bringing their spacecraft to life.

"Activating radio," said Cochran, reaching for the panels directly over his head. "And port side cockpit lighting. When you're done with your side, Walt, activate the CRTs. I'll check in with the control centers. Kennedy Launch Center, this is *Phoenix*. We are boarding the orbiter, do you copy?"

"This is Launch Control," Fernandez answered. "We copy. Radio check complete. Glad to have you with us, over."

"Nice of you to wait for us. *Phoenix*, out," Cochran turned a knob on his communications panel, switching to another frequency, this one putting him in touch with the Johnson Space Center, Houston. "Mission Control, this is *Phoenix*. Conducting radio check."

"Roger, *Phoenix*. This is FIDO," said Cochran. "Radio check complete. We'll be talking to you again, in one hour, thirty-five minutes to be exact. This is Mission Control, out."

"Ed, my communications panel is on and all three CRTs are up," said Post, pulling out of the flight data file the first of many launch procedure cue cards. "And it looks like we're getting the rest of our crew."

Paul Vachet and Julie Harrison climbed through the floor hatch next and occupied the remaining two seats in the cockpit. The other astronauts remained on the middle deck, where they stowed the crew's personal storage containers before taking their seats.

"What shall we do, Ed?" asked Vachet, as he finished locking his restraint belt. "How far are we along in the launch?"

24

"I'm ready to do the GPC status check and you'll test the intercom with Walt," said Cochran. "In ten minutes we'll do the abort systems check and get the advisory on the abort fields. By then we'll be on the fourth or fifth of these."

Cochran held up a velcro-backed cue card and attached it to the board between the cockpit's forward windows. There were more than a dozen such cards in the flight data file, located between the pilot seats. The cards were essential for enabling Cochran and Post to do the complex launch procedures and prepare the general purpose computer for flight.

"Launch Control to *Phoenix*. We're at T minus one hour, ten minutes, and counting. Your side hatch is being closed," said Fernandez. "Pad Leader, tell all pad teams to begin their final checkouts."

Ripley helped the ingress-egress team close and lock the side hatch, then took his seat with Simon and Pellerin. With the sealing the noise level on the middle deck and flight deck fell dramatically. The hissing of propellant boil-off from the external tank and the countless other noises that made the *Phoenix* an almost living creature were gone. Once the sealing was complete the shuttle's pressurization system stabilized crew compartment air pressure at normal atmospheric levels.

"Launch Control, pressure leak check complete," said Cochran. "Opening vent switches."

"Roger, *Phoenix*. We are at T minus one hour and counting. Feed in IMU preflight alignment."

"I'll do this, punching up launch pad coordinates on CRT Two," Post responded, using the GPC keyboard on his side of the center pedestal to enter the numbers that appeared on the display screen in front of him.

"Payload status check completed," said Vachet, glancing over at the panel where Julie was working. "Everything in the cargo bay is nominal. Ed, what do we do next?"

"After the Inertial Measurement Unit has been

stabilized, we'll be activating the nitrogen boilers," said Cochran. "Then we'll check the APUs, the environmental systems, and do the avionics software transfer. You finished, Walt? Launch Control, this is *Phoenix*. IMU pre-flight completed. We show latitude two-eight degrees, three-six minutes, three-zero point three-two seconds north, and longitude eight-zero degrees, three-six minutes, one-four point eight-eight seconds west. Over."

"Roger, *Phoenix*. Your IMU alignment is correct. We're at T minus fifty-five minutes. Commence boiler activation."

"Roger, Launch Control. Boilers being activated. The switches are on your side, Walt. Panel R-Two."

The nitrogen boilers were part of the first major system to be activated on the *Phoenix*. They were essential for controlling the crew compartment's atmosphere and supplying fuel to the auxiliary power units. Once the nitrogen supply system was operating, the environmental systems and APUs could be tested.

"Launch Control to *Phoenix*, we're at T minus thirty-two minutes and counting," said Fernandez. "Prepare GPC and BFS for primary avionics software transfer."

"Roger, Launch Control," responded Cochran's voice on the console speakers. "Switching GPC to mode five, and the standby light is on. Backup flight system ready for transfer."

"Looks like the egress team is ready to leave," said Reiss, studying the console's television monitor. On it he could see the interior of the crew access arm compartment and several people waving to the camera.

"Yes, it's almost their time," said Fernandez, pressing the transmit switch for his headset. "T minus thirty minutes and counting. The egress team has secured the white room. Launch Control to Pad Leader, begin evacuation of teams to their fall-back areas.

26

Commence switching launch pad systems from manual to automatic control."

"Launch Control, this is *Phoenix*. We're beginning OMS pressurization and activating compartment escape system, over."

"Roger, *Phoenix*. Advise when complete. Launch Control to Coast Guard, what's the status of the surface and airspace quarantine?"

"Port Canaveral Station reports both surface and airspace quarantines in full effect," answered the Coast Guard officer in the launch center. "They've finished towing in the protest ship and the FAA reports no civilian aircraft in the area. Military traffic is under full restriction."

"Damned religious fanatics," said Reiss. "Protesting 'Star Wars' when there aren't even any SDI experiments on this flight."

"Maybe after the launch we can tow them back out and let the Air Force drop a Midgetman missile on them," said Fernandez.

"Launch Control, this is *Phoenix*. OMS pressurization looks nominal. Compartment escape system, armed. Rocket motors, armed. Explosive cutting cords, armed. Drogue parachute mortars, armed. Escape system inhibitors, on."

"Roger, *Phoenix*. We're at T minus twenty-five minutes and counting. Conduct final voice check with Mission Control and prepare for the scheduled hold at the twenty minute-mark."

Cochran and Post reset their communication panels and talked with Mission Control in Houston. In addition to the test, they received updated weather reports from Corrigan on the abort fields. By the time he was finished, the countdown clock had stopped at twenty minutes.

This was the first of two preprogrammed, ten-minute holds in the countdown cycle. It allowed anyone who was delayed for any reason to get back on schedule. Mostly it was used by the launch pad teams or the global

27

tracking stations. As for the shuttle crew, their activity suddenly halted.

"Ed, how much longer?" asked Vachet, after his conversation with Julie Harrison had trailed off.

"It shouldn't be too much," said Cochran. "We've already reached ten minutes. This is one of the two most frustrating points in any launch. The other is the hold at the nine minute mark. Everything is ready and anything can go wrong."

"Are you eager to return?"

"What? After the bullshit we've had to put up with? The officials, the damn reporters. You bet I can't wait to return."

"Watch it, boss," Post warned, pointing to his headset microphone. "The channels are still open. And remember Reiss?"

"Yes, I know. He's still in the Launch Center," said Cochran. "Well, he's going to have to come out here with a can opener to get me out of this lady."

"What is it like when you go into space?" Vachet requested, hoping to change the subject.

"When you get into the upper stratosphere, you can see the curvature of the earth." Cochran's sharp tone quickly softened, and a smile grew on his face. "You see an endless sky . . . which becomes an endless night. And then the atmosphere's thin blue veil is below you, and you're in space."

"I thought I was the only poet here. Thank you, Edward."

"Launch Control to *Phoenix*, we're at T minus twenty minutes and we've resumed the count," Fernandez finally reported, breaking the calm that had hung over the cockpit. "Check and load OPS-One flight plan into GPC."

"Roger, Launch Control. Commencing flight plan load," said Cochran, reaching down for his GPC

28

keyboard. "Time to go back to work, boys and girls. Things are going to get a little fast around here."

Cochran and Post checked the shuttle's launch trajectory on their CRT screens before loading the flight plan software into the general purpose computer. They next fed the same plans to the backup flight system, ensuring they would have a ready reserve should the GPC fail.

Pressurization of the helium isolation system followed. This allowed the main engine systems, orbital maneuvering systems, and reaction control thrusters to keep their fuels separated until they were used. Not only did helium isolation allow the *Phoenix* to fly, it would prevent her from blowing up.

The range safety packages for the external tank and solid rocket boosters were armed. The abort systems were tested again and the final piece of emergency equipment to be activated was the armored rescue vehicle. It clanked out to a bunker a few hundred yards from the launch pad.

"Launch Control to all stations, we're at T minus nine minutes, forty-five seconds, and counting. We have decided not to conduct the scheduled hold at the nine minute mark. No one is reporting any delays, and you are all running on time and without serious problems. *Phoenix*, do you wish to conduct the scheduled ten-minute hold?"

"You should know the answer to that," Cochran replied, smiling slightly. "Let's get this lady into orbit, Ray."

"Roger, *Phoenix*. Prepare to start event timer in twenty seconds. Nineteen. Eighteen . . ."

Cochran easily programmed the digital clock on the cockpit's front instrument panel. He counted off the final seconds with Fernandez, then hit the clock's starting button.

"T minus nine minutes and counting and the event timer is on. The automatic ground launch sequencer is running; the orbiter is go for lift off. This is Launch Control to all stations, commence final countdown phase. Configure for lift-off!"

Moments later the radar stations in the Global Tracking Network began reporting to Fernandez, and synchronized with the ground launch sequencer. Through this, they were tied to the event timer in the shuttle's cockpit. Bit by bit, the *Phoenix* was taking control of its own launch.

"T minus seven minutes and counting. The crew access arm is being retracted. Launch Control to Pad Leader, evacuate remaining teams to fall-back areas. Switch crew access arm from manual to remote operation. We are now monitoring LOX and LH-Two fuel loading. Switch fueling sensors from manual to automatic."

The last of the pad teams boarded their vehicles and drove from the launch pad's parking lots. Their fall-back areas were beyond the perimeter road which surrounded it. Inside the perimeter the emergency crews remained, seated in either reinforced underground bunkers or the armored rescue vehicle. In a few minutes the only people that would be left on the pad itself would be the seven astronauts.

"T minus six minutes and counting. Initiate APU pre-start procedure, *Phoenix*."

Having activated their systems for more than an hour, Cochran and Post ran through the last checks for the three auxiliary power units. When Post opened the fuel lines to the first APU, Cochran, with a great amount of relief, watched the pressure indicator climb into the green. A minute later the other two had started up. The *Phoenix* now had all the electricity it needed.

"T minus four minutes, thirty seconds, and counting. The orbiter has switched to internal power. *Phoenix*, we are shutting down all external sources."

"Roger, Launch Control. All power levels are nominal," said Cochran.

The shuttle's only remaining link to any outside control was the automatic ground launch sequencer. It would run the countdown until the last forty seconds, when the GPC would take over.

"T minus four minutes and counting. *Phoenix*, all flight crew personnel are to lock down their helmet visors."

"Roger, Launch Control. Moving visors into place."

Cochran pulled down his tinted visor before he had finished answering and sealed it over his face. Post and the rest of the crew on the flight deck and middle deck did the same, then checked the emergency packs strapped to their seat backs.

"T minus three minutes, forty-five seconds, and counting. Launch Control to *Phoenix*, test orbiter aero surfaces and configure them for lift-off."

"It's about time we got to use these," said Cochran, grabbing hold of the diminutive control stick mounted on its own pedestal, and placing his feet on the rudder pedals.

Both he and Post worked the shuttle's flight controls in turn. Because they were unable to see the rudder, ailerons, and elevons themselves, they had to rely on the cockpit's aero surface indicators to tell them everything was working. Once finished, the surfaces were locked in their lift-off positions.

"T minus three minutes and counting. Launch Control to *Phoenix*, gimbal main engines to lift-off configuration."

"Roger, Launch Control. Gimbaling main engines."

Cochran tapped out commands on his pedestal keyboard and the GPC swivelled the trio of exhaust nozzles at the tail of the spaceplane. Each was moved a few degrees, enough to make maximum use of the thrust the main engines would develop.

"T minus two minutes, forty seconds, and counting. The liquid oxygen fueling vents have been closed. The LOX tank is full and we are commencing pressurization."

With the oxygen vents closed, the brief plumes of white mist curling from the top of the external tank ceased. One hundred and forty thousand gallons of liquid oxygen had been loaded into the upper portion of the tank.

"T minus two minutes and counting. The liquid oxygen tank is at flight pressure. The liquid hydrogen fueling vents have been closed and the LH-Two tank is being pressurized. We are retracting the fueling arm."

Three hundred and eighty thousand gallons of liquid hydrogen were now sitting in the lower section of the external tank. At the top of the tank, the fueling arm cap had been raised and was slowly retracting. In a minute it would be locked to the side of the service tower.

"T minus one minute, forty-five seconds, and counting. Launch Control to *Phoenix,* check inhibitor status."

"Roger, checking system inhibitors," said Post, grabbing one of the last cue cards from the file and reading through it. "Escape system inhibitors, range safety inhibitors, main engine start inhibitors, and OMS inhibitors are off. Escape system on automatic. Check list completed."

"Launch Control, this is *Phoenix.* GPC verifies readiness of main engines," said Cochran, reading his display screen.

"We copy. T minus one minute and counting. The firing system for the sound suppression water system has been armed."

Nearly eight hundred tons of liquid oxygen and hydrogen stood flight-ready in the cavernous external tank. The conduits from the tank to the shuttle were opened and through them flowed the super-cooled propellants to the main engines, where they would be heated and mixed when the ignition sequence was started.

"T minus fifty seconds and counting. The hydrogen ingiters have been armed."

The igniters were located under the spaceplane's main

exhaust nozzles, where any hydrogen leaks from the engines would eventually appear. This would set off the leaks to prevent a build-up and possible explosion on lift-off.

"T minus forty seconds and counting. Launch command has been switched to orbiter GPC. *Phoenix*, stand by for computer check for auto sequence start."

The automatic ground launch sequencer was no longer running the countdown. The system was reduced to monitoring the final events as the shuttle's computers took over and were tested by the Launch Control staff to see if they could run them.

"T minus thirty seconds and counting. We are go for auto sequence start. *Phoenix*, defeat manual engine start system."

"Manual engine start system, off," said Cochran, before he turned to Post. "Well, this is it. We're not only getting out of here on the first try, we're doing it ahead of schedule."

"T minus twenty-five seconds and counting. The solid rocket booster APUs have been started."

The shuttle, its external tank, and SRBs were all flight ready and under GPC command. Unless Cochran or Post stopped it, the computer system would finish the countdown. All Launch Control could do was ready the pad for lift-off.

"T minus twenty seconds and counting. The hydrogen igniters have been fired."

A curtain of sparks formed instantly around the spaceplane's exhaust nozzles. The occasional puff of flame indicated that the igniters were working as planned, burning off hydrogen gas as it leaked from the engines.

"T minus fifteen seconds and counting and the sound suppression water system has been activated."

Thousands of gallons of water flooded the blast deflectors under the nozzles and the lower levels of the launch platform. This dampened the acoustic shockwaves which formed on lift-off; these were otherwise capable of damaging not only the platform, but the shuttle's essential layer of heat tiles as well.

"T minus ten seconds. The orbiter is go for main engine start."

A surge of commands flowed from the GPC to the three main engines. Faster and more precisely than any human could manage it, each had its fuel and oxidizer pumps brought up to speed, its valves opened, and its main injector primed to deliver the right oxygen/hydrogen mix to the combustion chamber. They were programmed to start in sequence rather than simultaneously, and two seconds after the commands were given, the first engine ignited. The next one followed a tenth of a second later, the third a tenth of a second after that.

For each engine the initial spurt of flame was hydrogen rich and burned bright yellow. Then it became an iridescent blue when the proper mixture hit the combustion chamber. As thrust built up, the exhaust nozzles vibrated from the unleashed power and the shuttle lurched forward by three feet, compressing the struts which held it to the external tank. In the crew compartment, the sound of the engines was a distant, muffled roar.

"T minus six seconds and we have main engine start. Four seconds, three seconds . . ."

"Main engines at ninety percent thrust," said Post, watching the columns of light climb the propulsion system pressure scales. "Main engine status lights are green. SRB APUs are charging the igniters. Loading program One-Zero-Two."

At zero, the solid rocket boosters fired their igniters, generating temperatures of more than five thousand degrees. Exactly two point six seconds later the cakes of solid fuel were burning uncontrollably. The cables attached to the shuttle's umbilical panels were torn from their sockets, and incinerated as the spaceplane thundered off the pad. No one seemed to notice that the launch wasn't completed until three seconds after the countdown had ended.

"And lift-off! Lift-off of Mission Eighty-One L. The orbiter has cleared the tower."

The *Phoenix* rose on twin pillars of white-hot fire, supported by the faint blue exhaust jets of the main engines. Because of the time it had to spend on the pad, it ascended through billowing clouds of smoke and steam created by the vaporizing of water released by the sound suppression system. The moment it cleared the service tower, before Fernandez had finished his lift-off announcement, command of the flight had passed to Mission Control, Houston, and the Flight Information Dynamics Officer.

"*Phoenix*, this is FIDO. Are you commencing roll maneuver?" asked Bill Corrigan.

"Roger, Mission Control. GPC is commencing roll maneuver," said Cochran, after he switched frequencies on his com panel.

Some ten seconds after lift-off the GPC began to swivel the main engine and booster exhaust nozzles. It only had to move them a few degrees to make the shuttle, its huge external tank, and the solid rocket boosters roll slowly to the right. In twenty seconds the shuttle had rotated into a "heads-down" attitude. For the rest of the ascent it would climb on its back.

"Mission Control, this is *Phoenix*. Roll maneuver completed. APUs operating at one hundred and seven percent rpm."

"We copy. *Phoenix*, you are one point one nautical miles in altitude, one point seven nautical miles downrange," Corrigan answered.

During its ascent, all distances covered by the space-plane would be recorded in nautical miles, one of the few carry-overs from an earlier age of voyaging.

"*Phoenix*, this is Mission Control. Your airspeed is Mach One, throttle down to sixty-five percent power."

As it crossed the sound barrier, a build-up in atmospheric pressure around the shuttle, its tank, and boosters began. To prevent it from increasing to dangerous levels, the main engines were powered down by one-third for just under thirty seconds. At thirteen miles in altitude, the air was thin enough for the *Phoenix* to return to full thrust. At eighteen miles, the solid rocket boosters had consumed their eleven hundred tons of fuel.

"Mission Control, this is *Phoenix*. We have SRB burnout," said Cochran. "We're arming the separation motors."

"We copy, you are go for SRB separation."

A brief, luminescent glow filled the cockpit as Cochran hit the firing button for the separation rockets. The glow lasted until the booster casings broke their attachments to the external tank and pulled away. They decelerated immediately, but would not start falling for three minutes. By then the shuttle would be seventy miles up and skirting the edge of space.

"Mission Control to *Phoenix*, you're negative for RTLS abort."

"Roger, Houston. We're negative for return to launch site abort," Cochran affirmed. "Changing GPC abort programs."

"Better hurry up, boss. We might just need them," said Post, his voice suddenly quiet. "We've got trouble. Big trouble. Number one engine is losing power."

The left-hand column of light on the propulsion system pressure scale was below the level of the other two. Post quickly tapped out commands for the GPC to locate the problem, but by the time he had finished, the column had dropped to thirty percent and the engine status light was flashing red.

"To hell with finding the problem. Our flight might be over right here and now," said Cochran. "Houston, this is *Phoenix*. We've got an in-flight emergency. We're losing number one engine and we're changing to

36

abort mode."

"We copy. This is Mission Control to all stations, the orbiter is in abort mode," said Corrigan, an edge of nervousness apparent in his voice. "Rota Naval Air Station, prepare airstrip for use. Kennedy Center, alert all Atlantic rescue forces. *Phoenix*, what is your status?"

"We've shut down number one engine and our acceleration is slowing. We're ready for an abort decision."

"*Phoenix*, you're in the 'grey' zone. You cannot return to launch site. We cannot confirm you'll make it to Rota, or to orbit. We can only confirm an escape system abort. Those are your contingencies, the decision is yours."

The shuttle was at the most critical moment in its ascent. Houston could not determine if it had the altitude to glide halfway across the Atlantic to Rota, Spain, or the thrust to make it into space. The only sure way to end the emergency was to use the escape system. But this would mean destroying the *Phoenix*, by blasting the crew compartment out of its fuselage. Cochran had only a fleeting moment to weigh these options and choose the fate of his ship and crew.

"Switching escape system to manual operation," he said, pressing a toggle on one of his side panels. "Mission Control, we will throttle up and abort to orbit."

"Are you sure we can make it?" Post asked. "The way Corrigan was talking, we don't have the parameters."

"I say we do. Those parameters are based on the old engines. This lady has the new ones, with an extra fifty thousand pounds of thrust. Take us to the red line."

With the flipping of a control knob, Cochran put the shuttle in an abort to orbit mode. In a single action its systems were changed to accept the emergency conditions which allowed Post to shove his throttle to its gatestops. The remaining two main engines jumped from a hundred percent rated power to a hundred and fifteen percent. Though they took a beating, their increased thrust stopped the shuttle's deceleration.

37

By now the *Phoenix* was approaching the African continent. It had become ballistic, an airliner-sized artillery shell hurtling across the earth. As it consumed more fuel from the external tank it was riding under, the entire assembly became lighter. The shuttle's velocity increased, and so did its altitude.

"*Phoenix*, this is Mission Control. You are eighty-one nautical miles in altitude. You can throttle down your engines to ninety percent. We've rescheduled your MECO for three minutes from now. Prepare for Z minus translation dive."

The over-strained engines were powered back from their dangerous levels. At Corrigan's command, Cochran and Post swivelled their nozzles to push the shuttle into a shallow dive. It would have to give up some of its hard won altitude if it were to part company with the external tank. Three minutes later, the spaceplane was near the botton of its dive and the main engine cutoff point had been reached.

"Mission Control, this is *Phoenix*. We have MECO," Cochran sighed with relief. "We're closing the LOX and LH-Two valves for ET separation."

"We copy. You are go for ET separation."

At the bottom of its translation dive, the shuttle unlocked its fore and aft attachment joints and the external tank lifted away. A million and a half pounds lighter than it had been at launch, it slowed and fell behind the *Phoenix*. It would skip and tumble through the upper atmosphere, eventually to burn up over a remote area of the Indian Ocean.

"Mission Control to *Phoenix*, you are go for OMS-One burn."

"Roger, Mission Control," said Cochran, pressing the OMS arming buttons. "We are commencing burn."

The two largest nozzles at the end of the orbital maneuvering system pods flared brightly. Though they only had a fraction of the main engines' thrust, they would be enough to push the shuttle into space. After almost failing to reach it, the *Phoenix* entered a low-altitude orbit as the burn ended. Like any other flying machine, it was now in the element it was designed for. It was home.

Chapter Two

"This is Launch Operations to Pad Commander, complete checkout of steady arm counterweights and order the remaining crews to abandon the facility. We have control of the fueling procedure. The count is T minus four minutes and running. Yuri Pavelivich, what do our friends in orbit have to say?"

"They hope that the countdown delay hasn't spoiled some of their groceries," reported Yuri Pavelivich Sakolov, taking the one unoccupied seat next to his friend, Chief Flight Operations Officer Anatoly Ryumin. "The extra time has allowed them to complete some experiments without rushing them."

"T minus three minutes, thirty seconds. $\overline{W}$e have closed the liquid propellant tanks for the vehicle's primary and booster engines," said Anatoly Ruymin, before he turned to Sakolov. "I wish we could be given some extra time. Our delay has forced the GRU to hold the launch of their reconnaissance satellite from the Yangel area. They've called here about it several times already. Can you do something?"

"I am the Director of Manned Space Operations for Glavkosmos. I have few connections with military intelligence. I have as much influence on them as the moons of Jupiter have on our tides."

"T minus three minutes and the booster auxiliary motors have completed their pre-starts. Booster Control team, you are go for auxiliary motor start."

"Perhaps I can call in a favor," said Sakolov, reaching for a telephone. "At least I can make them stop bothering you until this launch is complete."

"Thanks, Yuri. What news do you have of the other launches? Today is very busy for space."

"The NASA shuttle launched on time but there was almost a second disaster. One of its main engines failed during ascent. They nearly killed another seven astronauts, and this time three of them would have been French. Yes, this is Director Yuri Sakolov and I wish to speak with Lieutenant General Bykovsky."

"The count is T minus two minutes, thirty seconds, and running. The kerosene tanks have been pressurized," Ryumin advised. "Pad commander has reported that his crews have completed their abandonment. Security, seal the perimeter of Launch Complex Twenty-one. Did I hear a touch of gloating in your comments?"

"And why should I not gloat?" Sakolov asked. There was a touch of arrogance in his reply. "We have not killed or even seriously endangered a single cosmonaut since 1971. For the last two decades our safety record has been superior to that of NASA."

"We have been lucky, my friend, and conservative. Our shuttle is still a year away from being operational. T minus two minutes. The liquid oxygen tanks have been pressurized. We have auxiliary motor start; the boosters are on internal power. What did military intelligence say to you?"

"They will stop harassing us until after the *Progress* has been launched. The General was sympathetic but wanted to know why our launch couldn't be hurried. After all, we are only launching an unmanned *Progress* tug."

"Manned or unmanned it is safety first," said Ryumin. "This vehicle is carrying essential supplies for our crew on the *Mir*. If, for whatever reason, it fails to dock with the station, they will be in jeopardy and may have to cut

40

short their stay. T minus one minute, thirty seconds. Commence alignment of first stage engine nozzles for lift-off."

"I should also tell you that the Chinese are proceeding with their launch today, in spite of our protests."

"While there may be political reasons for the protests, I don't see any safety problems. Even if their East Wind facility is only five degrees latitude south of us, it's more than two thousand miles downrange, and we are not using the same launch azimuths. We're coming up on the one minute mark. It will get very active here, my friend."

"I understand," said Sakolov, "I'm nothing more than an interested observer here."

"The count is T minus one minute and running. The computers have confirmed vehicle status. This is Baikonur Launch Operations to all commands, we are go for launch. Safety the liquid propellant conduits. Retract the umbilical tower. All vehicle systems are on internal power. Yuri . . . Yuri? What happened to our flight director?"

"The 'interested observer' has decided to get a better view," said Pietr Malyshev, Ryumin's deputy flight director. "He took the exit to our observation deck."

"He'll miss the best part of the launch," said Ryumin. "But I think I understand. I'll join him later."

From the bare platform atop the Glavkosmos mission control building, Sakolov could see Baikonur's Korolev launch area. The most densely grouped collection of space facilities in the world, only one of its pads was active today. Sakolov could barely see the *Progress* tug and its A-2 rocket among the forest of service towers, assembly buildings and cranes. He would get a better view of the pad on the operation center's main screen. But what he wanted to see most was the launch.

Barely half a minute after he had reached the platform, a plume of white smoke erupted from the base of the A-2.

41

A muffled roar hit the Glavkosmos building as the rocket climbed off its pad and into the afternoon sky. The smoke column it rose on curved gently to the east. Not until he turned to follow the vehicle's ascent did Sakolov realize there was someone behind him.

"Shouldn't you be watching that?" he asked, pointing to the trail.

"I left my deputy in command," said Ryumin. "Malyshev is a very competent man. He can do the rest of the launch and besides, it's only a *Progress*. We've sent up thirty like it."

"Maybe so, but it's still beautiful. I remember when our shuttle flew for the first time, how awesome it was, how proud I felt. I feel that every time we have a successful launch, yet people hardly look up at these. They should. Though these crafts aren't the public relations spectacles everyone loves, they represent our steady advance."

The initial, muffled roar quickly fell to a popping rumble as the A-2 flew farther downrange. Shaped like an inverted ice cream cone, it had an exceptionally wide base to accommodate over thirty exhaust nozzles. Two minutes after lift-off, most of them stopped burning as the boosters were shut down and peeled off. The rest of the A-2 continued to push the robot tug through the atmosphere. Once in orbit, the *Progress* would be flown by ground controllers. They would guide it to the rendezvous with the *Mir* and dock it to the space station.

"Comrade Director, our Lop Nor early warning station has picked up the Baiknour launch," advised a Chinese Air Force Colonel, as he entered the mission control center (also called the East Wind space facility) at Shuang Ch'eng-tzu.

"How far downrange has it travelled?" asked the flight director, Li K'uang Chou.

"Two hundred kilometers. Its first stage has separated

and it's going for orbit. Will we continue with our count-down?"

"Of course. We're not going to stop our operations simply because some Moscow imperialists have decided that our launch threatens theirs and that they must have priority. Do you see them? Our launch is just as important." K'uang Chou pointed to a glass-enclosed observation room where a group of Chinese and Indonesian officials were still deciding which seats to take. "The Americans failed them, but we're not about to. The Russians will not dictate to us when we can launch satellites. What they demand is an insult to both us and Indonesia."

In Houston, the flight director returned to his command console and spread word of the Soviets' launch of the *Progress* among his staff. On the main screen of the mission control room stood the *Long March 2*. The vehicle was on one of several launch pads serviced by a large, centralized gantry tower. It was still partly hidden by a number of work platforms, which would be retracted into the tower before launch. For now, all that could be seen of the Chinese rocket was the white, aerodynamic shell covering its payload: a Hughes-built, Palapa-D satellite for Indonesia, a replacement for the one the *Phoenix* had lost six months earlier.

"Mission Control, this is *Phoenix*. We have completed the OMS-Two burn," Cochran announced, when the pressure scales for the orbital maneuvering engines had fallen to zero.

"You're two hundred and forty miles in altitude, *Phoenix*," said Corrigan. "You're in orbit. Conduct post OMS-Two checkout. I'm turning you over to the CAP COM. This is FIDO, out."

"Thanks, Bill. We'll be talking to you on reentry. Walt, you finished with the APU check?"

"All APU systems are shut down, boss," said Post.

"Hydraulic pressure levels read zero."

"Good, we won't have to touch those until reentry. I'm changing the program in the GPC to One-Zero-Six."

Cochran tapped out the program number and accompanying instructions on his general purpose computer keyboard. With the program loaded, the system would monitor and help operate the shuttle while it was in orbit.

"Closing left and right external tank umbilical doors," Post advised. "Centerline attachment doors, closed and locked. Vehicle undersides have full reentry integrity."

"Good, we're in orbital conditions," said Cochran, changing to the intercom channel. "Commander to crew, remove your helmets and come topside for a little sightseeing."

With the exception of Cochran and Post, the astronauts unlocked their restraint belts and started gathering on the flight deck. Vachet and Harrison were the first to do so, floating to the cockpit area by simply pushing off from their seats. Those from the middle deck appeared a few moments later.

First to come gliding through the floor hatch was Renée Simon. The zero gravity that made her weightless also caused her long, blonde hair to stand out from her head. When motionless it formed a softly shimmering disc of light around her face, almost like a halo. Next to appear was George Pellerin, who was rubbing his forehead, and last came Ripley. Even though he had been in space before, and should have been first to appear, he had chosen to stay with his inexperienced crewmates to help them adjust to their initial experience of weightlessness.

"What happened to you?" Vachet asked, when he glanced away from the windows and caught sight of Pellerin.

"I tried to walk to the hatch and ended up hitting the roof," said Pellerin. "For a moment I forgot all I had been taught."

44

"There'll be more moments like that," Cochran warned. "This isn't like riding the 'vomit comet.' Those plane rides only gave you a taste of what zero-G is like. From now on, you won't have to run, walk or climb. You won't even have to sit. Only if you're part of the cockpit crew do you need to strap in."

"If you want a better view of the Earth you should use the skylights," said Ripley, after he had noticed Simon and Pellerin having difficulty looking past the people in front of them.

The "skylights" were the overhead windows at the back of the flight deck, in the aft crew station area. The *Phoenix* was still in the "heads-down" position it had rolled into shortly after lift-off. In effect, it was still flying on its back.

"Well, after hearing Ed talk about the view from up here, what do you have to say?" asked Post.

"Magnificent. One could easily be inspired by it," Vachet said quietly. "What a beautiful birthplace we have."

"Now that's a strange thing to say," said Cochran. "On my other flights, the first-timers would always talk about the Earth being our home. Not our birthplace."

"No, the Earth is not our home. It's our cradle, our nursery, and we cannot live in the cradle forever. Our true home is where our knowledge and imagination take us. Man is the only creature who dreams of living among the stars. We are the only ones who deserve it."

"You'll have to talk about that tomorrow, when we have our conference with the European press. It's a very original idea."

"Actually, it's not entirely mine," Vachet admitted. "It originated with a Russian scientist named Konstantin Tsiolkovsky. At the turn of the century he was creating theories on space flight. He's not well known in the West, probably because the stories of Wells and Jules Verne were more popular in his day."

"Even so, I'd still use it. I don't think many reporters

would know who you're stealing from."

"Yeah, boss. We all know your views on reporters," said Post, glancing at Cochran and Vachet. Then a movement over his shoulder caught his eye. "Now there's a sight we don't get much anymore, especially since the restrictions on hair length were implemented. Take a look behind us."

Vachet was forced to move to one side so Cochran and Post could see Renée Simon floating under the skylight windows. She had her arms raised above her head and was using her hands to keep herself positioned under the windows. The light from Earth which streamed through them made Renée's hair glow brightly. Every movement of her head caused her hair to swirl.

"That may be the most beautiful sight we'll ever have in orbit," Cochran finally remarked. "But we can't allow it to continue. NASA issued the guidelines for a reason. Long hair can get tangled in equipment, and that's both painful and dangerous. It's time for us to put on our head caps. Those who get done first are to stow the specialist seats."

With some regret, the crew members produced their head caps and pulled them on. As Cochran had ordered, those who were done first stowed the mission specialist seats on both the flight deck and the middle deck. Not until the shuttle was ready for its reentry would they be needed again.

"CAP COM to *Phoenix*, your cargo bay sensors are still showing a temperature increase," advised a new voice on the loudspeakers. It was Thomas Selisky, the first in a continuous relay of astronauts to be the capsule communicators.

"Roger, CAP COM, we'll take care of it," said Cochran. "Walt, prepare for roll maneuver. RCS thrusters, on. Setting digital autopilot for manual operation."

"GPC computing optimum rotation rate," said Post. "Bringing it up on CRTs One and Two."

Taking hold of his control stick, Post moved it slightly to the right, initiating a slow starboard roll which the GPC controlled by selecting the thrusters to fire. Except for those who were still strapped in, the crew members floated near the center of the deck they were on and watched the ship rotate around them. Once the *Phoenix* had completed rolling into a normal attitude, Cochran joined Post in unlocking the nearly three dozen latches to the cargo bay doors.

They folded the doors back from the top of the spaceplane, exposing an interior set of panels. These were slightly separated from the bay doors to allow the radiators they contained to dissipate the heat build-up from the launch, cooling down the *Phoenix* for its coming operations.

"East Wind Operations to downrange tracking, we are twenty seconds and counting to lift-off," K'uang Chou announced, enjoying the sound of his voice echoing through the mission control center. "Flight director to launch complex, switch gantry systems to remote operation."

On the center's main screen stood the *Long March 2*. The work platforms which had obscured most of it from view had since been retracted into the centralized gantry tower. Only the tower's steady arms remained attached to the rocket.

"We are ten seconds to lift-off. Commence auto start sequence on all first stage engines."

Seconds later the initial spurt of flames erupted from the *Long March 2*'s first stage and booster engines. By the final moments of the countdown, intense, yellow-white flames were bathing the pad's lower levels. At zero seconds the steady arms swung away and, freed at last, the rocket began a stately ascent.

Unlike the *Phoenix* or the Soviet A-2, the *Long March 2* didn't leave a trail of smoke across the sky. The fuels it used burned cleanly and lifted the rocket on a cluster of bright jets filled with high-speed shock diamonds. A minute after launch it acquired a cone of white mist, around its nose. The cone would remain until higher altitudes and lower air pressures were reached.

"I wish they would stop that noise," said K'uang Chou, glancing at the observation room where the Indonesian officials were celebrating. "This mission isn't over, it has just begun. Stand by for booster separation."

The center's main screen showed a view from one of East Wind's long-range tracking cameras. On it, the *Long March 2* was little more than a cluster of tail fires, and the outer ring was not glowing as brightly as the core. At K'uang Chou's command, the spent boosters were jettisoned. Free of what had become so much dead weight, the *Long March 2* accelerated even more rapidly.

Near the end of its first stage burn, it had almost reached escape velocity and was ready for orbital insertion. For the Indonesian satellite to continue its flight, the first and second stages had to separate. But fifteen seconds after the first stage engines had emptied their fuel tanks, the two sections were still attached.

"Comrade Director, something . . . something is wrong," said a nervous technician, his voice hushed, though it immediately attracted K'uang Chou's attention.

"I see it. Why has there been no separation?" he demanded.

"The first stage trusses have failed to unlock. If they don't, the second stage engines will not ignite."

"Then fire the explosive bolts. Range safety officer, prepare to detonate the abort charges."

"But, comrade Director, the explosive bolts are dangerous. Should we not try—"

"Do it now!" shouted K'uang Chou, cutting off the technician. "There's no time for anything else!"

With the flight director standing over him, the technician armed and fired the explosive bolt system.

48

The click of its button coincided with a set of white flashes on the main screen. The open, girder-like, trusses on the *Long March 2* had been disintegrated, and its inert first stage tumbled away. When the second-stage engines tried to ignite, however, jets of fire appeared along its body.

Fragments of the trusses had punctured the fuel tanks and damaged the combustion chambers. Before the range safety officer could detonate the abort charges, the *Long March 2* was shredded by an explosion and became a spiralling pillar of flame. It filled the main screen, the long-range camera pulling back to get the complete scene. Only then did anyone realize that something else was burning on its own. And climbing as well.

"This isn't possible," said another technician, who was in command of the satellite control console. "My board shows that the PAM motor is firing!"

The payload assist module was both transport cradle and third-stage engine for the satellite. The heat of the second stage's explosion had ignited the PAM's solid fuel motor, which was now pushing the satellite along an erratic, northeast trajectory. It had both the speed and altitude to achieve orbit.

"Colonel Nin, fire the payload assist module abort charges," K'uang Chou ordered.

"I'll try, comrade Director," said the Range Safety Officer. "They may not work under these conditions."

On the fourth try, the detonation signal to the PAM fired its explosive packs. The Hughes-built satellite and its module evaporated in a burst of flame and a cloud of glittering fragments. Gyrating wildly, they shot out from the fireball to assume the trajectory the satellite had been on, almost ninety degrees off the East Wind center's normal launch azimuth.

"Enough! Enough!" shouted K'uang Chou, to silence the cheering which broke out in the mission control room. "We have much to do. We must plot the orbits of the debris. They could interfere with other spacecraft, either our own or American, European or Russian. We must find out who is threatened and tell Beijing to warn them. Hurry! We may have only minutes to stop this disaster before it grows worse."

Chapter Three

"Baikonur, this is *Mir*. What's the condition of our groceries?" requested Colonel Frederick Andreivich Poplavsky, seated at the space station's command console. On one of its monitor screens he could see Yuri Sakolov and part of the manned flight operations center.

"The *Progress* is one hour, forty-five minutes from its transfer orbit burn," said Sakolov, reading from a mission update paper. "We are beginning vehicle checkout for the burn. We're three hours, fifty minutes from commencement of vehicle rendezvous. How are preparations going for you, Frederick Andreivich?"

"We're completing our round of experiments and will soon begin stowing equipment. We're ready to purge the fuel lines with nitrogen gas. Everything is go up here."

"Good. What is that shadow crossing over you?"

"It's Grachenko," said Poplavsky, "he's just coming in from the astronomics module. Arkady, stop and talk to one of our earthbound friends."

In front of the *Mir*'s command console, virtually at eye level with its operators, was the connecting hatch to the axial docking compartment. Arkady Grachenko was one of the other three cosmonauts manning the space station and its only civilian. He had floated in through the hatch until he was hovering just inches above his commander.

"Greetings, Arkady Alexiivich, you are fifteen minutes late getting out of that module," Sakolov noted, checking his watch. "As usual. What did you look at and dream about this time?"

"What else but the moons of Jupiter," said Grachenko, smiling slightly. "All the Galilean moons were visible. I think I even saw a volcanic eruption on Io."

"Really. Only NASA's Hubble telescope can do that. Ours does not have the resolution or the power. You have been dreaming again. You should be reprimanded."

"Now, Yuri. Arkady's next duty is to eat lunch," said Poplavsky. "It's unsupervised time and if he wishes to spend part of it dreaming of future space expeditions, then he can."

"Yes, and since he's also the nephew of our foreign minister, it would be embarrassing to reprimand him," conceded Sakolov. "After all, where would we be if the men before us had not dreamed? Only we shouldn't do it on active duty time, understood?"

"I understand, Director Sakolov," Grachenko answered, giving the image on the monitor screen a perfunctory salute and nearly hitting Poplavsky in the face. "Sorry, Colonel. If I may be excused, my lunch is being prepared for me."

Grachenko pushed away from the command console and floated to the back of the cabin, where he finally stood upright before entering the other section in the station's main module.

"We'll advise you on the status of the *Progress* at regular intervals," said Sakolov, a little irritated at Grachenko's response. "And if we have anything new on the Chinese launch failure, we'll pass it on. This is Baikonur, out."

"Roger, Baikonur, and in three hours, forty-five minutes this station will be ready for rendezvous," said Poplavsky, before the monitor he was talking to went blank. The audio channel from Baikonur was still open and on it he could hear the rest of the flight operations staff working on the unmanned *Progress* tug. For a few moments Poplavsky listened to the chatter, until he heard some noises behind him and turned to find two of his crewmen, Grachenko and Major Vassili Kostilev.

"I admire this man," said Kostilev, nodding to Grachenko. "It's not often that someone of privilege uses it properly."

"You mean by upsetting the authorities?" Poplavsky asked.

"Yes, that as well," said Grachenko, holding two trays of plastic tubes and small, sealed cartons. "I would prefer he meant the dreams I have of space exploration."

"Your 'Dreams of Future Man,' Arkady? Grand dreams that will cost billions of rubles and dollars. Is one of those trays for me?"

"Yes, Frederick, my dreams. It would be better for all of us if we could put our money into them, instead of better ways to kill ourselves. And no, this extra tray isn't for you, unless you talked to Yuri about us controlling the *Progress* tug?"

"No, I'm afraid I did not," said Poplavsky. "But I can tell you what his answer would have been. 'We've practiced remote dockings for more than a dozen years, and we're most efficient at it.' They will never let us control a docking, Arkady. Not unless the automatic systems fail."

"Then you'll have to get your own meal. This will be for Stefan, he's in the solar observatory. If anyone wants us, put them on hold until the flares are over."

Grachenko stepped backward then kicked off the floor of the cabin. Maneuvering his body, he was able to glide over his commander and shoot through the hatch without touching the sides. His destination was the far end of the space station, past the docking compartment, the medical resources and storage module, to the solar observation module where the fourth cosmonaut, Major Stefan Siprinoff, was using the spectroheliograph, x-ray sensors, and telescopes to watch the sun and record its activities.

"Here, Colonel," said Kostilev, handing another tray

to Poplavsky. "Will you order Grachenko and Siprinoff to eat with us? It's against regulations to eat anywhere but here."

"I know that," Poplavsky answered, taking one of the cartons from his tray and shaking it to mix the contents. "But I'm certain they will prevent food from contaminating their equipment. They may be dreamers, but they are both careful."

"Has there been anything new on that launch failure, or the American shuttle?"

"Both the *Phoenix* and what's left of the satellite are in orbit. At our altitudes, we and the Americans are safe. However, the debris can threaten our *Progress* tug. It's in eccentric, low-altitude orbits and it's difficult for Baikonur to track them. Ironically, had there been no launch delay, there wouldn't be this problem."

Looking like a segmented steel tube with faintly gleaming wings, the *Mir* was a two-hundred-foot long space station composed of five modules and an axial docking compartment. There were two modules on either side of the compartment, and most sprouted a wing-shaped array of solar electric cells. Above the compartment was the newest addition, the astronomics module. And at either end of the station was a *Soyuz-TM* spacecraft. Still the primary vehicle for Soviet manned flights, it had proven safe and reliable for more than twenty years.

"This is General Rosen, Space Defense Command to Mauna Kea Station. Give us your latest track of *Progress 31.* We'd like to compare it with our tracks of the Palapa debris."

Bernard Rosen leaned over his console to get the best view of his center's multi-story main screen. Once a part of NORAD, Space Defence Command now shared the underground Mount Cheyenne complex with its parent organization. Windowless and narrow, the SDC center

53

had three tiers of consoles on one side and a fifty-foot tall main screen on the other. Less than a minute after Rosen had made his request, the information arrived from the Spacetrack station on the Mauna Kea volcano in Hawaii. As the orbital track of *Progress 31* undulated across the screen's world map, he and the officers around him studied it.

"There's no change from its previous orbits," said Rosen. "The Soviets may be unaware of the danger it's in."

"They don't have a Cray-9, Bernie," answered Rosen's second in command, Colonel Lawrence Ericson. "In fact, the Russians don't have any computer advanced enough to do real-time predictions on something so complicated as this. In another ten or twelve hours they might figure it out."

"Okay, Larry, don't gloat. Does anyone here have a prediction as to when there'll be a rendezvous?"

"I do, General," said a woman who wore captain's bars on her shoulder boards. "The secondary group of Palapa debris will intercept the *Progress* vehicle in forty-seven minutes. The main group will intercept the vehicle in six hours and seventeen minutes. These predictions are based on the debris maintaining their orbital speeds and their current tracks."

"I see. Mary, do you have an estimate as to when the *Progress* will change orbit to rendezvous with the *Mir*?"

"If physics is the same for the Russians as for us, they should attempt a transfer orbit in fifty minutes," said Captain Mary Widmark.

"I can confirm that," Ericson added. "The windows for transfer orbits are very rigid. The Russians are in deep shit, they can't do anything before the window and the second one is four hours away. Any changes to *Progress 31*'s orbit would screw the whole mission up."

"So it's possible the Soviets really don't know the trouble they're in," said Rosen, taking another look at one of the center's side screens, where the future track of the *Progress* was displayed with the tracks of the Palapa debris groups. "Soviet Air Defence Forces have their best radar, but there's little love lost between them and Glavkosmos. *Their* civilian space agency has a lot of trouble with the military."

"What should we do, General?" Widmark asked.

"Sit back and watch the fireworks," Ericson suggested.

"Larry, please. This could result in the deaths of some brave men who don't deserve to die," said Rosen, angrily. "The best we can do is call the head of NORAD and hope he can convince the Pentagon and the State Department to send a warning to the Soviets. And if they won't do it, I have a friend who can try."

Since its launch, the *Progress* tug had remained in low earth orbit. Here its systems were tested by ground controllers and its main engine primed for the coming transfer orbit burn. The window for the maneuver was only a few minutes away. All the *Progress* had to do was avoid the Palapa-D satellite debris flowing around it.

One encounter with a debris cloud had been just barely avoided. Several miles behind it, the last remnants shot through the tug's path. The approaching cloud was much smaller, and went unseen by the Baikonur control staff until it was too late. Its first pieces drifted past the vehicle's docking probe. They were not jagged or massive like the earlier debris; on radar they were ghost-like and hardly noticeable.

However, some debris in this new cloud were made of denser material. Seconds after the first pieces appeared, the *Progress* was engulfed by a flurry of similar remnants. Most that hit it flew off in odd directions. But one fragment of metal became lodged in an attitude thruster nozzle, while another, much larger, remnant struck a glancing blow against a folded antenna boom on top of the tug. Since the antenna wasn't part of an activated system, its damage wasn't noticed.

"What are your conclusions, Anatoly?" Sakolov demanded.

"There were some collisions, but no apparent damage," said Ryumin, finishing his discussions with the console teams. "All control antennas on the vehicle are operating and there's been no drop in propellant pressurization. As far as we can tell, it's in perfect condition."

"Again, we've been lucky. If only we had radar tracking as modern as the military, this surprise would never have happened. Perhaps Dr. Fedarenko can use this incident at the next budget meeting to push for improved systems."

"You can discuss it with him later, Yuri. For now I need a decision, do we go ahead for the transfer orbit burn or not?"

"Proceed with the countdown," said Sakolov, his nervousness ebbing and an official tone returning to his voice. "Let's not delay our friends' supplies any longer."

Less than three minutes later, the tug's main engine fired. The sustained burn pushed it through an invisible window created by a mix of mathematics and physics. The *Progress* was on its way to its rendezvous with the *Mir* station. Not until then would the damage it had received become apparent.

"*Phoenix,* this is Houston. We have some news you'll be interested in," advised Tom Selisky, nearing the end of his tour as CAP COM. "And I'm afraid it's not good."

"We're sitting down and strapped in," said Post, for the moment Cochran was busy talking to Vachet. "We're ready."

"We just got this from Cape Canaveral. Ray Fernandez has been relieved of his duties as launch control officer."

"What? Would you mind repeating that?" asked Cochran, all conversation on the shuttle's flight deck coming to a quick end.

"Pending an investigation of your abort to orbit emergency, Fernandez is being relieved of all his duties. And Ed, you're going to have to do a lot of explaining when you return."

"What for? What are the charges, Tom?"

"You and Ray have been charged with violating NASA safety procedures when you cancelled the second hold at T minus nine minutes," said Selisky. "Management feels it contributed to your main engine loss. You've also been cited with violating flight rules for going to one hundred and fifteen percent power during your abort. You broke one of the post-*Challenger* rules, Ed. Not to overstress the engines."

"And what on earth was he supposed to do?" Vachet protested, as he plugged his headset into the nearest audio terminal. "What he ordered was the only way to save the mission, this spacecraft, and possibly our lives. I watched him carefully and he made the best decision anyone could make."

"Yeah and it was my hand on the throttle," Post added, "not Ed's. If they charge him they should charge me as well."

"I know, but Ed's the commander and he's the one responsible," said Selisky. "Hey, I'm just telling you what happened. It's not my fault. I smell George Reiss behind this."

"I understand," said Cochran. "So do I. I've been in hot water before and I guess he's going to parboil me this time. Does management want us to proceed with the satellite release?"

"No, they're making a change in the schedule."

"Now what? Do they want us to land so I can surrender?"

"Nothing so drastic. Your friend Bernie thinks something may happen when *Progress 31* docks with the *Mir*. The Pentagon wants you to deploy the reconnaissance camera package to record it. We'll give you more

57

details later. You're to stop work on the satellite launch. The big boys are talking to the French about it. They'll go along with a little delay."

"Especially if we share the information gathered," Vachet noted. "If Cochran's friend believes there could be trouble, will the Russians be warned?"

"The State Department is working on it," said Selisky. "And your government will probably get involved as well. After all that, we might warn the Russians before the docking begins."

"I should've guessed," said Cochran. "Do you know when the rendezvous will begin?"

"We think in about an hour, maybe less. We'll keep you busy until then. Prepare to switch to secure channel Alpha-Three in ten minutes. This is Houston, out."

"Roger, Houston. This is *Phoenix*, out. Renée, you can kill the activation of your navy's satellite. It looks like we're going on a little reconnaissance mission."

"Could the cosmonauts be in danger?" asked Renée.

"Yes, it could be very dangerous for them."

"Then why can't we contact them on our own? We can't just stand by and watch those men die."

"I'm afraid that's exactly what we will do," said Vachet, answering before Cochran. "Neither Houston nor Toulouse has given us permission to contact the Soviets, and even if they did, our communications equipment isn't compatible. We don't even have external navigation lights to flash at the Soviets."

"And at our closest approach we'll still be hundreds of miles away," said Cochran. "That's why we'll need to use the reconnaissance package. Julie, you can start activating it."

"This package, what is it?" Vachet asked.

"An automated camera with radar focussing," said Cochran, undoing his restraint belts and pushing out of his seat. "All we have to do is turn it on, program it, and point it in the right direction. The Pentagon and the CIA came up with it, and we carry one on every flight. Last

58

year, *Columbia* used theirs to film the break-up of a Cosmos ocean surveillance satellite. Let's see how Julie's doing. Walt, take care of the lady."

For the first time since boarding the *Phoenix*, Cochran got out of his commander's seat. Cramped from hours of immobility, he rubbed and exercised his legs as he floated to the aft crew station. Vachet followed him, and they joined Simon and Harrison who were busy working on the control panels at the station. While Simon shut down the satellite, Harrison was bringing the reconnaissance package to life.

"All systems on line, the unit is ready for programming," Julie Harrison advised. "Have they sent us our instructions?"

"No but they will," said Cochran. "Good work, Julie. The reconnaissance package is in the canister beside the manned maneuvering units, Paul. When we're ready to deploy we'll pop the lid."

"Yes, I see it," Vachet replied, looking down and to the starboard side of the cargo bay. "Are there other secret payloads on this flight?"

"Only what your country added. Remember, your specialists did most of the loading. All the Fleet Com satellites in the bay, and those we're going to refuel, are for your navy to maintain contact with its submarines. If there's anything secret with them, we won't know until you tell us."

"Touché, Edward, touché. All countries have their secrets. Tell me, is the identity of your friend a secret?"

"No, Bernie is General Bernard Rosen, commanding officer of Space Defence Command. In a few minutes we'll learn more about what he saw and what we're supposed to do. In the meantime, let's see if Walt's heard anything new. Until we get our instructions, there's little for us to work on."

A hook-shaped antenna swung out from the *Mir*'s axial

docking compartment. On its end was a bullet fairing that contained the radar to guide in the *Progress* tug during its final approach. It was the first sign of external activity related to the coming rendezvous on the space station.

"Baikonur, this is *Mir*. We've deployed the axial unit's radar docking system," said Poplavsky, glancing at a monitor screen on his command console. The screen showed Ryumin, and in the background could be seen the flight operations center.

"Roger, *Mir*. The *Progress* has made its de-transfer burn and is now in your orbit," said Ryumin. "Begin final preparations."

"Forward *Soyuz* secured," Grachenko reported, floating through the hatch in front of Poplavsky. "Solar observatory hatch, locked. Medical resources hatch, locked."

"Good, I want you down here with me," said Poplavsky. "Siprinoff will lock the forward hatch when he's finished with the astronomics module. Vassili will man the fueling control station after he arrives."

Grachenko pushed away from the main module's ceiling and squeezed himself into the chair beside the *Mir*'s commander. Like Poplavsky, he wore a pressure suit and found it laborious to pull restraint straps around it. He didn't finish before another figure appeared in the forward hatch.

It was Siprinoff, and he sealed the hatch before taking his seat at environmental control. Moments later Vassili Kostilev closed the aft hatch to the Modulny experiments platform. When he had taken his seat at fueling control, the entire crew was in the *Mir*'s safest module. From here they would await the rendezvous.

A hook-shaped antenna was being deployed along the top of the *Progress* tug. It took a little longer to raise into position than was normal and, when it began operation, here was a brief sparking near its base. At Baikonur the staff read it as a transient power surge in the radar docking system. The only warning they would receive had been dismissed as a momentary flutter on a single instrument in the vast control room. The robot ship continued toward the *Mir*. It had matched its orbit; now it had to match the space station's velocity.

"Your helmet, Arkady. Put it on while we have the time," said Poplavsky. "Stefan, report in."

"All right, I'm going under the fish bowl," said Grachenko. "But don't blame me if it's hard to hear what I say."

Grachenko pulled a helmet off the wall bracket beside him and lowered it over his head. Careful not to let its bottom ring scrape his nose, he sealed the helmet by screwing it onto his pressure suit's collar until the locks clicked.

"I'm reducing station atmosphere by seventy percent," Siprinoff advised. "All non-essential systems deactivated. Ready to switch off number one photovoltaic array."

"Switch off and retract the array," said Poplavsky. "Arkady, activate attitude thrusters and load maneuver program Eight-One."

"Station thruster banks activated," said Grachenko, watching a schematic of the *Mir* on one of his display screens. The points of light along it changed from red to green. "Program load finished on primary and backup flight computers."

"Then it's time to begin. Initiating maneuver."

As he spoke, Poplavsky tapped out the codes on his computer keyboard. The moment he hit the "run" switch, the nozzle groups along the station's exterior began firing in a precisely timed sequence. The pulses of flame swung the *Mir* around until it was flying sideways to the approaching *Progress*.

"You're finished with dinner already?" Ryumin asked, when Sakolov appeared in the center, and took a seat at his console.

"Of course. You think I would miss the best part of the flight?" said Sakolov.

"Then you're in luck, the best part is about to begin. Flight Officer to all stations, the *Mir* has assumed docking position, the event clock is on. Final approach will commence in fifteen minutes. Propulsion Control, in one minute I want a thirty-four second transposition burn on all forward thrusters. Rendezvous Control, switch docking system from long-range acquisition to rendezvous mode. Activate *Progress* data-link when we complete the transposition burn."

A ring of exhaust nozzles around the tug's nose fired in unison to slow its velocity. In half a minute it would almost match the *Mir*'s orbital speed. Behind the newly deployed radar was a parabolic dish mounted on a girder-like arm. The *Progress* would use it to communicate with the computers on the *Mir* after the first transposition burn had ended.

"Attitude thrusters on automatic position holding," said Grachenko. "The computer will maintain our position until the tug is docked."

"Colonel, I'm reducing the pressure in the empty propellant tanks from twenty atmospheres to four," Kostilev reported. "We'll be ready for the transfer soon."

"Good, everything's on schedule," said Poplavsky, scanning his monitor screens and status boards. "Stefan?"

"The array panels are horizontal and the retraction will be completed in four minutes," said Siprinoff.

The main module's portside solar wing collapsed slowly. Panel by panel, its photovoltaic cells were swung upright, by the sun tracking motors in the support beam, and folded against each other. The beam itself also retracted; the entire array would be flush against the station's side in minutes.

"Arkady, turn on the docking lights and TV camera," Poplavsky ordered. "Let's give our friends the usual light show."

A set of high-intensity lights snapped on around the docking compartment's port hatch while, above it, the camera began transmitting to the cosmonauts as well as to Baikonur. Should the automatic systems on the *Mir* or the *Progress* fail, the lights would be used by the ground staff to attempt a manual dock.

"Rendezvous Control, activate visual docking system," said Ryumin, before turning to an operator at his console. "Askyonov, put both the *Progress* and the *Mir*'s view on the main screen."

The screen's world map was quickly replaced by camera views from the tug and the space station. What they showed was nearly identical: a square of bright lights floating in the distance, with the dim outline of a vehicle around them. In a few minutes the outlines would be more distinct.

"Rendezvous Control to Flight Officer, request permission to switch from rendezvous to approach mode."

"Permission granted," Ryumin answered. "Flight Officer to all stations, we're seven minutes from final docking."

The docking lights and TV camera were activated moments after the tug's data-link system. Apart from giving Baikonur's staff a better view of the operation, they were of little use. The computers on the *Progress* and the *Mir* would control the rendezvous, and only those on the ground could change or override what they were doing.

"Data exchange between our computer and the *Progress* is getting heavy," said Grachenko. "The machines are taking over."

"This is Fueling Control. Propellant safety valves on automatic," Kostilev advised, glancing over his rows of status lights. "All systems at my station are under computer operation."

"This is Environmental Control, number one array is secure," said Siprinoff. "Environmental systems on automatic monitoring."

"Baikonur reports they have positive override capability," said Poplavsky. "Nothing left to do but watch our machines. Baikonur, this is *Mir*. Everything on our end is set; we can see our groceries."

By leaning over as far as he could, Poplavsky could see the approaching supply tug through a porthole beside the command console. Its powerful lights were clearly visible and in moments, as it glided in closer, the *Progress* would be further illuminated by those on the space station.

"Roger, Colonel. Everything is perfect here," said Ryumin, before he turned to the guest at his console. "This operation will be over in less than a minute, Yuri Pavelivich. Rendezvous Control, switch systems to docking mode."

"Yes, and I can still feel the exhilaration. Even after all these times," Sakolov replied. "I feel like I'm at a birth."

"Then I hope you have cigars and vodka ready for the celebration. We're about to make a delivery."

When it was five hundred yards out, the tug's radar changed from approach to docking mode. Ever since it had acquired the *Mir* at long-range, the *Progress* had been scanning it with increasingly narrow radar search cones and stronger pulses. As the radar changed modes, the robot commanded its aft thrusters to fireup to the acceleration necessary for making a hard dock. The surge in electricity caused the damaged antenna wires to begin arcing; in an instant the system had ceased operating.

At the same moment the thrusters in the tail of the *Progress* emitted jets of flame. An exhaust nozzle in the upper right corner had its jet partially blocked by a twisted fragment of metal. Made of magnesium, it melted in a flash of incandescent light. The intense heat exploded the tiny rocket engine and, with its loss, the robot vehicle flipped sideways and pitched its nose up. It was out of control.

"The devil take us," said Poplavsky, in a hushed voice. "Baikonur, this is *Mir*. What's happening with the tug?"

"All stations, manual overrides!" was the answer, and even on the monitor's small screen, the fear on Ryumin's face was apparent. "Propulsion Control, fire forward thrusters!"

"Rig for collision!" shouted Poplavsky, turning to his crew. "Baikonur can't control the tug!"

At two hundred yards the *Progress* attempted to correct its attitude, but when the control staff activated its manual override systems all thrusters stopped firing. The few seconds they had needed to coordinate their actions was enough; the *Progress* tumbled into the axial docking module on the *Mir*.

The impact caused the space station to bend; the sudden creaking the crew heard was the sound of the docking ports warping under the strain. In the main module they lost their lighting, followed by their communication link with Baikonur. More panels shorted out, but it wasn't until the *Progress* scraped past the module that the serious damage was done.

The tug pivoted after the initial collision and collapsed against the side of the station, shearing off the retracted solar array. Inside the module the secondary impact snapped the supports to Kostilev's seat and threw it to the floor with him still strapped in. The array's support beam motors were pushed against the tanks they backed, splitting them open at the seams. The impact the module took would've caused it to split open under normal circumstances. However, the lowered atmospheric pressure would allow it to survive for now.

"Arkady, help him!" Poplavsky ordered, pointing at Kostilev; who was lying on the floor behind them. "I'll try to regain Baikonur. Stefan, activate emergency systems!"

Without saying a word, Grachenko undid his restraint belts and pushed away from his seat. He sailed over to Kostilev, grabbing hold of the seat he was still attached to and reaching for the safety belt release.

"I got him free, but I think his right arm is broken," said Grachenko. "We can . . . I smell something. Look!"

He nodded to the port wall of the cabin, where streams of dark-colored, shimmering globules were spurting through its seams. The globules spread quickly around the cabin, carrying with them a rancid, obnoxious odor.

"The waste collection tanks have ruptured," said Poplavsky. "On top of everything else, we'll smell like a latrine."

"Colonel, we have to stop it," warned Siprinoff, almost shouting. "Arkady, get something to plug the leaks."

"No, I have to tend to Vassili," said Grachenko. "We have more dangerous things to worry about than a leaking piss tank."

"This is dangerous! Remember your basic biology. Urine is mostly sea water. If it makes contact with our electrical systems, it'll mean disaster!"

Though he didn't want to abandon his injured crew mate, Grachenko left Kostilev propped in his chair at the command console and went to work trying to plug the leaks. But by then it was too late.

66

The dark spheres rapidly spread through the main module and collapsed against whatever surface or object they hit. When it was an instrument panel, computer keyboard, or an electronic component of any kind, the splattering was soon followed by a fizzling. The human sea water worked its way into circuit boards and junction boxes, the ganglia of electric nerves essential to the running of the *Mir*. In moments there were puffs of smoke, flickering lights, and sparks throughout the module.

"Damn it!" shouted Grachenko, blowing to push away a sphere of urine from his face. Then he slapped down his helmet visor. "If you're going to regain Baikonur, you had better do it now! I don't think we're going to have emergency systems after this."

Grachenko had some success with a roll of electrician's tape from a work kit, but the damage was being done by what had already leaked out. Soon the other cosmonauts joined Grachenko in locking down their helmet visors, as much to escape being splattered as to avoid the rancid scent of urine and the acrid smell of the tiny electrical fires.

As much as the damage caused by the collision, the shortcircuiting created by the months of stored waste would doom the *Mir*. The collision had been read as a docking by its flight computer, which had turned off the position holding program. The shorting of the thruster control panel caused some of the attitude engines to fire up and remain firing. Though the crew had yet to notice it, the engines would propel the station into an increasingly faster tumble. It would not be able to correct the maneuver, and with so many other systems inoperative, the space station would become unsalvagable.

"Well? What do you think happened?" Cochran asked.

"Difficult to say," Vachet said, turning from the

monitors to the remote arm TV cameras. "These sets are black and white, and we saw very little detail. But I believe there was a collision."

"Unfortunately, I think you're right. Though we really won't know until what the package has recorded is analyzed. Julie, get in here and retract it. The intelligence boys will be eager to see what we got."

Perched some forty feet above the *Phoenix*, the remote reconnaissance package hung on the end of the manipulator arm. Its programmed operations over, the barrel-like package was slowly lowered into the cargo bay. Once it had been returned to its transport canister, its information would be transmitted to Earth. Only then would the details of the accident be known to anyone outside the Soviet Union, and ever after that only a select few would ever see what the package had recorded.

Chapter Four

"Mr. Reiss, the computer enhancement is ready," advised a technician, stepping up to a group of visitors in Canaveral's photography and imaging center.

"Finally. Now we'll see what really happened," said Reiss. "Bring it up and run it in slow motion first, then in normal speed."

Reiss, and the officials he had brought with him, turned their attention to the long-dead television monitors beside them. When they flickered to life they displayed a much sharper version of the footage transmitted from the *Phoenix*. On the monitors hovered the segmented tube of the *Mir* station. Approaching it, in a halting glide, was the *Progress* tug. While the station was brightly illuminated and distinct, the *Progress* remained a faint outline until a sudden and prolonged flash lit up its tail.

The spacecraft raised its nose and began to swing to the right. In the collision one of the station's solar wings was crushed. The docking lights went out, though beyond that little damage to either craft was apparent. The *Mir* remained intact and the *Progress* tumbled away without exploding. After waiting more than an hour, the officials at last had something to talk about. They turned to Reiss for answers.

Reiss, however, proved unable to give anything except general information. And he grew resentful when it was suggested that the obvious experts be brought in to view the footage.

"I don't see what your objections are to having some of the astronauts see this," said the State Department official. "They certainly have the experience."

"They also have a lack of discipline," said Reiss. "I've found that out in the last year. If any were to see this footage, it would imperil the shuttle's mission."

"How so? You just finished telling us the shuttle was in no danger from this accident."

"Not directly, not even from the *Progress* tug tumbling all over the place. The danger to the mission comes from the astronauts themselves. If they were to see this, they'd get word to the *Phoenix* about how badly damaged the space station is. I know Cochran, he'd want to fly a rescue flight. And unless the Russians ask for one, I won't even consider it."

"This sounds like Langley," observed the CIA official, ruefully. "Don't let the people in the field know the truth."

"Don't tell me how to run the astronaut corps," Reiss said angrily. "You'll all be given copies of this footage. You can take it back to your own experts for analysis."

"In my branch, we don't have many space experts," said the State Department man. "Maybe I could ask the Soviets? After all, their Foreign Minister has a relative on the *Mir*."

"Our experts will be available to you," offered a respresentative from the National Security Agency. "Have the French and the military put in their requests for the footage?"

"Yes, Space Defence Command especially," said Reiss. "But they'll have to learn to wait their turn. They're not first in line. You people are, and I want you to promise me that you won't show any of this to the astronaut corps. I have enough problems with them already. This would only fan the flames."

"I've manually closed the valves to the fuel lines," said Grachenko, appearing at the main cabin's rear entrance. "The thrusters will stop firing once the propellants in the lines have been used up. What are the rest of our problems like?"

"We may still smell like a latrine, but the leaks have been sealed," Siprinoff answered. "However, the damage has been done and can't be reversed. Most of our electronics are out and we're on emergency power."

"Once the thrusters have stopped, could we activate others and halt this spin?" asked Poplavsky, the only one of the four cosmonauts to be seated at a console. He reached over and switched the communications panel to "receive only" mode, giving him and his crew a little privacy from Baikonur.

"I'm afraid not Colonel," said Grachenko. "The attitude control system is entirely computer operated, even the backup, and we lost the computers in the initial collision. Vassili, how are you feeling, my friend?"

Grachenko floated to the center of the *Mir*'s main module, where he joined Siprinoff and Kostilev. Siprinoff had finished attaching plastic splints to Kostilev's right arm and was attempting to put it in a sling, though the bulky pressure suits everyone wore made things difficult.

70

"I think this confirms that the leaching of calcium from our skeletons can be dangerous," said Kostilev, wincing in pain as Siprinoff got the sling around his neck. "Considering the time I've spent in orbit, I must have the bones of a seventy-year-old."

"No, Vassili. You were just unlucky," Siprinoff answered. "You landed on your elbow in exactly the wrong way. There, this should be enough for you until we return to Earth. And when will that be, Frederick Andreivich?"

"Not soon. Baikonur and Moscow are still trying to decide our fate," said Poplavsky. "We may become victims of politics. Moscow may decide our national image will suffer if we abandon this station. They may order us to stay and repair it."

"Out of the question. I may only be a medical specialist, but I think this station can't be repaired. Arkady Alexiivich, what do you say?"

"Not even if we could take it back to the factory could we repair it," said Grachenko. "Not only have most of our electronics failed, we also have structural damage and the emergency power system has been affected. The collision damaged many of the power cells. What's left will be drained in less than a day. If we don't leave in the *Soyuz* craft soon, either structural failure or power failure will doom us."

"How can we leave when the auto dock system has shorted out?" asked Kostilev.

"One of us must stay on board to release the others," said Poplavsky. "Then he can escape by undocking the remaining *Soyuz* externally. In theory it works, but no one's ever done it before."

"We may have to put theory into practice," Grachenko added. "It'll be very dangerous for the one left aboard. He could end up adrift between the station and his *Soyuz*. We had better do all we can to convince Moscow that we must abandon this station, before the

71

disaster becomes too critical. Dead cosmonauts will not do much for our national image either."

"CAP COM, this is *Phoenix*. Number one satellite is in deployment position. Spin-up is complete, the bird is at launch rotation speed. We're ready to deploy."

Ripley was now carrying out most of the communications between *Phoenix* and Houston. For the last twenty-five minutes, he and Harrison had been reactivating the first of the French navy satellites. Joining them at the aft crew station were Simon and Pellerin, who would take over the next day. For the first time since lift-off, the command team of Cochran, Post, and Vachet had little to do. They remained in the cockpit section of the flight deck where they wouldn't interfere with the mission specialists.

"Roger, *Phoenix*. You are go for deployment," announced the voice on the deck's loudspeakers.

"Thanks, CAP COM. Julie, you can have the honors," said Ripley. "I think someone else should have the fun."

"Houston, we're deploying number one Fleet Com," said Harrison as she armed the release controls and pressed the brightly flashing buttons on the payload service panel.

Through the skylight and aft bulkhead windows the astronauts watched the spinning disc of silver and gold sail out of its storage pallet. In a few minutes the satellite would be far enough away from the shuttle for it to unfold its solar cell arrays. By then it would be controlled by the CNES center, in Toulouse, which would complete its activation. As for the *Phoenix*, for the last half-hour it had been flown by those at the aft crew station. But with the Fleet Com's release, the command team would once again control the spaceplane.

"Houston, this is Cochran. Loading program Two-Zero-Five into GPC. We're unlocking cockpit flight controls and setting the digital auto pilot for manual operation."

"Roger, *Phoenix*. You are go for return to parking orbit attitude," advised the CAP COM.

"Thanks, Houston, here we go. Jack, lock down the aft station flight controls. Julie, deactivate all payload launch systems. Walt, they've stood her on her head long enough."

For the satellite launch, the shuttle had assumed a perpendicular attitude; in effect, it was flying on its nose. As Post took hold of his control stick, a soft jolt rippled through the airliner-sized spaceplane and its nose started to rise. The panorama of white, brown, and blue visible from the cockpit disappeared, replaced by the curvature of the Earth and the distant blackness of space. Half a mile in front of the *Phoenix* was the Fleet Com; its delicate solar wings were just starting to unfold.

"Magnificent. You think you can repeat this tomorrow?" Vachet asked, as Simon and Pellerin floated up to him.

"After we gain more experience with the OPF recovery, yes," said Pellerin. "Are you ready for what happens before that?"

"You mean our press conference? Almost. I still have to do the most difficult part, write a small piece on my thoughts and views. My journalist friends told me they'd ask for it."

"Well, that's one group of people the rest of us don't consider too friendly," said Post. "Right, boss?"

"Don't ask me about reporters," Cochran advised. "NASA has told me my official answer should be 'no comment.'"

"I agree with you," said Julie Harrison, floating into the cockpit area. "If one more reporter asks, 'What is it like to be the second black woman in space?' I'll scream."

"Your experiences with the press have been most unfortunate," said Vachet. "You've seen their unprofes-

73

sional side. I can understand your reaction, Julie. You must work in the shadow of someone of great achievement. Dr. Wendelle was the first astronaut to be awarded a Nobel prize for science. Being of the same race and sex will naturally bring comparisons. You must be strong enough to face them."

"I know. All I want to do on this mission is perform my duties well enough to be assigned to another one. I can never equal what Ruth did. But even she needed two missions to make her breakthroughs for the Orbital Pharmaceutical Factory."

"If the first astronaut to win a Nobel prize had been a man, I wonder if the vultures would've taken after Walt or Jack, or myself?" said Cochran, asking the question as much to himself as the others in the suddenly jammed cockpit.

"I doubt it," Post answered. "Hopefully the Europeans will harp on it less. After all, they got their own to talk to. What did you mean by the writing is the difficult part? I always heard it's the rewriting that's difficult."

"I do very few rewrites," said Vachet. "The difficulty I have is in the initial rendering. The secret of writing is learning how to see. It's difficult to decide which point of view, which eye, I'll see something through. And I also need serenity. Something I might not get here until later tonight."

"What you just said reminds me of what I once read about another Frenchman," Cochran recalled. "Right here and now I can't remember his name. But I will—"

"*Phoenix*, this is CAP COM. We have started countdown for transfer orbit burn. Are your preparations under way?"

The capsule communicator's voice jolted most the shuttle's crew. For a few moments they had forgotten about Houston, and the constant flow of commands from its mission staff. It took Cochran another moment to change his thoughts and give an answer.

"Not just yet, Houston. We'll begin them shortly.

Well, boys and girls, it looks like we won't get a free moment until we're scheduled for one."

"Come in, Pietr Arkadivich. Have a seat," offered Nikolai Grigorivich Grachenko when the door to his office opened yet again. "You're early. Comrade Fedarenko has just arrived."

The army marshal who entered the foreign minister's office removed his wheel cap and great coat and hung them on the stand. Though the snow which had dusted them had since turned to water, Defence Minister Pietr Nagorny could still feel the bitter cold of Moscow's spring in his nose and cheeks.

"Dr. Fedarenko," he greeted, as he rubbed his face to get the blood circulating again. "I must admit I was once envious of your easy life in the academy of sciences. I don't feel that way anymore. These last hours must have been very hard for you. And you too, Nikolai Grigorivich."

"Thank you, my friend," said Grachenko. "I don't know which is worse, dealing with inquiries from other governments or from my family. My brother and his wife have been very persistent."

"I can understand. What's happened on the *Mir*?"

"Conditions have stabilized for now, though we can't expect it to remain that way," said Fedarenko, reciting the summaries from the reports he had brought along. "There's been heavy structural damage, most systems are inoperative, and emergency power will fail soon. The cosmonauts are requesting permission to abandon the *Mir*."

"What do you mean? I thought your agency was predicting that the station could be repaired?" Nagorny responded.

"That was issued when the Politburo was demanding answers," said Grachenko. "When the Politburo wants something, you give it to them. Even if it's premature."

"You're right, I know that problem well. What can you tell me about China's responsibility for this disaster?"

"The Chinese are indeed culpable and responsible for the disaster. Dr. Fedarenko's reports are most conclusive." Grachenko motioned toward the stack of folders on his desk. "I've already drafted a position statement I'll give to the Premier."

"And what about American complicity?" Nagorny asked.

"How can you say that? This was a Chinese launch," said Fedarenko, shocked and turning pale.

"Of an American-built satellite. And don't you think it strange the Americans offered so quickly to rescue our men?"

"Both the American *and* the French embassies offered to use the shuttle to rescue the *Mir* crew," said Grachenko, holding up a pair of telegrams. "I believe the Americans did so because President Bush wants to be seen as a man of peace in the coming elections."

"He also wants another triumph against us," said Nagorny. "He had one a year ago with the defection and hijacking of our missile submarine. Another triumph would ensure his reelection. This disaster was no accident, it was planned."

"Perhaps. No doubt there are those in the Politburo who feel the same way and who will order me to reject the American and French offers," said Grachenko, raising his hand to Fedarenko to stop the protests he knew would come. "There are considerations of state security and national pride involved here."

"If we have to reject the Americans, then you must urge the Politburo to have the *Mir* abandoned," said Fedarenko. "For the safety of your nephew and the other cosmonauts, it must be done soon. It will not help national pride if they die."

* * *

"Paul, what are you doing up so early?" Cochran asked, his head appearing in the floor hatch. "We still have more than an hour before our wake-up call."

Cochran propelled the rest of his body through the hatch with a gentle push and easily maneuvered around to his command seat, while Vachet occupied the pilot's seat. Balls of crumpled paper drifted near him, rotating like miniature satellites.

"I still have more than half my speech to write," Vachet admitted, glancing up from his clipboard. "It was too hectic before. Now, all is serene and I have this 'endless sky, this endless night' for inspiration, to borrow your phrase."

Vachet extended his hand and gestured toward the panorama visible from the cockpit. The Earth hovered in the lower portion of its windows. At its rim could be seen the faintly blue envelope of the upper atmosphere. The sun's harsh glare had yet to return; for now the Earth was framed by the silky blackness of space.

"I remembered the name of the writer I was trying to compare you to," said Cochran. "Antoine Saint-Exupéry. What you've told us reminds me of his writings, especially *Night Flight*."

"You humble me with that comparison," said Vachet. "But I'm grateful for it. Few have compared me to the poet laureate of aviation, perhaps because not many remember his name. He had the bad luck to go missing in combat. He should be remembered for more than just creating a children's fable."

"I'm sure that won't happen to you. You'll be famous for being the first pilot of the *Hermes*, while I'll end up in the Twilight Zone. Because of what happened at the start of this flight, this may be my last mission."

"Conditions can change, Edward. There have been many unique events today. Who knows how they'll be resolved? They could work to our benefit. Incidents have a way of creating opportunities, and we must be ready to take advantage of them."

"You mean my space rescue idea?" Cochran asked. "Well, right now I don't think it'll happen. We haven't heard much about the collision since it occurred. No one will say how serious it is, except that one of the cosmonauts was injured."

"No one is saying, but we can find out," said Vachet. "You have your friends, I have mine. Jacques Daurat is one of my closest, and he's mission control director at Toulouse."

"I hope you have a few favors you can call in, Saint Ex."

"I have, and in his own way Daurat admires what I write. Perhaps my speech can help to persuade him, though I dare not direct it at him, or specifically mention your rescue plans."

"You think you can finish it in time?"

"With hard work, and a little solitude," Vachet answered. "I have some difficulty with overwriting the poetic side of this piece. I was right, what we have here is very inspiring."

"And by solitude, I take it you mean you'd like to be left alone?" said Cochran.

"I'm sorry, my friend, but even an audience of one can be intimidating. I know how I want to end this. I just don't know how to get there from here . . ."

Vachet held up his clipboard for Cochran to view. In the minutes since his arrival, whatever Vachet had written was crossed out. He still had half the page to complete and there would be several more beyond that before he would be finished.

"You mean you don't know just yet," said Cochran. "I'm sure you will, especially if I'm not hovering around you. I'd like to see that before we begin the press conference tomorrow, just to see how you finished it."

"Good night," Cochran added as he used his fingers to push off from his seat. He sailed backward, using the handholds to guide his way out of the cockpit, then to change his attitude and drop toward the flight deck's floor hatch. Partway through the hatch, Cochran stopped and turned back to Vachet.

"Here, something to keep you company," he offered, reaching into one of his flight suit pockets. "It's one of those transforming toys Walt got from his kids to bring along."

Cochran tossed the miniature jet fighter as he would a paper airplane. Instead of dropping to the floor with a hard thud, the metal and plastic toy sailed gracefully to Vachet. As Cochran returned to the middle deck, the Frenchman caught the fighter. He allowed it to hover in front of him, where it began to gleam and sparkle as the sun rose above the Earth's rim.

Chapter Five

"*Mir*, this is Baikonur. We've completed our analysis of your situation," announced a solemn Anatoly Ryumin. "Are all of you awake, Colonel? And are you present in the main module?"

Ryumin was forced to ask his questions because television contact had been lost for the last twenty hours. Beginning just seconds after the collision, the only reliable way to maintain contact with the *Mir* was by emergency radio. Even that would fade due to the station's erratic, and dangerous, rotation.

"Arkady is with me," said Poplavsky, who was strapped in with Grachenko at the *Mir*'s command console. "But Stefan and Vassili are still sleeping. They relieved us two hours ago and I would like them to have their rest, especially Vassili."

"Agreed. You and Arkady are the ones we need most to talk to. You're the ones who can best understand our decisions. Our analysis agrees with your analysis. We see no way for you to repair all the damage, and Moscow has agreed to a strategic redeployment for you."

"Somehow, that doesn't sound like we are abandoning the *Mir* and returning to Earth," Grachenko observed. "Explain 'strategic redeploment' to us."

"Anatoly, I'll handle this," said another voice on the radio, one both cosmonauts recognized as that of Sakolov. "I'm sorry. We tried to get you back directly, but Moscow decided it would be too embarrassing. Instead, you will abandon the *Mir* and rendezvous with the *Salyut* 7."

"But the *Salyut* is little more than a satellite. It hasn't been occupied for nearly two years."

"We know, it's not man-rated. However, we will reactivate it and prepare it for you. This will take several hours and you must take with you all the supplies you can."

"How long do you estimate we'll need?" Poplavsky asked, pausing for a moment as a faint groan echoed through the connecting hatch in front of him. Somewhere in the station, something was being overstressed by its ceaseless tumbling.

"At least six hours for you," said Ryumin. "We'll need up to eight hours to reactivate the *Salyut* 7. Remember, our estimate for you includes preparation of both the *Soyuz* and shutting down the *Mir* as best you can. I must warn you that your estimate also coincides with some of our computer projections for station self-destruction. Whether by centrifugal stress, or ignition of leaking fuel, the *Mir* will last no longer than fourteen hours."

"Thank you, Baikonur. We'll keep it in mind," said Poplavsky. "Have you decided which of us will undock the other three?"

"You will," said Sakolov. "We know all of you volunteered to stay, even Kostilev. But you, Frederick, were judged to have the best chance for success. Grachenko will of course command the first *Soyuz*."

80

"We agree with your choices, though as commander of the *Mir*, I would've countermanded your decisions had they been different. We'll begin work immediately. Arkady will go forward to activate his spacecraft, and I will commence a shut-down of station systems. This is *Mir*, out."

Poplavsky switched the emergency radio to its "receive only" mode before turning to Grachenko. This allowed them to hear any messages from Baikonur while having a private conversation.

"Curious. I wonder why Ryumin claims we'll need six hours to abandon this station?" said Grachenko, lost in thought for a moment. "It will certainly take a lot of hard work, but we could do it in less time."

"You believe they could have another reason, Arkady?"

"Yes, the NASA shuttle. Just as we perform reconnaissance duties for the army, the shuttle does the same for the American military. It's possible that the *Phoenix* can watch us and Moscow doesn't want us to do anything while it's in range. Placing us in greater danger isn't as important as trying to control this disaster and put a good face on it."

"For a relative of our foreign minister, you're remarkably cynical," said Poplavsky. "You're probably also correct. What do you propose we should do?"

"We're tied to the ground, so there's little we can do independently," said Grachenko, hitting the release for his shoulder harness. "I'm going forward to prepare my *Soyuz*. I'll hook into the intercom when I reach it. I'm not going to be a pawn to politics. We must be ready for any contingency, and do everything to survive."

The moment he threw off his harness straps, Grachenko started drifting out of his seat. The station's centrifugal force created a slight gravity effect, pulling him away from the command console and toward the module's ceiling. Before he reached it he kicked off from his seat and maneuvered for the connecting hatch. In spite of his bulky pressure suit he squeezed through it, then the hatches to the next two modules before reaching his *Soyuz*. There, he would bring the long dormant spacecraft back to life.

"Mrs. Harrison, my readers want to know what it's like to be the second black woman in space," requested a reporter, appearing on one of the television monitors at the aft crew station.

The smile on Julie's face disappeared as she let out a soft hiss which was, fortunately, covered by Ripley's moaning.

"Alain, please. If you wish an answer to that question you can get it from the reporters at Canaveral," said Vachet, moving to defend his crew mates. "Julie's answered it enough times already. Please, ask her another question."

"All right. Mrs. Harrison, what are your goals for your career?" said the French reporter, who had stopped to think for a moment.

"To perform my duties well enough on this mission to be included on future ones," Harrison answered.

"Thank you, Mrs. Harrison. Now comes the question many of us here have been wanting to ask," said the reporter in charge of the conference. "Monsieur Vachet, you've now had a full day in space. A day in which to gain impressions and write about them. What do you have for us?"

"Something which I can't promise is too polished," said Vachet. "This was written in what little free time I had."

As he spoke, Vachet opened one of the breast pockets on his flight suit and pulled out a set of folded sheets. They were filled with a neat, airy script, though they did have sections where passages had been crossed out and rewritten.

"My impressions of this realm were years in the

making," he began, reading slowly so the transmission static would not scramble his words. "But nothing I had read or was told about prepared me for what I've experienced after only one day. I've never witnessed such beauty as I have seen up here, nor felt such solitude. What you've seen on television can only give you a hint of what it's truly like.

"Here we drift between two worlds, both the comfortable, familiar place of our birth and an unknown world filled with the cold beauty of numberless suns lure us. We fly between man's past and his future. In our ship we cannot touch the stars—that voyage is reserved for mightier craft—but we can touch the future. In this solitude, where I have neither the shouting wind nor even gravity for a distraction, I can feel the stars beckon us.

"I know this to be our destiny. Not just the destiny of my profession, but the collective destiny of all nations reaching to space, and through them, mankind itself. Not all men are brothers, and space will not resolve our differences—in this we must be realists. But we can cooperate to a greater degree here than in any other realm. We face dangers so great and share so many goals that cooperation and joint efforts are the best answer.

"As we skirt the edge of our last frontier, my crew mates and I realize that after more than thirty years of space exploration, mankind is still only beginning. In comparison to earlier ages of exploration, we have not yet reached the age of the Phoenicians or the Vikings. Our Drakes and Captain Cooks have yet to be born and we may never live to see them voyage from these shores. But up here, with only our machine and our dreams for companions, we know it will one day come to be."

Vachet refolded the pages, though when he tried to reinsert them in his pocket, he started to drift away from the rest of the crew, who had to grab him to keep him in place.

"After speaking so eloquently of this realm, you forgot

you were in it," said Cochran, who then addressed the TV camera his crew had been facing for more than forty minutes. "Do any of you have any additional questions for us?"

"I do. Is this piece going to be the start of a new book, Monsieur Vachet?" responded one of the reporters on the monitors.

"It'll be part, but not the start," said Vachet. "I've already written a few items and hope to do more while in orbit."

"Will this book become the first book written in space?" asked another.

"Will you transmit this book to your editors while you're still in orbit?" said a third.

"All right, enough," said Vachet, making it a gentle order. "I think your questions are wandering onto a banal terrain. We should be talking about our mission, not my literary efforts."

"I can answer some of your questions," Cochran offered. "As one of the pilots of the *Phoenix*, Paul is going to be a little too busy to write an entire book. Today we'll be recovering the OPF and launching another Fleet Com. And in the days to come we'll be refueling and repairing satellites already in orbit. Since the allotted time for this conference is almost up, this would be a good point at which to end it."

"Yes, thank you for your time, Commander," said the lead reporter, ignoring the last-minute questions from the rest. "We thank you all for this opportunity and hope to repeat it again."

The two monitor screens blacked out a few moments after the conference had ended, and Cochran immediately reached forward to switch off the video camera mounted beside them. As he moved back to his crew, Cochran picked the diminutive microphones off their flight suits. It took him less than a minute to collect them all, then he turned to the intercom and started unplugging their lines.

"I'm afraid my compatriots weren't much better than the reporters at Canaveral," said Vachet. "For that I am sorry."

"At least you were better able to control them than we were," offered Post. "Why did you read your article in English instead of French? This was a conference for European reporters."

"In Europe, English is a very common second language. A lot of people will understand me, for those who can't there will be subtitles, and this way I have a better chance of being shown in America. And besides, this is an American spacecraft."

"And I suppose you kept the reading short so it would have a better chance of getting on television?" Cochran noted, as he joined the group. "This post-press conference gripe session is over with, let's get back to work. Julie's already in the cockpit, working on the program for the OPF rendezvous. George and Renée have gone below to check out the spacesuits for our EVA walk. Jack, since you're going to make the walk, you should be down there helping them. And make sure you and George start breathing pure oxygen right away. Walt, get forward and help Julie with the new program."

To reach the middle deck, all Ripley did was move to the floor hatch and push away from the ceiling. As he sailed through the opening, Post made for his seat in the cockpit. In moments only Vachet and Cochran were left at the aft crew station.

"What are my duties to be?" Vachet asked.

"You'll work here with Julie once she's done with the program," said Cochran. "You think what you've read will have an impact on your friend in Toulouse?"

"Hard to say. The press conference originated from there, so Daurat should've heard it. What I've done is plant a seed. We must wait until later to see if it's taken root. For the present we have other duties to occupy us."

*　　　*　　　*

85

"You think we should send this to your friend in orbit?" Ericson inquired, after the newly arrived video of the *Mir*'s collision had finished its run. "We got the uplink facilities, and I'm certain he'd like to know."

"Yes, probably the entire crew would like to see this," said General Rosen, motioning to the TV monitor he and the others had been watching. "If only it had arrived sooner than half an hour ago. Right now the *Phoenix* is recovering that OPF satellite."

"The NASA official I talked to claimed there was a long waiting list for this tape," said Mary Widmark. "There were just a lot of people ahead of us."

"I bet. It certainly seems odd that the people who first warn about the disaster are the last to see the results. Who's got the latest on Soviet activity?"

"I do," said Ericson. "The *Mir* is continuing to wobble while it's rotating. Glenn thinks it may be the result of crew activity inside the station. With the loss of its attitude thrusters, the *Mir* is subject to every movement by its crew."

"In space, every action does indeed have an equal and opposite reaction," Rosen noted. "What's new on the *Salyut 7*?"

"Reactivation continuing. Baikonur appears to be readying the station to receive the cosmonauts. All indications show they'll abandon the *Mir* in four or five hours."

"Looks like Cochran won't get his chance to pull off his space rescue, and pull himself out of the doghouse. Mary, what did NASA have to say about his rescue plan?"

"Nothing. Who I talked to couldn't tell me anything. He suggested I contact George Reiss, but I didn't try."

"A good idea. Reiss has been known to eat captains, and even colonels, for breakfast. I don't know how a man like that ever got to be director of flight operations. Perhaps I can get an answer out of him. Is he still at the Cape?"

"As far as I know, he's still there," said Widmark.

"Well, let's find out," Rosen answered, lifting the

telephone beside his chair and punching one of the buttons on its control console. He first got a switchboard operator in the NORAD complex, who gave him one of the secure outside lines and put his call through to Cape Canaveral. Next it was a NASA operator and finally, several minutes later, Reiss himself came on the line. For all the time it had taken Rosen to get him, his conversation with Reiss lasted little over a minute.

"Well, what did he say?" asked Ericson, after the telephone receiver was jammed back on its cradle.

"The man has a definite attitude problem," Rosen grumbled. "He was more interested in finding out where I heard of the rescue mission than in telling me about it. He forgets we can listen to any conversation with a spacecraft. As for the rescue itself, Reiss considers the idea dead. Then he claimed he had to get back to more important matters."

"What can he be doing? All flight operations are controlled by Houston," said Santiago.

"I had interrupted a conference with some intelligence people. I think they're planning another reconnaissance mission for the *Phoenix*. They probably want another look at the *Mir*."

"And what should we do?" Ericson asked. "Contact the *Phoenix* on our own? I'll bet Mr. Reiss hasn't shown this video to its crew. He'd enjoy keeping them in the dark."

"When the time's right, we'll contact Ed," Rosen answered, and started to smile. "But knowing Ed, he may try reaching us. You and Mary are to report back to the ops center and continue monitoring the Soviets, only now you'll have to keep a watch on the *Phoenix* as well. I'll take this video tape to the commander and deputy commander of NORAD. I want to keep them abreast of what's happening."

The *Phoenix* was once again standing on its nose, flying

perpendicular to the Earth. Again its cargo bay doors were open, only this time a satellite already hovered before the shuttle. In the cargo bay two astronauts were backing into the manned maneuvering units.

"Houston, this is *Phoenix*. Pellerin and Ripley have completed their rebuilding of the storage pallet and are donning their MMUs," said Cochran.

"Roger, *Phoenix*. Make sure they check all contamination monitors before deactivating the OPF," advised the CAP COM.

"Will do. We'll relay the orders to them once they're out of the bay. *Phoenix*, out. Paul, how are the fly boys doing?"

"Getting ready for takeoff," said Vachet, glancing through the aft station windows. "It looks like George will be first."

"This is Pellerin to *Phoenix*, all systems have checked out," George Pellerin reported, stepping forward after Ripley had unlocked his MMU's storage braces. "Nitrogen tanks are full, batteries at full charge. Adding one-quarter vertical thrust."

As he pushed his right-hand maneuvering lever, the nozzle groups at the base of Pellerin's MMU expelled jets of nitrogen gas. They were enough to lift him off the floor, and, maintaining the thrust, he climbed slowly out of the cargo bay. The moment he was away, Ripley locked his own MMU to his backpack and hit the storage brace releases.

"Ripley to *Phoenix*, all systems are go and I'm away."

Unlike Pellerin, Ripley wasn't making the first flight of a prototype unit. He had on his back a familiar machine and he was home. He stepped forward and lifted off the floor in one smooth motion. His ascent angle was steep; Ripley had to raise his legs to clear the OPF pallet.

Broadly similar in design, the French and American MMUs were chair-like machines worn by their astronaut/pilots. Both mounted their flight controls on retractable arms, but the French unit had its thrusters grouped in a triangular arrangement, with two groups at the MMU's base and the third behind Pellerin's head. It was simpler than the American design, which had two dozen nozzles scattered along its exterior.

"*Phoenix* to Ripley, check all contamination and status monitors on the OPF before proceeding with shutdown," Harrison advised, watching the astronauts through the overhead skylights.

"Ripley to *Phoenix*, I copy. We'll do this one by the numbers. George, I'm coming up on your left side."

Following their initial ascent from the shuttle's cargo bay, Ripley and Pellerin fired their maneuvering jets until they were facing the OPF. The Orbital Pharmaceutical Factory was several hundred feet in front of them, an octagonal-shaped column some fifteen-feet long and topped by an X-pattern array of solar cells. The automated satellite processed medicines that could only be made in zero gravity. After lining up on it, Ripley and Pellerin slowed their velocity.

"Ripley to *Phoenix*, I estimate we'll reach the OPF in less than two minutes."

"Roger, Jack. We're activating the remote arm," said Harrison, glancing over the RMS controls below the aft bulkhead windows.

"Aft station to cockpit, we're activating remote arm and flight controls," Vachet advised.

"Roger, Paul. We're safetying ours and putting our systems on standby," said Cochran, punching out the disengage commands on his GPC keyboard. "Take care of my lady."

Until the end of the recovery operation, Vachet would fly the shuttle, while Harrison flew the remote manipulator system. Anchored on the cargo bay's port side, the fifty-foot arm had shoulder, elbow, and wrist joints which gave it the dexterity, though not the speed, of a human arm.

"Software programs to standby. RMS on manual control," said Harrison. "Rotation and translation hand controls, on. Elbow and end effector cameras, on. TV downlink, enabled. RMS latches, unlocked. *Phoenix* to Ripley, the remote arm is active. We'll be ready to grapple the OPF by the time you're finished inspecting it. Deploy and activate your video system."

"Roger, *Phoenix*, deploying camera. We're about twenty feet from the OPF."

Ripley and Pellerin separated as they approached the slowly rotating satellite, coming to a halt when they were close enough to touch it. They were near its base, where they could see its first tier of processing modules. The display panels were inactive, the condition they had been left in when the *Columbia* had put the satellite in orbit eight months before.

"Ripley to *Phoenix*, the OPF looks good. We're activating Tier One displays. George, how's your maneuvering unit working?"

"So far, it's fine," Pellerin answered. "I can arrest forward motion quite easily and it's simple to maintain position. I'll do more flight testing after we recover the OPF."

"Will do. Now the way the OPF's rotating, I'll turn the displays on and you watch for anything unusual. Especially the contamination monitors. *Phoenix*, my video system is on. Are you picking up the transmission?"

"You're coming in clear," said Harrison. "We're taping your show for later broadcast to Houston."

On the top right corner of Ripley's MMU, a TV camera had popped out of its stowage position and was sitting above his shoulder. It allowed his crew mates on the *Phoenix*, and later Mission Control in Houston, to watch him activate the module display panels as they rotated past him. Despite the fact that they had been dormant for eight months, the panels came on immediately and were checked by both Pellerin and Ripley.

"Ripley to *Phoenix*, Tier One contamination monitors read negative. We're moving to the Tier Two modules."

By firing the vertical jets on their MMUs, the astronauts rose to the processing modules above them. They repeated the procedure of activating the displays, and reporting back to the shuttle on their condition.

"*Phoenix* to Ripley, commence full system shut down," Harrison answered. "I'm maneuvering the remote arm into position. When you're finished we'll move in to make the capture."

"Roger, *Phoenix*. George, shut down all Tier One modules. I'll take care of these and the photovoltaic array."

Only minutes after switching them on, Ripley began turning the displays off. First he deactivated the processing modules themselves, before doing the same to their display panels. When he had finished, he moved to the satellite's solar power array controls and hit the deployment motor button.

The dozens of photovoltaic panels in the X-shaped array swung into their upright positions and the support arms started pulling them in. The wings became noticeably shorter as they folded into their storage compartment on top of the OPF. It was a slow procedure, which allowed Vachet to bring the *Phoenix* several hundred feet closer, while Harrison raised and maneuvered the remote arm until its end effector was hovering over the satellite.

"*Phoenix* to Ripley, I'm ready to make the capture," said Harrison, her attention focussed on the monitor screens beside her. "Unless I run into difficulties, we won't need you and Pellerin's help until we actually load the OPF onto its pallet."

"Roger, *Phoenix*. George and I will continue flight testing his MMU. If you have any trouble, let us know."

Ripley and Pellerin moved away from the satellite as Harrison pushed the end effector over its grapple probe. Instead of using the observation windows, she concentrated on the monitors. They displayed views from the remote arm's cameras, and showed the grapple disappearing inside the effector. A squeeze of the trigger on the rotation hand grip caused the capture wires to snare the grapple. Moments later, the flashing status lights on Harrison's control panel indicated that a secure lock had been made. All she had to do now was swing the hundred-million-dollar payload over to the shuttle's cargo bay and lower it onto the rebuilt storage pallet.

"He just arrived, comrade Premier," said Grachenko, when he saw Fedarenko being led through the door by his secretary. "Yes, I will ask him, I'll ring you back. Well, Doctor, that was Premier Gussarov. He too would like to know why the operation you pushed so hard for has been delayed for more than an hour?"

"Because of the Americans," Fedarenko quickly answered, taking the same chair he had used in the last meeting. "The *Phoenix* received coded transmissions over two hours ago, after it recovered a civilian satellite. Since then it has not been performing its declared mission. Air Defence reports the spacecraft has assumed an attitude similar to the one it used previously to spy on the *Mir*."

"I was not aware that you had a close friendship with the commander of our air defence forces?"

"I do not. Marshal Suvorov and I agree on very little." Fedarenko shifted restlessly in his chair, Grachenko's suggestion made him uncomfortable. "He treats me as if I were a peasant. But on matters of state security he is quick to react. He called me from his headquarters about the shuttle's apparent change in operations. I ordered the abandonment of the *Mir* to be delayed until it was out of range."

"Did you not say earlier there was a time limit beyond which the crew is in danger of dying in an explosion?" Grachenko recalled. "And are we not reaching that limit?"

"I'm afraid we are, we're eating into its safety margin.

92

Though with some luck we . . ."

Fedarenko's voice trailed off as one of the telephones on the foreign minister's desk started to beep shrilly. It caught both men by surprise, and Grachenko hesitated until the phone's third blast before lifting the receiver off its cradle.

"Odd, I thought Gussarov would wait until I called him," he said. "Yes, Leena. Who is it? I see . . . It's your office, Doctor. They say it's urgent."

Grachenko handed his guest the telephone receiver, then eased back in his chair. Though eager for any news about the disaster, he didn't want to put Fedarenko under any additional pressure. Instead, Grachenko waited patiently for the brief conversation to end before making his demands.

"The shuttle has moved out of range," Fedarenko said, as he returned the telephone receiver to its cradle. "I gave orders for the abandonment to resume at once. In the next three minutes the cosmonauts will be given their orders."

"Good, but I suspect from your end of the conversation that that wasn't all you discussed. Has something happened up there?"

"We may not have as much of a safety margin as I had thought." While Fedarenko's words were sober, the grave look on his face was an even better indication of the seriousness of events. "The problem of fuel leaks is becoming critical sooner than we expected. Perhaps you should contact Premier Gussarov now. Should I return to my office, or go to his?"

"The premier's would likely be better," said Grachenko, stabbing one of the buttons on his telephone's control panel. "In times of national emergencies, it's best for leaders to present a unified front."

Chapter Six

"*Mir,* this is Baikonur. We have the go-ahead," said Ryumin. "Proceed at once with your evacuation. Keep the lines open and contact us when you are free of the *Mir.*"

"Thank you, Anatoly. If we still have a little luck, we will," Poplavsky answered, reaching for one of the few controls still active in the main module. "*Mir,* out. You realize, this is the last time anyone will ever say that?"

"Yes, and this station was launched with such hopes," said Grachenko. "What do you want me to tell Stefan and Vassili?"

"Prepare them for full depressurization. Since this is the manual cabin air purge, once I start it, I cannot reverse it."

Poplavsky waited until Grachenko got a response before rotating the dial he had his hand on. They both heard a slight hissing through their helmets and, since the associated monitor panel had shorted out, it would be the only indication that the station's remaining atmosphere was being vented to space. The cosmonauts were now totally reliant on their pressure suits to keep them alive.

"After you, Arkady," said Poplavsky. "I have to see how you move between the modules so easily."

For the last time, they unlocked their harness straps and rose out of their seats at the command console. Following Poplavsky's orders, Grachenko moved first to the connecting hatch. He grabbed its rim with his fingers and pulled himself through in one smooth motion, like a diver swimming around a sunken ship. Behind him, Poplavsky had more trouble with the maneuver.

"My chest pack is catching on the hatches," he said, caught halfway inside the axial docking compartment.

"Inhale as you reach the hatch, it'll hold the pack closer to your chest. Give me your hand."

Grachenko pulled his commander through the docking compartment. The force of his ejection propelled the two across the medical module to its opposite end. At the next hatch, Poplavsky found the maneuver easier as he followed Grachenko's advice.

On the other side was the solar observatory. More cramped than the medical module, this actually made it easier for Grachenko and Poplavsky. They used the handholds and bulky equipment mounts for guides to make their way to the end of the station, where they found an equally cramped *Soyuz TM*.

"We were debating if you two had forgotten about us," said Siprinoff, from the second compartment of the *Soyuz*. "Our power levels are still high. All systems are mission-ready."

"Good, we have permission to leave," Grachenko advised. "Clear my seat. I'm boarding the spacecraft."

Grachenko raised his legs and slid into the lead compartment feet first. Called the orbital module, it had been loaded with essential supplies scavenged from the *Mir*. Once inside, he turned his body upright and faced his commander one final time.

"Take care, Arkady Alexiivich," said Poplavsky, extending his hand. "I'll see you on the *Salyut 7* in four hours."

"Take care, Frederick," said Grachenko, as he shook the offered hand. "I still think I should do what you're doing."

"I'm the test pilot, not you. This situation is familiar to me. Of all the cosmonauts I've flown with, you're the true sailor of the universe. Voyage well, my friend."

Poplavsky unhooked and lowered a docking hatch from the interior of the observatory while Grachenko did the same inside the orbital module. Their twin, echoing clanks meant they had been sealed. As Poplavsky got ready to release the *Soyuz*, Grachenko backed into its command module.

Siprinoff grabbed his boots and guided him through

the hatch between the orbital and command modules. Grachenko moved to the left and slid onto the pilot's couch behind the instrument panels. On his right was Siprinoff, in the center couch. Kostilev was in the starboard one.

"Vassili, how are you feeling?" Grachenko asked, while he deployed the flight control mounts.

"Uncomfortable. I need more of Stefan's pills," said Kostilev. "So let's get an atmosphere back in this thing."

"As soon as we launch, which is coming up. Grachenko to Poplavsky, can you hear me?"

"You're coming in clear," was the reply, with a minimal amount of distortion. "I'm preparing the manual release controls. When do you wish to undock?"

"As we come off the bottom of this spin," said Grachenko. "Try to make it close to our original attitude."

"I'll try. Ready your ship and wait for my signal."

Poplavsky had already pulled down the manual release system handles on either side of the hatch. He put his feet on it and grabbed the handles again; he needed all his strength to free the *Soyuz*. Poplavsky used one of the observation ports to watch the dizzying spin of Earth and space. After a few moments he had the station's rotation rate timed, and when the Earth appeared again, he tugged on the handles with all his strength.

"Now, Arkady, now!" he shouted. In the same moment he felt the resistance in the handles' end. The module jarred sluggishly. The *Soyuz* was free.

"Two second burn on all forward thrusters," said Grachenko, working the attitude control stick with one hand and programming the duration of the burn with the other. "Begin repressurization of the ship, Stefan."

Jets of flame briefly erupted from the thruster quads on the service module behind the *Soyuz* command module. It was the extra kick the ship needed to clear the station before the opposite end came around. Through the observation port on his side of the cabin, Grachenko watched the *Mir* as he backed away. He saw its underside and the array of antennas on it, then the second *Soyuz TM* when the other end rotated past.

"Repressurizing under way," said Siprinoff. "We'll have a normal atmosphere in two minutes."

"Good. Let me see if I can still reach Poplavsky," said Grachenko, turning up the volume on his communications set. "*Soyuz 71* to Mir, Frederick, can you hear me? Over."

"Can hear . . . faintly. I'm head . . . other *Soyuz*. Will join you . . ." And from there the answer became too distant and broken for Grachenko to understand.

"What did he say, Arkady?" Kostilev finally asked.

"He'll join us soon," said Grachenko. "Time to put us around and prepare for our transfer orbit to the *Salyut* station. Since we departed late, the window is fast approaching. Deploy the wide-scan periscope, Vassili. Prepare for rotational maneuver. Port and starboard thrusters activated."

The thruster quads on the *Soyuz* service module began firing in a seemingly random pattern. It swung the spacecraft until it had turned a hundred and eighty degrees and its main engines were facing the *Mir*. A box-shaped pod was lowered from the command module's underside as the maneuver finished. Normally used for rendezvous and docking operations, the crew had deployed the sighting periscope for one last look at their home.

"I have the station," said Kostilev, pushing the view finder over to Grachenko. "Will you try to reach Frederick?"

"No, we're beyond range of our communication systems," said Grachenko. "And besides, the Colonel is far too busy for talking. We'll wait here until he escapes."

The moment Poplavsky saw that his crew was away, he spun around and flew to the observatory's other end. This time, the equipment mounts which had helped to guide him earlier became obstacles. They snagged his suit, blocked his helmet, and, like the connecting hatches, caught his chest pack.

He maneuvered easily between the solar observatory and the medical module. But at the station's midpoint he ran into trouble again with the axial docking compartment. His chest pack caught on a hatch rim and he had to back up to free it. Poplavsky was still in the compartment when it twisted violently. Though it felt like the entire station was coming apart, it was only the module above him.

"The dreams of Future Man . . . God, no," Grachenko uttered, in a hushed voice. Then he turned the view finder so the others could see the start of the *Mir*'s destruction. "Frederick, get out of there. It'll happen quickly now."

The astronomics module tilted in the direction of the *Mir*'s spin before ripping away at its base. The resulting shock wave rippled through the station's structure, further damaging already weakened equipment. After detaching, the module tumbled into a higher orbit, scattering more debris along its trajectory. It would arc several miles above the station before its momentum would give out. What had once been a platform for space exploration and research had become so much junk, the flotsam and jetsam of a new age.

Poplavsky struggled through the axial compartment, hoping its quake-like spasms would not catch and crush him. He pushed his way into the main module, sailing over the command console before standing upright. As he drifted through it, Poplavsky saw that the sparking from still active systems had increased visibly; the waste tanks were leaking again and a new fluid was seeping through the wall seams. It was light-colored, and Poplavsky recognized it immediately. Monomethyl hydrazine.

Some of the light-colored spheres made contact with a glowing circuit, erupting into blossoms of flame. They generated an intense heat Poplavsky could feel through his insulated pressure suit. As the blossoms expanded they ignited other hydrazine spheres. In an instant the flashes were snaking their way across the cabin to their source.

Poplavsky made for the hatch at the end of the main module. He had barely pushed off the floor when the wall the hydrazine had originated from exploded. The blinding eruption of light filled his helmet, before the pressure wave cracked it. He was thrown against something solid and, mercifully, lost consciousness.

"He'll get out. He'll . . . ," Siprinoff's assurance trailed off as he watched the view finder.

"No! Rig for collision!" Grachenko shouted, after he turned the view finder so he could see. "Stefan, lock this down! Watch your fault sensors! Starting main engine."

Fire raced through the axial docking compartment and entered the medical module, where it found more materials to consume. The Moduluny Platform contained little that would burn, but the *Soyuz* attached to it had full oxygen tanks and fuel cells. In seconds most of the two-hundred-foot long station had been overtaken by the growing fireball.

Last to go was the solar observatory. Like the platform, it held nothing explosive; what tore it apart was the force of the blast. What had taken nearly a decade to assemble and had performed so flawlessly in that time, was gone in a matter of moments. Only *Soyuz 71* survived, provided it could flee the cloud of flame and debris.

Grachenko had just ignited the main engine when the shock wave from the explosion reached the spacecraft and rippled through it, compressing and jarring its structure. In the command module the crew was thrown forward. Fortunately their restraint belts kept them from crashing against their instruments. In that instant, most of the sensor lights snapped on, then went off. But because of the confusion, no one could remember which had come on or for how long they had burned.

"I think every light on my board came on," said Kostilev, resettling into his couch. "I can't tell if they were momentary shorts or indicative of real damage."

"You'll have to check them as we proceed to the transfer orbit window," Grachenko advised. "It's too dangerous to remain in this area."

"But shouldn't we at least try to find out if the colonel is alive?" said Siprinoff.

"No one could survive that explosion, and we may not if we stay here. The immediate vicinity is filling with debris. We have no choice. Transmit to Baikonur, tell them Poplavsky is dead and we're heading for the transfer window. Building engine thrust to sixty-five percent."

The increase pushed the *Soyuz* ahead of the expanding sphere of debris from the *Mir* explosion. The fireball quickly burned itself out, leaving behind the wreckage of what had once been mankind's most successful space station. Fleeing it was the *Soyuz*, which in a few minutes would change direction and fire its main engine again, putting it on course for the one haven open to its crew.

"Do you want me to ask Siprinoff to confirm?" Ryumin asked, after he had acknowledged *Soyuz 71*'s latest message.

"No, no need," said Sakolov, wiping the tears from his eyes. "Our console displays show he's telling the truth. They don't need to hear any demands from us. Who knows how badly their ship was damaged by the explosion? They must both check it out and prepare for the transfer orbit. While I'm gone, grant them any information requests they make."

"While you're . . . Where are you going, Yuri?" said Ryumin, caught off guard by Sakolov's orders.

"Someone has to tell Moscow, Anatoly. This is one time I'll not complain about passing a decision to higher authority."

Sakolov rose out of his chair at the command console and turned to leave the operations center. Behind him the stunned and silent control staff returned to some degree of normal activity as they started to feed information to Ryumin. Like the crew of *Soyuz 71*, they could afford only momentary sorrow at the loss of one of their friends.

"Mr. Reiss. Mr. Reiss, I have a priority call from Mount Cheyenne," announced a secretary on the meeting room's intercom. "It's General Rosen himself. He says it's very urgent."

"What in hell's going on?" Reiss demanded, reaching for the intercom controls on his telephone. "First Houston, now NORAD. Okay, Paula, I'll take this one. Christ, I've heard more from this son of a bitch in the last two days than I have in two months."

Reiss switched off the intercom and lifted the telephone receiver to his ear. His irritated tone lasted for the duration of his greeting to Rosen. He then suddenly took great interest in what he was being told, waving at the other people in the room to stop their talk so he could hear better.

"Yes, this does change things," he finally said. "No wonder Houston's been trying to reach me. What's the current condition of the remaining *Soyuz?* I see . . . No, they don't know yet. No, I can't tell if this will revive Cochran's rescue idea or not. It has to be discussed. Thank you for informing me, General."

"What's going on?" asked the State Department official.

"The *Mir* station exploded fifteen minutes ago. One cosmonaut is dead, the other three are on *Soyuz 71*. They're heading for the *Salyut* station but they may have some control damage. Their entry into the transfer orbit window was ragged."

"What was that about the space rescue? Is it still alive?"

"As soon as the orbiter crew hears about this it will be," Reiss answered. "Since we were discussing future mission changes, we're in a good position to decide. Does the State Department have any objections?"

"No, not really, provided the Soviets agree to it in the first place," said the official.

"I think the NSA will object," responded another. "We put a lot of sensitive equipment on these shuttles. Bringing those Russians on the *Phoenix* could compromise it."

"Yeah, those guys haven't seen an issue of *Aviation Week and Space Technology* for months," said the CIA representative.

"Let's not have any dissent in our ranks," said Reiss, cutting off the argument. "When we leave here we have to present a united front, especially to the astronaut corps."

"Here we go again. You're talking as if the astronauts are the enemy. It's the Russians who are the enemy."

"Don't tell me my job! I've done a year as head of manned flight and I know these people. We can't let them divide us. I'll call Houston. The rest of you should call Washington and learn what your agencies and departments are doing."

"I agree, but you're forgetting about the French and the military," said the State Department official. "What about them?"

"We'll freeze them out," said Reiss, "if we can't keep them in line. And somehow I doubt that we can. After the problems we've had with our space mission, this disaster couldn't have happened at a worse time. It looks like we're going to have to do a little more damage control because of it."

"Comrade Doctor, you forgot your coat," said a secretary, emerging from the premier's office with an overcoat in her arms. "And I would like to say that my friends and I are very sorry over the death of Colonel Poplavsky. Please tell his family that they are in our thoughts."

"Yes, yes I will. Thank you," said Fedarenko, in a dazed, toneless voice. He accepted the coat and folded it over his arm, instead of pulling it over his shoulders. As with almost everything else, he seemed oblivious to the spring snowstorm outside. "What can we tell our people? How will we tell the world?"

"My ministry is organizing a press conference," Grachenko replied, as ashen-faced as the Glavkosmos chairman. "You must be there, I'll be there, and so will our best spokesmen. They must already know of the tragedy. Even now they're probably writing anti-Star Wars speeches, for use at the conference."

"Star Wars? The *Mir* wasn't shot down, it blew up. Star Wars had nothing to do with this."

"Of course not, but the propagandists will not miss this opportunity, I guarantee you. And it does serve a purpose. It'll deflect the hard questions the foreign press will ask."

"So everything must serve the interests of the state. We just lost a brave and courageous man. Will we be allowed to mourn his death, or will it be used for political purposes?"

"It will, but stop and listen. The mourning is already happening. You can hear the news spreading through the building, just as it's probably spreading throughout Moscow."

Grachenko and Fedarenko stopped long enough to hear the whispers and startled conversations moving through the offices around them. They could see small groups of workers clustering to hear the news, and they saw tears.

"A reaction like this only happens when a high official dies," Grachenko added, turning and waving his hand around the hall. "Not for a mere colonel, not unless he's a cosmonaut."

"Frederick Andreivich would appreciate it," said Fedarenko. "Now that I think of it, there's an ironic side to this. A year and a half ago, Poplavsky fought successfully to retain the *Salyut* 7. Now it will be a lifeboat for the others."

"We must get moving again, my friend. At the Foreign Ministry we'll prepare for the conference. Here, let me help you."

As they resumed their stride, Grachenko took the coat draped over Fedarenko's arm and helped him into it. At the end of the hall they entered an elevator reserved for executive use. For a short time they would be alone and Grachenko felt comfortable enough to ask a more personal question.

"What of my nephew, Doctor?" he inquired. "Will Arkady Alexiivich remain commander of the spacecraft?"

"Yes, even though he's a civilian. The military may request a change, but he's the original commander of *Soyuz 71*. I just realized something—what about the American shuttle? What will NASA do?"

"Apparently you didn't hear much after news of the disaster reached Gussarov's office. Marshal Suvorov will increase surveillance of the *Phoenix*. He and the Premier believe the Americans may try to take advantage of our misfortune. If they repropose their rescue offer, I'm to politely reject it."

"There's no need for them to offer it," said Fedarenko. "Your nephew and the other cosmonauts will rendezvous with the *Salyut* 7. From there, they'll return to earth. Considering Major Kostilev's injuries, they have to. Though I doubt you'd want that revealed at the press conference. If I'm to be there, you must tell me what I can and cannot say."

"When did it happen, Houston?" Cochran asked, somberly.

"An hour and forty minutes ago," said Caroline Ross,

who was beginning her tour as CAP COM. "We knew about the explosion fifteen minutes after it occurred. We wanted to tell you then, but management had to make the decision first."

"Another management decision," Post commented. "I think Reiss was behind this one as well. If it were up to him, he'd keep us in the dark until we landed."

"If only we hadn't made the attempt to spy on them. I can't help but feel we're responsible," said Simon. Like most of the crew, she stood directly behind the command seats in the shuttle's cockpit. While her tears welled up, they did not roll down her face.

"You have no reason to feel guilty," said Vachet, digging through his pockets for a tissue. "Our reconnaissance pass may have delayed them, but it was their decision to wait. We all have free will. They should've exercised theirs."

"I agree with Paul. In this environment, it must always be safety first," said Cochran, turning in his seat to see his crew. "We can't be held responsible for someone else's paranoia. CAP COM, do you have any idea which of the cosmonauts was killed?"

"We believe it was Colonel Frederick Poplavsky," Caroline answered. "The survivors are all aboard *Soyuz 71* and they're in a transfer orbit for the *Salyut 7*. It appears that the old station has been reactivated."

"I doubt that can work, the *Salyut* is very old. Has my idea been reconsidered? Now would be a good time for a rescue."

"You sure know how to ask the hard questions, Ed. We've not heard much about your idea since it was first rejected. In fact, we've been told not to discuss it with the press."

"That's probably the one management decision I can agree with," said Cochran. "We don't want this idea to be prematurely exposed and flogged to death. We'd like to start making preparations up here. You think we'd have any trouble with it?"

"On a standby basis, I don't think so. But final approval would have to come from the State Department, the White House, the Pentagon, and the French. Not just Bob Engleberg."

"We understand. We'd just like to do something so we won't feel so helpless."

"Well, barring any complaints from Reiss or Engleberg, go right ahead," said Caroline. "Though I should add you can only work on these plans when you don't have some scheduled activity. Which, by the way, are piling up. We're twenty-three minutes from handing you over to CNES control."

"Of course, but before we begin, there's something we want." Cochran shifted in his command chair again and glanced at his crew. He got a nod of approval from each before completing his transmission. "We want a moment of silence for a very brave man."

At first there were some protests from the mission control staff. However, when they realized no one was answering them, they too fell silent. Apart from the humming and clicking of some equipment, a somber quiet spread through the *Phoenix*. For half a minute the astronauts bowed their heads and closed their eyes. At the end of the moment they returned to work. The noise level on the spaceplane jumped dramatically. All too soon, all too fleetingly, the first memorial service to occur in space was over.

Chapter Seven

"Baikonur, this is *Soyuz 71*. We have the *Salyut* on our rendezvous system," Grachenko advised. "We're still having trouble with our attitude thrusters. We'll have to vary their firing duration in the first transposition burn."

"We understand," said Ryumin, who was back to watching the cosmonauts on his console's monitor screen instead of just listening to them. "Since it's impossible to isolate the damage, we cannot help you with this. You must do it as you think best. Sakolov wants to know if you'd like to hold the rendezvous for one orbit, and see if conditions improve."

"No, we should finish it now. The sooner we dock, the sooner we can begin repairing this ship. Your politically motivated strategic redeployment may prove very useful."

"Moscow will be happy to hear that. You're coming up on transposition burn one. T minus five minutes starting now."

"Was it the keel thrusters we were having problems with?" Grachenko asked, before he started programming the ship's thruster quads to slow it for the rendezvous.

"Yes, they were the ones producing only intermittent power," said Siprinoff. "I'm picking up the *Salyut*'s docking radar. We're wide of the mark but it's sweeping us."

"That will change once this maneuver is over. Programming of forward thrusters completed. Two minutes, thirty-four seconds to first transposition burn."

Grachenko switched the flight system to automatic and recited the countdown with a team from the Baikonur control staff. When the count ended, the front nozzles on the *Soyuz* thruster quads emitted jets of blue-white flame. Those on the top and sides of the spacecraft didn't burn as brightly as the keel thruster. The latter, however, did not fire as smoothly and, only seconds into the burn, cut out. Then the entire quad disappeared in a jarring flash.

"Lock down your helmets!" Grachenko shouted,

slapping his own visor over his face. "Stefan, check pressurization! Manual overrides, on! Baikonur, we have an in-orbit emergency!"

All activated thruster engines stopped firing as Grachenko brought his fist down on a red plunger switch. But the momentum they created was causing the *Soyuz* to tumble, nose over tail, toward the *Salyut 7* station.

"Arkady, we have damage to the keel thruster quad," said Kostilev. "I'll try to isolate it."

"All right, just don't shut down the entire system," said Grachenko. "Topside thrusters, one hundred percent."

By the time the engines he had selected were firing, the *Soyuz* was upside down and flying backwards. They immediately slowed its tumbling and, a few seconds later, it came to a halt, standing on its head.

"Our atmosphere is normal. The pressure shell hasn't been ruptured," Siprinoff reported.

"*Soyuz*, this is Baikonur. What's your condition, over?"

"Our condition is difficult but stabilizing," said Grachenko. "Please compute our closure rate and rendezvous time with the station. Vassili, close the fuel lines if you have to. I'd rather loose thrusters than more fuel."

"*Soyuz*, this is Baikonur," said Ryumin, his face no longer appearing on the instrument panel monitors. Until the ship was righted there could be no video transmission. "Your orbital velocity and closure rate remain the same. You'll overtake the *Salyut* in eight minutes, fifty seconds. Do you still wish to try for a rendezvous?"

"I'm afraid not with this damage," Grachenko answered.

"Then you must program another burn. You moved enough laterally to put you in danger of colliding with the *Salyut*."

"Roger, Baikonur. Preparing side thrusters two and

four. They'll fire at seventy percent thrust. I'll control the duration of the burn. Stand by."

Grachenko quickly activated the portside thrusters and fired them manually. They halted the drift started by the original maneuver and pushed the *Soyuz* along its y-axis, away from a collision with the rapidly approaching space station. Grachenko shut off the thrusters after receiving the word his ship was out of danger. A few minutes later the navigation and docking lights of the *Salyut 7* came into view.

"So close and yet so far," Siprinoff commented, looking past his commander's shoulder.

"Yes, we can almost reach out and touch it," said Grachenko. "But it might as well be orbiting with the moons of Jupiter. Baikonur, this is *Soyuz 71*. We have passed the station. We cannot, repeat cannot, dock with it. We request permission to begin the earliest possible re-entry."

"We need to talk with Moscow first," Ryumin warned. "I'll contact Dr. Fedarenko immediately. Stabilize your ship as best you can and we'll bring you home, I promise. Good luck, Arkady. This is Baikonur, out."

"Christ, did you see that? It flew right by the station," said Ericson, pointing to the lines on the main screen.

"Of course I see it," Rosen answered. "Instead of being obvious, Larry, bring up a magnification on screen 1-A."

On the multi-story screen in SDC's control center, the orbital tracks of *Soyuz 71* and the *Salyut 7* had been merging for the last ten minutes. Now, however, the *Soyuz* track was passing the station's and had begun to flash, indicating something had gone wrong with the expected rendezvous.

"Magnification coming up, General," said Ericson, as he finished giving instructions to the center's display control.

On the uppermost left-hand screen an enhanced and enlarged version of the missed rendezvous was shown. It presented more information than the main screen: the velocities of the two craft, the distance of their separation, their altitudes and attitudes. Rosen and those with him only had to study the side screen for a moment before they realized something was indeed wrong.

"Good God, it's almost perpendicular to the Earth," said a Major. "What the hell happened?"

"Let's piece it together," said Rosen, tapping a button on his communications panel. "Command One to Satellite Control, I want SARSAT and AMEWS pictures of the *Soyuz 71*. Bring them up on side screens 1-B and 1-C."

Activity in the lower tiers of consoles increased after Rosen gave his orders. Commands went out to the chains of synthetic aperture radar satellites, and advanced missile early warning satellites in high polar orbits. What the SARSATs couldn't gain through their radar-imaging systems, the AMEWS would detect by infrared. Several minutes later, the information arrived at Space Defence Command, having first gone through NORAD, and was put on the two side screens.

"SARSAT scan coming in," Ericson observed. "And it looks like the AMEWS data will arrive on time, for a change."

The radar and infrared images were identical, though etched differently. The radar one was made of sharp, green lines and had the clarity of a black and white photograph. The infrared image was painted in surrealistic hues of black, yellow and red, revealing the various temperatures on the surface of the *Soyuz*.

"So it is perpendicular," said Rosen, leaning forward. "Damn, what's the glowing spot on the bottom of the ship? It's too hot just to be the thruster engines."

"It's in the location of the bottom thruster quad," said Ericson. "Could there be a fire on the ship?"

"If there was a fire, the *Soyuz* would've been destroyed by now." Rosen shifted his chair and glanced at the main

110

screen, where the track of *Soyuz 71* continued to snake its way across the map. "The heat's probably from an explosion. We've got a seriously damaged spacecraft here. It won't be able to dock with the *Salyut* station."

"What's going to happen to the crew?" asked the Major.

"If the ship can still do it, the cosmonauts will make a reentry. I should add that's a pretty big if."

"What about NASA?" Ericson asked, "Should we contact them?"

"Yes and no," said Rosen, getting an angry look in his eyes. "I'm growing tired of talking to the non-astronaut about space matters. And I bet he won't tell the ones who count."

"Then who should we tell?"

"The ones who count. The time's right for contacting Ed. We won't do it through our own facilities, there's no need to. The *Phoenix* is being directed by Toulouse Mission Control, and NORAD has secure channels to the French Air Force's Défence Aérienne command. They can tie us directly into their mission control, and the non-astronaut will never have to know."

Rosen took one last glance at the information displayed on the screens in front of him before turning his attention to his communications panel. Through NORAD's channels he would hopefully reach CNES mission control in the southern French city of Toulouse.

"Brad, you're late," said Clay Reynolds, when he noticed another figure entering the astronauts' lounge. "Where have you been? Talking to your wife?"

"No way, not me," said Bradford Harrison, astronaut Julie Harrison's husband, as he approached the men and women who were clustered in front of the lounge's TV set. "The *Phoenix* is still under French control. I can't talk to Julie until later. What's happening here?"

"A live press conference from Moscow. They got the

111

Foreign Minister, the Glavkosmos chairman, plus the usual mouthpieces. They've admitted the disaster, but they're using it to kick around Star Wars again."

"Hey you guys, Fedarenko's talking about the survivors," said one of the other astronauts. "Pipe down and listen."

Once Reynolds and Harrison ended their conversation, Fedarenko's voice was heard clearly, along with the rapid fire clicking of still cameras. Even though the press conference had been a hastily organized one, it was heavily attended by camera crews and reporters. Many were not the regulars assigned to Moscow, but they had been sent specifically to cover the *Mir* disaster. As novices, they did not know the rules for interviewing Soviet officials and were asking more and more difficult questions, with a noticeable effect on Fedarenko.

"No, the remaining *Soyuz* has changed orbits to rendezvous with the *Salyut 7* station," he answered, becoming visibly confused. "No, I cannot say if the *Soyuz* was damaged by the explosion. No, I see no reason why it can't return if it has to. Why do you ask these questions? Do you wish to see further disaster? You want the rest of our cosmonauts to die?"

"Poor bastard, he's letting the press apes get to him," said Reynolds. "Sort of like someone in orbit we know."

"Yes, and even though they're upsetting the Russians, those questions do have a use for us," Harrison added. "We can find out how badly damaged the *Soyuz* is, and perhaps improve chances for Cochran's rescue plan."

"Cochran better worry about how he can rescue his career, instead of saving Russians."

The remark and the familiar voice took everyone in the lounge by surprise. It was George Reiss. He had entered the room virtually unnoticed and, from the look in his eyes, the astronauts could tell he was in a vindictive mood.

"I knew I'd find you here," he continued. "You always gather at a tragedy. I've come to tell you there isn't going to be a rescue mission, in spite of what happened today. The Soviets have said 'nyet' to our offer again, and the issue is dead."

"But what if the ship can't dock with the station?" Reynolds asked. "Or reenter because of damage? What then? We should still be doing the background work for a rescue operation, just in case it's needed."

"Yes, we should keep making the offer to the Russians until they accept it," said Harrison, recovering from his shock. "Conditions can change."

"I didn't come to argue this with you," said Reiss, his ill mood growing worse. "I'm here to tell you the issue is dead and to warn you not to try anything behind my back. Your communication privileges are suspended until the *Phoenix* lands."

"You always were a dickhead, Reiss," said Reynolds. "But this should get you the Dildo of the Month award."

"That's going to cost you the command of *Discovery's* next flight. Keep it up and you'll be looking for another job."

Reiss turned and stormed noisily out the lounge in direct contrast to the way he had so quietly slipped in.

"God, how I wish we had Richard Truly back," said one of the other astronauts. "What will you do now, Clay?"

"I'll tell you what he'll do," said Harrison. "He's going to find a way to skin Reiss and hang him out to dry."

"A nice idea but, business before pleasure," Reynolds admitted, a smile on his face. "There's more than one way to talk to a spacecraft. And I know a few."

"*Phoenix*, this is Toulouse. Is the Fleet Com deploying?" asked Raquel Jordan, the senior French Capsule Communicator.

"Yes, my dear, she's just as magnificent as the first one," said Vachet. "The rest of her activation is up to you."

"Roger, *Phoenix*. Our satellite control team is taking command. Daurat would like to have a word with you."

Raquel gave up her seat at mission control's command console to the man standing behind her. Jacques-Chaumie Daurat had the headset on and was talking to the shuttle before he had finished sitting down and adjusting the chair to suit his much shorter frame.

"This is Mission Control Director to *Phoenix*," he announced, enjoying the chance to use his title. "Paul, I have some news for you and Commander Cochran. It came from an unusual source, a General Bernard Rosen."

"Yes, Bernie is certainly odd," said Cochran. "Only he would think of sending a message through you."

"For a general, he's proving very resourceful," said Vachet. "What news do you have?"

"The *Soyuz* has missed its rendezvous with the derelict station. Rosen believes it is too badly damaged to attempt a docking. The craft is changing to a lower orbit."

"Do you think it's preparing for reentry, my friend?"

"I believe so," said Daurat. "And if the craft has lost some of its flight controls, then the reentry will be very rough for its crew. They're not out of danger yet, though it does mean an end to your rescue plans. I'm sorry, Commander, yours was a noble idea and we would've liked to have been part of it."

"Don't be sorry. To fly the rescue would've required new flight programs and a lot of ground help NASA isn't about to give," Cochran answered, the sadness in his voice coming over clearly on the headsets and console speakers. "Though I still think those cosmonauts would be safer returning with us."

"No doubt they would, but your nobility must remain stillborn. Paul, I know you supported Commander Cochran. I'm sorry for both of you."

"It was Edward's original inspiration. I only supported it, and articulated it," said Vachet.

"But you did it so well," Daurat responded. "I

114

understood what you were talking about earlier today. If only the officials at NASA and in Moscow would listen to you. I guess they don't have time for eloquence . . . Do you wish to be kept informed of *Soyuz 71's* flight?"

"We'd appreciate it," said Cochran. "This disaster isn't over yet. A lot of things still could happen."

"Consider it done. I'm turning you back to Raquel. Good luck, *Phoenix.*" Daurat stripped off his headset and returned both it and the chair at the command console to Raquel Jordan. "Make sure they receive updates from the tracking net."

"You think this crisis is finished?" she asked.

"No, it has yet to play itself out. What the American said is true, and I'll go even farther. Until the *Soyuz* command capsule is on the ground, those men are in danger and may need our help."

"Baikonur, this is *Soyuz 71.* The command module has been sealed," Grachenko advised. "We're ready to jettison the orbital module."

"Roger, *Soyuz.* You may proceed," said Ryumin. "You're five minutes, nineteen seconds, from your reentry window."

"Thank you, Baikonur. *Soyuz 71,* out. Stefan, unlock the collar. After all those hours it took to load them, we can now wave good-bye to our groceries."

Siprinoff reached for a wheel over the main instrument panel and began turning it counterclockwise. Despite the advanced, modern systems aboard the *Soyuz TM,* some equipment was still manually operated. When a soft clank vibrated through the spacecraft, followed by the hiss of out-rushing air, the cosmonauts knew the module in front of theirs had detached.

Grachenko tapped the controls for the remaining forward thrusters and the *Soyuz* pulled away from its orbital module, which at once started to decelerate and tumble. In several hours it would enter the atmosphere

115

and, since it lacked a heat shield, would burn up. The moment he was finished with the forward thrusters, Grachenko fired another set of attitude jets to realign his craft for the upcoming reentry window.

"*Soyuz 71*, this is Baikonur. You are T minus one minute from your de-orbit burn," Ryumin announced. "Check fuel pressure and commence pre-ignition sequence."

"Roger, Baikonur. We've finished retracting the photovoltaic arrays," said Grachenko. "Pre-ignition sequence has begun."

"The arrays are secured, Arkady," Siprinoff added. "All systems are on internal batteries."

"Good. Vassili?"

"Main engine fuel lines have been pressurized," said Kostilev, rechecking his panel status lights. "They are nominal."

"*Soyuz*, this is Baikonur. You are T minus thirty seconds."

"Roger, Baikonur. Main engine control has been switched to the flight computer," said Grachenko, getting into the rhythm of the operation; he was at last feeling comfortable. "Manual flight controls and overrides on standby."

"Life support is nominal, Arkady," said Siprinoff. "It looks like this nightmare is finally ending."

"*Soyuz*, this is Baikonur. You are T minus twenty seconds. Lock down your helmets," Ryumin ordered.

"Roger, Baikonur. Locking helmets."

In unison, the cosmonauts lowered their visors and sealed them. Despite the fact the command module had normal atmospheric pressure, the safety precaution had been taken on every *Soyuz* reentry for the last twenty years, ever since *Soyuz 11* had depressurized by accident, killing its crew.

"*Soyuz 71*, this is Baikonur. You are T minus fifteen seconds. Are you go for automatic ignition?"

"Roger, Baikonur. Final computer check confirms we are set for auto sequence firing," said Grachenko.

"Excellent, *Soyuz*. You're T minus ten seconds and

116

your auto sequence is initiating. T minus seven seconds, six . . ."

Grachenko eased onto his couch in preparation for the burn. Apart from detaching the service module after the de-orbit maneuver was completed, there was nothing left for him to do until touchdown. When Ryumin reached zero, the *Soyuz* was jarred by the initial firing of the main engine. As it built up thrust, Grachenko could feel the deceleration it caused. He also saw it in the drop-off of speed and altitude on his panel displays. In half an hour, he guessed, the disaster would be over.

"Arkady. Arkady, there's trouble," Kostilev warned, talking above a shrill beeping. "My heat shield sensor is on."

"What? God, no," said Grachenko, his pleasant daydream shattering. "Check it, make sure it's not a sensor fault."

He reached for the manual shut-off button but stopped short of hitting it. Most of the damage his ship had suffered was electrical, and Grachenko wanted to make sure the alert was more than just a glitch before taking the irreversible actions which would end the maneuver.

"It's no sensor fault, Arkady," said Kostilev. "Something is definitely wrong with the heat shield. I think it's cracking from the pressure of the de-orbit firing."

"Warn Baikonur!" said Grachenko. "I'm killing the burn!"

First he hit the shut-off button, then the manual overrides, to free the flight controls. The *Soyuz* had lost a critical thousand kilometers per hour in velocity and fifteen kilometers in altitude. If he did not regain them, the drag created by ploughing through the upper atmosphere would doom his ship.

"Baikonur, this is *Soyuz*. We are aborting reentry," said Siprinoff. "We've suffered heat shield failure."

"Understood, *Soyuz*. We'll compute your burn time to regain orbit," said Ryumin. "Do nothing until then. Baikonur to all stations, we have an orbital emergency."

"Arkady, didn't you hear Ryumin? He said we're to do nothing until he talks to us."

"Let the devil take him, Stefan," Grachenko replied. "We have only minutes to do something before it's too late."

The *Soyuz* had been flying backwards ever since achieving its reentry orbit; this allowed it to use its main engine for braking. Now, to regain the position that had been lost, Grachenko reactivated his thrusters and tumbled his spacecraft a hundred and eighty degrees until he had the engine pointing in the right direction.

"But what about Ryumin?" Siprinoff repeated. "He's—"

"Not here," said Grachenko. "We are, and every second of inaction takes us closer to our deaths."

As he spoke, Grachenko tapped the manual ignition button for the main engine. The response was the familiar kick as it fired up, ending the ship's fatal descent and speed loss.

"*Soyuz*, this is Baikonur. Why have you restarted your engine?" Ryumin demanded. "You were ordered to wait."

"Anatoly, shut up," said Sakolov, who, because he didn't have a microphone on his voice, sounded more distant to the cosmonauts. "They couldn't wait for you. Recompute burn time from the moment they restarted their engine."

"Hurry, Anatoly," Grachenko added. "I don't have the fuel to stop and restart this thing."

"Enough! I'm trying, I'm trying!" Ryumin said nervously. "All right. Try two minutes at my mark . . . Mark."

Grachenko immediately started to count off the seconds of the remaining main engine's burn time by using his panel chronometer. Siprinoff and Kostilev joined in and, exactly one hundred and twenty seconds later, the manual shut-off button was hit again.

"Vehicle speed is 28,000 kilometers an hour," said

Grachenko. "And we're back at our original altitude. For now, we're safe."

"But for how long?" Siprinoff asked. "We're low on fuel and oxygen, and we have no other supplies. We can't reenter and we can't return to the *Salyut* station. Unless our friends at Baikonur can come up with another miracle, I'm afraid our options have just run out."

Chapter Eight

"Thank you for seeing me at this hour, Nikolai Grigorivich," said Defence Minister Nagorny, when a familiar face greeted him at the entrance to the foreign minister's residence. "I appreciate it. I know you have the full story, and I would like to hear it before the official version comes out."

"Thank you for coming at such a time," Grachenko somberly responded. "It gives me someone to talk with. Please, come in."

Nagorny emerged from the chill night and went to the closet to hang his overcoat. When he was finished, he accompanied his friend to the one illuminated room in the otherwise darkened house, the first-floor study. Warm and familiar, it was richly appointed with collections of czarist-era paintings and other art works. After they entered, Nagorny selected his favorite chair in front of the study's fireplace, while Grachenko took a seat opposite his.

"What did Fedarenko tell you of your nephew and the other cosmonauts?" Nagorny asked, settling into his chair.

"They're stranded in orbit. They're almost out of fuel, their heat shield has failed, and in a matter of hours they will exhaust their oxygen. It would take Glavkosmos two

119

weeks to prepare another *Soyuz*, or the shuttle, for a mission. Fedarenko says his agency has run out of options."

"Are they doing anything? In the army, we would try something to rescue our people."

"The wives and children of the cosmonauts are gathering at Baikonur," said Grachenko. "From there, they will say their farewells. Don't blame the space agency for doing little; you must understand the conditions they work with. What's the army doing in this crisis, Pietr Arkadivich? There are some unsettling rumors."

"You've heard what Suvorov in Air Defence is doing," said Nagorny, shifting nervously in his chair. "That's how I first found out there was something wrong with the reentry. Yes, certain forces in his command are on second-stage alert."

"Such as the satellite interceptor forces at Volgograd and the Northern Cosmodrome?" Grachenko added.

"Yes, they are very active."

"And are they not preparing the new Hydra anti-satellite weapons for launch?"

"Your information is remarkable, my friend,' said Nagorny, surprised at the revelation. "Marshal Suvorov is readying the Hydras for launch, as many as he can. He still believes the Americans can take advantage of this disaster, and his actions have the support of many in the Politburo."

"In honesty, I wish the Americans would try. They can do something more than mount a ghoulish death watch on our cosmonauts. Do you see the equipment over there? From this room I can talk to almost anyone in the world."

Grachenko rose from his chair and walked over to his desk, where he laid a hand on a modern communications console. It was out of place with the room's furnishings, but it allowed Grachenko to perform the duties of his position.

120

"From here I could talk directly with Washington," he continued. "I could talk to the Secretary of State, and accept the offer to use their shuttle to rescue our men. You don't know how much the thought appeals to me."

"Nikolai, it would do no good," said Nagorny. "You would be replaced and your successor would disavow your acceptance. Please don't end your career this way."

"I know you're right, but it does not help my conscience rest any easier. The only actions I'm being allowed to take are to prepare our country for the impending tragedy, and to warn the only people who can save our men not to try."

"Marshal, we have an update from the Volgograd battalion," warned a Lieutenant General as he entered the darkened room. "You said you wanted to see it the moment it came in."

"Yes. Yes," replied the figure which lay on a bed. "Let me have the report."

Marshal Vitali Suvorov was irritated by the disturbance and grumbled as he rolled upright to sit on the edge of his bed. He switched on a reading light and held the paper his deputy had given him under its bright glare. The scowl on his face quickly changed to a satisfied smile as he read through the report.

"I knew he would succeed," said Suvorov, handing the sheet back. "Colonel Aksyonov is a good man when threatened. What of the Northern Cosmodrome battalion, any news from them?"

"Since they were on schedule, I didn't feel it necessary to question them."

"General, I want to know what's happening at all times. Hand me my jacket and cap, I'm coming out."

The deputy, Lieutenant General Alexei Jurkov, retrieved Suvorov's jacket and wheel cap from a nearby closet and handed them to him after he was finished tying his shoes. He would then return to the command center to gather the latest information while Suvorov completed dressing.

"Alexei, I also want to know about the American shuttle," he added. "Especially any change in its orbit or attitude."

A few minutes later, Suvorov had finished grooming himself and emerged from his bunker-like quarters. He had only to walk a dozen yards before entering the command center to his Voyska PVO, the National Air Defence Forces.

The center had a low, domed ceiling which made it oppressively closed in. In the middle of the room was a raised platform for the command consoles, and along one section of the wall were maps of the Soviet Union and the world. Suvorov made his way through the outer rings of consoles and mounted the command platform.

"The Northern Cosmodrome reports their first Hydra is thirty minutes away from operational status," said Jurkov, as he finished his salute. "Their second is ninety minutes away. In three hours all satellite interceptors will be flight ready."

"After the years we spent perfecting this system we may at last see it used," said Suvorov, turning to another officer on the platform. "Colonel, what's the status of the shuttle?"

"It has not changed altitude or orbit for the last four hours since its crew went to sleep," the officer answered. "Though there has been a new development."

Suvorov walked to the section of the platform which faced the wall maps and quickly found the orbital track of the *Phoenix* on the world chart. Its track a yellow line snaking across the land masses, the symbol for the shuttle was approaching the western shore of Australia. Suvorov studied it for several moments, then turned to face his staff.

"Development? What development?" he asked. "I see no change in its speed, track, or altitude."

"The change is in who's controlling it," said the

122

Colonel. "The French Mission Center at Toulouse was originally to control the shuttle. But now it's in direct contact with NORAD command in America, probably their space defence forces."

"Can you intercept what they're saying?"

"We can, but we can't decipher it. The Americans are using secure military channels."

"I see. And what should this lead us to conclude?" asked Suvorov.

"Further evidence of the dissimulation of America's claims that their space program is run by civilians," said the General, as if he were reading the response.

"No, Jurkov. That is too broad, for now."

"The Americans obviously know of our problems," said the Colonel who had first warned of the transmissions. "The military is talking to the shuttle crew about them. Perhaps they're planning to take advantage of our misfortune."

"Yes, Colonel. That's exactly what they're doing," Suvorov replied. "We must tighten our surveillance of the *Phoenix*. This conspiracy of the Americans and the Chinese is about to succeed. I wish the fools and appeasers in Glavkosmos and the Foreign Ministry would see it, but they're too concerned with politics and coexistence."

"Do you think the French are involved in the conspiracy?" asked Jurkov. "They're quite independent of the Americans."

"Of course they're involved. The Western Allies think alike on these matters. I want increased surveillance on all their launch bases. General, make sure all shifts understand the order. Like the others, it will stay in effect until this crisis with our spacecraft ends."

"I think we've got everyone," said Cochran, checking the crew who were on the flight deck. "No, wait. Where's Jack?"

123

"Space veteran is having a little trouble getting out of his hammock," Post answered. "Either he'll be here soon or we'll hear some gagging from the middle deck."

"Well, there's enough of us here. What do you want to tell us, Bernie? I hope it's worth getting us up two hours early and taking the chance at Reiss's anger."

"Believe me, it is," said Rosen, his voice coming over the flight deck's loudspeakers. "We may have a day, or even less, before this crisis ends fatally for our Soviet friends."

"What happened? We were told they'd be reentering during our sleep period," said Vachet.

"They attempted a reentry, but stopped only moments into their de-orbit burn. From the transmissions Fort Mead deciphered, we believe their heat shield has failed. Their oxygen supplies are minimal, and they don't have the fuel to return to the *Salyut* station. So your plan, Ed, is the only option left to them."

"I can't deny that I feel a certain elation over this," Cochran admitted, the gloom which had been hanging over him for the last several hours suddenly lifting. "Though I feel sorry the Russians couldn't get out of it on their own."

"Can't they rescue themselves by reentering with their service module attached?" Post asked. "After all, John Glenn came back with the retro-rocket package still attached to his capsule because of a possible heat shield failure."

"A service module isn't a simple package of solid-fuel rocket engines," said Rosen. "It has tanks of liquid fuel and oxygen, and there's enough left in them to cause one hell of an explosion when they reach ignition temperature."

"Then a rescue has become a matter of necessity," Vachet concluded, "not just a noble and eloquent gesture, not just an adventure. It's truly life or death, and we're the only ones with the power to change the fate of these men."

124

"Problem is, we need ground support," said Cochran, his mind racing to plan out all the particulars the operation would need. "Houston would love to help, though they'd all be fired if they did. Toulouse doesn't have enough ground tracking facilities. Which means the only space center that can help us is yours, Bernie. You've got the staff and the computers to do our flight programs, and you have both Spacetrack and the navy's Space Surveillance System."

"Now hold on, Ed. I'm taking a hell of a chance just contacting you," said Rosen, the surprise in his voice noticeable even two hundred and forty miles up and half a world away. "My staff wants to help, and I'm pretty sure the air force wouldn't mind us getting involved, but I can't commit us any further. Perhaps with the situation changed, Reiss and the rest of NASA management will look upon your idea differently."

"I understand. But remember, the Defence Department owns half the orbiter fleet to begin with. I doubt NASA will do much to upset the arrangement. You have anything else for us, Bernie?"

"No, I've covered it. We'll keep monitoring the situation, and let you know if something happens. We've smoothed out our communications with the French. Getting in touch will be easier in the future. This is Space Defence Command, out."

A soft click brought the transmissions to an end and Cochran motioned for his crew to unplug their headsets. He turned in his cockpit seat to find Ripley hovering above the floor hatch.

"How much did you hear, Jack?" Cochran requested.

"Enough to know we could be back in business," said Ripley. "Your friend certainly knows the fine difference between getting involved and being committed."

"What difference is there?" Vachet asked.

"Well let me put it this way. In ham and eggs, it's the chicken that's involved but the pig that's committed."

"An appropriate comparison," said Cochran. "Bernie

125

doesn't want to get his fat fried over this. It's not his career on the line, and this isn't his ship. It's mine on both counts."

"Still, let's not give up on your friend so completely," said Vachet. "He shares many traits in common with Daurat. And I do admire him because of his reluctance to get civilian officials angry at him. Only in totalitarian regimes do the generals feel they have an immunity to civilian rule."

"Then I hope we can wear down both your friend and mine, Saint Ex. Frankly, I don't give them much chance of turning NASA around. Speaking of your friend, shouldn't he or the Toulouse CAP COM be trying to contact us?"

"Perhaps they don't know our conversation with General Rosen has ended? Let me set the Toulouse frequency and see if someone there is on duty, or at least waking up."

Vachet squeezed his way through the crowd and slid into the pilot's seat. He reset the overhead communications panel to the CNES frequency and only had to ask once before getting a response from the mission control staff.

"They know of the problems the Russians are facing and want to know if General Rosen gave us anything new," said Vachet. "They tell me Daurat is waking up and will come to the center."

"So, in spite of the fact that we have ninety minutes of sleep time left, we've got work to do," said Cochran. "Not all of us need to be up here. I suggest some of you catch the rest of your sleep if you want to. We're going to have a busy day."

Most of the crew followed Cochran's advice and returned to the middle deck to complete their sleep. Only Ripley stayed behind to hear what he had missed. After several minutes, he too disappeared through the floor hatch, leaving Cochran and Vachet to themselves once again. But this time they weren't mourning what might

126

have been; they were discussing what had to be.

"*Soyuz 71*, this is Baikonur. Have you corrected your tumble?" Ryumin asked, as he plugged in his headset.

"Anatoly, you're back," said Grachenko, his voice coming over clearly. "Yes, we had some trouble while you were off-duty but we corrected it. Though we did use most of our remaining fuel to stop it."

"What difference does that make?" Siprinoff complained. "We're going to die, Arkady. Ryumin had come back to start a death watch. We're going to die."

"Please, Stefan. None of this is easy for any of us." Ryumin spoke quietly and tried to keep the emotion he felt out of his voice. He had thought, had hoped, that this would not happen until much later. He quickly understood the ordeal he was in for. "When I woke up, I read you had confirmed heat shield failure visually. How did you do it?"

"We turned the wide-scan periscope to watch our back," said Grachenko. "Eventually we saw pieces of the ablative shield flake off and drift away. We also completed our assessment, would you care to hear it?"

"Yes, please. It wasn't completed in time for me to read."

"Most of our food, water, and oxygen supplies were in the orbital module we released. We have only fourteen to sixteen hours of oxygen left, including our pressure suit supplies. We have our emergency rations of food and water, so we won't go hungry while we wait for our atmosphere to give out. We do have our medical kit, and we know which drugs to take when the time comes. We don't have enough fuel left for our main engine, though we can use our attitude thrusters."

"Why not use the rest of our fuel now and begin a reentry?" asked Kostilev. "I'm in enough pain already. Why not finish it quickly?"

"Because we learned with Komarov on the *Soyuz 1*

that burn-up during reentry can be very painful," said Ryumin. "We want to make this as painless for you as we can. And there's still a chance we can come to an agreement with NASA."

Ryumin lowered his voice and whispered the last part of his response. Political officials at Baikonur had ruled the topic a non-subject. Nevertheless it had been widely discussed, though Ryumin's mention was the first time anyone had raised it openly.

"Any straw in the wind is worth grasping," said Grachenko, the pessimism in his voice lifting a little. "Apart from your hopes for an agreement, what else have you been planning?"

"Our journalists will visit here shortly. They're to do a story on how dedicated and professional Glavkosmos is, in wake of criticisms in the western press. After them, we'll bring in your families. We'll limit it to your wives and older children, no parents or other relatives. You're to set your TV camera on ground control, and we'll keep it in operation until the end of this crisis. Be prepared to say good-bye, my friends. We'll give you as much time as is reasonable."

"What's to happen after we die, Anatoly Victorvich? Has anything been decided?"

"Moscow is already planning memorials to you in the days to come," Ryumin answered, choking back the emotion he could feel tightening his throat. "As for us, we have two choices. One is to let your orbit deteriorate naturally and allow you to burn up. The other is to change the *Soyuz* over to Ground Control and attempt to keep you in orbit until we launch the shuttle. Yuri Sakolov has already ordered an Energiya booster and the *Baran* shuttle to be stacked ahead of schedule. However, there are certain groups who want nothing done."

"We understand. Better to have bronze plaques and statues to dedicate than bodies to bury," Grachenko soberly remarked. "If you don't mind, Anatoly, we'd like to have a little time to ourselves. We need time to prepare."

128

"Of course. If you wish for anything, contact us at once. This is Baikonur, out."

When transmissions from the *Soyuz* ended, Ryumin pulled off his headset and rose to his feet. He glanced around the center, its activity level considerably subdued beyond what was normal, then fixed his gaze on the main screen. On it the tracks of the *Soyuz*, the *Mir* remnants, and the *Phoenix* were displayed.

"You took considerable risk bringing up the NASA option," said deputy flight officer Malyshev. "Political Affairs has been very active trying to defeat the idea. They almost make it sound as if we're at war with the Americans."

"I know. Even after all these years of glasnost, they still find an idea dangerous. The NASA shuttle could easily rescue our friends, if only reality didn't stand in the way."

"Yes, comrade. If only we could contact NASA on our own, I'm certain we would reach an agreement."

"You just took a considerable risk in mentioning that," said Ryumin, smiling. At least he found something which could lighten his mood. "Political Affairs is probably listening to everything. The only ones who don't have to worry about what they say are our friends in orbit. I hope we can make their last hours as comfortable as possible, though it will not be comfortable for us."

Chapter Nine

"This looks like a familiar scene," Reynolds observed, as he walked into the lounge and noticed his friends clustered around its television set. "I suppose if we can't be astronauts we can at least be couch potatoes. What's on the tube?"

"Something that's also become familiar," said Brad Harrison. "And this time you're missing it. We got another conference from Moscow. Better get over here."

At first Reynolds was only dimly aware of the voices coming from the TV. But the closer he got, the more recognizable they became, especially one which spoke in stiff, lightly accented English. When he reached the set, he could see Fedarenko manning a panel with the usual Soviet spokesmen and propagandists.

"He doesn't sound as combative as yesterday," said Reynolds, taking a seat across from Harrison. "What happened? Did he get kicked in the head? He sounds like he's in shock."

"I think he is," said the woman sitting next to Harrison. "They can't get their men out of orbit. Just listen."

"No, the *Soyuz* has not gone back to the *Salyut 7*," Fedarenko answered, slowly and painfully. "All our options are being studied at the present time."

"Dr. Fedarenko, why don't you just ask NASA for help?" demanded an off-camera reporter, in a loud, dominating, voice. "Why don't you just admit the crisis is out of control and ask NASA to rescue your cosmonauts?"

"Yes, jerk, why don't you get the most dedicated spacefaring nation on the planet to admit it can't get three guys out of Low Earth Orbit," said Reynolds.

"Keep it down, Clay," said Harrison. "We'd like to hear the answer to this."

"The crisis is not out of control," replied one of the foreign ministry spokesmen, cutting in on Fedarenko. "Our best experts are working on it. We've not asked NASA for its assistance because we understand the shuttle they have in orbit is very busy conducting SDI experiments. These experiments are classified, and the Americans would not wish to compromise them by bringing our cosmonauts on board. We can understand this, but of course we cannot condone your country's

130

desire to militarize space. If it weren't for this, we would ask."

The response brought out a mixture of groans and laughter from the astronauts. Those who were angry with it wanted the program changed, but a majority held out and the show continued to run, though its audience seemed much less interested.

"Trust the fucking Russians to turn a disaster into an anti-Star Wars speech," Reynolds remarked bitterly. "What jerks."

"Sounds to me like everyone on this show is a jerk to you," said Harrison, trying to be humorous.

"Everyone but him." Reynolds pointed to the screen, where Dr. Fedarenko was once again being shown. "Poor bastard, the one figure of dignity and intelligence in a sea of assholes."

"We better realize statements like theirs aren't going to help our cause much," said an astronaut who sided with Reynolds. "When this conference started, I had hoped Reiss would watch it. Now I hope he doesn't hear about it."

"Yes, having the Russians insult us won't make it easy to sell the rescue to NASA management. By the way, where is Reiss? I don't see him sneaking around here."

"In another meeting, Clay. I heard he's in a teleconference with Houston and Space Defence Command. Looks like he's going to call your friend on the carpet for talking with the orbiter."

"Reiss can bitch at Bernie and make him feel uncomfortable," said Reynolds. "But he can't do much else."

"Well, we'd better be ready when his meeting ends," Harrison advised. "In spite of what's being said, it's more important than ever that we fly a rescue mission. I don't know about you two, but I'm not going to let my wife down."

"*Soyuz*, this is Baikonur. We're receiving your transmissions, you're coming in clear," said Ryumin, glancing between the monitor at his console and the identical image on the main screen. "Are you receiving ours?"

"Only a test pattern, but it's clear," Grachenko replied, looking down at the monitors on the main control panel.

"Good. Your family will go first, Arkady."

Ryumin turned to the visitors' booth at the back of the operations center and motioned for the live transmissions to begin. Inside the booth a makeshift television studio had been set up and, aside from its crew, the only people in it were a statuesque blonde and a young girl, barely a teenager. The moment Ryumin gave his signal, their image appeared on the monitor Grachenko had been staring at.

"Natalia," he said, leaning more to left for a better view of the screen. "Natalia, you look so beautiful. Just like I've always dreamed about you, and always will. I'd give my soul to hold you once more."

"I know, Arkady. I love you," Natalia responded, leaning closer to her monitor as well, until the crew told her she was leaning out of the frame. "I'm sorry. I'm sorry for so many things. I'm sorry we argued before you left."

"I'm the one who should be sorry. I don't want you to feel guilty for anything. Remember only the good times, Natalia, there were so many more of them. Remember the dreams we shared, remember my dreams for Future Man. After I am gone, it'll be up to you to carry them on. I'll never leave you, Natalia. Think only of our dreams and I'll be there."

"Father, why must you die?" asked Grachenko's daughter. "Why can't all these people save you?"

"Tatanya, my dear. You can be so adult, and yet so much a child," said Grachenko, a smile breaking over his face. "We've done everything, but we are only human. Like your mother, I want you to remember the good times. My one regret is that I will not have more of those

132

times with you and your brothers. In the days to come I need you to be strong, Tatanya, for your brothers, your grandparents, and to help your mother. Always remember that what I did was to serve all humanity."

"Arkady, I'll do everything you told me," said Natalia, tears beginning to form in the corners of her eyes. She struggled to get out everything she wanted to say. "I love you, you're the only man I will ever love. I'll keep you alive, Arkady. I promise. I promise . . ."

Whatever his wife said afterwards Grachenko couldn't hear. Her crying obscured the rest of the transmission, even what his daughter tried to say. Grachenko reached out and stroked the black and white image on the monitor. He could feel the tears collect in his own eyes. More than ever he wanted to hold her, but he was reduced to merely touching a poor-quality electronic reproduction of her.

"Good-bye, Natalia. I'll never leave you," Grachenko uttered when technicians entered the frame and lifted his wife out of her chair. "Tatanya, be strong for your mother."

"Ryumin was correct when he told us none of this would be easy," said Siprinoff, reaching over to the monitor and pulling Grachenko's hand away. "My wife will appear next, and so will my daughters. They're probably old enough to appear. I don't know what I'll do if they start crying like Natalia. You'll probably have to pull me off one of these screens."

Siprinoff nodded to the panel monitors on either side of him. The one on his left was the one Grachenko had used, while the one on the right would be used by Kostilev when his time came. Siprinoff at least would have a choice in how to view his family.

"*Soyuz*, this is Baikonur. We're sorry, Arkady," said Ryumin, appearing on the screens. "We're sorry we couldn't leave Natalia on any longer. I hope you understand."

"I do. It would only have been torture," Grachenko

133

replied, rubbing his eyes to force out the tears which were blurring his vision. "In the time we had, I told her what really needed to be said. I only wish . . . I only wish I could have just looked at her for a little while longer."

"I know. I wish we could've done this some other way, but Stefan and Vassili deserve time. Stefan, your family is next."

Ryumin disappeared from the monitor screens and was replaced moments later by a dark-haired woman not as tall as Grachenko's wife. On either side of her stood Siprinoff's daughters, neither of whom was yet old enough to be called a teenager.

What Siprinoff said to his wife was similar to what Grachenko had said to his family: be strong, remember only the good times. Siprinoff maintained his composure for a time, until he made a request to the camera crew for close-ups of his wife and children.

As the camera panned over the faces of his daughters, his words began to catch in his throat. When it stopped on his wife, all he could do was kiss his fingertips and place them over her mouth. As he had warned, Siprinoff tried to throw himself on one of the monitors, but was held back by Grachenko.

"Stefan, stop it!" he ordered, forcing his crew mate into his couch. "Touch the right controls and we'll be doomed now."

"I'm sorry, Arkady," Siprinoff cried. "If only I could hold her and touch her one more time. If only I could hold them all once more, I would die a happy man."

"I know, it would make all our souls rest easier," said Grachenko. "I'm afraid your time is nearly at an end. It's Kostilev's turn next."

After Siprinoff and his wife said their good-byes, Ryumin briefly reappeared on the monitors, then was replaced by Kostilev's wife. Of the three wives she was the youngest and, while her ten-month-old son wasn't officially old enough to be included, no one had had the heart to tell her no.

Of the three cosmonauts, Kostilev broke down the quickest, crying almost from the moment their conversation started, though he did refrain from attempting to throw himself on the nearest screen. Like the others, he reached out to the monitor and stroked its image. Most of his good-bye could not be understood as he half-sobbed it to his wife. His time on camera ended with a request for a close-up of his son, who had gone from a happy, bubbling infant to a quiet one as his mother held him and cried.

"Hold him for me, Svetlana. Every night, hold him for me," he managed to say coherently, just before the monitors faded out. Afterwards he buried his head in his hands and cried quietly.

"Baikonur, this is *Soyuz*. Thank you," Grachenko finally said. "As much as it hurt us, we are all thankful for it. If you could give us a minute to recover before your next order?"

"You have it, Arkady," said Ryumin. "You can have some free time before your next duties. We're sorry it could not have been longer, but your families are emotionally exhausted. And to be truthful, so are we. This is Baikonur, out."

"BERNIE: WE'RE GETTING A DIRECT FEED FROM NSA ON LATEST SOYUZ CHATTER, WITH TRANSLATION. MARY SAYS IT'S IMPORTANT."

Rosen glanced down at the note Ericson had slipped on top of his folders, taking his eyes off the television monitors he'd been talking to for the first time in almost twenty minutes.

"What are you getting from Fort Mead?" he asked, leaning over to Ericson. "And why's it so important?"

"It's a video signal," Ericson said quietly. "And we're getting both the *Soyuz* and Baikonur signals. From what Mary told me, the crew's saying good-bye to their families."

"I'll bet it's pretty emotional. I'd like to—"

"General, far be it from us to interfere with vital air force communications," announced an arrogant voice from one of the monitors. "But I thought you were part of this conference?"

Rosen turned back to the screens and found both Houston and Cape Canaveral waiting for him. It had been the first time that he had taken his attention away from the teleconference, and he had been caught by Reiss.

"Well, General, are you going to let us in?" Reiss continued. "Or is it classified?"

"No, as a matter of fact it's not," said Rosen. "Fort Mead has been intercepting and translating video signals between *Soyuz 71* and Baikonur. My people tell me that the cosmonauts are having their final words with their families."

"The topic here is unauthorized communications with the *Phoenix,* not what the Russians are saying to their spaceship."

"Did the IQs in this conversation drop sharply while I was distracted? The reason I talked to the *Phoenix* is because of what's happening on the *Soyuz.* And it's the reason for most of the illegal communications from Houston."

Rosen could feel the hate in Reiss's stare, and he was glad it came from half a continent away instead of from across a table. And yet, he also took great pleasure in sparking Reiss's anger, especially since he knew he alone could get away with it.

"We'll get nowhere with those kind of remarks, General," Reiss said with a measured voice and fire in his eyes.

"Well, at least we're being consistent," said Ericson.

"General, control your aide. We don't need to hear any comments from him."

"Yes, Mr. Reiss," said Rosen with mock seriousness. "Colonel, you'll have to stand in the corner for this."

"Excuse me, General. Could you tell us more about these transmissions?" asked one of the people in Houston. "We haven't heard about them yet."

136

"You'll find out about them when I decide!" Reiss stormed, causing those in Houston to cower again. "They'll cause unnecessary emotion and will be restricted. The CAP COMs are not to know about them, Mr. Corrigan, and those I've identified are to be punished. General Rosen, I want your command to stop its communications with the *Phoenix*. What you're doing can only have a detrimental effect on its crew. Is it your desire to ruin this mission?"

"Of course not," said Rosen, a resentful tone in his voice. "In fact I'll make a note right here and now to my command not to interfere with the rest of this mission."

"Very good, General. Now as for your malcontents, Mr. Corrigan. I want Tom Selisky to be removed from the crew roster for the next flight of *Atlantis . . .*"

While Reiss busied himself with punishments for the CAP COMs, Rosen took a nearby legal pad and wrote a brief message on it, which he then handed to Ericson.

"LARRY: AFTER ALL TRANSMISSIONS HAVE BEEN RECORDED, CONTACT TOULOUSE. WE'LL LET THE FRENCH SEND THEM AND THE NON-ASTRONAUT WILL NEVER HAVE TO KNOW."

"Well, my friend. I hope you understand I did my best to make them accept the offer," said Grachenko, when he met up with the Glavkosmos director outside the Politburo's meeting hall.

"No one could have been more eloquent or forceful than you," Fedarenko offered. "But your oratory ran into the brick wall of national interest. What makes this outcome worse is that you're the one who must contact the American and French embassies and tell them their offer's been rejected, for the final time."

"I may not have signed my nephew's death warrant, but I feel as though I'm being made his executioner. I'm not going to like my duties over the next few hours."

Grachenko walked slowly as he and Fedarenko left the

137

meeting hall. Immediately after the Politburo session ended there had been a flurry of activity as its members and their staffs filed out, rushing either to their offices or to their limousines for the drive to their homes outside the city. The session had been a late one and had been called at the last minute, upsetting the evening schedules of many members. Now, they hurried away while Grachenko moved wearily to his car. From there he would be driven to the Foreign Ministry, where the most difficult part of the day's ordeal awaited him.

"Nikolai Grigorivich, you were most persuasive back there," said Nagorny, intercepting Grachenko by emerging from a side corridor. "I'm sorry I couldn't support you more than I did."

"I wouldn't call merely withholding your vote much of a support," Fedarenko said bitterly.

"Comrade Doctor, you must understand that as defence minister, I'm torn between two loyalties. One is to the state and the other is to the army. Remember, two of the men who will die up there are air force officers. And yet, state security cannot be violated. We can't allow the Americans and the French to learn any secrets from our spacecraft."

"That is the weakest of arguments against the rescue. The *Soyuz* design is twenty-five years old, and apart from the film packs for the Cyclops camera, there's little in the vehicle that is sensitive."

"The Cyclops Three was the most advanced reconnaissance camera on the *Mir*," Nagorny replied. "The West could learn virtually all of its capabilities from those film packs."

"Is that worth killing three men for, comrade?"

"Please, please," said Grachenko, stepping between the two adversaries. "Must I be a diplomat before I even reach the ministry? Doctor, it took some political courage for Nagorny to do what he did. Inside the army itself he had factions to contend with. The commanders of the Strategic Rocket Forces and Air Defence wanted

138

him to vote no. The commanders of the air force and land forces wanted him to vote yes. In the Politburo, even not voting is making a statement."

"I see, but I still don't like the outcome," said Fedarenko. "It still means three of our bravest men are going to die. I was told their farewells to their wives grew very emotional."

"At least they had that," Nagorny said quietly. "Many heroes of the Soviet Union have died lonely deaths without the chance to say good-bye."

"But remember, Pietr, one of the three who will die is my nephew," Grachenko added, a hint of resentment in his own voice. "I helped Arkady get his original appointment to the space program and now, instead of helping him once again, I'll be instrumental in sealing his fate."

"I understand, Nikolai. Would you care to have us accompany you to your office? I don't have much to go to."

"Thank you, but no. This is something I must do as foreign minister, and I would like to do it alone."

Grachenko shook Nagorny's hand, then Fedarenko's, before he continued slowly down the corridor, leaving the two adversaries behind.

"It's remarkable how this crisis has aged Nikolai," said Nagorny. "Much more so than any previous one."

"And what you in the Politburo handed him doesn't make it any easier," said Fedarenko. "Marshal, are you responsible for the death watch enacted by the Air Defence Forces?"

"Suvorov is a Marshal of the Soviet army, same rank as mine. He doesn't need my approval of every operation he undertakes, only those which involve the possibility of combat. Though I must admit what he's done makes me feel uneasy. His paranoia is a constant source of problems for me."

*　　*　　*

"We've got everyone here," Cochran noted. "Time to go on line. Hit the camera, Jack."

"I wish I could give this camera a big fucking hit," said Ripley. "That would sure screw up Reiss's conference."

"Watch it, Jack. He could already be listening to us."

Ripley tapped the power and video transmission buttons on the TV camera, while Harrison watched the uplink and downlink panels at her aft crew station. In moments she confirmed that the *Phoenix* was both sending and receiving signals.

"We're getting a video transmission," said Harrison. "I'm putting it up on monitor one."

With the flip of a switch, the top monitor screen at the aft station came to life. On it was George Reiss, adjusting his microphone. While the *Phoenix* crew was ready, those who had ordered the conference were not.

"Cochran, what's the meaning of this?" Reiss demanded, when he noticed the crew on one of the studio monitors. "We weren't supposed to begin for another two minutes."

"We got an incoming signal and we put it on the set," Cochran answered. "We thought everything was ready."

"Well, if we can see each other we might as well begin. I asked for this conference because of some recent incidents, the most important of which is that the Russians have again rejected our rescue offer. It's unfortunate, but what's even more unfortunate is all the time and effort wasted on a futile gesture."

"And I bet you knew all along it would be futile," said Post, his sarcasm cutting through the crew's swearing.

"It was futile for you to have wasted valuable mission time!" Reiss's burst of anger was so sudden it took most of the shuttle crew by surprise. "It was unprofessional of you to have involved so many others! You put your whole mission at jeopardy, as well as the future of joint operations."

"Mr. Reiss, I can assure you that the actions of your astronauts will in no way endanger future cooperation with the CNES," Vachet replied, using a calm, modulated voice. "In fact, Ed Cochran showed the very highest professionalism when he proposed this rescue mission."

"Mr. Vachet, I don't want to argue with you. Your people are guests on this flight. This only concerns NASA personnel."

"Guests? I'll remind you that the French government has paid more than half the costs of this flight, and if you wish to know, I fully support Edward's rescue idea."

"I'm sorry to hear that," said Reiss. "You have a lot to learn about the real world of space operations, Mr. Vachet."

"You've a lot to learn about humanity," said Vachet, moving close enough to the monitor to look in Reiss's eyes, which were averted as he stared at a monitor screen as well.

"I didn't arrange this conference to argue with you. I'm here to discipline the NASA personnel in the crew. Cochran, your behavior in the past has tried my patience, but this time you've passed the limit. I can assure you this is your last space flight. Then again, you already knew that."

"Yes, isn't it amazing how much trouble you can get into for doing the right thing," Cochran observed, moving next to Vachet. "Or would you have preferred the destruction of this orbiter on lift-off, by blowing out the crew compartment?"

"I'm not here to discuss NASA safety procedures. If you had a problem with them, you should've scheduled a hearing to air your complaints."

"Yeah, the first thing we should do in an emergency is request a hearing on safety procedures," said Post, bitterly. "Trust a bureaucrat to say that."

"Reiss, why don't you do us all a favor and go fuck yourself," said Ripley. Like Post, he was at the back of the group and so could not be easily seen.

"All right, who said that?" Reiss demanded, bending over to get a better look at his monitor and nearly

141

disappearing out of the frame. "Who told me to fuck myself?"

"This is Walter Post, negative on the fuck you," Post advised. Then he nudged Harrison in the arm.

"This is Harrison, negative fuck you."

"This is Pellerin, I'm in a negative fucking mode," Pellerin said, managing to do so without even the hint of a smile.

"Enough! I don't want to hear another word out of you!" Reiss shouted. "Not a syllable of a word from any of you! You've displayed the most unprofessional behavior I've ever witnessed in a shuttle crew. At the end of this flight you'll all be reprimanded. Now listen to this and understand it well. As much as it pains you, there will be no rescue. In a special Politburo session the Russians vetoed it, and if they didn't authorize it, we're not going to risk it. You can all stop fantasizing about being heroes! There will be no more unauthorized communications with Space Defence Command. You're to return to work by the time the French reassume control. Perform the rest of your mission, damn it, and maybe you'll have another space flight in your lifetimes."

Chapter Ten

"Houston, this is Toulouse, we're ready to assume orbiter control," Daurat advised, seated at the command console.

"Roger, Toulouse. We got the *Phoenix* ready for handover," said the NASA CAP COM on the console monitor. "The orbiter is yours. Good luck with your operations."

"Thank you, Houston. We'll switch the orbiter to secure Marine Nationale channels for most of our communications."

"Roger, Toulouse. We won't even try to listen in."

"Roger, Houston. We'll contact you in three hours," said Daurat. "Raquel, see if you can raise the *Phoenix*."

The senior CAP COM reached the shuttle on her first try and got Vachet, who sounded very downcast. Everyone in the Toulouse mission control center heard it in his voice, especially Daurat, who motioned to Raquel Jordan that he would take over the line.

"Is there trouble aboard the *Phoenix*, Paul?" he asked. "Something's wrong and I can hear it."

"Nothing's wrong up here," Vachet replied, strapped into the pilot's seat; for the next three hours he would be flying the shuttle. "The problems are elsewhere. From the way NASA lectured us, I feel we've become the first penal colony in space."

"Things may change, my friend. Switch to secure voice channel zero-three and activate your secure video uplinks as well. We have some fresh information for you."

"Roger, Toulouse, Making the switch now." Vachet reached for his overhead communications panel and flipped the toggles, switching from the open NASA channels to a scrambled channel used by CNES and the French navy. "Julie, turn on the monitors."

Harrison and Simon turned from the satellite control panel at the aft crew station to the television monitors which were again brought on line to receive a ground transmission. Most of the crew joined them, except for Cochran, who remained in his seat to operate the *Phoenix*.

"The tapes you're about to see came from General Rosen, who received them from the National Security Agency," said Daurat, his voice coming over the flight deck speakers. "They also supplied the English translation. The first channel will show the *Soyuz* transmissions, the second channel, the transmissions from Baikonur. I must warn you they're difficult to watch."

The tapes began their runs simultaneously. In spite of this, there was little overlap between the audio portions

143

of the two. The only real problem the crew had was with the translations. All were read by men, which made it confusing when the women spoke. Still, the taped farewells had an effect on the crew. Cochran soon joined them at the aft station.

"I've set as many systems as I can on automatic," he said, floating down from the cockpit. "But I'll have to go back in about ten minutes to reset some. Who's this guy?"

"I believe he's Stefan Siprinoff," Vachet answered. "He's the medical specialist. What do you think of this so far?"

"Who was the first one up? Was it the *Soyuz* commander?"

"Yes, Arkady Grachenko. The foreign minister's relative. What did you think of him?"

"I say a man that eloquent has to be rescued. Let's give him his dreams, Saint Ex, instead of allowing him to become just a memory. Watch the rest if you want. I've already made my decision. When it's over we'll have to make some choices."

Cochran pushed himself back to the cockpit, but kept an ear turned to the aft station, as much to hear the translations of what the cosmonauts said as the response it provoked from his crew. When the tapes finished their run, they turned to face Cochran, almost as if he had ordered them to.

"Well, boss? What's your decision?" Post asked.

"Whether or not we have NASA's help or Russia's permission, I say we do the rescue," said Cochran, slipping his headset back onto his ears. "Now I can order all of you to do it, but I'd prefer we reach a consensus on this. What do you say?"

"I don't care if they're Russians, and I don't give a fuck if we have permission," said Ripley. "I say we fly the mission."

"It would be hypocritical of me to back away from what I said earlier," Renée Simon observed. "Of course

144

we should go."

"I'm concerned about who we can get to help us," said Pellerin. "It's obvious we'll need some form of ground control to perform this kind of mission. Who can you get to help us?"

"I think I know who," said Cochran. "Toulouse, this is *Phoenix*. Did General Rosen send a message with those tapes?"

"Yes, he did. I wrote it down," Daurat replied. "His message is, 'The non-astronaut didn't want you to see these, but I felt you should. If you need anything, just let us know. Bernie.'"

"Thank you, Toulouse. We'll be back in touch soon. *Phoenix*, out. Well, I think we have our ground support."

"I'll start work immediately," said Pellerin.

"And what about the rest of you?" Cochran asked, turning to face his crew. "Saint Ex, I know how you feel. But Walt, Julie, you had better realize this could mean the end of your careers as astronauts. Understand that right here and now, what you decide will effect the rest of your lives."

"It will of course affect more than your careers," Vachet added. "It could change the future of space exploration. The deaths of four men would be a serious blow to all space efforts. By rescuing the survivors, we can nullify the disaster."

"We can always hope NASA will look on this as an unscheduled flight," said Post, after thinking it over. "At Pax River we had a saying about unscheduled flights: 'It's easier to get forgiveness than permission.' Of course I'll go along. If NASA doesn't want me, I can always go back to the navy."

"Well I'm not going to be the one to stand in the way of history," said Harrison. "Looks like I won't get my wish of flying again. But at least it's one way for the second black woman in space to make her mark."

"Then the first international rescue mission in the history of space flight is about to begin," Cochran

145

announced, reinserting his headset jack into the inter-com. "We do this for the men we'll rescue, and for the future of man in space. Toulouse, this is *Phoenix*. We're cancelling our planned operations in favor of what you called a noble idea. We can bypass you and go straight to Space Defence Command. But if we go through you, NASA will never have to know. We can't force you to cooperate, though we'd like it just the same."

"To participate in so historic an undertaking would be an honor," said Daurat. "Don't worry about the trouble, Commander. Something which angers both Russia and America is so, so French. My country must take its rightful place with the other world powers in all areas. What do you want from us? Over."

"We'll fly the first part of our refueling operation as planned. We'll rendezvous with the Fleet Com satellite, but we'll refuel our own OMS and RCS systems. Contact General Rosen, tell him we'll need his computers and radars. I'll have a more detailed list of our needs in a few minutes. *Phoenix*, out."

"We'll be ready for you, Mr. Cochran. Your noble idea is about to be born. Toulouse, out."

"Awaiting your orders, Commander," said Vachet, standing in front of the rest of the crew. "What do you want done?"

"We have a rendezvous coming up in one hour," said Cochran. "We'll start our mission there. Ripley, George, Julie, get your oxygen packs on and prepare for an EVA. Renée, you help them. Paul and I will fly the lady. Walt, dump some of our old programs and get ready to load the new ones. We're an outcast crew in a jinxed ship, and from here on out we'll be making history."

"I knew I'd find you here. If you weren't in the lounge, I knew this was where you'd be," said Harrison, walking up to a lone figure standing amidst a forest of larger statues.

Reynolds glanced over his shoulder and smiled at Brad

Harrison as he approached him. Reynolds was in the middle of the memorial's arc of free standing statues, directly across from the one of Gregory Jarvis. The memorial had no other visitors as it was closed to the general public. For the rest of the evening only base personnel could approach it.

"I just had to get away from the crap," Reynolds finally said. "Everyone's waiting for those poor bastards to die, and management wants us to carry on as if nothing's happened."

"And yet they won't let us be interviewed by the press," Harrison added. "This is one time where I wouldn't mind being interviewed. You know what they're saying about us?"

"Yes, every network and newspaper is asking the same questions: 'Why not rescue them on our own?' 'Do these men have to die in the name of Russian paranoia?' 'Why's NASA hiding behind the White House?' God, I'd sure like to give them some answers. That's part of the reason why I came here, where you can both have solitude and be with people who understand you."

"I see someone else had the same idea. We got company."

Harrison pointed to a set of headlights coming down the spit of land the astronauts' memorial stood on. Occasionally, above the sound of the waves hitting the nearby shore, the whisper of the car driving along the road could be heard.

"Probably more of our friends," said Reynolds. "I think this place is going to get a lot of use today."

While Reynolds turned back to his contemplations, Harrison kept an eye on the approaching dark-colored sedan. Since it wasn't the usual astronaut's sports car, it got his curiosity, then aroused his suspicions when it drove past the parking lot to stop in front of the memorial. He identified the sedan's lone occupant the moment the driver's door opened.

"I don't believe it. This is in-fucking-credible," said

147

Harrison, tapping Reynolds on the shoulder. "It's Reiss."

Reiss halted momentarily when he realized he had been identified. He resumed walking toward the two astronauts and tried an unconvincing smile.

"Do we even have to put up with you here?" Reynolds asked sarcastically. "Haven't you had enough arguments for one day?"

"No, I didn't come here for a fight," said Reiss, the hard look returning to his eyes. "I heard you took the final Soviet rejection of our rescue offer very hard. I wanted you to know I did my best with the State Department and the White House."

"That's a damn lie. We heard that Space Defence Command has tapes of the cosmonauts saying good-bye to their families. But you were one of the people who decided not to show them. Not to us, not to the White House, and most especially not to the *Phoenix*."

"Showing those tapes would serve no purpose. They'd cloud the issue with emotions, and we can't decide this crisis on emotion. That's not the way a government operates."

"Then you didn't push our views," said Harrison. "You pushed the NASA management line, which isn't the same as ours."

"Of course I pushed the management line," Reiss answered. "Flying an unapproved rescue mission would be dangerous, and we can't afford another disaster with our shuttle fleet."

"This is what we get when the director of manned flight is a bureaucrat and not an astronaut," Reynolds sniped.

"Bureaucrats know how to deal with budgets, Mr. Reynolds. Another shuttle disaster would ruin our support from Congress and the current administration. For the future of the manned space program, there can be no rescue without Soviet approval. I know there's been some grumbling about flying the mission anyway. You

148

can just forget it. The Russians could easily shoot down the *Phoenix*, and then we'd have to put another seven statues in this park. Think about it. Especially you, Brad."

Reiss didn't say good-bye, but ended the conversation by turning around and walking back to his car. Reynolds continued to watch him from the corner of his eye, waiting for the director to pull away before he would speak.

"Well that was certainly unique," said Harrison, beating him to the first remark. "It's rare to see Reiss so conciliatory and willing to explain his actions."

"Yes, he did extend an olive branch," Reynolds admitted. "And whacked us in the face with it. Well, I've thought enough about it. Ed once told me he accepted responsibilities like this. I think his destiny and the destiny of his lady are intertwined. And if there's any way I can help them, I will. Still, our friends will be taking one hell of a risk. And for you, it also means your wife. What do you say, Brad?"

"I'll support whatever decision Julie makes, but I hope it's one to save three brave men. And I think those who are here would support it as well."

"Toulouse, this is *Phoenix*. Ripley and Pellerin are beginning their EVA," said Cochran. "Renée, how's Julie doing?"

"The airlock is repressurized and she's ready to climb in," Simon reported, standing beside the lock's entrance hatch.

"Tell her to proceed. They'll be needing her out there."

With all the control panel status lights reading green, Simon opened the hatch and Harrison glided into the bulky drum at the back of the middle deck. Like Pellerin and Ripley, she had on her ventilation suit and a scuba-like portable oxygen system. Julie had used it for the past hour to wash the dissolved nitrogen out of her bloodstream. Had this not been done, the oxygen-rich, low-pressure environment of her space suit would have given her the bends, just like a deep sea diver.

"*Phoenix*, this is Toulouse. You are one hour, fifty minutes from return to NASA control," said Raquel. "Have you started refueling?"

"We're just about to," Cochran replied. "What's it like at your end? We're ready to receive our new flight programs."

"Daurat is talking with your Space Defence Command. We're having trouble with our computers. Let me get General Rosen for you."

"Commander, this is Renée. Julie's putting her suit on. She'll be ready for EVA in five minutes."

Once sealed in the airlock, Harrison took the lower torso assembly of her suit from its storage frame. The assembly contained every garmet she would need from the waist down and, inspite of its awkwardness, she easily pulled it over her legs. She removed her portable oxygen system and activated the chest pack computer on her upper torso assembly. When all its systems came on line, she let the upper section float in midair as she wiggled into it.

She connected her ventilation suit umbilicals to the lines inside the assembly; then joined the upper and lower torsos by snapping the waist rings together. She attached the last major component of her space suit by sitting under its storage frame and pulling herself up on its guide rails. When the rail locks clicked, she had her life-support backpack in place.

"*Phoenix*, this is Mount Cheyenne. We've got a small problem here," said Rosen, finally reaching the shuttle after the cockpit team had waited several minutes for him.

"Yes, you need a new telephone operator," said Cochran.

"Well, that too. The more serious problem is that our

computers can't interface with the CNES main frames. Their languages aren't compatible and we have a snag with the flight programs. No one here's an experienced astronaut and we've had trouble planning the fastest reentry for you."

"I should've guessed problems like this would crop up, especially with a plan that's been dead as many times as mine. We could help you with the flight plans, but we're busy with every other aspect of the rescue."

"What about the astronauts at Canaveral and Houston?" Vachet asked. "Wouldn't they help?"

"I'm sure they would," said Cochran. "Though contacting anyone in Houston is just too risky. Most there have duties as CAP COMs. Try Clay Reynolds, Bernie. I think the son of a Flying Tiger ace would find breaking the rules a family tradition. If you can't reach him, try Brad Harrison."

"Will do," said Rosen, "but we still have the problems of getting the programs to you. And there's only one answer for it."

"I know, we'll have to go with a direct link instead of through the French. How long would you need?"

"It would only take two or three minutes for the transfer orbit and rendezvous programs we already have."

"Okay, Bernie. We'll set things up at this end. Contact us when you're ready. *Phoenix*, out," Cochran advised, just before Post tapped him on the shoulder.

"Better switch to the short-range channel," he said. "Julie's getting ready to go."

"I'm deploying the water feed line," said Harrison, pulling a tube out of a pack on her right shoulder. "I'm all set to begin. Tell Jack I'll be joining him soon."

The last part of her suit she attached was the spherical helmet. She already had on her gloves, head cap, and wireless headset, and with the locking of the helmet neck rings she was encased in a self-contained environment which would allow her to work in a far more hostile one.

"Renée, once the airlock's been secured I want you at the aft crew station," said Cochran, changing back to the ship's intercom. "I want you to monitor activities in the cargo bay. Post has been doing double duty between that and the GPC, and I want his full attention on reprogramming."

"Understood, commander. I'll be there in a minute," said Simon, as the airlock's pressure scale fell to zero.

Harrison watched a similar scale in the chamber's interior and, when it registered near-vacuum conditions, she opened the hatch to the cargo bay. She stepped out into the harsh glare of the sun. To prevent it from blinding her, she immediately slapped down her helmet's gold anodized visor.

"Nice to see the maid service is finally here," Ripley commented, looking up from his work on the fuel tank at the cargo bay's far end. "You can start on the silverware, honey."

"All right, knock it off," said Post, moving to the windows at the aft station. "Julie, the fuel tank has been pressurized for propellant transfer. The tanks for the OMS engines have also been pressurized, the isolation valves are on."

"Thanks, Walter. I'm going down to join the comedians," said Harrison. "I'll be there in a minute."

She reached up and attached her safety line to the EVA guide rail on the starboard side of the cargo bay. Once secured, she easily climbed over the pallets containing the Orbital Pharmaceutical Factory and the remaining Frency navy satellites. She hopped from one pallet to another, reaching Pellerin and Ripley in less than a minute.

"Watch your feet," Renée warned, rising out of the floor hatch. "I've safetied the airlock, the middle deck is empty."

"Good, action's getting heavy back here," said Post. "This is the panel for the tank and this is the panel for the OMS engines. Monitor them, watch them for any pressure spikes. We don't want any surges or broken lines. Not with these chemicals."

"Don't worry, there won't be any."

"I hope not. If you need me for anything, I'll be here."

Post removed his headset jack from the intercom box at the aft station and transferred it to the mission specialist console. From there he could talk to the cockpit team and those on the ground.

"*Phoenix,* this is Mount Cheyenne. We're ready to transmit the transfer orbit and rendezvous programs," said Rosen.

"Good. I think we're ready up here," said Cochran. "Walt, how are you doing?"

"Just a minute. I'm dumping the launch programs," Post advised moving from the computer keyboard at his console to the overhead GPC panels behind Vachet. "Even with the improvements, we're going to need all the memory we can use."

"Trust the navy to slow things up. C'mon, Walt, hurry it along. We're on a direct line to the SDC."

"Okay, everything's set. We're ready to receive."

"Fire away, Bernie," said Cochran. "Everything's clear."

"Transmitting now," answered Rosen, and a few moments later the mission specialist station indicated the new programs were coming in. It would take just over two minutes for them to be sent, even using high-speed transmissions facilities.

"*Phoenix,* this is Ripley. I'm ready to connect the lines to the starboard OMS pod. Read me the checklist."

"Roger, Jack. Checklist for starboard OMS pod," said Simon, glancing at the panels Post had ordered her to watch. "Fuel and oxidizer cells, pressurized for transfer. Helium isolation valves, open. Cross-feed systems valves, closed. Starboard OMS access panels have been unlatched. You're clear to proceed."

"Thanks, Renée. Here we go, attaching hydrazine line."

Ripley had climbed onto the back of the *Phoenix* and

was standing at the base of its tail fin. When two hatches on the starboard engine housing popped open, he lifted the one marked "MMH." He attached the feed line he held to the valve he found under it, then tightened down the connection with a wrench from the tool caddy on his chest pack.

"The line's hooked up," said Ripley. "And the head valve is open. Time to open it at your end."

"Roger, here we go," said Harrison.

She threw a lever on the right side of the cargo bay tank, and immediately the silver line floating above her became rigid as it filled with monomethyl hydrazine.

"*Phoenix*, this is Ripley. We're ready to start fueling."

"Roger, you may proceed," said Simon. "I'll monitor the tank from here and advise you when it's full."

"Thanks, Renée. Opening fuel tank valve."

Ripley twisted a small wheel on the valve stem, starting the flow of hydrazine into the OMS tank. To make the operation possible it had been repressurized to a level lower than that of the cargo bay tank. It was the only way to perform the transfer without the use of pumps.

"George, hand me the nitrogen line," said Ripley, turning back to his team members. "Renée's going to watch the hydrazine tank. We better get the oxidizer transfer underway."

Pellerin grabbed the feed line attached to his side of the cargo bay tank and pushed its end toward Ripley. He uncoiled the rest like it was a length of rope. Though it started to drift, Ripley easily snagged the line and connected it to the valve behind the second access hatch.

Nitrogen tetroxide was the oxidizer for the OMS and RCS systems. While stored in the twin-chambered bay tank with the hydrazine, it would have its own cell in the OMS pod. Its transfer operation was identical, and Simon would monitor both from the aft crew station.

"Ed, transmission's over. We got our new programs," said Post, shutting down one of the communications panels at the mission specialist station. "When do we get the rest?"

"Let's ask," Cochran answered. "Mount Cheyenne, this is *Phoenix*. Initial software transfer is complete. When do we get the new de-orbit, reentry, and landing programs?"

"Hard to say," said Rosen. "We got Clay Reynolds, but it's going to take us time. At least another hour, maybe more."

"More? We only got ninety minutes left before we go back to Houston. You transmit after that and they'll damn well know."

"Take a look at your new programs, Ed. In about ninety-two minutes you're to begin transfer orbit maneuvers. By then, believe me, they'll know."

"I guess so," said Cochran. "Still, get the rest of the plans to us as soon as possible. We'll be switching back to French navy channels, Bernie. Contact us through Toulouse, *Phoenix*, out. Renée, how's the fueling operation doing?"

"The starboard OMS pod is nearly full," Simon advised. "I'm cutting in its RCS system so its tanks can be filled. *Phoenix* to Julie, standby to cut hydrazine flow."

A minute later Harrison pulled the control lever on the hydrazine line, shutting off the fuel at its source. What was left in the line quickly emptied into the various cells in the starboard OMS pod. Ripley closed the line's head valve, then the tank valve, and finally disconnected the line. While he was working, Simon ordered Pellerin to shut-down the nitrogen flow.

In moments the lines would be reconnected to the port side OMS pod and the fueling procedure repeated. It would take less than half an hour to complete, though the team's work still wouldn't be done. They would have to stow the equipment, then work on the manned maneuvering units. They had to replace the battery packs, recharge the nitrogen cylinders, and do a systems check for any malfunctions. If no problems were encountered, the *Phoenix* would be ready for its rescue mission at about the same time it was due to be handed back to NASA.

"Arkady, this is Baikonur. They're gone," said Ryumin. "The press and party officials are continuing their interviews outside the operations building. There's no one here but staff."

"Good, that's the way it should be," said Grachenko. "Tell me, is Sakolov with you? I can't see him on the monitor."

"Yuri Pavelivich is with the party officials. He's arguing with them about the shuttle mission he's planned to retrieve you. They want him to cancel it. We all hope he wins. If he doesn't, we'll file a letter of protest with the premier's office."

"Thank you, my friends. We know the risks of such a heretical act. Have you heard anything from my uncle?"

"We know the foreign minister argued in the last Politburo session for the American rescue offer," said Ryumin. "Your uncle is a brilliant diplomat, but he's no miracle worker. Have you taken your tranquilizers?"

"Vassili has and Stefan is about to, I haven't just yet." Grachenko ran his thumb over the foil pack he held in his hand. Through the heavy material of his gloves he could feel the two capsules inside the pack. "I must admit I'm reluctant to."

"I understand, but it would be better . . ."

"You don't understand," Siprinoff snapped, cutting off Ryumin. "These pills won't make it easier or quicker, they'll just make dying from asphyxiation a little less painful."

"Or burn-up," said Grachenko. "I think I used what little fuel we had left restabilizing us. Soon we'll begin tumbling again. In a few hours we'll probably be reentering. Your hard-fought plan to recover our bodies may come to nothing."

"We will still make the effort," said Ryumin. "Work is progressing very well on the *Baran*. With some round-the-clock shifts we could achieve a miracle."

"But not one which can save us. The only ones who could were officially warned not to do so."

"Yes, NASA could do it. If only reality didn't stand in the way . . . Better take your pills before you eat, Arkady."

"Yes, we might as well start our banquet," said Grachenko, taking a firm hold of the foil pack and tearing it open. He grabbed the capsules before they floated away and placed both in his mouth. Siprinoff handed him a water bottle which, after he took a sip from its tube, allowed him to swallow the tranquilizers. Grachenko then turned to the still active camera and forced a smile on his face. "Are you satisfied, Anatoly?"

"I'm satisfied. We'll leave you until you're done with your meal. Let us know when you're through."

"We will. Thank you, my friend."

Ryumin reached for the monitor controls on his console and turned the screen off. After it went blank, he shifted his gaze to the center's main screen; where he studied the orbital tracks of the vehicles it displayed.

"If only reality didn't stand in the way," he sadly repeated, focussing his attention on the track of the *Phoenix*. "I could change things . . . With the communications net we have here, I could contact NASA and on my authority authorize a rescue."

"That would only result in further embarrassment to our country and your arrest," said Ryumin's deputy. "And it would be my responsibility to notify security. All of us wish things could be different, but they can't. We have no way of changing fate."

"Yes, yes. But knowing this won't make the next few hours any easier. It's going to be hard, so very hard, to watch our friends die. Even if they are hundreds of kilometers above us."

Chapter Eleven

"*Phoenix,* this is Toulouse. You are nineteen minutes from return to NASA control," said Raquel. "Your fueling team should be finishing their EVA."

"Roger, CAP COM. The last of the team has just entered the airlock," said Vachet. "Our countdown shows we're at T minus twenty minutes, twenty-nine seconds to first OMS burn."

"Commander, Pellerin's going to help Jack at the airlock," Harrison informed Cochran. "Where do you want me?"

"With Renée," said Cochran, glancing over his shoulder. "Make sure the cargo bay doors are closed properly."

Still wearing her ventilation suit, Harrison rose through the floor hatch, then pushed off for the aft crew station. Below her, on the middle deck, Pellerin was just opening the airlock's inner hatch. Despite the fact that the air pressure between the crew compartment and the chamber was almost equal, there was still an audible hissing when the hatch's seal was broken.

"Here, take this over to the recharge system," said Ripley, handing Pellerin one of the backpacks floating in the chamber. "We're going to have to refill all three packs for the rescue, and get Renée out of storage as well."

"We're lucky Canaveral gave us the new suits," said Pellerin. "The old ones had the pack permanently attached to the upper torso assembly. This deck would be filled with space suits if we had to charge them."

Pellerin moved to one of the middle deck's equipment bays, where he mounted the pack on a set of brackets. He connected a high-pressure line to one of its valves and started refilling the pack's liquid oxygen supply. He would also replace the lithium hydroxide cartridge and check the batteries. Simon's backpack needed to be

158

checked out completely before it could be used. To prepare all four packs would take almost an hour; they would be ready for the astronauts just in time.

"Commander, this is Julie. We are closing the cargo bay doors. Activating motors. Renée, stand by on the latches."

Together with their interior sets of radiators, the sixty-foot-long main doors rose smoothly and closed over the shuttle's cargo bay. Once their latches were sealed, the *Phoenix* would be externally ready for the transfer orbit maneuvers.

"Toulouse, this is *Phoenix*. We are T minus fourteen minutes and counting to OMS-One burn," said Cochran. "Our countdown is on schedule. Have you been contacted by Houston yet?"

"Yes, *Phoenix*. And they want to know why the satellite alongside you hasn't been refueled," said Raquel Jordan. "Daurat told them there was trouble with your fueling equipment."

"So they have been watching us. Did they say anything about us being contacted by Space Defence Command?"

"No, nothing about your contacts."

"Well then they're not watching us too closely. We're going to move away from the satellite to prepare for the transfer orbit," Cochran advised, punching in the maneuvering controls on the cockpit's center pedestal. "Paul, unlock your joystick."

Cochran reached for one of the overhead panels and started activating the reaction control systems. When finished, Vachet entered a program number into the GPC and squeezed the control stick. A computer-selected series of thrusters fired briefly, pushing the *Phoenix* away from the satellite it had been parked beside for almost two hours. A second squeeze of the control stick fired thrusters on the spaceplane's opposite side to halt its slide out of its entry window.

"Saint Ex, it's time to give up the pilot's seat," said

Cochran. "For the upcoming maneuvers we need our best man."

"I quite agree," said Vachet, unlocking his restraint belts. "But I hope you won't mind if I stay up here."

"Of course not, we're all fathers to this scheme."

Vachet pushed off from the seat and glided backwards from the cockpit. His feet were just clearing the headrest as Post climbed into position.

"Commander, all latches to the cargo bay doors have been locked," reported Harrison. "The cargo bay is secure."

"Shut down the aft station and come forward," Cochran ordered. "The fun's about to begin. T minus nine minutes, thirty seconds to OMS-One burn. Walt, let's turn the lady around. Load program Two-Three-Zero into the GPC."

Once the general purpose computer had its new instructions, Post swung the *Phoenix* a perfect one hundred and eighty degrees. Now flying tail first, it would only remain so until after its initial transfer orbit maneuver was finished.

"T minus seven minutes and counting to OMS-One burn. Toulouse, this is *Phoenix*. Anything new from Houston?"

"Yes, *Phoenix*. They're aware that something is going on," said Jordan. "They want us to hand you back immediately."

"Just keep them off us for another five minutes and we'll be okay," said Cochran. "I don't want to hear any bitching until we're ready for it. Julie, standby on the communications panels. Commencing OMS pressurization, OMS engines armed. Helium isolation system, on. Stand by to open fuel and oxidizer tanks."

As the OMS engines were prepared for firing, their exhaust nozzles were pitched up to the travel limits of their gimbal mounts. This would slow the shuttle's velocity and push it to a lower altitude, both of which were necessary if they were to make the approaching

160

transfer orbit.

"Switching OMS to GPC control," said Post. "Commencing primary software transfer for rescue mission."

"Hey, boss, are we missing anything up here?" Ripley asked, poking his head through the floor hatch.

"Just a little history," said Cochran. "T minus four minutes, fifteen seconds to OMS-One burn. Toulouse, this is *Phoenix*. We're ready for handover to NASA. How do they sound?"

"Angry, though it may just be a result of Daurat arguing with them," said Jordan. "Here, I'll let you talk with him."

"Commander, they're asking questions about everything," Daurat warned, his voice coming in a few moments later. "They want to know about your attitude change, why the satellite wasn't refueled, and why I refuse to hand you back to them."

"You might as well do it, Mr. Daurat," said Cochran. "All our preparations are complete. They can't interfere with us."

"Very well. Personally I would've preferred to continue arguing with your officials, but if you wish to do so . . . Stand by to switch to NASA command channels."

"Okay, you heard the man. Julie, get ready. We change on Raquel's orders. Walt, is the software transfer complete?"

"Program loading for GPC and BFS, finished," said Post.

"*Phoenix*, this is Toulouse. You may switch to NASA command channels," said Jordan. "And from all of us here, Godspeed."

"Thank you, Toulouse. Changing now," Cochran ordered, as he motioned for Harrison to start flipping toggles on the communications panels. For a moment his headset was silent, then the voice of Houston's CAP COM rang in his ears as he hit the transmit button. "Houston, this is Rescue One. We are T minus two minutes and counting from OMS burn."

161

"Rescue what? Ed, what the hell's going on?" the new CAP COM asked, a confused tone to his voice.

"What's going on is something we should've done hours ago, Don. I only hope we're not too late. We're going to rescue those poor bastards, whether you want us to or not."

"What in God's name? Are you guys crazy? You'll be arrested for this. You're stealing a spaceship!"

"Hold it down, Epstein," said Post. "Don't freak out on us just yet. We took a vote and we're going to fly Ed's rescue mission. Tell the administrators they got a mutiny here."

"I'm . . . I'm getting the on-duty flight officer," said Epstein. "He can handle this."

"You do that," said Cochran. "Only don't make it sound like you're calling the vice-principal on us. And Don, when you get the on-duty F.O., tell him we're T minus one minute, fifteen seconds and counting to OMS burn."

Cochran activated the flight deck's speakers in time for the rest of the crew to hear Epstein drop his headset and leave his chair. They also heard the faint murmur of other staff members talking and distant, scattered applause. Closer to the headset's microphone came the heavy stamping of feet as someone rushed up to the CAP COM's console.

"This is Flight Officer Richard McMains. What the hell's going on Cochran?" a louder, angrier, voice demanded.

"T minus eighteen seconds to OMS-One burn," Cochran answered. "We're doing what has to be done, Rich."

"Ed, what you're doing is illegal. It'll ruin your career and the careers of your entire crew."

"We've all decided our careers are a small price to pay for the lives of three men. T minus nine seconds."

"We can stop you. There are remote systems."

"We turned those off," said Cochran, a smile breaking

162

over his face. "Two seconds, one . . . OMS ignition commencing."

Neither Cochran or Post fired the engines; the GPC handled the operation. The upturned nozzles on the orbital maneuvering pods emitted bright flashes of light. In seconds the engines had increased to full power and were decelerating the *Phoenix* and pushing it into a lower orbit.

For the crew members who were not strapped in, the initial reduction in speed caught them by surprise. Vachet and Harrison clutched the headrests to the cockpit seats, while Ripley grabbed some hand holds on the flight deck's roof. Pellerin and Simon sailed back to the aft crew station, where they grabbed the orbiter and remote arm control grips to stop their flight. They all adjusted to the sustained deceleration created by the burn and quickly made their way up to the cockpit.

"*Phoenix,* you've lost fifteen miles in altitude," said McMains. "If you kill the burn now, you can return to orbit and we'll forget this ever happened."

"McMains, don't beg," said Post. "It's not dignified. Remember your position."

"I'll remember my position all right. When NASA reassigns me to a tracking station on some God-forsaken island."

"In NASA, they don't kill the bearer of bad news," Cochran remarked. "If they did so, every flight officer I've known would either be serving in the Australian outback or Ascension. Go do your duty, McMains. Tell Engleberg, tell Reiss, tell whomever you like, but get one thing straight. This is a rescue mission, not only for those cosmonauts but the future of man in space. Thirty-two seconds to end of OMS burn. Walt, prepare to change attitude for transfer orbit entry."

Half a minute later the OMS engines ceased firing, causing a soft ripple throughout the airliner-sized spaceplane. It was now hundreds of miles behind the satellite it had parked beside and more than fifty miles

163

below it. Now at the same altitude as the *Soyuz*, *Phoenix* had completed the first step of the rescue. In moments Post would change its attitude by a hundred and twenty degrees and begin another countdown. This would launch the shuttle through its transfer orbit window, eventually to intercept the orbit of the *Soyuz*.

"Marshal, the computers confirm it," said Jurkov, meeting his commander at the entrance to the Voyska PVO headquarters. "The *Phoenix* is on an intercept course."

He handed Suvorov one sheet of paper, then another. Suvorov stopped so he could better examine his command's lastest information. He began smiling, but grew irritated when his deputy tried to explain what he was obviously enjoying.

"Yes, Jurkov. I know how to read the formula of an orbital track," he said. "This clearly is an intercept course. And you've also detected a communications from NORAD. This confirms the military nature of the shuttle's mission. Good work."

Suvorov resumed his stride and quickly reached the center's command platform, where the personnel gave him the latest information as he circled around its consoles.

"The transmissions from NORAD lasted only for seven minutes total, three minutes of which was a high-speed data transfer," said the Colonel from the intelligence section.

"Were the transmissions scrambled?" asked Suvorov.

"Yes, and the Americans are using an encryption system we're not familiar with. I should add that most of the shuttle's communications were with the CNES mission center in Toulouse."

"It makes no difference. The French are helping the Americans. They always were their lackeys. Maintain surveillance of the spacecraft. I want to know everyone it talks to."

"Yes, Marshal, we will," said the officer. "They are currently talking to NASA headquarters, Houston."

"Good. Colonel Gubarev, what's the status of the Hydra battalions?" Suvorov requested, turning to another console.

"Both Volgograd and the Northern Cosmodrome can begin their countdowns once they receive orders to fire," said Gubarev.

Suvorov walked to the section of the platform facing the center's display maps. He gave only a cursory glance to the world map and the track of the *Phoenix*. Instead Suvorov concentrated on the Soviet chart, on the markers for Volgograd and the Northern Cosmodrome, and the data blocks running beside them.

"Tell them to commence their countdown operations," he ordered. "We must have warheads in orbit as soon as possible."

"But, Marshal. Orders to launch have not yet arrived from the Premier and Defence Minister Nagorny," said Jurkov, approaching his commander. "We cannot launch without their permission."

"I know that. However, I'm certain we'll receive those orders shortly. We have enough evidence to prove an American-Chinese conspiracy. The appeasers and fools in Glavkosmos will look on this act as humanitarian. There's nothing humanitarian about it. We shall have our orders within half an hour. Yes, Colonel, what is it?"

"It's the *Phoenix*, sir," said the intelligence officer, rushing from his console. "They're communicating with NORAD again. Both voice links and now data transmission."

"Excellent, Colonel. They give us more proof, more ammunition by the minute. I will contact Marshal Nagorny from my office. When I return, I want a new status report on the Hydras."

*   *   *

165

"Security desk reports Reiss just arrived," said Canaveral's deputy launch officer, as he placed a telephone back on its cradle. "And they say he's on the warpath. Clayton, are you sure you want to be here?"

"He'll find out what I've done sooner or later," Reynolds observed, standing on the observation platform behind the command consoles. "I'd like dickhead to hear it from me. Besides, what else can he do to me after taking *Discovery* away?"

"Plenty. You could be the first astronaut executed by . . ."

The launch officer's remark trailed off when the center's main doors flew open as if they had been kicked. Reiss stormed through them, his rage blinding him to the people he almost knocked down as he marched to the one active command console.

"Give me an uplink to the *Phoenix*," he demanded, slipping a headset over his ears. "Houston, this is Canaveral, get off the air. I have a priority override. Cochran, are you reading me? You're a disgrace to the entire astronaut corps!"

"Commander Cochran isn't in just now, but if you leave your name and number at the tone I'll see that he gets back in touch with you," said Post, before a shrill beep filled the launch center's speakers.

A ripple of laughter swept through the center's skeleton staff, until Reiss started shouting at them to shut up or he would have everyone fired.

"I'm here, George," said Cochran, after the threats had ended. "How can I help you?"

"Cochran, I'm ordering you to stop this hijacking and land that spacecraft immediately. We'll send you programs to land either here or at Edwards."

"Sorry, we already got programs to land at Northrup Strip or Rota. We'll see you in about two hours."

"Where the hell did you get those flight programs?"

"Fifteen minutes ago the orbiter received a coded transmission," said the flight officer. "It came through the TDRS satellites, and from the way it was encoded I'd say it was military in origin."

"I knew they had to have ground support," said Reiss. "Was it the French? Or was it Rosen and his crew?"

"I helped him, if you want to know," Reynolds answered.

Reiss spun around and glared at him. Instead of just a voice on the speakers, Reiss had an immediate and personal focus for his anger. For just a moment Reynolds had to wonder if Reiss would actually attack him. But the director held off, preferring at the moment to give him a hateful, silent stare.

"Get security in here. I want him arrested," he ordered, pointing at Reynolds. "When I'm through with you, Mister, you'll lose that shit-eating grin."

"Don't worry, Clayton. We'll send you a cake with a hacksaw blade in it," said Cochran. "You happy with yourself, Reiss? You have one small victory, but you haven't stopped us."

"Well perhaps this might. Your career is over, Cochran. The rest of you can still have yours, if you give up following him on this dangerous flight of fancy."

"I can speak for the rest of the Americans in this crew," said Post. "Ed's our commander and we've voted to follow him. In the words of someone else on this ship, go fuck yourself."

"It's easy for you to anger me," said Reiss. "You can always go back to the navy. And what of the French personnel on your ship? Do they agree with this insanity?"

"We're following a higher rule of law than yours," Vachet offered. "Your orders castrate us from our nature. What we're doing restores it. In this, the people I command fully agree."

"This isn't the time for poetry, Mr. Vachet. It's time for reality, and your participation in Cochran's scheme could ruin future ventures between your country and NASA."

"Like other risks, that's one we must take if there's to be a future for man in space. And if we're successful, my country might find future cooperation with the Soviets much easier."

"What you're doing will have the exact opposite effect on the Russians," said Reiss. "When they rejected our help, Moscow warned us not to take advantage of their crisis. This will be seen as a provocation. Is that what you want?"

"We want three men who aren't much different from us to live," said Cochran. "If Moscow has a problem with that, then get on the phone to them. You have thirty-one minutes before our transfer orbit maneuvers end, and in another twenty we'll overtake the *Soyuz*. As director of manned flight operations, why don't you do your bit for our future."

Cochran reached up to his communications panel and hit one of the toggles, cutting off Reiss's answer in mid-sentence. Since his communications panel controlled the flight deck's speaker system, no one else got to hear Reiss, except for Post, who could operate his panel independently.

"Looks like we'll have one hell of a reception waiting for us when we return," Ripley observed, his voice muffled by the face mask he was wearing. "We'll either be arrested as criminals or treated like heroes."

"I doubt they'll treat heroes as criminals," said Vachet. "Especially if the press knows, and Daurat will inform them."

"Yes, it's a little ironic that the people I hate the most may end up being our best ally," said Cochran.

"I feel sorry for Clayton," Harrison added, wearing a face mask similar to Ripley's. "He's being arrested simply because he helped us with the new flight programs."

"Don't worry, Brad will go to his rescue once he finds out what happened. How's your half of the operation going?"

"We finished our meals and have been on oxygen for

168

fifteen or twenty minutes," said Ripley. "Renée got lightheaded until we adjusted her flow rate and George is on the space potty."

"I see you're making them follow your patented EVA rules," said Cochran. "Full stomachs and empty bladders. Will you be ready by the time we intercept the *Soyuz?*"

"We'll be ready. I just hope those guys will be conscious enough to help us rescue them. It'll be a hell of a letdown if we get there and can't do anything."

'Pietr Arkadivich, have you seen the Premier already?" asked Grachenko, surprised when he saw a familiar face coming from Gussarov's office. "And why did you bring along an aide?"

"Following procedures, my friend," said Nagorny, motioning his aide to fall back. "The colonel is responsible for safeguarding the codes to launch strategic weapons. Since we placed the satellite interceptors in that category, it was necessary to bring him to the meeting."

"You mean . . . You mean the orders have already been given?" Grachenko's surprise turned to shock when he realized the full implication of what he'd been told. The color drained out of his face and he took an involuntary step backward before he steadied himself. "Firing on an American spacecraft . . . This is insane! Have the missiles already been launched?"

"The Hydras will launch in one hour. Marshal Suvorov has enough evidence to prove the shuttle is on a military operation. It received coded orders and data transmissions from the American Space Defence Command. And for several hours before it changed orbit, the shuttle was controlled by the French navy. What we have here can be viewed as a classic conspiracy by Western military and intelligence services. I don't know how else you can view the evidence."

"Neither do I . . . But there are people who can. I must get ahold of Dr. Fedarenko. We'll contact the Americans and the French, and discover the truth. I can't believe they would steal our spacecraft after offering so many times to rescue its crew."

"I suggest you do it quickly," Nagorny advised, he motioned again to his aide; this time to join him and he put his cap on in preparation to leave. "I fully realize what we've done is a dangerous provocation. However, as a military man, it's the only response I can see, given the evidence and the circumstances. In a way, Nikolai Grigorivich, I hope you succeed."

Chapter Twelve

"*Soyuz 71*, this is Baikonur. *Soyuz 71*, please respond," Ryumin asked, watching his console monitor for any sign of activity from the cosmonauts. "Arkady. Arkady, please answer."

"Are you getting anything from them?" said Sakolov, stepping up to the console and glancing over Ryumin's shoulder.

"Nothing, the drugs have already taken effect. At least with Stefan and Vassili."

"Why is the picture breaking up every few minutes?"

"The spacecraft is tumbling again," said Ryumin. "Which causes the signal to weaken every so often. With almost no fuel for the thrusters, there's little we can do about it."

Sakolov straightened up and looked at the center's main screen, where the new orbital track of the *Phoenix* had intercepted that of the *Soyuz*. The *Phoenix* was now matching its orbit, and slowly overtaking it. The data blocks beside them indicated the two vehicles were less than a dozen kilometers apart, and the shuttle was decelerating.

"When I first heard that the NASA shuttle was changing orbits, I thought it was the answer to all our prayers," said Sakolov, to no one in particular. "However, with the way Suvorov in Air Defence is reacting, it could just be a continuation of the nightmare."

"We're getting a reaction from Arkady," said Ryumin. "Look!"

Sakolov glanced back down at the console in time to see Grachenko lean forward and place a hand on the control panel. Unlike Siprinoff and Kostilev, his actions were deliberate. He was, for the moment, still conscious.

"Arkady, Arkady! This is Anatoly, answer me please. The American shuttle is closing on you, we think the crew will rescue you. Arkady, answer me!"

"This, is Arkady. Why are you waking me?" Grachenko finally asked, fighting through his drug-induced haze.

"Arkady, the NASA shuttle is closing in on you!" said Ryumin, speaking loudly and slowly, to ensure Grachenko would understand at least part of what he was saying. "We believe it's there to rescue you. Please answer me, over."

"Anatoly, I just realized something," said Sakolov, grabbing Ryumin by the shoulder. "If NASA is to rescue our cosmonauts, they must enter the module. When that happens, the atmosphere will leave. Our cosmonauts are wearing their suits, but their visors are up."

It only took an instant for Ryumin to comprehend what he'd been staring at for the last twelve hours. While all three cosmonauts were wearing their complete pressure suits, none of them had their helmet visors sealed. Though the monitor's picture quality was mediocre, that small detail immediately became obvious to Ryumin.

"Arkady, listen to me! You must lock down your

helmet visor," he ordered. "And you must lock down the visors of your crew. Do it, Arkady! Do it!"

The voice still sounded distant. However, it had taken on a sudden urgency and was issuing him instructions. At first Grachenko wanted to turn his headset off so the voice wouldn't bother him. Then, his years of training and space operations took over and he slowly closed his visor; sealing it after the distant voice had told him repeatedly to do so.

"Good, Arkady. Now lock down the visors of your crew," said Ryumin, again loudly and slowly. "They're unconscious. You have to do it for them, Arkady! Do it! Turn to your right!"

More instructions. Grachenko turned as far as his restraint belts would allow and reached for Siprinoff's helmet. Fortunately, Siprinoff's head was tilted in his direction and he managed to close the visor with one hand, then locked the sealing latches.

"Director, you have an urgent message from Voyska PVO headquarters," said one of the command console operators, handing a telephone to Sakolov.

"This is Director Sakolov, what's the message?" He tried to be as cordial as possible and at first listened patiently to the Air Defence spokesman, but this did not last for long. "You tell the marshal he can feed his ideas to the pigs! We don't take orders from him!"

"What the hell was that?" Ryumin asked, jumping when the telephone receiver was smashed back on its cradle.

"Air Defence says their Krasnoyarsk radar has the shuttle less than two kilometers from our craft," said Sakolov. "Marshal Suvorov wants our men to resist the American 'attack.' He's mad, insane. What's happening with Arkady?"

172

"He's locked Stefan's helmet, I'm trying to get him to do the same for Vassili. Arkady, you must unlock your belts. Reach down! Unlock your belt!!"

The haze was darkening and Grachenko could barely feel anything with his fingers. He attempted to do what the voice was telling him, but the belt catches had disappeared into the folds of his bulky spacesuit. His attempts to reach them quickly exhausted him, causing the darkness to rush in faster. Grachenko thought it was the tranquilizers and morphine tightening their grip on him, then he realized there was no longer any Earth-light streaming through the observation windows.

"God help me. The Devil has come to take us," Grachenko managed to say, before his speech became so slurred no one at Baikonur could understand it.

"Arkady, the NASA shuttle must be upon you," said Ryumin. "Can you see it? Can you see it! Yuri, I'm not getting any response from him."

"Keep trying," urged Sakolov. "He has to help Vassili and the Americans. This rescue will not be easy."

The distant voice had retreated to infinity. Grachenko no longer cared about it, no longer felt the terror he had experienced when the module's interior grew dark. The haze closed in around him, shutting off all remaining light. The devil had come to take him and he was no longer afraid of the death he had held off for so long.

"*Phoenix* to rescue team. Stand by, I'm opening the payload doors," said Vachet, glancing around for the right panel of switches at the aft crew station.

The *Phoenix* was hovering less than two hundred feet, the closest Cochran and Post dared bring their spaceplane, below the slowly rotating *Soyuz*. They had matched its speed and orbit; the rest of the operation was up to the men and women waiting in the cargo bay.

"Paul, the door controls are on panel R-Thirteen," said Harrison, growing impatient.

"Yes, I have them. Opening payload doors."

Vachet's hand glided over the right line of switches, hitting them in the correct sequence to activate the motors. The work lights inside the cargo bay snapped out just before the massive doors raised and folded back. They revealed the crippled *Soyuz*, appearing lifeless and out of control, framed against a coldly beautiful star field.

"This is rescue team commander to *Phoenix*, the MMUs are flight-ready," said Ripley, checking the display on his chest pack computer. "Lifelines are secured. We're ready for EVA."

"You're cleared to begin," Vachet answered. "Good luck, my friends. And remember, you're writing history."

"Roger, *Phoenix*. Okay, George, let's do it your way. One-third vertical power."

Ripley and Pellerin fired their manned maneuvering units simultaneously and both rose off the floor of the cargo bay on barely visible jets of nitrogen gas. They left Simon and Harrison behind, though not for long. Harrison was attached to Ripley by a thirty-foot-long tether, as was Simon to Pellerin. They waited a few moments for the lines to run taut, then jumped so they wouldn't be pulled off the bay floor.

"The rescue team is outbound," said Vachet, moving from the mission specialist position at the aft crew station to the pilot's position. "I'm activating the flight controls."

"And I'm switching off mine," Post responded. "Handle her gently, Paul, and don't let that deathtrap get too close to us."

"I hope Jack and the others can do it," said Cochran, reaching for a switch on his com panel. "I didn't expect to find it tumbling the way it is. Mount Cheyenne, this is *Phoenix*. Has there been any change in radio traffic to

174

the *Soyuz?*"

"No change from what we can read," answered Colonel Ericson. "They're still using Glavkosmos channels and it's voice transmissions out, video transmissions back."

"Larry? Is that you? What's going on? I was just talking to Bernie five minutes ago."

"He's now talking with Reiss. He was smart enough to put two and two together, so it looks like we're going to catch a little hell from NASA."

"Well, at least you're not in jail like Clayton. Let us know if anything changes with the Russians. *Phoenix*, out."

"Julie, this is Ripley. How are you two doing back there?"

"We're catching up on you a little but so far, so good."

"You had both better shorten your lines. We're pretty close to the *Soyuz* and we're going to stop here. George, how fast do you estimate it's spinning?"

"About one revolution every fifty-four seconds," said Pellerin, using his chest pack chronometer to measure the rotation rate. "Not dangerous, but it will give us trouble. I'm ready on my flight controls, when do we slow?"

"I want two-thirds forward power in ten seconds. Ready? Mark . . ."

Ripley counted off the seconds, giving Simon and Harrison enough time to gather up most of their tethers. Pellerin activated his forward thrusters in unison with Ripley. As they slowed to a virtual hover, Simon and Harrison drifted past them, jerking to a stop only when their tethers became taut.

The team was some forty feet away from the crippled *Soyuz*, close enough to read its external markings and to peer through the observation windows when they came by. Even though what remained of the spacecraft could be easily placed inside the cargo bay of the *Phoenix*, it was still a dauntingly massive vehicle to the four astronauts poised beside it.

"Ripley to team, activate helmet lights."

Ripley took his hands off his flight controls and reached for the tiny boxes mounted on either side of his helmet. When he clicked their switches, powerful beams washed over the Soyuz. As his lights combined with those of the other team members, the Soviet craft was no longer rotating in and out of shadow.

"I see them!" Simon shouted, at first forgetting the proper radio procedure, then hastily adding, "Simon to Ripley, I can see the cosmonauts."

"That's better. Can you see any movement?"

"No, but they're still wearing their space suits and helmets."

"Good, we'll have no problems making the transfer," said Ripley. "George, if we were to grab hold of this thing, do you think we could slow its rotation with our MMUs?"

"We could, though it might also make the problem worse," said Pellerin. "Remember when the Solar Max satellite was rescued eight years ago? The astronauts tried stopping it by hand first and only made things worse. Still, slowing this vehicle could only help with the rescue."

"Then we'll try it. I want you and Renée to circle around, and make sure you avoid the ship. We'll grab the EVA handrail around the docking hatch."

"That light. It's coming from outside the ship," said Ryumin, when the interior of the *Soyuz* suddenly grew brighter. "It must be from the Americans."

"How could it be? The shuttle is too far away to use its external lights," Sakolov recalled.

"It must be some of the astronauts. They're using their maneuvering packs to approach our craft. I told you they would not use their remote arm."

"They'll still have to remove those packs before they enter the module. And Kostilev's helmet visor is still

176

unlocked. If only we could talk to the *Phoenix* . . . I should call Moscow direct. Perhaps Fedarenko can tell NASA, or will allow us to talk to the shuttle."

Sakolov reached for one of the specially marked telephones on Ryumin's command console and immediately got the long-distance operator. He would not go to the communications office and talk under the watch, and with the consent of, a political officer. There wasn't time for such formal procedures, if indeed there was time for any communications.

With Simon in tow, Pellerin maneuvered out of range of the tumbling spacecraft. The pair executed a wide, careful turn and closed on Ripley, eventually stopping a few feet away from him. During the long minutes the operation took to complete, the *Soyuz* kept rotating, end over end, in front of Ripley.

"Ripley to Pellerin, you guys ready?" he asked.

"Ready, how do you want me to grab the handrail?"

"You'll have to grab it with your left hand, which means you must operate your translation control with your right hand. Can you do it?"

"It will be difficult, but yes, I can," said Pellerin.

"Good. Renée, Julie, you'll sail past us when George and I begin braking this thing. I want both of you to climb onto it, either by grabbing the solar cell panels or the ring of antennas that separates the service and command modules."

"We can do it," said Harrison, answering for both herself and Simon.

"All right, stand by for twenty second countdown. Ripley to *Phoenix*, we're going to try slowing the vehicle's rotation. Still no sign of activity from it."

As Ripley spoke, the tail of the *Soyuz* glided between him and Pellerin. After it had passed them, he began his countdown, watching the nose of the spacecraft swing toward him. The circular handrail around its hatch

177

gleamed brightly in the combination of sunlight and artificial light. Ripley glanced over at Pellerin and watched him release the translation knob at the end of the MMU's left control arm. Pellerin then grabbed the handrail with his left hand just as the nose of the *Soyuz* dipped into view.

"Three seconds, two seconds, one . . . Catch it, George!" Ripley shouted, as his own right hand wrapped around the gleaming chrome rail. "Stand by for full power."

The astronauts had been relatively motionless while they waited for the nose to swing into range. The moment they grabbed its handrail, they were pulled gently along by the multi-ton vehicle. They both had the urge to fire their maneuvering units immediately, but Ripley ordered Pellerin to hold off until all members of the team were moving.

"Julie. Renée. Are you with us?" he asked.

"I'm sailing right behind you, Jack. And so is Renée."

"Roger. Initiate full power on forward thrusters, George."

Steams of nitrogen gas poured from the exhaust nozzles on the front end of each MMU. Pellerin and Ripley felt the strain suddenly increase in their arms and shoulders. It wasn't apparent to them that they were having any effect on the vehicle's rotation rate until Harrison and Simon warned that they were overtaking them.

"Ripley, I'm almost on top of you," said Julie. "Here goes, I'm touching the ship."

Harrison made contact with the *Soyuz* by grabbing one of its folded solar cell wings. She decelerated and crashed softly against the side of the spacecraft. Simon made contact further down its body by catching hold of the antenna ring and placing her feet on the EVA handrail.

"Renée, you're standing on my fingers," said Pellerin. "If you can move, do it!"

"Roger, I'm moving. If I can stand between you and

Jack, I'll be able to look through one of the view ports."

By grabbing one antenna in the ring after another, Simon managed to inch her way around the *Soyuz* until, no longer crushing Pellerin's hand, she could look through the observation window. She had to bend down to do so, but she had the first close look at the cosmonauts.

Inside Simon could see Grachenko lying partly in his couch, and partly over Siprinoff. Siprinoff and Kostilev lay peacefully in their own couches—too peacefully. Apart from their arms, which floated in a neutral body position, Simon could detect no movement.

"Ripley, it looks like they're dead," she warned. "Julie, can you see anything at the other window?"

"I'm just climbing down to it," said Harrison, grabbing one of the flat-blade antennas in the mid-body ring. "Below me, watch your hands."

"Roger, Julie. So far I've used nearly one-third of my propellant," said Ripley. "George, how are you doing?"

"About the same," Pellerin advised, glancing at his chest pack display. "I think we're having some effect on its rotation rate though."

"The only effect I can feel is my arm being pulled out of its socket. Ripley to *Phoenix*, are we making any difference to this tin can?"

"Yes, you are," said Vachet, watching the team's activities through the skylight windows. "Its rotation rate has slowed to one revolution every ninety seconds. But I doubt that you can stop it completely."

"Understood, *Phoenix*. George, prepare to shut down on my mark. Let's save some fuel for the rest of the operation. Three seconds, two, one. Mark."

Pellerin and Ripley killed their MMU thrusters simultaneously, easing the strain they felt in their arms. For a few moments they continued to hold onto the EVA handrail, until they were certain they were matching the rotation rate of the *Soyuz*. When they released their grip, the weak centrifugal force generated by the spacecraft caused Ripley and Pellerin to drift away until they used their MMUs to correct it.

"Lights. More lights, Yuri," said Ryumin, tapping the director's arm. "They're brighter. The astronauts must be closer, right outside the craft."

Sakolov lowered his telephone receiver for a moment and examined the console monitor. Renée's helmet lights overpowered the on-board camera; when the angle was right they filled the screen with a blinding white glare.

"I've still not reached Fedarenko," Sakolov finally commented. "Incredible, they might actually do it. I'll try another number. I've got to reach Konstantin. Anatoly, try contacting Grachenko again. He's got to help his rescuers."

"I can see the cosmonauts," said Harrison, getting her helmet's front bubble as close as she could to the observation window. "At least one of them. He's either asleep or unconscious, but he's alive, I can see him breathing."

"Thank God. We'll proceed with the rescue," said Ripley.

"Not so fast, we've got another problem. This man's helmet isn't sealed. If we open the docking hatch, we'll kill him."

"Shit. This'll fuck things up. *Phoenix*, this is Ripley. If you've been listening, we do have a problem."

"Paul, I'll take this," said Cochran, hitting another toggle on his communications panel. "Jack, this is Ed. We may have a hard decision to make. We may have to kill one man to rescue two. How long do you think it'll take you to open that hatch?"

"At least a minute, probably more," said Ripley, hovering directly in front of the *Soyuz* nose hatch. "The command module will depressurize the moment we start

180

turning the wheel lock. It'll take three people to unlock this thing, raise it, and move inside the module. It'll take time, and no one can survive a vacuum for more than a few seconds."

"Wait. Before we kill someone, there's another way," Vachet advised. "Jack, you're a little too close to the problem. Take a look where Renée is standing."

Ripley looked up and to the right, to the point where Renée Simon was standing on the EVA handrail. Beside her legs he could make out a series of pictograms, with a line of boldly printed cyrillic words above it. While he could't read Russian, Ripley quickly understood the pictograms.

"It's an escape system!" he shouted. "The hatch can be ejected. That's what I think it means."

"Jack, deploy your camera," said Cochran. "Paul, switch on the monitors. I'm coming back."

Cochran unlocked his restraint belts as he gave his orders. Once he was finished, he pushed on his armrests and sailed out of his command seat. For several feet he glided head first, then grabbed a pair of handholds in the cabin roof to arrest his flight and push his body into an upright position. When he spun around to face the aft crew station, Cochran found Vachet activating the two black and white TV monitors.

"Switching screen one to MMU transmission," said Vachet, turning a knob on the video control panel. "And we're not getting anything from Ripley. What else should I do?"

"Switch the second screen to the interior camera," said Cochran. "Activate video recorder. Enable TV downlinks. Walt, tell Houston we're going to send them some pictures. Where's the intercom box at this station? Thanks. Ripley, this is Ed. How are you coming?"

"Video system deploying. I'll be on the air soon."

Once again the TV camera rose out of its storage position and locked into place over Ripley's right shoulder. Unlike its use during the OPF retrieval, this

181

time it would be used for more than just recording the show. The moment Ripley hit the "video transmit" button on his chest pack, the monitor at the shuttle's aft crew station showed the *Soyuz* docking hatch, and Simon's boots on the handrail encircling it.

"*Phoenix* to Ripley, pan up a little," said Cochran, watching the image on the top monitor. "There, I can see the stencilling. Pan up a little more so I can read the label. Emergency . . . Hatch. Jettison . . . It's an escape system all right. The other line warns you not to stand in front of the hatch when you fire it. Follow the symbols and the system will operate much like ours. The only suggestion I'll add is don't fire it when the nose is pointing at the *Phoenix*. Let's not hurt the lady."

"Roger, *Phoenix*. We'll keep it in mind," said Ripley. "We're going to have to change our plans, boys and girls. Simon, can you read the pictograms?"

"Yes, they're similar to our procedures. Very easy to understand."

"Good, you operate the escape system. Julie, since you're the smallest member of our team, and you know which cosmonaut has his visor up, you get to enter the module. I'll push you in once the hatch is blown. George, stand by in case any of us need help. Does everyone understand what they're to do?"

The team members responded that they did, and immediately went to work. Simon opened the panel next to the operating diagrams and pulled the safety pins off the arming lever. Harrison climbed off the *Soyuz* while Ripley backed away from it, aligning himself not directly in front of the hatch but just below it. Ripley had also to match the rotation rate of the *Soyuz* before he hauled Harrison in using her tether. With little to do for the moment, Pellerin maneuvered until he was alongside the vehicle's nose, within a few feet of Simon, and in a direct line to Ripley.

"I got you," Ripley advised, grabbing hold of Harrison's boots. "Unlock your safety line and pass it back to me. You'll need all the freedom we can give you."

"Simon to Ripley, I'm ready to arm the system's explosive bolts."

"Proceed with arming, Renée. Julie, I've got your safety line. I'm unhitching its other end from the MMU and I'm placing it in my accessory pack. Ripley to *Phoenix*, we're ready to enter the *Soyuz*. We'll hold off firing the escape system until we're approaching our zenith."

"Thanks, Ripley," said Cochran. "And good luck."

Simon pulled back the escape system's arming lever until the indicator flag changed from green to red. The explosive bolts were ready for firing. All Simon had to do was return the lever to its original position and the hatch would be blown away, though she would have to wait until the nose of the *Soyuz* had cleared the tail of the *Phoenix*.

"Ripley to team, stand by. Julie, make sure you hold your arms in front of you when I push you off."

"Don't worry, I'll fly into that capsule just like superman," Harrison replied. "You make sure you point me in the right direction."

"I've got you sighted in. Ripley to team, here we go. Fire the system, Renée."

The *Soyuz* was nearly vertical; for the next thirty seconds the *Phoenix* would be safe. Simon threw the lever again and the Soviet spacecraft rippled with the detonation of the explosive bolts. The hinges and locking mechanism disintegrated instantly, unsealing the hatch and blowing it clear of the *Soyuz*. Inside its command module there was a flash of light followed by a shower of metal fragments, most of which were sucked out when the module's atmosphere was lost to space.

Outside, the hatch plate flew past Harrison's helmet, tumbling end over end. A stream of metal fragments and other debris followed it, but the operation didn't wait for them to clear. Ripley pushed Harrison away with all his strength, then had to grab his maneuvering unit controls to correct the drift caused by his actions. Harrison sailed through the debris stream and closed in on the open nose of the *Soyuz*. She was just starting to drift towards Pellerin when she caught the hatch rim and corrected it.

Harrison glided easily into the command module, her only hindrance a sharp bump she felt as something struck her backpack. She maneuvered over Grachenko and reached out for Kostilev, slapping down his visor in one swift motion. When she got closer, Julie groped around for the latches to lock the visor, eventually finding them farther back on Kostilev's helmet than she had expected.

"I've done it! I've done it!" she finally shouted. "His helmet is sealed and I think he's still alive."

"Good, Julie. Now unlock his belts and start pulling him out," said Ripley. "George, move in and help her."

Harrison backed away from Kostilev, enough to allow her to look down and find the catches to the restraint belts. Only when she started to move her hands to grab the catches did she realize how cramped the module had become. With Grachenko pressed against her right side, there remained just enough free room for her to release the catches. A feeling of claustrophobia set in, and it became especially sharp after she started having difficulty moving any farther backwards. Then, a hand took hold of her boot and pulled Harrison from the module. She let out a startled cry until she realized it was Pellerin doing what Ripley had ordered him to.

"Oh, thank God," Julie said, emerging from the nose hatch. "This is one of those times I feel lucky to be black, so you won't see how embarrassed I am."

"Your skin may hide it but your eyes don't," said Pellerin. "Have you freed our first passenger?"

"Almost. Let me go back in and get him."

Julie partially reentered the hatch to complete her work on Kostilev. After a few moments, she advised her team she was ready and, once again, Pellerin hauled her out. This time, she brought Kostilev with her. By then Ripley had flown back to the *Soyuz* and handed Harrison

184

her safety line.

"Reattach yourself to my MMU," Ripley ordered, grabbing Kostilev while Harrison rehooked her line to her belt. "This must be the injured cosmonaut. I'm glad we got him out first. George, we'll be returning to the orbiter with him. I want you and Renée to get the Russian commander out next. Don't leave the vehicle until we come back."

"Understood," said Pellerin. "Renée, stand by to enter the command module. The cosmonaut we're to rescue is the one lying across the other."

"Ripley to *Phoenix*, we're inbound with a survivor. Stand by on the airlock and break out the medical kit."

"Roger, Jack. We'll be ready for you," said Cochran, reaching for his line to the intercom box. "*Phoenix*, out."

Cochran unplugged himself and slipped off his communications headset. He stowed it in the same aft crew station locker he had removed the shuttle's television camera from, along with a set of mounting brackets and coaxial cables.

"Ed, what are you doing with that?" Vachet asked, looking away from the skylight windows.

"I'm making a slight change in plans. We're going to shoot the recovery of the cosmonauts. Houston seems really afraid that Russia will try something because of our rescue. If they do, NASA can show 'em this footage. I'll switch to a wireless microphone stored on the middle deck. Let me know when our astronauts reach the cargo bay."

"Video control confirms it, Yuri," said Ryumin, holding a telephone receiver to his ear. "Video transmission was cut off at the source. Something happened on the *Soyuz* in those final moments of its broadcast."

"This is becoming futile. I can't reach our illustrious chairman anywhere," said Sakolov, a receiver still pressed to his own ear. "Ask the video team to replay the last twenty seconds of the broadcast. Tell them to run it in slow motion."

"Flight Officer to Video Control. Replay in slow motion the last twenty seconds of the *Soyuz* tape. Yes, replay it on the main screen."

Ryumin and Sakolov hung up their telephones simultaneously and turned their attention to the main screen. The curtain of snow which had filled it after the transmission had been cut was replaced by a second showing of the events aboard the *Soyuz*. The tape was run at one-quarter normal speed, making it appear at first as if nothing were happening.

Then, an extended burst of light filled the screen. The bodies of the cosmonauts rippled as if hit by a shockwave and the cabin filled with debris. Even at the tape's reduced running speed, the debris hung in the air for only a moment before it magically disappeared. The camera lens misted up slightly, obscuring the image. Just as it cleared, a blur rushed under the camera and was approaching the cosmonauts when the curtain of snow appeared.

"I didn't see that flash the first time," Sakolov admitted. "I was distracted. It looks to be an explosion. Do you think the astronauts did it?"

"Yes, I believe they're responsible," said Ryumin. "It was an explosion, but what? And the way those fragments disappeared? Almost as if they were sucked out by a vacuum."

"A vacuum? That's it! The debris, the clouding of the lense, it all fits. There was a decompression in the module."

"The NASA astronauts! They fired the explosive bolts on the docking hatch. Then the blur we saw before the picture cut out was . . . Hello, Video Control. I want the last five seconds of the Soyuz tape run again, and freeze it when I tell you."

Ryumin hung onto the telephone receiver as the final moments of the transmission were played once more. He shouted into it for the image to stop when the blur entered the frame, then he and Sakolov studied the main screen carefully.

"I can see arms, and hands on that thing," said Sakolov, pointing out what he was describing. "It is an astronaut."

"Yes, and he's heading to Vassili," Ryumin added, "to close his helmet. This is a rescue! You must try Moscow again, Yuri. If you can't get ahold of Fedarenko, then try the Foreign Ministry. Arkady's uncle will listen to us."

"Ripley to *Phoenix*, I'm going to change course and let Harrison enter the cargo bay. Julie, can you handle our guest alone?"

"I think so, just move out of our way. We're coming up on you fast."

After crossing the gap between the *Soyuz* and the *Phoenix* as rapidly as he could, Ripley slowed to a halt in front of the aft crew station windows, then moved sideways. Harrison and Kostilev had been trailing behind him for most of the transit; now they sailed past him, still travelling at their original velocity. They nearly crashed onto the floor of the cargo bay, but their tether snapped taut and they jerked to a stop a few inches above it.

"Ripley, I'm unhooking my safety line," said Harrison. "I can take him the rest of the way to the airlock."

Tension in the line caused Harrison and her passenger to rise, until she released it from her belt. When she lowered her feet they barely touched the cargo bay floor, though with a gentle kick the contact was enough to send her toward the airlock's hatch.

She held onto Kostilev with one hand while reaching for the hatch with the other. Julie managed to wrap her fingers around one of the ingress-egress assistance bars next to the hatch, arresting her flight. For a few moments she released Kostilev and allowed him to hover beside her as she unlocked and opened the airlock. The unconscious cosmonaut didn't drift very far before Julie had grabbed him again, pulling him to the open hatch in the cargo bay's forward bulkhead.

"Ripley to Julie, you need any help down there?"

"No. I almost have him in the airlock," said Harrison. "I just have to turn him the right way. Get ready to toss me my safety line."

As she hauled Kostilev in, she was forced to keep one hand on the assistance bar. It made handling Kostilev difficult, but Harrison managed to spin him slowly with her free hand until he was oriented in the right attitude and pointed in the right direction.

"Sorry I can't make this any gentler," she told him, as she guided him into the airlock. "But you'll get some TLC later."

When Kostilev's boots cleared the hatch, Harrison closed and sealed it. She turned away from it in time to catch the line Ripley threw down to her. In moments she was reattached and being carried back up to the *Soyuz*, where Pellerin and Simon were extracting the second cosmonaut.

"Middle deck to pilots. I'm pressurizing the chamber," said Cochran. "Paul, the camera's on. Downlink it to Houston."

Cochran had the TV camera mounted on the lockers at the middle deck's front end. Its power and transmission cables ran through the roof hatch to the aft crew station. While a haphazard arrangement, it at least worked. Cochran had to lie on the roof to use the camera's viewfinder. Once its focus had been set, he sailed back to check the airlock's control panel.

While the chamber pressurized rapidly, it would still take nearly two minutes to equalize its atmosphere with the crew compartment's. With no way for Cochran to monitor the man inside the airlock, he stood helplessly beside it until remembering that Ripley had asked for the medical kit.

"Post to Cochran, you're on line in Houston. They say

you should do your flying with a red cape and blue body stocking."

"Sorry, the phone booth up here is occupied," said Cochran, pulling a fabric case out of a forward locker. "They're going to have to make do with a mild-mannered shuttle commander."

An alarm warned Cochran that the airlock was approaching normal air pressure. He threw a salute to the camera and returned to the airlock control panel, where he decided the pressure scale reading was close enough to open it. He mounted the medical kit on some velcro pads at the galley station and grabbed a lever on the airlock's hatch.

Though the few pounds of difference in air pressure hadn't seemed like much to Cochran, he quickly discovered how difficult it was to unseal the hatch. His first attempt barely moved the lever. Only when he used both hands did the middle deck fill with the explosive hiss of air rushing into the chamber. Once pressures were equal, the hatch slid up and to the left.

Cochran grabbed the figure inside the airlock by its life-support backpack. He pushed Kostilev up until he caught his legs, then pulled him out feet first and upside down. Cochran rolled him upright as he cleared the entry hatch and practically tore the visor open to get a good look at Kostilev's face.

"Middle deck to pilots, I'm not getting any response here. I don't like it," said Cochran, who at first could not detect any signs of life from Kostilev. "C'mon, breathe, damn it!"

Cochran shook the cosmonaut, then slapped his face, but it didn't produce the results he wanted. As his desperation turned to panic, he remembered the medical kit. He flew to it and unzipped its lid, pulling a stethoscope from one of its packages. Cochran turned back to Kostilev and unlocked the glove on his left hand. After sliding it off by its connecting ring, Cochran laid the stethoscope's disc on the bottom of the exposed wrist to hunt for a pulse.

"Post to Cochran, the guy could be comatose. Bernie warned us the cosmonauts were told to take drugs."

"I know," Cochran replied. "I got a pulse. Walt, he's alive! Paul, tell our rescue team to bring back the *Soyuz* medical kit. We've got to find out what they're on."

"Roger. What will you do with our guest, Ed? Is he the injured one?" Vachet asked.

"Yes, he's got a broken arm. Christ, his suit's covered with something that smells like urine. I wonder why?"

"Ripley to Pellerin, are you guys ready to depart?"

"We're ready," said Pellerin, moving away from the *Soyuz*. "Did you have any problems getting your man into the airlock?"

"Just make sure you're out of Simon's way when you reach the orbiter," said Ripley. "Did you find the medical kit?"

"I'm afraid not. By the time Vachet told us to look, we already had Commander Grachenko out."

"Don't worry, Harrison will look for it. Get your tail back to the *Phoenix*. Don't return to the *Soyuz*. Once Julie and I are finished, that'll be it. All we want is the crew."

As Ripley and Harrison climbed toward the *Soyuz*, Pellerin and Simon, Grachenko cradled in her arms, were departing. Ripley slowed for his return to the crippled spacecraft. This caused Harrison to again sail past him, until she grabbed her tether and started to haul herself back to him.

Since the firing of its hatch, the *Soyuz* had begun to wobble. Soon it would be tumbling erratically, hastening its certain doom. While not dangerous for now, the wobble did create problems for Harrison as she prepared to reenter the ship.

"I can't time the way it's moving," she said. "If you point me left or right, I could miss the hatch entirely."

"Okay, straight ahead you go," said Ripley. "Let me grab your feet. I'll match the rotation after you're aboard."

190

Harrison and Ripley hovered before the *Soyuz* as the hatch swung into view.

"I'm unhooking your safety line," Ripley advised, removing the tether clip from Julie's belt. "Are you ready?"

"All set, Jack. I'm A-OK."

"Good. Here you go."

Ripley pushed her away with less force than before. Still, he had to immediately start correcting the drift the thrust had caused. As he backed up, he watched Harrison glide to the *Soyuz* with her arms outstretched to catch its nose hatch if it moved out of her path.

In the few seconds it took her to fly the twenty-odd feet to the spacecraft, the hatch did indeed shift to the right, causing her to catch it first with her right hand, then with her left. For a moment Harrison had to pause and realign herself; then she charged the rest of the way into the command module.

Even with two of the cosmonauts removed, the cramped interior brought on her claustrophobia once more. She was not only apprehensive about the module but was growing to fear her own space suit and how it confined her. She fought off her terror by concentrating on the tasks assigned to her. Ignoring the cosmonaut lying in front of her, Harrison swung her head from side to side, searching for the ship's medical kit. On her third scan she found it, stuffed behind the headrests to the couches.

"Harrison to Ripley, I've spotted the kit. I'm going to remove it before unbuckling the cosmonaut."

To retrieve the medical kit meant going deeper into the module. Harrison swallowed a mouthful of water from her shoulder pack and took hold of the headrests, then pulled herself in an extra two feet. The medical kit was a black leather valise the size of a doctor's traditional medical bag. It was open, though most of its contents did not appear to have been disturbed. Harrison zipped the valise shut and, after a few attempts, pried it out of the nook it had been stuffed in.

191

"You're pretty far in there, Julie," Ripley observed, hovering in front of the docking hatch. "I can hardly see your boots. You enjoying yourself in that cave?"

"Jack, I'm going to kill you when I get out of here," she said, and for the moment she meant it.

Harrison placed the medical kit on Kostilev's empty couch, then backed up to free Siprinoff. She unlocked the buckles on his restraint belts and threw them off him. He started to float, but she held him down while she grabbed the kit and backed out. Harrison managed to get halfway through the hatch when, suddenly, she could move no further. There was something pressing against her right side, though she was unable to see it.

"Jack, I'm stuck," Julie said, her fear beginning to turn into panic. "Something's caught me, it's under my right arm."

"Hold on, I'm moving in."

Ripley fired the thrusters on the port side of his MMU, turning him to the right. He fired his top thrusters as well, swinging him under Harrison and allowing him to move a few inches closer to the *Soyuz*. Ripley slid his left hand over the hatch rim and groped until he felt a cylindrical object wedged between his teammate and the rim.

"Julie, breathe in hard," he ordered, wiggling and twisting the object until it popped out of the hatch and floated in front of him. "Good God it's a camera lens. Looks like it got sheared off at its mount. Can you move now?"

"Yes, I'm coming out," said Harrison, breathing easier.

"Good, bring the medical kit with you. It'll be easier for me to handle while you go back in for our friend."

"Finally! Finally, I've got him," said Sakolov, cupping his hand over the telephone's mouthpiece. "Your idea was genius, Anatoly. Yes, Doctor, we've been following the rendezvous of the *Soyuz 71* and the NASA shuttle. No, we think it's a rescue flight. Here, I'll let Ryumin tell

192

you why."

"Doctor, what's happening isn't a hijacking or a kidnapping," Ryumin answered, after he had accepted the receiver from Sakolov and heard a familiar voice on the other end. "This is humanitarian. It's a rescue flight and we have evidence to prove it."

"Evidence? Describe it to me," said Fedarenko, his voice rising with anticipation. "Nikolai, get on your phone."

Ryumin heard a click on the other end, indicating that another telephone had been picked up. He didn't need to hear the new listener identify himself to know it was the foreign minister.

"We have a tape of *Soyuz 71's* transmission," said Ryumin. "In its final moments it shows what we believe is a NASA astronaut heading to save one of our cosmonauts. If you wish, we can transmit it directly to the Foreign Ministry."

"Yes, make the preparations," said Grachenko. "We can use anything you can give us. Have you any other evidence?"

"I must admit the rest of what we have isn't very strong. The shuttle isn't trying to recover the *Soyuz*, and the KGB tells us it is also transmitting video signals to earth. We believe they're recording the rescue."

"Did the KGB also inform you the shuttle was talking with America's space defence forces?" Grachenko asked. "That they did so on scrambled military channels?"

"Yes, and I cannot explain it," Ryumin admitted. "Parts of this rescue flight do confuse me. However, I've still seen nothing to convince me that this is anything but a humanitarian act. Director Sakolov agrees with me and so does everyone else in this operations center, comrade Foreign Minister."

"Thank you, Flight Officer. Could you put Director Sakolov on the line? Fedarenko and I wish to speak with him."

"Yes, of course. Yuri?"

Ryumin handed the receiver back to Sakolov, who spoke for a little over a minute to the director of Glavkosmos and the foreign minister before ending the conversation.

"Well, we had better let Communications handle the video transmission," said Sakolov, placing the receiver back in its cradle. "We don't have much time to meet their deadline."

"Do you think the foreign minister believes this is a rescue flight?" Ryumin asked. "Does he believe our evidence?"

"I think he believes what NASA is doing is a rescue. But I doubt he had much confidence in our evidence. He needs more conclusive proof than what we have. Understand, the people he has to convince aren't space experts, they're politicians."

"If only we could talk to the shuttle, that would end our problems. Flight Officer to Video Control, prepare to transfer the last *Soyuz* tape to the Communications Office. Make sure you include the slow-motion version of its final moments."

"Ripley to *Phoenix*, we've recovered the medical kit and we're inbound with our last guest."

"Roger. Will you be needing the other part of your team, Jack?" Vachet asked.

"No, we got all we need from that deathtrap. How much time do we have before the first transfer orbit window?"

"The event timer shows twenty-one minutes. If we can't make the first window, we'll have to stay in this orbit an additional fifty-five minutes before we can use the next one."

"Roger, *Phoenix*. It's not much time, but we'll be ready for the first window. Ripley to Simon, I want you to enter the airlock with your cosmonaut. Ed's going to need your help. Pellerin, begin stowing your MMU. We're almost finished."

Once again, Ripley and Harrison were returning to the *Phoenix*. They carried with them the last of the *Soyuz* crew and its medical kit. Behind them they left a crippled derelict. In a few days, what was left of the *Soyuz* would be burning up on reentry, though fortunately it would be a lifeless, empty shell.

Approximately a hundred feet below them, Ripley and Harrison could see Simon entering the shuttle's airlock with Grachenko in tow. Unlike Harrison, she entered the chamber with her comatose charge and locked the hatch after her.

"Simon to *Phoenix*. I'm pressurizing the chamber," said Renée, a gentle hiss growing audible in her helmet.

"Open the commander's helmet as soon as you have a breathable atmosphere," Vachet ordered. "When pressurization is complete, Ed wants you on the middle deck. Don't try to remove and store your pressure suit. He needs you now."

After he was finished with Simon, Vachet worked the flight controls at the aft crew station to correct a drift he had noted. The response was a series of brief flashes around the OMS pods at the tail of the *Phoenix*. This pushed the shuttle back under the *Soyuz*, and the descending trio of astronauts.

"Ripley to Pellerin, you need any help down there?"

"No, my storage operation is moving easily."

"Good. Help Julie when she arrives with her guest."

To stow his maneuvering unit, Pellerin undid the latches connecting it to his backpack and walked out of it. When he turned around, the MMU was hovering where he had left it. He deactivated its propulsion system and its batteries, and refolded its control arms. He locked the unit into its storage braces, completing the operation in time to assist Harrison when she touched down with Siprinoff.

As before, the momentum of her descent from the *Soyuz* carried Harrison and her guest to the floor of the

195

shuttle's cargo bay after Ripley had pulled to a stop. Together with Pellerin, she carried Siprinoff up to the airlock, where they were forced to wait until it was cleared for their use.

"Pass him to me and then climb out," said Cochran, when the airlock's interior hatch rolled open.

"Here he comes, Commander," said Simon. "Watch his head."

Grachenko's body was bent at the waist and bent at the knees; even so, Simon had to push his head down in order for him to clear the hatch. Once through it, Grachenko began to relax as Cochran maneuvered him around the compartment.

"Get your helmet and gloves off," he ordered. "Just discard them. Prepare the chamber for the next group."

Simon emerged from the airlock and rolled the hatch shut. She hit the buttons on its control panel to evacuate its atmosphere; in a few minutes it would again be ready for use. She stripped off her gloves and helmet and let them drift away as she'd been told to.

"I've checked him for vital signs," said Cochran, working on Grachenko, while Kostilev floated beside him. "He's alive. His suit has a permanent backpack, just like our old ones."

"What should I do, Commander?" Simon asked, moving to the other side of Grachenko. "Work on the injured man?"

"No, first we have to find out how these suits are constructed. Help me find the mid-body ring."

"All right. Have you any idea why they smell so bad? Did their waste system malfunction?"

"It must have," said Cochran. "We'll get rid of the smell when we remove these suits. Here's the body flap. Christ, it's sealed by snaps. Why can't the Russians steal velcro?"

The body flap to Grachenko's suit was a ridge held together by a row of snap buttons. As with the NASA suits, the body flap covered the waist ring connecting the upper and lower assemblies. Once Renée and Cochran had unlocked it, they pulled the upper torso off Grachenko. They would examine its construction, before trying to cut the same thing off Kostilev.

"This is Volgograd Launch Control to all ground crews. We are T minus thirty-four seconds and counting to first launch, T minus sixteen minutes and counting to second launch."

The warning echoed across an empty row of gentry-style pads and missile silos. No rockets were on the pads, and there was no activity around the silos, now given a wide berth by all personnel in Volgograd's primary launch facility.

North of the Black Sea, near the town of Kapustin Yar on the Volga River, the Volgograd Cosmodrome was one of three Soviet launch centers. Similar to the White Sands test range, it was also one of the most secret, with few scientific or civilian launches since the late 1980s. And unlike White Sands, Volgograd was an operational base as well as a test facility.

Approximately half a minute after the last warning, the thin shell over one of the silos exploded away. A white plume of gas shot into the air, and a one-hundred-foot long missile was ejected from the silo. It rose nearly twice its length before the engines at its base ignited.

The roar of the SS-18's initial launch was deafening and shook the ground, but it was minor compared to the thunder created when the first-stage nozzles emitted a sheet of flame. In spite of the altitude, the ground surrounding the silo was bathed in fire. Trees up to a mile away swayed in the shock wave caused by the main engine ignition. Even at the distant control center, the windows rattled loudly.

Unlike the SS-18s in the Strategic Rocket Forces, this one did not swing into a highly slanted ballistic arc. It did not head north for a sub-orbital polar flight. In the hands of the Air Defence forces, it was no longer a nuclear-tipped ICBM but had become a Mark 1 Hydra satellite interceptor.

Like all orbital vehicles leaving Volgograd, the Hydra climbed along an easterly launch azimuth. After two and a half minutes of firing, the first stage would shut down and separate. From there the Hydra would go into low earth orbit, where it was programmed to release its interceptors.

After more than two decades of development, experimentation, and flight testing, the first operational launch of an anti-satellite weapon had been made. The opening shots in history's first space war were being fired.

"Hey, there's my wife! And she's got the third Russian with her!" Harrison shouted, pointing to the main screen in the suddenly crowded launch center. "They got 'em all!"

Harrison's remarks coincided with a burst of applause and cheering from the assembled personnel. Canaveral had tapped into the video transmissions from the *Phoenix,* and each time a cosmonaut was pulled from the airlock, the crowd celebrated it. This time, however, Reiss had finally had enough.

"Shut up already, this isn't a damn football game!" he shouted, immediately silencing the crowd. "That goes especially for you, Harrison. If you had anything to do with this stunt, you'll be sharing a jail cell with Reynolds."

"It was only luck he got the call and not me," said Harrison. "I would've been glad to help in this, the most important space event since the moon landings."

"It may well be, but it could also lead to a confrontation with the Russians. I had to wake up Engleberg and all I got was the duty officer at the State Department. I haven't heard back from either of them yet."

"I know the Russians are touchy, but you've been acting like they could start a war over what the *Phoenix* has done," commented the deputy launch officer. "This is a rescue, a mercy flight."

"It's also unauthorized, and the Russians know it," said Reiss. "And when things start going wrong, they turn paranoid."

"You could be right," said Harrison, his euphoria cooling down. "We better hope that either Washington can make them listen to reason, or that Cochran gets the orbiter down before they can react."

"What's going on? Why's your friend leaving the two girls with the Russians?" asked Ericson, watching a feed of the shuttle's video transmission on an auxiliary screen.

"According to the clock, they have ten minutes before the first transfer orbit window," said Rosen. "Ed's probably going to the flight deck to help prepare."

"This is NORAD Combat Operations Center to Space Defence Command," announced a voice which filled the room. "We show three Red Birds on lift off. How come you guys didn't catch them?"

"What? Where? Larry, find out what's happening," said Rosen, embarrassed at being caught off guard. "Chris, is that you? What are the launch points for the Red Birds?"

"Yes, this is Chris. Two are from Volgograd Station and one's from the Northern Cosmodrome. What went wrong, Bernie?"

"We were preoccupied with the *Phoenix*, sorry about that. Colonel, what do we have?"

"The AMEWS satellites confirm it," said Ericson. "We got missile launches from the two military cosmodromes. All the data is coming up on the main screen."

Largely ignored in favor of the action being shown on

the smaller auxiliaries, the center's main screen displayed the bright red tracks of three missiles lifting out of the Soviet Union. Initial information came solely from the AMEWS net. Once the missiles climbed above the atmosphere, the SARSAT satellites and ground-based radars would provide more data.

"General, our weekly schedule says nothing about these launches," Mary Widmark advised. "Could this be a missile attack?"

"Not likely," said Rosen. "Two of these birds are on an East-West trajectory. ICBMs follow a North-South one. They're going into orbit, and I'm afraid I know what they are."

"SARSAT scan on the first Volgograd bird is coming in," said Ericson, a telephone receiver pressed to his ear. "Display Control is putting it on screen 1-B."

On the monitor below the one showing the shuttle's middle deck, an eerily sharp image from the synthetic aperture radar satellite was shown, along with the missile's exact dimensions. It only took Rosen a moment to confirm his fears.

"It's an SS-18 in satellite interceptor configuration," he said in a low voice. "And I bet the others are the same way. Soviet Air Defence is using their best, they're launching Hydras. This is Command One to NORAD Combat Operations Center. We have hostile military action by the Soviet Union; our confidence is high. We suggest you go to Def Con Three."

"Roger, Command One," said the voice that had first warned of the launches. "Stand by, Bernie. We'll need a lot of your information in the next few minutes."

"We'll be here. We'll try to figure out the Hydra deployments. This is Space Defence Command, out."

"What do we do, General?" Widmark asked. "And more important, what do we do about the *Phoenix?*"

"Tell Communications to standby on the secure channels," said Rosen. "Alert the Cobra Dane site, and the Spacetrack chain. We won't contact our heroes just yet. The Hydra is a nasty weapon but it takes time to deploy. With a little luck, and if they make this transfer orbit window, they'll land without ever really having been in danger."

Minutes after Rosen gave his commands, the main screen lit up with the reactions. The Cobra Dane radar in the Aleutians started to scan for the rapidly approaching missiles, while the Spacetrack bases scattered across the globe stepped up their surveillance. And at the top of the screen, the defence condition display advanced to Def Con Three. The readiness of NORAD and U.S. strategic forces had just been raised to a higher level.

"Glad to have you back, Ed," said Post, when Cochran glided up to his chair. "What's the aroma I've been smelling?"

"It's our guests," said Cochran, strapping himself in. "Their pressure suits are covered with urine. I gave orders for the suits to be stuffed in the airlock after the rest of our team's aboard. Speaking of which, what's Ripley doing?"

"He didn't enter the airlock with George," Vachet responded. "He claimed the medical kit didn't allow him enough room."

"Bullshit. What's he doing now?"

"Recharging the nitrogen tanks on his MMU."

"What? Let me talk to him," said Cochran, reaching for his com panel and reactivating it. "*Phoenix* to Ripley. Jack, this is Ed, what the hell are you doing?"

"I have to refuel the MMU," said Ripley. "If we had an emergency of our own, we'd need one right away."

"Okay, just make sure you're in the airlock the moment it's depressurized. Cochran, out. Paul, move us away from the *Soyuz* and prepare to return flight control to Walt."

Vachet glanced at the spacecraft through the skylight windows before pulling the translation grip. The thrusters grouped next to the OMS nozzles fired briefly, producing enough of a kick to move the *Phoenix* out from under what was now a hazard to navigation. Vachet quickly deactivated his controls and returned flight authority to Post. He remained at the aft crew station, even though it was virtually shut down.

"Loading program Two-Three-Nine into GPC," said Post, tapping out commands on his computer keyboard. "Program load to BFS completed. Initiating OMS firing sequence."

"OMS engines, armed." Cochran pressed a set of buttons on his side of the cockpit's center pedestal which activated the orbital maneuvering system. Midway through his procedure he hesitated, then reached for one of his earphones.

"Boss, what's going on?" Post asked. "You're turning pale. I didn't know you could lose color like that in zero-G."

"It's Mount Cheyenne," said Cochran, though only after being prodded. "They broke in on the NASA channels. We're in deep shit, Walt. Bernie, can you repeat what you told me? I'm switching you to the PA system."

Cochran hit more controls on his communications panel, and moments later Rosen's voice was heard on both the flight deck and the middle deck.

"This is Space Defence Command, we're tracking the lift-offs of three Hydra satellite interceptor missiles from the Volgograd complex and the Northern Cosmodrome. All three are on their second stage burns and we . . . We have a fourth launch. *Phoenix,* we've detected a fourth launch, the second lift-off from the Northern Cosmodrome. We suspect it's another Hydra."

"Jesus Christ, you were right," said Post, who was now turning pale. "Traffic's going to get pretty busy up here. How much time do you think we have?"

"If we're lucky, enough to make the White Sands reentry," said Cochran. "Bernie, do you agree?"

"Yes, Ed. Provided you make the upcoming transfer orbit," Rosen added. "I didn't want to tell you, but the situation is changing. We'll keep you abreast of it. Mount Cheyenne, out."

"Thanks, Bernie. *Phoenix*, out." When the transmission ended, Cochran switched to both the crew intercom and the short-range radio. "Okay, you heard the man. Complete OMS activation. Paul, prepare to close cargo bay doors. Ripley, we're committed to this window. Are you in the airlock yet?"

"Ed, what about us and the Russians?" Harrison asked.

"It'll be a half hour before we reenter," said Cochran. "Tend to our guests as I instructed and stuff their suits in the airlock. How are they?"

"We know which drugs they took, but we haven't treated them yet. We got most of their suits off, except for Kostilev's upper torso assembly. We're waiting for Jack to help us."

"Good, stay on them. If anything happens, let me know."

"OMS armed and ready for firing," said Post, checking through the list on his CRT screen. "Transferring OMS to GPC control. T minus two minutes, forty-six seconds, and counting to transfer orbit burn."

"Let's bring the lady around," Cochran ordered. "Commander to crew, stand by for attitude change."

Post twisted his joystick grip slightly, and started the *Phoenix* pivoting sixty degrees to port. On the flight deck, the maneuver caused few problems. On the middle deck, the situation was different. As the compartment swung around them, Harrison, Simon, and Pellerin had to move their patients so they wouldn't collide with the side walls. They also had to knock floating objects out of the way.

"We should put these men on our ECG equipment so we can send their vital signs to the doctors in Houston," said Julie, pushing a space suit away from Grachenko.

"A good idea, though we should wait until after the

OMS burn to do it," Pellerin suggested. "The leads would be snapped off if we put them on now."

"All right, we'll wait. Renée, could you check the airlock? Jack should finally be in it."

"I'm safetying my flight controls," said Post, twisting the lock pins in his joystick pedestal. "We're all set for OMS burn. T minus two minutes and counting to ignition."

"We're not ready yet," said Cochran. "My CRT shows the cargo bay doors haven't been closed. Paul, what's the holdup?"

"I wanted to wait until Jack was in the airlock before closing them," Vachet admitted. "Looks like I'll have to wait until after the OMS burn."

"What? Ripley, we are leaving! We got big trouble and we've got to make this first window."

"I know, I know! But I have to safety the nitrogen fueling line," said Ripley. "Don't worry about me, I'll be in."

"You'd better. This is serious."

"Ed, you want me to stop the countdown?" Post reached for a group of toggles on a side panel and held his fingers over them. The moment they were touched they would deactivate the OMS engines, effectively killing the shuttle's transfer orbit attempt. "We're at T minus one minute, thirty seconds."

"No, get your hand away from those inhibitors," Cochran ordered. "We can't wait for the next window with ASATs flying around. Don't worry, Jack knows he had better get his ass in here."

As Ripley finished looping the fueling line around its storage rack, he swung the cover plate down and locked it. The nitrogen station was secure, as were the two maneuvering units mounted on the cargo bay's forward bulkhead. Between the MMUs was the airlock hatch, which Ripley easily reached after pushing off from the bay's port side. During the glide he looked at the time display on his chest pack and realized he barely had a minute left before the OMS burn.

The moment he got his hand around the hatch lever he threw it, unsealing the airlock. By grabbing hold of an ingress assistance bar, Ripley steadied himself while he jerked open the hatch. He raised his legs and sailed easily through the opening feet first. The only trouble he had with his entry was the hatch itself. Ripley had used so much strength to open it, the hatch was resting on the travel stops of its hinges, forcing him to lean back out in order to grab its handle.

"This is Ripley, I'm in. I've sealed the outer hatch and I'm pressurizing the chamber."

"We're at T minus twenty-four seconds," said Cochran. "You made it by the skin of your teeth, Jack. Commander to crew, grab something that's nailed down. T minus fifteen seconds and counting."

To prepare themselves and their patients, Harrison, Simon, and Pellerin each grabbed a cosmonaut by his feet and braced themselves against either the airlock or the middle deck's back wall. Inside the airlock, Ripley hung on to some pressure suit frames. At the aft crew station Vachet already had his feet secured; he only needed to put his hands on the shuttle control grips to prevent himself from being pushed against the instrument panels.

The fifteen seconds had given them barely enough time to prepare. At zero seconds the shuttle's general purpose computer fired the orbital engines. To the crew, the acceleration felt like the afterburner kicking in on a jet fighter. The *Phoenix* trembled as it moved out of the orbit it had been in for little more than an hour. For the next thirty-two minutes it would head north, to intercept the orbit which would then take it far enough south to land at White Sands. The rescue was a success. All the *Phoenix* had to do now was return to Earth.

Chapter Thirteen

Nine minutes after liftoff, the lead Hydra shut down its second stage engines and coasted powerless. It had flown nearly a thousand miles downrange from Volgograd at orbital speed and had almost reached its operational altitude. During the time it coasted, the separation motors fired, detaching the now useless second stage.

What remained of the Hydra was the delivery bus for the interceptor vehicles. These were still hidden beneath the missile's segmented nose cap, where they would stay until they reached their release point. At the base of the delivery bus the in-orbit maneuvering engines pivoted, then fired, causing it to climb to the same altitude as the *Phoenix*.

Far behind the lead Hydra, its Volgograd sister, its wing man, was still on its second stage burn. In the next few minutes it would achieve orbital insertion, but would immediately change its trajectory. By the time the Volgograd Hydras reached their release points they would be hundreds of miles apart, allowing their interceptor vehicles maximum deployment spreads.

While they tracked across the eastern horizon, the Northern Cosmodrome Hydras climbed toward the North Pole. The first one had just completed its second stage burn and was shedding the empty section. It had the speed and altitude for orbital insertion, and would be at its release point in twenty minutes.

Though the first of the Northern Cosmodrome Hydras was in fact the third to be launched, the dictates of orbital mechanics meant it would deploy its interceptors almost an hour ahead of the Volgograd pair. A hundred miles below it, the second Northern Cosmodrome missile was still on its first stage burn. Already its trajectory was several degrees farther east, and this would increase once the boost phase was over, when the delivery bus was following its flight program to its own release point. If nothing stopped them, the Hydras would deploy their web of anti-satellite vehicles in just over an hour.

"Madness. Pure madness," Sakolov uttered, as he watched the main screen plot the orbital tracks of the ascending Hydras. "Though I'm surprised Marshal Tukavsky hasn't joined Suvorov in launching an attack with our Strategic Rocket Forces."

"Please, don't make this nightmare any worse than it is," said Ryumin. "Has Air Defence responded to our requests?"

"No, not since I told them what they could do with Suvorov's ideas. I keep hoping, Anatoly Victorvich, that I'll wake up and find this is only a dream."

"Comrade Flight Officer, we've made our calculations on the shuttle's new orbit," said a technician, laying a graph in front of Ryumin. "If the *Phoenix* changes orbit again in twenty minutes, it'll be committed to the White Sands reentry window."

"A military field," said Sakolov. "More and more this rescue sounds like a Pentagon operation. Perhaps Suvorov is not entirely wrong."

"Yuri, don't be paranoid," Ryumin commanded, looking up from the newly delivered graph. "Leave that to Suvorov. I'm still convinced it's a humanitarian act."

"Then why didn't NASA warn us they were going ahead with it? How difficult would it have been?"

"Very. The hot line runs between Washington and Moscow, not between us and Houston. We do not have direct links with NASA. Valery, can the shuttle make its reentry before the Hydras deploy?"

"I doubt it," said the technician. "The interceptors could start deploying in the next few minutes, or not until the *Phoenix* approaches the reentry window. We don't know the deployment pattern Air Defence has selected. However, the *Phoenix* can land before all the interceptors are in position. With a little luck, it could beat out Suvorov's attempt to destroy it."

"A little luck . . . It seems as though every time we get some, a mountain of problems falls on us," said Ryumin, handing back the graph. "We should wish for less luck and more communication. For now, all we can do is watch."

"Jesus, what smells in here?" Ripley asked, grimacing as he stepped out of the airlock. "Did the toilet back up?"

"Ours didn't, but theirs might have," said Pellerin, motioning to the three cosmonauts. "Their suits are coated with urine. We have to stow the sections in the airlock. Here."

Pellerin handed Ripley an upper torso assembly. Unlike the others, its right arm had been cut off at the shoulder and there was a long, jagged slit down its right side. Both the waist ring and collar had been bent out of shape so that the cosmonaut inside the suit could be easily removed.

"Good God, what kind of party have you guys been throwing?" said Ripley, examining the torn suit.

"A coming out party," said Pellerin. "It was the only way we could free Mr. Kostilev without injuring his arm further. Is there room inside the airlock for everything?"

"Not unless we take a lot out." Ripley's voice echoed slightly as he reentered the chamber. He pushed in Kostilev's upper torso assembly, then unclipped something from the inner wall. "We've already got three complete suits in here."

Ripley emerged from the airlock carrying a detached backpack. He pushed it over to the recharging station, then grabbed another drifting section of Soviet pressure suit. The shuttle's middle deck was filled with the torso assemblies, helmets, and gloves which Pellerin and the others had pulled off the cosmonauts.

"How long will it take to clear this mess?" Harrison asked.

"Too long with just Ripley and me," said Pellerin, moving to the roof hatch. "Paul, are you going to join us?"

"In a minute. I have to finish locking the cargo bay doors," Vachet advised. "Just give me a little more time."

"We're running around like someone stepped on the ant hill," said Ripley. "Why are we in such a damn hurry, George?"

"That's right, you didn't hear General Rosen," said Pellerin. "The Soviets have responded to our rescue of their men. They've launched Hydra anti-satellite weapons."

"We risk everything to save these guys and now they want to shoot us down. That's what I call fucking gratitude."

"Well, whatever kind of gratitude it is, it means we'll all have to work fast. Take this."

Pellerin grabbed a lower torso assembly and handed it to Ripley, who stuffed it inside the airlock. He emerged carrying another backpack, which he sent gliding over to the recharge station before selecting another pressure suit half.

"Cargo doors closed. Activating centerline and bulkhead latches," said Vachet, running his hand down the rows of latch switches at the aft crew station. When the status lights had changed from red to green, the operation was complete. "Ed, what are your orders for the middle deck team?"

"Stabilize our guests as best they can," said Cochran. "And strap them into the horizontal bunks. When you're done, break out the seats for reentry. I'll do the same up here."

Vachet acknowledged his instructions and disappeared through the hatch. He had barely gone when Cochran pushed himself out of his chair. Leaving Post to operate the *Phoenix*, he sailed to a locker under the satellite control panels. He pulled from it the mission specialist

209

seats. Stowed since the time the *Phoenix* had achieved orbit, Cochran unfolded each seat and deployed its support legs. He found the attachment points in the deck's flooring and locked them down by inserting their anchor posts.

"God, the smell is much worse down here," Vachet observed, as he dropped from the ceiling to the middle deck floor.

"It'll end once we finish stowing their suits," said Ripley. "We're almost done."

The bulky torso halves had since been packed into the airlock chamber. Ripley and Pellerin were now collecting the smaller items for stowage, their hands were filled with discarded helmets and gloves.

"Paul, we got vital signs on all three cosmonauts," Julie advised. "They're low but stable. They're all in a drug-induced sleep, almost comatose. What should we do with them?"

"Ed wants us to stabilize them," said Vachet, moving around the Russians to where Harrison was standing. "Then strap them into the first three bunks. Break out the endo-tracheal tubes and prepare to give these people some detox injections. What's the residue on your hands, Julie?"

"It's the urine from their space suits. It's been rubbing off and turning sticky. And it smells terrible."

"Not to mention that it's highly unsanitary. Before we start giving injections, you and Renée should clean up. I'll take him."

Vachet grabbed Grachenko and Kostilev by the shoulders as Harrison released them and turned to the galley. On one side was the personal hygiene station, a clear plastic bubble with two openings, the zero-gravity sink. After adjusting the temperature control, Julie stuck her hands through the openings and hit the circulation button.

Streams of hot water and germicidal soap sprayed into the bubble. A vacuum was started, sucking away the water and the foul-smelling grease Harrison rubbed from her hands. In moments they were as clean as a surgeon's. When she was finished, her place at the hygiene station was taken by Simon, who found it difficult to push her hands inside the bubble because of the connecting rings on the arms of her pressure suit.

"The lithium hydroxide canisters are still active," said Ripley, closing a panel in the middle deck's floor, below which was the shuttle's life support system. "The best way to clear the smell is to enable the cabin vents and put the circulation fans on high blower."

"There, all cleaned up," said Pellerin, rolling the hatch plate down and sealing the airlock, which was now filled with space suit parts. "I'll give Edward your orders."

Pellerin glided to the roof hatch and poked his head through it. On the flight deck he found Cochran finishing the reinstallation of the second mission specialist seat.

"How's it going?" Cochran asked. "You sound busy."

"We're getting the job done, but we need some help with the smell. Jack wants you to enable the cabin air vents and switch the circulation fans to high blower."

"It'll get pretty noisy around here, but I guess it's the only way. Have you started treating our guests?"

"Not yet. Paul ordered the women to scrub down before doing any medical procedures," said Pellerin. "I suppose Jack and I will have to as well."

"You'd better. You look as if you've been cleaning out the toilet. Be sure to remind Paul we don't have much time left. Walt, how long do we have?"

"Fourteen minutes, fifty-seven seconds," said Post, checking the cockpit's event timer. "And we'll have to change the ship's attitude before we make the de-transfer orbit burn."

"Will do," Pellerin replied. He pushed away from the hatch and returned to the middle deck, touching down next to Simon at the shuttle's galley. "Did the rest of you hear? We have less than fifteen minutes to the

211

next orbit."

"That doesn't give us much time to treat our friends," said Vachet. "George, take Renée's place at the hygiene station. Renée, we need two hypodermics from the medical kit. Five hundred milligrams of epinephrine and five hundred of naloxone. At least we can start their treatments."

"Yes, ambassador, I believe this action was humanitarian," said Grachenko, motioning for the Glavkosmos Director to take a seat while he kept the telephone receiver to his ear. "But I need proof, do you have it? Yes, interesting. Interesting . . . I suggest, Mr. Lovell, that you have your space officials transmit those tapes to us. They would be quite compelling. Good day, and, please, time is important."

"Was that the American Ambassador?" asked Fedarenko, seated in front of Grachenko's desk. "What did he tell you?"

"Unless Mr. Lovell has changed nationalities, yes it was. He said NASA has visual evidence of the rescue. It would be useful, but how good is our evidence?"

"Anything NASA has will certainly be better than ours. I'm afraid Sakolov and Ryumin were a little too enthusiastic in their description of their 'evidence.' All I saw was a blur with arms, an instant before the tape ended. It wasn't convincing. Whatever the Americans have has to be better."

"I believe it is," Grachenko answered. "Their shuttle crew filmed the entire rescue. Ambassador Lovell will see about transmitting the tapes to us. I hope we can see them soon. Together with our influence, they could be what we need to stop this madness from going any further."

"My influence," said Fedarenko, his voice trailing off and his mood darkening further. "There's a saying in my agency: 'we have as much influence on events as the

212

moons of Jupiter have on our tides.' We used it with a touch of fatalism, but I never knew it would be this fatal. How can we stop the Hydras?"

"I'm not a weapons expert, but I do know of self-destruct systems. The Hydras are classified as a strategic weapon and all strategic weapons in our arsenal are equipped to self-destruct. However, only the premier, with the recommendation of the defence minister, can order a self-destruct. So beyond us, there's one man who needs to see the NASA footage when it arrives."

Grachenko picked up his desk phone and, instead of ordering his secretary to place his call, made it himself, tapping out a long series of numbers on the phone's keypad.

"Are you calling Gussarov?" Fedarenko asked. "I can tell you're dialing a private line."

"The premier will eventually see the tapes," said Grachenko, the telephone receiver back on his ear. "But it's Pietr Nagorny I'm calling first. Remember what I just told you, the defence minister must recommend the self-destruct to the premier. You, Pietr, and I must view the tapes first. Yes . . . Yes, this is Grachenko. Is Pietr Arkadivich in? Good, put me through at once. Your influence alone, Konstantin, may be no more than that of the moons of Jupiter. But with Pietr's and mine, it will bring an end to this crisis."

Minutes after shedding its second stage, the lead Northern Cosmodrome Hydra began firing its thruster quads. The selection and duration of the burns was controlled by the delivery bus computer. The Hydra was no longer under ground control, but had become completely autonomous. In moments the delivery bus had achieved its optimum rotation rate, increasing its stability and creating the right amount of centrifugal force.

A compressed gas charge fired in the vehicle's nose cap, splitting it open. The centrifugal force caused the sections to fly away, revealing a dense cluster of Hydra interceptors. There were six in all, half with blunt tips and half with sharper tips encircled by rings of tiny windows. The blunt-tipped warheads were the radar-guided Hydras, the others were infrared guided.

The delivery bus was now high over the North Pole. Its wing man still lagged far behind it but had completed its second stage burn. This was the last of the Hydras to achieve orbit. Now all four were heading for their release points.

To the south, the Volgograd Hydras crossed the Soviet Union's Pacific coast, and were approaching the Japanese island of Hokkaido. They were both down to their delivery buses, even their nose caps having been ejected. They were ready for deployment, though they wouldn't reach their release points until they were over the North Atlantic Ocean. Which meant if there was to be an early interception of the *Phoenix*, it would be done by one of the Northern Cosmodrome interceptors.

"All right, brace yourselves," Vachet warned, grabbing Siprinoff's right arm. "Here goes his second injection."

Pellerin and Ripley each placed a foot against the middle deck bunks and took hold of Siprinoff's left side. Like before, the hypodermic met some resistance as it punctured the skin. However, Vachet prevented its shaft from bending or bowing as he pushed it into the upper arm muscle. In seconds, five hundred milligrams of nalaxone were injected into Siprinoff. This would counteract the demerol he had taken, while the epinephrine would fight the tranquilizers.

"There, we're finished," said Vachet, withdrawing the needle and handing it to Simon. "Julie, how are the other two doing?"

"Kostilev's respiration and pulse rate have increased," she said. "But Grachenko's vital signs haven't yet improved."

"I know, intramuscular isn't as fast as intravenous would be. Jack, how much time to the de-transfer orbit maneuvers?"

"Four minutes, thirty-nine seconds," Ripley answered, after checking his wristwatch. "And we have two and a half minutes before Walt reorientates the orbiter."

"We better load our friends," said Pellerin. "Who goes first? I'd suggest this one, he's closest to the bunks."

"No, we'll load Kostilev," said Vachet. "He's stabilizing and his arm requires special handling. Jack, you help me."

Vachet squeezed around Harrison and took hold of Kostilev by his shoulders. With eight people, the middle deck was extremely cramped, yet Vachet was able to maneuver Kostilev over to the bunks on the starboard side with little difficulty.

Ripley prepared the uppermost bunk and helped slide the injured cosmonaut into it while Harrison and Pellerin held the other two. Kostilev entered his padded enclosure feet first, with Ripley guiding him and Vachet immobilizing his right arm.

The fit inside the bunk was tight. Though more than six feet long, it was barely thirty inches wide, which made it difficult to maneuver Kostilev whenever his feet snagged on the sleep restraint bag. Vachet and Ripley placed him on top of the bag instead of inside it. This made it faster and easier for them to strap him down.

"Commander to crew, we are T minus one minute and counting to attitude change," Cochran warned, his voice drowning out all conversations on the middle deck.

"We can get one more in if we hurry," said Vachet. "George, we'll go with your man. Turn him around, he goes in feet first. Jack, you help him. I'll prepare the second bunk."

"RCS thrusters to manual control," said Post, tapping out more instructions on his computer keyboard. "I'm bringing up the attitude change on CRT One and Two."

When Post was finished with his keyboard, an outline

of the shuttle appeared on the display screens in front of him and Cochran. The outline showed the *Phoenix* in its current attitude, graphs beside it indicating what its new position would be.

"I could start the change now, boss," Post continued. "You want me to? The computers don't care so long as we're in the proper attitude before the de-orbit burn."

"No, we can wait another forty-odd seconds," said Cochran, glancing over his left shoulder and down through the floor hatch in an effort to see any activity on the middle deck. "It sounds to me like they're still busy below us."

"How about calling Space Defence Command? I'd like to know what those ASATs are doing."

"Bernie said he'd warn us if they do anything. If we get lucky we'll be reentering just as they start deploying. Unlock your joystick, we're coming up on the half minute mark."

"Open the base panel and pull his feet down," Vachet ordered, after Siprinoff's feet had snagged yet again on the restraint bag. "Renée, are you finished with the medical kit?"

"Repacked and closed," said Simon, sliding the last package into the kit and zipping its lid shut. "Should I stow it?"

"For now leave it attached to the galley. Who knows if we may need something from it."

"Paul, he's in," said Ripley, clinging to the middle deck's front bulkhead like a fly. It was the only position that would allow him to reach inside the cramped end of the bunk.

"Strap him down," said Vachet, glancing at his watch. "We have ten seconds. Julie, Renée, stand on either side of Grachenko. George, how are you doing?"

"Finished," Pellerin answered, tightening the belt around Siprinoff's chest.

"Commander to crew, we're initiating attitude change."

216

With a brief rumbling from the nose module thrusters, the compartment tilted up and rotated to the left. The floor pushed gently against everyone's feet as the entire spaceplane rose a few inches. As it rotated, the compartment's wall swung into the astronauts, pinning Grachenko against Simon.

"Julie, pull him toward you," she said, as she pushed Grachenko away. "It's getting tight."

Fortunately, Simon's pressure suit kept her from being too seriously squeezed. Harrison pulled Grachenko until he was once again in the middle of the compartment. And suddenly, the attitude maneuver was over. The *Phoenix* was aligned for its new orbit and had only to wait for the upcoming transfer window.

"Commander to crew, we are T minus two minutes and counting to the de-transfer orbit burn," Cochran advised. "Let me know when you've finished stowing our guests. We'll be using the OMS engines to make the change."

"Two minutes. We'll have enough time to load him," said Vachet, pointing to Grachenko. "Julie, turn him around. Renée, stow the medical kit. George, stow those backpacks."

"Keep the RCS system on line," said Cochran, after he was finished with his announcement. "The OMS engines check out and they're ready for use."

"Good, I'll switch them and the thrusters to GPC control," Post replied, reaching for one of his overhead panels. "I'll have us ready in less than a minute."

"Just enough time to check everything before the maneuver starts. It looks like we're going to get lucky."

"General Rosen? Welcome to Combat Ops," said a startled general at the director's console. "This is surprising. I thought Space Defence was too busy for you to leave?"

Brigadier General Christopher Stewart rose from his

chair and moved to the back of the glass-enclosed room, where he greeted Rosen and Mary Widmark. The same grade as Rosen, Stewart wore the uniform of Canadian Armed Forces. As deputy commander of NORAD, he was in charge of air defences for the entire continent until the return of Eldridge.

"It's the calm before the storm," said Rosen, once the greetings were over. "The *Phoenix* will have to abandon its reentry. All Hydra delivery buses are in orbit and they'll be releasing their warheads soon. Mary, show Chris our projections for warhead deployment."

With Stewart's consent, Captain Widmark took over one of the room's computer terminals and began calling up information from Space Defence Command's Cray-9. In moments, the screen in front of her displayed half a dozen double track lines rising over the North Pole and descending across the hemisphere. Then she painted in the shuttle's orbital track.

"These trajectories are for the Hydras in polar orbit only," Mary advised. "They'd be the ones to deploy first."

"It looks like the *Phoenix* could be intercepted in two locations if it maintains this path," said Stewart, studying the screen. To escape, it will have to maintain its speed and altitude."

"Yes, and by the next orbit the remaining Hydras will have deployed," said Rosen. "Until we find a way to land it, we'll have to ride shotgun over the *Phoenix*. That means the Three-eighteenth and the Forty-eighth."

"I knew it would. As deputy commander I can turn those squadrons over to you. But wouldn't you rather wait for Eldridge to return? I know I would."

"It takes time to get the planes, pilots and ASATs ready. By the time Eldridge returns, it could be too late."

"All right, I've seen enough," Stewart concluded, returning to his operations chair and reaching for one of the telephones beside it. "I'll take the risk of getting my commander angry and turn the squadrons over to you.

Now your command will have some teeth."

"Thanks, Chris. I know the kind of trouble you can get in if Eldridge disagrees with your decision," said Rosen. "Look at it this way, if NASA does to me what it's threatened, then we can have our fat fried at the same barbecue."

All Hydra delivery buses were now at their optimum rotation rate, one revolution every five seconds, twelve every minute. The Northern Cosmodrome Hydras were coming down over Baffin Bay to the east, and the Beaufort Sea to the west. The delivery bus over the Beaufort Sea was the first the Northern Cosmodrome had launched, and it was the first to release its interceptors.

One of the blunt-tipped Hydras was ejected from the cramped bus by a shot of compressed gas. Its front end was shaped like a truncated cone, its back end like the base of an egg, and its center section was ringed with thruster quads. The aft nozzles on the quads fired moments after the interceptor's initial release, accelerating it away from the still rotating bus.

The release and ignition of the first Hydra did little to destablilize its launch platform. Even though it was bathed with exhaust flames from the thruster engines, the bus continued its rotation and, fifteen seconds later, ejected a second warhead.

This was one of the sharp-tipped, infrared-guided interceptors, similar in overall design to the radar-guided version except for its nose section. Immediately after its release, the second warhead started obeying its on-board programming. Its guidance sensors locked onto the nearest infrared source, the first warhead, and fired up its thruster quads to overtake it.

In moments the two interceptors were abreast of each other and had established a data transfer link between their computers. In unison they fired their thrusters again and veered out of the delivery bus's track. They set up a new orbit farther to the west, one that would bring them down over the Hawaiian Islands. Fifteen seconds later, another radar-guided Hydra was released, followed by a second infrared-guided interceptor.

They too linked up and moved into a different orbit, as did a third pair of Hydras. The pairs swung off to the east while the delivery bus continued along its original track down the west coast of Canada and the United States. Eventually, its retro-rockets would fire and it would burn up over the southern Indian Ocean.

It took just over a minute and a half for the first pairs of Hydras to be released. And the operation was still going on over the Beaufort Sea when the second delivery bus above Baffin Bay started firing its interceptors.

For the most part the operation was identical: the Hydra warheads were ejected separately, then paired and entered new orbits—except for the last pair. The radar-guided Hydra deployed normally and began moving east to assume an orbital track straight down the middle of the Atlantic. When its mate was ejected, however, the thruster quads fired for only a few moments before shorting out one by one.

The sequence in which the engines died caused the infrared interceptor to start yawing erratically. It slowed and lost altitude. In minutes it would be behind and below the delivery bus; in hours it would be reentering the atmosphere uncontrollably. For a second or two its radar-guided mate reduced power on the thruster jets it was firing, almost as if it were waiting for the other to catch up.

But when it failed to achieve a data link-up or receive any communications at all, the remaining Hydra accelerated to full power and moved off to its new orbit. The first half of the web had been set; the pursuit of the *Phoenix* was about to begin.

Chapter Fourteen

"Marshal, this is an honor," said the watch officer, snapping to full attention. "What do you wish from us?"

"For you and your staff to take a break," Suvorov responded, as he entered the headquarters' code room. "You deserve it, and don't return until we are finished in here."

The on-duty watch officer, together with the rest of his staff, saluted their commanding officers as they abandoned the code room. While Jurkov closed and locked the door, Suvorov walked to the back shelves filled with code books.

"Vitali Vassilivich, are you certain this is an activity we should be doing?" Jurkov asked, one of the few times he used something other than Suvorov's official rank.

"Yes, General. What we do here will ultimately be viewed as patriotic. We can't allow the appeasers to stop our justified response."

Suvorov removed one of the smaller loose-leaf note books from the shelves and brought it forward. Using one of the keys from his massive key ring, he opened it. It did not take him long to find what he wanted, though Suvorov did check the pages to make sure he had the correct ones.

"Jurkov, go to the files and select binder Samyii-Seven-Three-One-Seven," he ordered. "We will destroy both the originals and the duplicates."

While his deputy followed his instructions, Suvorov removed the pages he had checked, smiling slightly as he fanned through them. Jurkov came to him with a note book of similar size and opened it with his own set of keys.

"Are these the codes you want?" he asked, holding up some sheets he had removed from the book.

"Yes, the Hydra self-destruct codes," said Suvorov. "Also the codes that order them to abort their orbits.

With the elimination of these, the Hydras will be locked on their autonomous search and destroy programming."

Jurkov pulled a few more pages from his binder before handing them all to Suvorov. In turn, he took them all to the room's document shredder. The quietly humming machine buzzed loudly as one page after another was fed into it. Confetti-like bits of paper, virtually impossible to reconstruct into a document, showered out of its disposal chute. When he was finished, Suvorov and Jurkov locked their respective notebooks.

"There, it's done," he said, taking the notebooks back to the shelves. "We may be arrested, Alexei, but in the end we'll be looked upon as patriots. Are you prepared for that?"

"I'm the general of the Soviet Air Defence Force, and you are my commander. Yours are the orders I will obey." Jurkov's response was automatic, almost as if he were reading it from a book. In his eyes, however, there was a faint glimmer of fear.

"Excellent, General, excellent." Survorov displayed a confident smile, ignoring the glimmer. "We must be prepared to be heroes. Unlock the door and let the captain back in."

"We're through the window," Cochran announced, hitting the public address button on his communications panel. "Commander to crew, begin preparations for reentry. De-orbit OMS burn will commence in two minutes, thirty-nine seconds. Stand by for radical attitude change."

"RCS system to manual control," said Post. "I'll begin the change as soon as I get the DAP readout."

Post waited for the digital autopilot to present the latest flight information before working his joystick. The pulses of fire from the RCS engines rotated the *Phoenix* to the left, swinging it one hundred and eighty degrees. A further series of thruster burns slowed the rotation until the spaceplane was flying backwards.

On the middle deck the reorientation was the most extreme the crew had experienced, and yet, one of the easiest for them to tolerate. With the cosmonauts stowed in their bunks, and all other floating materials packed away, the astronauts only had to stay in the center of the cabin and watch it swing around them.

"God, this is making me dizzy," said Simon, when the engines had stopped rumbling and the room finally ceased moving.

"You'll experience worse during reentry and landing," Ripley promised. "Here, we'd better get you out of your suit."

Ripley took hold of Simon's backpack, unlocked its catches, and pushed it up, while she grabbed the bunks' support frame and held herself down. As the life-support pack slid off her space suit, Harrison helped Simon unlock her suit's waist ring. What would normally have taken an individual nearly ten minutes to accomplish would be done in a little over two.

"Returning RCS system to GPC control," said Post, before he started to grimace. "There's that smell again. What gives? Haven't they cleaned up the middle deck yet?"

"Cabin air will only mix completely during an attitude or orbit change," said Cochran. "Cathy in Life Sciences told me that. At least it'll help the life support system clean out the smell. We're T minus one minute, five seconds to OMS burn."

"Flight Program Three-Zero-Two loaded into GPC and BFS. Auxiliary power unit fuel tank valves closed." Post ran his hands over his side panels and the cockpit's center pedestal, reactivating systems which hadn't been used since the *Phoenix* had achieved orbit. If it were to land safely, everything had to be on line and operating. "There. All APU systems in pre-start conditions."

"Good, let's see what Mission Control has to say. Houston, this is *Phoenix*. We're ready for your Go/No

Go decision."

"Just a minute, *Phoenix*. Things are still a little crazy around here," answered the CAP COM.

"We don't have a minute," said Cochran. "We got thirty-five seconds to OMS burn. Is White Sands ready to receive us and do your computers confirm the validity of our re-entry program?"

"White Sands has advised they'll be ready for you. Preliminary computer check confirms your reentry profile."

"We'll take that as a 'Go.' Safety the OMS inhibitors, Walt. T minus twelve seconds and counting . . ."

In the remaining time Cochran warned his crew to brace themselves for the de-orbit burn. They were still lining up against the front bulkhead on the middle deck when the OMS engines fired, shaking the entire spacecraft.

The immediate and most powerful effect was the deceleration from escape velocity, which pinned everyone on the middle deck to the bulkhead and pulled Post and Cochran out of their seats. Their restraint belts digging into them, they grabbed their locked joysticks to push themselves back.

This would continue until the end of the firing as both ship and crew decelerated at the same rate. Normally, the firing would last for two or three minutes. But only a minute into the operation, Cochran put his hand to his ear so he could listen to Mission Control better.

"Ed, what's going on?" Post asked.

"Jesus Christ, kill the burn!" Cochran shouted.

"Since when is he flying this vehicle?"

"Don't be funny, damn it. Houston just got word from Bernie that if we continue de-orbit maneuvers we'll be intercepted. Kill the burn and turn us around!"

Working in concert, commander and pilot moved swiftly to stop the reentry operation. The orbital maneuvering engines were inhibited and their fuel flow cut. The general purpose computer ceased its program

224

run and had its newly loaded plan dumped from its memory.

"I'm ending the APU start," said Post, one hand flying over the side panels while the other reached for the overhead controls. "RCS system to manual control. Cross feed lines open. What flight program do you want me to load?"

"I don't know, let me check," Cochran replied, reaching into the flight data file for the program codes.

"Ed, why did you stop the OMS engines?" asked Vachet, popping through the floor hatch. With the burn ended, the deceleration had ceased and the crew found they were free to move around.

"We've got trouble, Saint Ex. We'll be intercepted by ASATs over Hawaii if we reenter at this time. We're going to get trapped in orbit, and we need a program to stay up here. Two-Zero-One, that's it. I'll do the GPC load. Walt, you swing us around. Saint Ex, tell everyone on the middle deck we're returning to orbit."

"We've lost a thousand miles an hour," said Post. "We'll get it back if we do everything right away."

Vachet could see Post unlocking his joystick and Cochran working his GPC keyboard. The Frenchman pushed himself back through the floor hatch to warn the rest of the crew that while the reentry was over, the crisis was not.

Cochran entered Two-Zero-One and commands for the computer to pull the identified program from its memory. The GPC finished within seconds, and Cochran pressed the "mode five" button, transferring the software to the backup flight system.

"GPC and BFS reprogramming completed," said Cochran. "OPS Two-Zero-One has been loaded. Are you ready?"

"As soon as I get the new flight attitude from the digital autopilot," said Post, reaching for the center pedestal. "Better tell everyone I'm going to bring her around."

Cochran was still warning the crew when the information Post needed appeared on the CRT screens. He carefully squeezed the joystick grip, causing the preselected RCS thrusters to fire and initiate the maneuver.

On the middle deck, the rest of the astronauts again gathered in the center. The cabin rotated around them, a little faster than before, as the *Phoenix* returned to its original heading. Barely perceptible to them was the slight nose-up pitch Post gave the shuttle after he finished swinging it back.

"Grab something on the airlock or the commode stall," said Vachet. "They'll fire the OMS engines to keep us in orbit."

"Grab something, hell. The space potty's mine," Ripley warned, opening the stall door and climbing on top of the closed toilet. "Would either of you ladies care to join me?"

"We're at the same point in our orbit as our OMS-Two burn," said Post. "We can return if the engines are ready."

"They're armed and on line," Cochran answered. "Just enter a manual ignition command."

Unlike the RCS thrusters or even the main engines, the OMS engines could not be started or throttled by manual controls, but could only be armed or stopped; the rest was done by computer. Post quickly entered a command on his GPC keyboard and, as he hit the "execute" key, the OMS engines fired up.

The acceleration effect gently pushed Cochran and Post into their seats. It wasn't as sharp as the deceleration experienced in the de-orbit burn and even the crew on the middle deck rode comfortably through it. The radar altimeter began recording a slow increase in altitude and the accelerometer showed a gain. The *Phoenix* was returning to orbit, though how long it would have to remain was a question no one could answer.

* * *

"Colonel, they're all in the briefing room," said a master sergeant as he entered the squadron operations center.

"Good. Lieutenant, is there anything new from Mount Cheyenne?" Colonel Frank DeCarlo inquired, gathering the telex sheets he'd been reading.

"No, sir. Nothing new has come in on the machines."

"Then I'll go with what I have. Major, if there are any new reports from the flight line, I want to hear about them. Let's go, Henry."

Accompanied by the master sergeant, DeCarlo left his squadron's operations center and walked down the corridor to the briefing room. The moment they entered, the assembled personnel jumped to attention. Most were officers; the few enlisted men were, like the sergeant, part of security, and they sealed the room while DeCarlo took the center podium.

"As of this moment, we're on full alert," he announced, looking directly at his pilots. Then he glanced down at his telex file and selected the ones he would read. "About twenty minutes ago, we and the Forty-eighth were transferred from NORAD to Space Defence Command. We're about to become part of the catastrophe in orbit we've been watching."

"What are we going to do, Frank? Shoot those poor bastards down?" asked one of the pilots, half seriously, half jokingly.

"No. Just over an hour ago, the crew of the space shuttle *Phoenix* rescued the cosmonauts trapped in the *Soyuz* module."

Applause and a ragged cheer swept through the pilots, staff officers, and security men. Though DeCarlo had expected it, the response still surprised him, and he had to use a little more effort than usual to quiet them down.

"All right already, that was the good news. The bad news is that, in response to our guys pulling their guys out of the fire, Soviet Air Defence has launched four

Hydra ASATs. Two have just deployed their interceptors; the other two will do so shortly. You'd better look forward to some high-altitude flying, because it'll be up to us on the West Coast, and the Forty-eighth on the East, to protect the shuttle until it can land.

"All our aircraft, and every available Vought ASAT at this base, is being readied for flight. However, we have only four ASATs and eight pressure suits. We can only prepare a limited number of aircraft for high-altitude flight. I informed Space Defence of this, and they've decided to send most of you south to Edwards Air Force Base and China Lake Naval Weapons Center. Between the navy, and the air force, and NASA, there'll be enough equipment to outfit and arm you."

"Have you picked who's going to stay, Colonel?" asked another pilot. "And who has to go?"

"Yes. Riddick, Kilmer, Tyrell, and myself will stay," said DeCarlo. "The moment this briefing ends, the four of us will head for the high-altitude preparation room. The rest of you will find your flight plans in the ops center. Yes?"

"Colonel, what about the four birds we got in the alert hangers?" asked a third pilot.

"They're being disarmed. The Voughts will be the only weapons we'll carry. All Eagles will also be equipped with FAST packs before they depart. After you've been armed, you'll be dispersed to bases up and down the West Coast, from Twenty-nine Palms to Comox. Since the Hydras are in pairs, we'll deploy in pairs. If there are no more questions, then the heavens really do await us. I want all of you to fly like you really deserve the thirty-million-dollar planes you've been given. Good luck."

DeCarlo stayed in the briefing room long enough to collect the pilots he had named. He led them out a separate door from the rest of the men. While most of the squadron would dress in regulation flying suits, DeCarlo and his team entered what was virtually a laboratory to begin a more involved suiting up.

They commenced breathing pure oxygen, to wash the nitrogen from their bloodstreams, and were given medical exams before dressing for high-altitude flight. The suits they wore were of essentially the same make as those the *Phoenix* crew had worn during their EVA operations. The pilots would be flying to the frontier of space, and they needed the same protection as the astronauts they would defend.

On the flight line a similar activity was growing. In front of the base's main hangars were two rows of ten F-15s. The huge, angular fighters were being prepared for flight. They would depart from McChord Air Base and head south to Edwards and China Lake in California. Apart from having fuel and sensor tactical (FAST) packs attached to their sides, they would be given no other equipment, including weapons. The rest they would receive in California.

At a smaller set of hangars closer to McChord's runways, a more involved operation was underway. The four F-15s in them were already flyable and combat ready. But their quartets of AIM-7 Sparrow and AIM-9 Sidewinder missiles were being removed. Even their Sidewinder launching rails and centerline fuel tanks would be carted off. In their place went the FAST packs, and the Vought anit-satellite weapons.

Roughly the same size and shape as a cruise missile, the Voughts didn't have wings folded against their sides or prominent air intakes. Their only control surfaces were cruciform tail fins, and their center sections, which separated their first and second stages, were pinched. Only when the Voughts were mated to the fighters and the pilots had finished suiting up would Space Defence Command have its satellite interceptor forces.

"Well, they've managed to trap themselves in orbit," Reiss commented, watching the velocity and altitude numbers for the *Phoenix* climb back to their original levels. "I'd like to hear Vachet talk about the future of man in space now."

"Reiss, why don't you shove it?" said Reynolds, back in his old position on the launch center's observation deck.

The center's staff and visitors froze into silence when Reynolds made his remark. Reiss whirled around and glared at him.

"Still playing at being cocky, aren't you mister? Keep it up and you'll find yourself in detention again so fast they'll put your ass in another cell."

"Hold it, you guys. Hold it," said Harrison, stepping in front of Reiss. "We're better at fighting amongst ourselves than with the Russians. Let's solve our problems, instead of arguing over how they originated. And we've got one hell of a problem."

Brad Harrison pointed at the center's main screen, forcing Reiss to turn back and watch the *Phoenix* regain its orbit. Also painted on the screen were partial tracks of the deployed Hydra warheads. Canaveral had no direct data link with Space Defence Command but had to rely on what Mission Control in Houston would send it, which was a good deal less than instantaneous.

"Houston says the other Hydras will deploy soon," said the deputy launch officer. "Right now they're approaching the West Coast. We'll put them up when we get the track data."

"When they do we'll have anti-satellite weapons in intersecting polar and equatorial orbits," Harrison predicted. "Their tracks will take them over every known landing site whenever the *Phoenix* approaches one. Houston will have to move her into an orbit where she won't be threatened."

"Yes, that's our first order of business," said Reiss. "Bill Corrigan is already working on it. Second order is to get a billion-dollar vehicle and seven people down safely."

"Correction. A *three*-billion-dollar spaceship and *ten*

230

people. There must be a hole in this web the Russians are spinning. If we find it, we could bring the *Phoenix* in, but where do we land her? There's the real problem.''

"What about the footage Cochran sent to us?'' Reynolds asked, leaning over the guard rail on the observation deck. "What's being done with it? Why don't we send it to the Russians?''

"It is going to Russia,'' said Reiss, trying to cut off what he considered useless questioning.

"George, he doesn't know,'' said Harrison. "You only freed him a half hour ago. The Soviet foreign minister, defence minister, and your buddy, Fedarenko, will view the tapes, Clay. Let's hope he's as intelligent as you think he is.''

"And in the meantime what should we be doing?'' asked another astronaut.

"What Harrison just said,'' Reiss advised. "Let the computers find the holes in this web. You find the fields where the shuttle can land. You people know what to look for. I'll tell Houston to get the astronauts there on the same project. I want you to come up with every landing field the shuttle can use.''

"We better get the portable microwave landing systems ready for transport,'' said Harrison. "And there's something else we should consider. With ten people instead of seven, life support on the *Phoenix* will become critical. Especially oxygen, which they'll use forty percent faster than before. We'd better find out how long they can stay in orbit.''

"*Phoenix*, this is Houston. You are back in flight conditions prior to de-orbit burn,'' said the latest CAP COM. "Has orbiter control been returned to the GPC?''

"Roger, the lady's now under GPC command,'' Cochran answered, before a puzzled look crossed his face. "Susan? Did we change CAP COMs? Did things really get that hot up here?''

231

"I was brought in while you and Post were doing the manual OMS burn. Corrigan said you did it as well as the GPC."

"Well, that's one of the nice things about the human mind—it has a great on-demand programming feature."

"Yes, it's called 'panic,'" Post injected.

"Shut up, Walt, you're too close to the truth," said Cochran. "What's Bill doing there, Sue? He's not supposed to be on duty for a couple of hours yet."

"He came in when he heard you were rescuing the Soviets," said Susan. "He's working on a new flight program to keep you out of danger until we decide how and where to land you."

"Heard? Did he hear about us through the grapevine?"

"Of course. We've got a complete press blackout on your activities and they're going crazy. Since you're stuck in orbit, we're going to have to release something. Maybe it'll help ease this standoff with the Russians."

"It's going to take a lot to convince them we only did a rescue mission," Cochran replied. "Tell us if anything new comes up, Houston. *Phoenix*, out. Yes, Paul, what do you need?"

"It's our guests," said Vachet, hovering above the floor hatch he just rose through. "If we can't reenter for some time, we should resume treating them up here."

"You're right. Break them out, put them on the ECG equipment if you can, and continue with the epinephrine and naloxone."

"Roger, we'll bring them around. Who knows, maybe they can end up helping us."

To steady himself, Vachet had wrapped his fingers around one of the handholds in the cabin roof. All he had to do was push away from it and he was sailing back to the middle deck.

"Paul, we think we can hear one of them moaning," said Simon, as Vachet arrived. "What do we do?"

"Get them out and resume treatment. If we need to, we'll put them on the electrocardiograph. Which one

232

is moaning?"

"We think it's Siprinoff. We'll find out soon."

As Vachet recited the orders, the rest of the crew went to work. Pellerin removed the medical kit from its locker while Ripley and Harrison opened the bunk side panels. When they slid back the panel on the middle bunk, Siprinoff groaned and turned his head to avoid the harsh light.

"He's semi-conscious," said Harrison, reaching inside the bunk to unlock the straps. "Those drugs we gave him are working."

"Good. Renée, prepare more doses of epinephrine and naloxone," Vachet ordered. "Jack, how's Grachenko?"

"He's not responding," said Ripley, switching on the lower bunk's reading light. "Maybe we should give him the shots?"

"No, we'll give them to the man who can come out of it faster. Let's hope he speaks English. Bring him out, Julie."

On Earth, Harrison would have weighed 105 pounds and Siprinoff, 195. She would barely have had the strength to drag him. But in orbit, she easily pulled him out of the bunk with one hand while using the other to grab the bunks' support frame and steady herself.

Harrison handed Siprinoff over to Vachet, who ordered a stethoscope, a blood pressure cuff, and a pencil flashlight. Pellerin removed each from the tightly packed medical kit and threw them as if they were darts. They glided or tumbled slowly to Vachet, who picked them out of the air and either stuffed them in his flightsuit pockets, or used them on Siprinoff.

Vachet checked the cosmonaut's heartbeat, then strapped the blood pressure cuff to his arm. Harrison helped him get the systolic and diastolic readings from Siprinoff by repeatedly inflating the pressure cuff. Finally, Vachet tested Siprinoff's eyes with the flashlight. His pupils dilated when exposed to the strong beam.

"How's he doing?" Ripley asked, joining Vachet

and Harrison.

"He's got low blood pressure and he feels cold to the touch," said Vachet. "But he's coming around. Another set of injections should do it. Jack, you and Julie will have to help me. Renée, when you're finished with the injections, activate the galley. Brew the strongest coffee you can. This man and the others will need it when they awaken."

Ripley and Harrison aligned themselves on Siprinoff's right side and took hold of him. Simon gave the first hypodermic to Vachet, and handed the second to Pellerin before turning to the galley. She opened the food pantry and took out several packets of freeze-dried coffee. In the lower compartment Simon found the water heater and zero-G cups. It would take her five minutes to brew the coffee, and hopefully by then Siprinoff would be conscious enough to drink it.

"*Phoenix*, this is Houston. We've just had an urgent request from Space Defence Command," warned the CAP COM. "They want us to turn you over to them. Can you do it?"

"Susan, we've done it so often we can do it in our sleep," said Cochran. "Why does Bernie want to talk to us?"

"They say they've spotted something serious and that time can't be wasted passing it through us. Are you ready?"

"We're all set, just give us the word. *Phoenix*, out."

At Houston's command, Post started flipping toggles on the overhead and side panels. Cochran repeated the sequence on his own panel and, in moments, the spaceplane had switched from NASA command channels to the secure military channels of SDC.

"Mount Cheyenne, this is *Phoenix*," said Cochran. "What's the trouble, Bernie?"

"It's big," Rosen answered immediately, as if he'd been waiting for the question. "We should've spotted this earlier but we fucked up. You're going to be

234

intercepted by a Hydra."

"What? I thought we avoided that when we aborted the reentry. What the hell's happening?"

"Our earlier projections were based on comparing the Hydra trajectories with your reentry track. We never compared them to your orbital track, until now. Our computers show you'll be intercepted over the North Atlantic Ocean. We've got the information ready for transmission. You can display it on your CRTs."

"Enable the data uplinks," Cochran told Post while reaching for the display controls. "I'll put the info on CRT Three."

The third CRT screen was set in the middle of the front instrument panel, the pilot's and commander's CRTs flanking it. While their screens showed flight and shuttle operations data, the middle one displayed general information. It also showed ground transmissions and, with the uplink activated, a map of North America and the North Atlantic Ocean soon appeared.

Across the map snaked the west-to-east path of the *Phoenix* and the polar tracks of the newly deployed ASATs. Because of the shuttle's speed, it outran most of them, except for one descending over the Atlantic.

"This doesn't look good," said Post. "What the hell can we do? General, will your F-15s be able to intercept them?"

"The East Coast F-15s won't be operational in time," said Rosen. "However, my staff has another way to stop the Hydras."

"What's that? Write our wills and throw 'em at those things?" Cochran asked cynically.

"Almost. How many satellites do you still have?"

Cochran didn't need to answer the question, or hear the rest of Rosen's idea to understand it. His fear abated and a mischievous smile broke over his face.

"You want us to lay decoys," he responded. "How many satellites do you want us to use?"

"Just one. There's only one Hydra in the track which

235

intercepts you," said Rosen. "Its mate failed to deploy after release. We think it's the radar-guided ASAT, and if we can give it a big enough target, we'll fool it into exploding."

"Yes, it could work," said Post, after thinking over the idea. "But we'll need all the help we can get from you."

"That's the reason I asked Houston to turn you over to us. You've got twenty minutes to prepare, and the clock's running."

"Roger, Mount Cheyenne. I'll put someone on it right away. Walt, find out what Bernie wants done," Cochran ordered, before he changed his communications panel to the public address system. "Harrison, Simon, report to the flight deck immediately."

Cochran loosened his restraint belts so he could turn in his seat to look over his headrest. Moments later, Harrison and Simon came sailing up from the middle deck and gathered behind his seat.

"As Walt would say, what's up, boss?" Harrison queried, hovering a few inches away from Cochran.

"We've got big trouble waiting for us on the horizon," he said. "Space Defence Command has just identified an ASAT that's going to intercept us. Unless we do something to stop it, we'll make the *Mir's* explosion look like second-rate fireworks."

"What can we do? Throw stones at it?" asked Simon. "What about your fighters and their anti-satellite missiles?"

"They're not ready yet. We've got to handle this ASAT right here and now. We can't throw rocks, but we can toss a decoy in its path. How long do you need to activate a Fleet Com?"

"I need more than an hour to make it fully operational. Though if you only want it powered up, I can do it in ten minutes."

"Then get your butt over there." Cochran nodded at the starboard side of the flight deck. "Julie, open the cargo bay and activate the remote arm. We got a

236

deployment to do."

Simon and Harrison turned and made their way around the seats still anchored in the middle of the deck. Simon went to the payload control panels, while Harrison moved to the aft crew station. She placed her feet in the zero-gravity shoe attachments at the station before reaching for the cargo bay controls.

Inactive since being prepared for reentry, the bay, its contents, and controls, had to be turned on if there was to be any deployment. Harrison ran her fingers down the rows of latch switches, their status lights changing from green to red. With the cargo bay doors unsealed, she hit the buttons for their drive motors. In just over a minute they would be open.

The moment the doors separated a dazzling light flooded the bay. It illuminated the two remaining Fleet Com satellites, the OMS fuel tank, and the Orbital Pharmaceutical Factory with a harsh glare. The light poured through the bulkhead observation windows, causing Harrison to avert her gaze.

"Cargo bay doors opening," she said, blinking until her eyes could take the light. "Which satellite are you using?"

"Fleet Com Three," Simon answered. "Main and auxiliary power, on line. Activation sequencer to manual control. I'll have it ready for you in a few minutes."

"Good. Aft station to cockpit. You guys have any specific instructions for me?"

"We'll be getting some on the teleprinter soon," said Post. "Activate the remote arm and deploy the satellite."

"Roger. Punching in the RMS."

Julie shifted her attention to the remote manipulator system and switched its control panels on. She activated the rotation and translation hand grips, the arm's shoulder, elbow and wrist joints, then unlocked the latches holding the arm to the cargo bay's port side. Lastly, she put the software programs on line instead of changing the arm to manual operations.

"Selecting program number three," said Julie, tapping one of the auto load buttons. "Stand by for computer operation."

She hit the auto sequence proceed toggle when the ready light above it started to flash. The remote arm rose smoothly from its stowed position, its wrist and elbow joints pivoting as it rose. The elbow swung the upper part of the arm over the open cargo bay and the wrist pointed the end effector down. Under computer command it could be programmed to move in all three axes at once.

"What the hell's going on here?" Ripley asked, appearing on the flight deck. "Has Houston gone crazy?"

"Houston isn't controlling us," said Cochran. "Mount Cheyenne is. They report that one of the Hydras will intercept us, so one of the Fleet Coms is about to become the most expensive decoy in history. Jack, could you get that?"

A soft clacking had started up during Cochran's answer; the teleprinter was processing instructions from Space Defence Command. Ripley turned to the flight deck's port side and grabbed the scroll of paper floating out of the printer. It had scarcely stopped when Ripley tore off its roller bar.

"Here. They need me on the middle deck," he said, handing the paper to Cochran. "It looks like Siprinoff is coming around."

Ripley glanced through the aft crew station windows as he returned to his companions. He briefly caught sight of the remote arm's end effector, dropping swiftly and precisely toward the pallet containing the third Fleet Communications satellite.

"Julie, you had better halt the RMS," Simon advised. "I don't have the Fleet Com ready yet."

"Roger, halting RMS," said Harrison, tapping the software stop button on the remote arm panel. An instant later its end effector froze just above the satellite's grapple pin. The arm was still under computer control, though until it received another command it would

238

remain suspended over the cargo bay.

"Renée, what's wrong? We don't have a lot of time left," said Cochran, glancing up from the instructions.

"I'm going to auxiliary power for the attitude system," said Renée, pressing her controls so hard that she was moving away from her station. "Just give me a minute to test it."

"Julie, grab her or she'll be bouncing around the cabin."

With her operation on hold, Harrison had little to do and was within easy reach of the satellite control panels. She turned in time to catch Simon by the shoulder and push her back down. All the while, Renée Simon kept working on her procedures.

"Attitude system on line," she finally said. "I'll have flight command. Unlocking pallet latches. Ejection system safetied. You can proceed with the extraction."

All Harrison had to do was tap the striped button on the RMS panel and the arm instantly resumed its programmed operation. The end effector dropped over the grapple pin, its wires quickly snaring it. Once the arm had its own confirmation of the capture, it smoothly lifted the multi-ton satellite out of its pallet. The computer-guided operation came to an end with the Fleet Com hovering some fifty feet above the cargo bay.

"Program run has ended," said Harrison, her hands gliding over the RMS panels. "Switching remote arm to manual control."

"These are for you," Cochran answered, tossing over the instruction scroll, which he had flattened out and folded into a rectangle of paper. Each fold contained a separate set of orders. "I tried to divide them between you and Renée."

Julie Harrison caught the spinning rectangle and immediately unfolded it. She found each grouping of instructions separated from the other by a heavy crease,

239

as Cochran had arranged. She placed the sheet in the clipboard normally used by the aft station pilot, where both she and Simon could readily view it.

"These look complicated," said Simon. "Can we study them?"

"No, just do them," Harrison said sharply. "Activating rotational and translation hand controllers."

She unlocked the safeties to the remote arm grips and selected the operating mode for the wrist joint. Glancing through the skylight window, Harrison raised the satellite until it resembled a cap sitting atop a slender, fifty-foot pole.

"Changing RMS modes to shoulder yaw," Harrison advised. "Ed, you'll be able to see the Fleet Com when I'm finished."

The fifty-foot pole tilted to the left, as if its base had given way. It fell at a steady rate until it was almost level with the shuttle's port wing. Harrison slowed the arm's descent, and after a few moments it came to a halt with hardly a quiver, in spite of the multi-ton payload sitting at its end.

"I got it, Julie," said Cochran, craning his neck over his left shoulder. "Just a couple of degrees above the horizontal."

"Good, changing RMS modes to elbow control," she said. "You'll have to warn me when it gets close to the nose."

With the middle joint activated, the arm bent until it was almost V-shaped, moving the Fleet Com toward the shuttle's nose. With the arm out of Harrison's view, she had to rely on her instruments to tell her its velocity and on Cochran to tell her how close it was approaching.

"Slow it down," he warned. "It's ten feet from my window."

"All right, but I have to move the arm into the angle given by the instructions," said Harrison.

The satellite stopped when its rim was barely six feet from Cochran's side window. Harrison's last task in the decoy launch was to reactivate the wrist and swing the satellite ninety degrees until it was pointing away from the shuttle.

"Fleet Com in launch position and attitude," she announced. "Renée, have you been following your instructions?"

"To the letter. Commander, how much time do I have left?"

"You have forty-five seconds," said Cochran, glancing at the cockpit's event timer. "Would you like a countdown?"

"Yes, start it at T minus fifteen," said Simon. "That should give me enough time for the last checks."

She took the instruction sheet from the clipboard for the aft station pilot and transferred it to her own. With the exception of the payload release, all of the remaining orders were hers. Simon checked her list one more time. Near the end, she could hear Cochran begin the countdown.

"Twelve. Eleven. Ten . . ." he recited, as the final seconds flashed on the timer.

"Julie, get ready on the end effector," said Simon, reaching for a set of diminutive joysticks on one of her panels. "Manual flight controls, on. Activation sequence, completed."

"Two. One . . . Release!"

Harrison hit both the derigid and open buttons on her RMS panel. The capture wires moved the grapple pin to the effector's front end and sprang back to their stowed positions. The tiny kick the satellite received started it on its trajectory toward the unseen Hydra. A moment later it got a more substantial increase in velocity when Simon fired the attitude control thrusters.

"God, that smarts," said Cochran, turning away from the burst of light flooding through his side window.

"You're lucky we're not using the main engine," said Simon. "I think it would melt the orbiter. Ask your Space Command if they're tracking the Fleet Com."

241

"Mount Cheyenne says they have both us and the satellite," Post reported, the only one on the flight deck still wearing his headset. "They say its trajectory is good enough to intercept the Hydra. Proceed with the rest of the operation."

"Roger. Initiating rotation," said Simon.

Normally, the Fleet Com satellites were spun to their launch rotation speed by the electric motors in their cargo pallets. In an emergency, when they were launched by the remote arm, the rotation speed would be achieved after launch by using the attitude thrusters. It was a tricky manual operation, but Simon had been practicing it for months.

She delicately worked the attitude control joysticks, causing the lateral thrusters to fire. At the distance the satellite had already travelled from the *Phoenix*, its exhaust flames could be seen as bright points of light. Moments after they were first ignited, the thrusters were seen rotating at a visibly increasing rate. By the time the Fleet Com was at normal launch speed, the thruster jets appeared as a ring of light.

"Spin up, completed. Rotation rate is nominal," said Simon. "What does Space Command advise?"

"Another burn on the aft thrusters to increase velocity," said Post. "They'll let us know when it's at the right speed. They say to stand by on the solar wing release."

"Roger, going for second velocity burn. Harrison, what are you doing?"

"Stowing the remote arm," Harrison answered, working the rotational hand grip. "I might as well do something. All we can do is hope the Air Force got their plan right."

What had only minutes before been painful and blinding to watch was now merely a set of glowing jewels on the back of a silver and gold disc. Simon kept the satellite's translation joystick pulled back until Post

242

relayed the message that optimum velocity had been achieved.

The Fleet Com moved rapidly toward the northern horizon. Cochran kept an eye on its flight, until farther in the distance a faint pulse of light caught his attention. It appeared to the right of the Fleet Com, and as he focused his attention on it, he could just make out a nucleus of darkness above Iceland.

"Boys and girls, I think I just spotted our ASAT," Cochran announced, in a hushed voice. "This had better work."

"It will," said Post. "Renée, hit the release."

The last command to the Fleet Com was for it to deploy its solar cell arrays. The frail, iridescent wings unfolded from the satellite's main body, greatly increasing its radar image. Almost at once there was another pulse of light from the Hydra as it fired its thruster quads. The sudden appearance of a large target in its vicinity set off its radar tracking system. The Hydra veered sharply from its intercept path, ignoring the distant shuttle, and closed on the first target to enter its search cone.

"Walt, you're right," said Cochran. "It's going to work."

Seconds later the Hydra was within proximity fuse range of the Fleet Com. It evaporated in a dazzling flash, both its explosives and remaining fuel detonating at once. The fireball and the expanding cloud of debris and shrapnel overtook the Fleet Com. Its solar wings and stowed communications antennas were torn off, followed by panels from the satellite's main body. Shrapnel punctured its fuel cells, creating a fireball just as the initial flash was dying out.

On the *Phoenix* they never heard the explosions or felt their shockwaves. The only effect they were subjected to was a sudden increase in brightness, which even those on the middle deck noticed. The shuttle easily outran the cloud of debris. For the moment it had escaped, but it was far from safe. It would have to climb to a high altitude to avoid the debris on later orbits, and there were still more than twenty deployed ASATs hunting it. The *Phoenix* would not be out of danger until it had landed, and everyone aboard her who was conscious knew it.

Chapter Fifteen

The light was powerful and painful to look at even through closed eyelids. It was the first sensation Grachenko felt and his initial thought was to turn it off. But no matter how he tried, he couldn't make his arms move, or pronounce hs orders clearly enough to be understood.

Then the harsh light vanished, replaced with a softer glow which didn't hurt his eyes. The snug, confined, feeling he had also become aware of disappeared as well. He was floating free and there were people around him. There was pain, a brief, sharp pain in one arm and a dull one in the other. A painfully bright light was also flashed repeatedly in his eyes. Somewhere around the eighth or tenth time Grachenko raised his hand to block the light, which brought a noisy response from the people nearby.

They may have been near, even standing beside him, but to Grachenko they were a thousand miles away, or at least far enough for him to be confused by what they were saying. Until he gradually became aware that most of them were speaking English, not Russian.

The only voice he could identify among them was that of Siprinoff, who spoke both English and Russian. When he could finally open and focus his eyes, the first thing Grachenko saw was a petite, blonde-haired woman wearing a bright blue flightsuit.

"A *devushka?*" he mumbled, though he realized he

should've called her angel, instead of just a girl. In any event, the response to what he uttered was still more cheering.

One of the people in blue flightsuits pushed a container in his mouth and told him in Russian to drink. It was coffee, strong and hot, and he accepted it a little at a time, its warmth slowly flowing through him.

The people around him became less distant. He could understand what they were saying and grew aware of the small room they were in. Grachenko was helped upright to face one of the men who had been working on him. Though conscious, he was still weak and when his feet touched the floor, his legs gave way. He would have collapsed, had he not been in zero gravity.

"Commander Grachenko, I am Paul Vachet," said the man he was facing. "Senior French astronaut on the American space shuttle *Phoenix*. We've also rescued Mr. Siprinoff and Mr. Kostilev."

Vachet motioned to the bunks on the middle deck's starboard side. Siprinoff and Pellerin were examining Kostilev. Siprinoff turned and gave Grachenko a brief smile and a salute, then went back to working on their crew mate.

"Welcome to United States territory," Vachet continued. "We're still in orbit, but we're hoping to land soon. It's fortunate Mr. Siprinoff is a medical research specialist. Mr. Kostilev appears to be heavily sedated."

"Yes, he was taking pain killers since he had broken his arm," said Grachenko. "The last dose probably put him deeply under. We and our flight operations staff wondered if you would rescue us. For all of them, I thank you."

"You're most welcome. We did it for ourselves as well as for you and your dreams for Future Man."

"How did you know that? Did I say it earlier?"

"I shall explain later. Jack, tell Walt and Ed that another of our guests is awake."

Ripley acknowledged his order and jumped off the

middle deck floor. As he emerged from the hatch on the flight deck, he found Harrison stowing the last mission specialist seat while Cochran and Post were talking, in a somber way, to Space Defence Command.

"I don't like the sound of this," said Ripley, standing behind the cockpit seats. "We heading for more trouble, boss?"

"I'm afraid we are," said Cochran. "But this time Bernie says his command can handle it. A pair of ASATs will intercept us over the Western Pacific. I hope your news is better."

"It is. The *Soyuz* commander is awake and reasonably coherent. In a few minutes we should be able to bring him up."

"Good. Perhaps he can give us some information on the Hydras. What about the other two? Especially Siprinoff?"

"He's up and fully conscious," Ripley explained. "In fact, he helped us revive Grachenko and now he's working on Kostilev."

"Do they know that their Air Defence Forces are hunting us with anti-satellite weapons?" Post asked.

"One thing at a time, Walt. We'd just like to get them up and moving. Kostilev will be very difficult to bring around."

"But I want them told," said Cochran. "And who knows? After we've saved them they may just end up saving us."

"Gentlemen, this will be my last speech. I promise," said a man wearing a bulky white pressure suit. He stepped in front of a group of similarly dressed men. They all carried portable air conditioning units, and were breathing oxygen through scuba-like mouthpieces. Because of the suits, none of them wore their rank insignia, in fact, many of the suits didn't even have U.S. Air Force badges. But there could be no doubt that the man in front of them was their commanding officer.

"Don't talk for too long, Steve," warned one of the other pilots, briefly removing his own mouthpiece. "Or the doctors will say you're contaminating your bloodstream."

"Hopefully just with nitrogen," said Colonel Steven Hall. "You all have your individual assignments, and you all know what our mission is. The fate of ten brave men and women will be riding on what we and the pilots of the Three-eighteenth do. These are the first space combat missions in history, and they'll be dangerous for everyone involved. Where we're going there will be no margin for error. That means I don't want anyone playing Luke Skywalker, especially you, Tony."

The warning and example brought a scattering of laughter from the pilots as well as the technicians still working on them. When it ended, Colonel Hall finished his speech.

"This is the last time we'll be together as a squadron," he continued. "And I hope we'll all meet here after it's over. Good luck and don't end up a dead hero, because a dead hero can't help that spaceship."

Instead of using his breathing gear again, Hall turned to a NASA technician beside him and bent his giant frame. One of the tallest pilots in his squadron, he was part of a substantial segment of his men who had to be suited up by NASA's Flight Research Center at Langley. The technician lowered a helmet over his head, then helped him seal its locking ring.

The rest of the pilots of the Forty-eighth Fighter Interceptor Squadron did the same, removing their portable oxygen breathing systems and donning a variety of helmets and plexiglass bubbles. To outfit the Forty-eighth's two dozen pilots and aircraft, the resources of every Langley-based unit had been used.

In addition to the squadron and NASA's facilities, they had brought in the First Tactical Fighter Wing. Also equipped with the F-15, the wing's ground crews helped

247

prepare the Forty-eight's Eagles for high-altitude flight and armed them with the available Vought anti-satellite weapons. NASA concentrated on equipping the pilots. They had the largest stock of specialized flying gear and the most experience with such operations.

As a result, more than half of the interceptors departing from Langley were mission-ready. Only those heading south would have to pick up their Vought ASATs at Eglin Air Force Base in Florida before being declared operational. Though they had started much later than the 318th, the Forty-eighth Fighter Interceptor Squadron would be deployed and ready at nearly the same time.

"Space Defence Operations, this is Iceman Blue One. My wingman and I are at forty thousand feet and awaiting orders," said Colonel DeCarlo, completing the trim-out of his F-15.

"Roger, Iceman One. Stand by for intercept vectors. You and your wingman are go for ASAT activation."

"Roger, Operations. We'll stand by for vectors. Kilmer, arm your Vought. Looks like we're going to use them."

After advising his wingman, DeCarlo ran his hand over the armament panels on the cockpit's right side. His Vought's warhead was an array of infrared sensors and thrusters that would keep the package on target. It wasn't armed so much as activated, as were the rest of the systems on the two-stage missile. The activation was completed when DeCarlo linked the ASAT to his F-15's fire control system.

"Iceman Two to Iceman Lead, my ASAT's Christmas tree is full green," said the wingman. "Frank, how do you like Jay's ship? He sure bitched when you wouldn't let him take it."

"I can understand why," said Decarlo. "He's made this bird very responsive. Let's see how she does in the high blue."

248

"Iceman One, this is Space Defence Operations. What is your weapon status?"

"Operations, our ASATs are full green."

"Roger, Iceman One. Separate and come to heading three-three-five, true. The *Phoenix* is over the Hawaiian Islands and we have a pair of Hydras on an intercept track."

"Roger, Operations. Kilmer, jettison your wing tanks."

Both F-15s released their external tanks before swinging due north. DeCarlo pulled a tighter turn than his wingman, opening the distance between the two. By the time they came to their new course they were separated by five miles. To each other they became grey shadows skirting the similarly colored overcast above the North Pacific.

"Iceman One, this is Operations. Stand by for zoom climb and ASAT release at eighty thousand feet. Your Regional Operations Command Center reports no other traffic in your area. Thirty second countdown commencing now."

DeCarlo and his wingman braced themselves for the pending maneuver as the intercept control officer read off the seconds before ordering them to dive. They checked their pressure suits to make sure they were operating properly; at fifteen miles up any problem would be serious, and they'd have no time to correct it.

When the countdown reached zero, DeCarlo and Kilmer nosed their fighters over. The huge, angular machines dropped from the sky as if they had lost their wings. Even without afterburners they quickly built up speed and the momentum they would need if they were to make it to 80,000 feet.

Moments after starting, DeCarlo and Kilmer plunged into the overcast they had been skirting. The world outside their canopies became a formless grey mass with an occasional flash of light as they passed between cloud layers. DeCarlo and Kilmer concentrated on the changing numbers of their head-up displays and the voice of the intercept control officer.

"Iceman One, you're approaching twenty-eight thousand feet. Initiate pull-out."

"Iceman One to Iceman Two, start pulling her up," DeCarlo relayed. "We're going for the high blue."

G-forces immediately started to build as the pilots hauled back their control sticks. The F-15s used an extra three thousand feet to end their dives, and the moment the altitude numbers on the HUDs started to reverse themselves, DeCarlo and Kilmer hit their afterburners.

The sudden kick pressed them firmly against their seats; the additional power made up for any loss in velocity. With their speed already at Mach 1, the fighters quickly passed Mach 2 as raw fuel dumped into their engine exhausts.

A little over a minute after the F-15s had dropped into the overcast, they came rocketing out of it. At their speed, and given the buildup of air in front of the fighters, they punched holes through the overcast as they emerged. They were still on their intercept course, still separated by some five miles. Above the overcast the sky was dark blue and growing darker.

Above 40,000 feet the air rapidly grew thinner. For the moment this meant little to the F-100 engines in the fighters. Their box-like intakes allowed them to swallow prodigious quantities of air. Flight control, however, was becoming more difficult. Soon the massive stabilizers, twin rudders, and ailerons would be of little use in controlling either aircraft.

"Iceman One to Space Defence Operations, we're coming up on Armstrong's Line," said DeCarlo.

"Roger, Iceman. You and your wingman are on your vectors. No changes need be made."

At 63,000 feet the fighters crossed Armstrong's Line, the unofficial boundary to space. More than ninety-five percent of the atmosphere was behind them. With no longer enough air to maneuver, they were now ballistic, thirty-ton projectiles with the speed and trajectories of artillery shells. They would be propelled the remaining three miles to their launch altitude by diminishing levels of engine thrust and inertia.

Above Armstrong's Line the sky changed from dark blue, to violet, then black. It had been early afternoon when DeCarlo and Kilmer left McChord; now the stars were coming out. Though they were still on afterburner, their planes grew eerily silent; there was no longer enough air for effective sound transmission.

"Iceman One, you're at seventy thousand feet. You and your wingman should have the target satellites on your screens."

"Roger, Operations. I have it on my CRT and my HUD," said DeCarlo, glancing between the head-up display atop his instrument panel and the radar screen which dominated its left side. "I have enough information for a weapons' lock."

With the F-15's APG radar set at extreme range, the Hydra ASATs appeared at the top of the left-hand screen. Normally it had a range of less than a hundred miles. But under present conditions, line-of-sight with no ground clutter or atmospheric disturbances to degrade it, it could scan nearly three hundred miles, enough to pick up satellites in low earth orbit and to provide the HUD with acceptable targeting information.

The HUD itself was on long-range interception mode. It showed a target blip surrounded by a contracting circle of green light. The numbers displayed around it gave the fighter's altitude, heading, and target distance. All the information being shown to the pilot was also fed to the Vought ASAT. When the contracting circle and target blip started to flash, both pilot and missile knew they had a lock.

"Iceman One to Operations, I have a lock on the first target. My wingman has a lock on the second."

"Roger, you are go for weapons release."

DeCarlo hit one of the buttons on his control stick,

initiating the launch procedure. The Vought's main engine was ignited while the missile was still attached to the pylon, its guidance system receiving a final burst of data. Seconds later, with the engine burning at full thrust, the pylons's support pins snapped down, kicking the missile away.

The Vought fell less than a dozen feet before it started to move forward. It arced out in front of DeCarlo's F-15, already following its own programmed trajectory. When the ASAT's exhaust plume briefly obscured his forward view, DeCarlo glanced over at his wingman and found Kilmer's missile also climbing away.

"Iceman One to Operations, both launches are successful. We're coming down from the high blue."

While the Voughts accelerated and rose higher into the ionosphere, the fighters decelerated. With their afterburners turned off, they rapidly lost airspeed. They were reaching the apex of their zoom climbs, and at 83,000 feet DeCarlo and Kilmer pulled their control sticks.

The Eagles responded by falling onto their backs, then turning in brief loops. As they had followed ballistic trajectories to reach their altitude, they would now follow similar arcs in their return flight to the planet which, at the moment, seemed so far away. Their part of the mission was over; it was up to the machines they had launched to complete the interceptions.

"Commander Cochran, I would like to introduce to you Commander Arkady Grachenko," Vachet announced, standing next to a bedraggled, unshaven figure in an orange ventilation suit.

"Commander, this is indeed a pleasure," said Cochran, undoing his restraint belts and sliding out of his chair.

"And on behalf of my men, I thank you," said Grachenko.

The two shook hands as Cochran moved out of the

cramped cockpit area. Grachenko then embraced him; it was not a strong hug, though it did catch Cochran off guard.

"In space, all men are brothers," Grachenko continued.

"If that's true, I don't think I'm going to let one marry my sister, to quote one of my favorite science-fiction stories," said Cochran. "Paul, does he know about our problem?"

"No, I thought he should hear it from you," said Vachet.

"I suppose so. Commander, the rescue of you and your men was done without the knowledge of my country or the permission of yours. They've seen fit to call it a hijacking.. They've launched nearly two dozen Hydra anti-satellite weapons. We're trapped in orbit, and we're hoping you can help us."

"That's . . . That's not possible," Grachenko responded, his English momentarily breaking down. "My uncle . . . He's the foreign minister! He fought to have us rescued."

"He was out-voted," said Vachet. "It appears as though your Air Defence Forces had a greater influence."

"I can't believe you . . . I can't believe this is happening. Not even Suvorov would be this crazy."

"Well, the sooner you believe it, the better it'll be for all of us," Post added. "Boss, SDC reports they've had two ASAT launches. Interception will take place in five minutes."

"Ask them if we'll be able to see it," said Cochran. "Whether or not you want to believe it, Arkady, it's happening. There are twenty-one Hydra interceptors in orbit. One failed to deploy properly, we destroyed its mate, and a third just intercepted a Japanese research satellite. Its mate is still in orbit, acting as a lone wolf. If you can tell us anything about these weapons, we'd be grateful for it."

"I . . . I must think about it," said Grachenko. "I still have to believe I'm not a dead man."

"You still might end up that way if we don't defeat those weapons," said Post. "SDC reports we'll see the intercepts all right. We got a good seat for the fireworks."

"Paul, see if you can pry Siprinoff away from his patient," Cochran ordered. "I'd like both him and Grachenko to witness these fireworks. Sorry Grachenko, but we need any information we can beg, cajole, or coerce out of you."

"Bernie, the Intercept Control Officer reports that the weapons are approaching first stage separation," said Ericson. "All systems are go. What's happening with the *Phoenix*."

"Their Soviet guests are waking up," answered Rosen. "And they'll be in visual range of the intercepts. Mary, how are you coming with your orbital evaluation?"

"I think we may have something," said Mary Widmark, glancing away from her computer screen. "I think we've found a hole in this web. In two orbits the *Phoenix* can land at Rota, Spain."

"If it can survive the next three minutes," said Rosen, as he glanced at the center's main screen, where the shuttle's track and those of the Hydras and Voughts were closing on each other. "And if NASA will let it land in Spain. Larry, when this is over I'll want to talk to Daurat. Perhaps the CNES would be best for bringing the *Phoenix* in."

At 400,000 feet, roughly seventy-five miles, the first-stage engines on the Voughts finally burned out. The missiles separated at their pinched center sections, nearly two-thirds of their bodies falling away. An instant later their second-stage Altair rocket engines ignited.

All that remained of the two weapons were their infrared sensors, thruster systems, guidance packages, and the spin motor platforms everything sat on. When the first stages separated, the spin motors had shut down, leaving the upper stages rotating at twenty revolutions per second.

The Altair engines would remain burning for only a minute before dying and being jettisoned with the spin motor platforms. By then the upper stages would be at escape velocity. They would need additional thrust only to maintain course for the last two and a half minutes of their flight.

Already the infrared sensor arrays were tracking their targets; each time the Hydras fired their thrusters the arrays had a fresh reference point. By contrast, the thrusters on the ascending Voughts used nitrogen bled from the cryogenic system to keep the sensors cool. The brief spurts of freezing gas would not be sensed by any infrared device.

The Hydras were still more than a hundred miles higher than the Voughts and several hundred miles up-range. But at a combined closure rate of 35,000 miles an hour, the distance would be crossed in the minutes which remained.

"There, Arkady, can you see them?" Cochran asked, back in his command seat and pointing into the distance. "They look like two faint stars just above the disc of the Earth."

"Yes, I can see them," said Grachenko. "Though just barely."

To use the cockpit's side window, Grachenko had to squeeze himself between Cochran's seat and the cockpit wall. He could only fit his head into the narrow space, and with his face pressed so close to the window, his field of view was limited.

"That doesn't look very comfortable," said Cochran, turning to see how Grachenko was positioned. "I think we should find a better way for you to see this."

"How about rotating the orbiter ninety degrees?" Post offered. "They could use the front windows."

"Yes, but let's not make the maneuver too compli-

255

cated. It'd be simpler just to roll the lady ninety degrees. Activate the RCS system. Paul, how did it go with Siprinoff?"

"I managed to convince him that Kostilev will be left in good hands," said Vachet, rising out of the hatch. "Here he is, Commander. Major Stefan Siprinoff."

Another bedraggled figure in an orange ventilation suit appeared on the flight deck, this one shorter and fairer than Grachenko. At first he appeared dazed, though in truth he was simply awed by the advanced technology he had seen.

"Commander, I'm so grateful for what you and your crew did," said Siprinoff, shaking Cochran's hand. "I had lost all hope. Your ship is quite amazing. Arkady, have you ever seen the like? It is so much more sophisticated than our shuttle. Do you believe it?"

"I believe what I see," said Grachenko, moving below the skylights. "But Commander Cochran wants to show us something I can only half believe. Come stand with me. Commander, we're ready."

"Good, just stay where you are, we'll do the rest," Cochran replied. "Okay, Walt, go ahead."

"Roger, RCS system to manual control," said Post. "Digital autopilot has selected the rotation rate."

Post activated the roll thrusters, and gently squeezed his joystick grip. The *Phoenix* responded by dipping its left wing and continuing a steady roll until it was flying on its side. Vachet, Grachenko and Siprinoff hovered near the middle of the flight deck and watched the cabin swing around them. In seconds, the skylight windows were sitting in front of them.

Though he was aware of what was being done, the maneuver still affected Grachenko. He had yet to fully recover from his drug overdose, and the swirling cabin made him feel as if he were falling. He closed his eyes, swaying groggily until Vachet took hold of him.

"I'm . . . I'm all right," Grachenko mumbled. "I guess I'm still not strong enough."

256

When his mind cleared, he found he had an unobstructed view out what had become the shuttle's port side. He could see parts of the Hawaiian Island chain through the broken cloud cover over the Pacific. And above the clouds he saw two black discs with a faint flashing discernible around their rims.

"There, Stefan," said Grachenko, in a low voice. "The Devil take us, it is a hunter-killer pair of our Hydras."

"And even at this range they have a lock on us," said Siprinoff. "Madness. How could they let Suvorov do this?"

"What are you saying? Suvorov is commander of our Air Defence Forces, he's a Marshal of the Soviet Union! He wouldn't act so irresponsibly."

"Sometimes, Arkady Alexiivich, you are too naive. Do you think everyone in our country believes in your dreams for Future Man? The people who voted to let us die could just as easily vote to kill us, especially if Suvorov alters the facts to support his views. We're expendable, Arkady."

"Gentlemen! You can continue the political reality lesson later," Cochran advised, raising his voice until the others quieted down. "Space Defence Command reports we're one minute to interception. You should be seeing our ASATs soon."

"All right, we'll talk later," said Grachenko. "Commander, what type of warhead do your weapons use?"

"None. When you hit something at over 17,000 miles per hour, kinetic energy is all you need."

"Ed, I think I can see our interceptors," said Vachet. "There, in the lower corner."

Vachet's warning turned Siprinoff and Grachenko's attention back to the converging pairs of anti-satellite weapons. With a little help they spotted the ascending Voughts, which had since jettisoned their spin motor tables and second-stage engines. Now just rotating cylinders of infrared sensors and thrusters, they were at escape velocity and on track.

Because of the observers' perspective, the American ASATs appeared to be moving faster than the Hydras. Nearly invisible, even against a background of white overcast, the Voughts were like bullets. Too small, too fast for any of their features to be discerned, they were also too small for the radar-guided Hydra to detect them, too cold for the infrared mate to see them.

The Hydras never attempted to avoid them and first one, then the other, evaporated in a flash like a nuclear detonation, followed by a shower of glittering fragments. In an instant the fuel and explosives aboard the Hydras were ignited by the impacts and consumed. Unlike the earlier interception, no wreckage remained. The missiles had been so pulverized by the collisions that none of the debris was larger than a grain of rice.

For nearly a minute, showers resulting from the explosion sparkled brightly in the harsh sunlight. Grachenko, Siprinoff, and Vachet watched silently until the remnants had dispersed so widely they were no longer visible, except for the occasional glint.

"Impressive, and most sobering," Grachenko finally observed, moving away from the skylights. "No one could've arranged this as a trick. I'm sorry I did not believe you earlier."

"Don't worry about it," said Post, while Cochran talked with Ground Control. "Just so long as you can help us stay out of danger until we land, wherever and whenever that may be."

"It could end up being sooner than you expect," said Cochran. "Thanks, Bernie. We're changing back to Mission Control."

"What's happening?" Grachenko asked. "Are we landing?"

"Yes. My friends at Space Defence Command think they've found a hole in the Hydra 'web,' as they call it. We might be able to land in Rota, Spain in another two orbits, provided everything goes right both up here and on the ground."

258

"That will give us three hours," said Vachet. "More than enough time to prepare ourselves properly for reentry. Is there anything special we need to do?"

"Stay out of danger," said Cochran. "Which means going for a higher orbit, or so Mount Cheyenne thinks."

"Yes, that would be true," Siprinoff added. "Once the Hydras are deployed at a certain altitude they don't vary much from it. It was assumed that most of their targets would be satellites in fixed orbits. In the case of a manned vehicle, then the Hydras were to be deployed in several altitudes, forming a type of space minefield, or deployed at reentry altitude. Which is what Suvorov has done here."

"Arkady, do you agree with what he said?"

"I can't say. I am not an expert in this area," Grachenko admitted. "I'm a civilian cosmonaut, not military. But Stefan's advisory does sound like something I once heard."

"Good. That little bit of information will be useful to us," said Cochran, reaching over his head to reset his com panel. "I'll tell NASA to put us at a high orbital altitude, and we'll make a rapid descent before our deorbit burn. Looks like I was right. Now that we've rescued you, you'll have to rescue us."

"Well, that's that," said Rosen. "The *Phoenix* is back under NASA control. Larry, is Toulouse on the line?"

"Yes, and it's Jacques Daurat," Ericson answered. "He's on outside line number four."

"Then let's not keep him waiting." Rosen turned to his communications panel and, after a little hunting, pressed one of the buttons marked "external." "Director Daurat, sorry to take this long in getting to you. I trust you've been listening?"

"But of course, the events concern French astronauts as much as American," said Daurat, a rumbling of impatience in his voice. "And we're greatly interested in your evaluation of the orbiter's situation. Do you believe NASA will land it in Spain?"

"Well, they'd better listen to reason now. And I've been thinking Houston shouldn't guide the landing. NASA's never done a shuttle test landing at any of the overseas emergency sites. In your case, however, you actually carried out several landings at Rota with the flying prototype of the *Hermes*."

"Yes, we did them last year with the aerodynamic test vehicle, before we sent it to Kourou. In fact, Vachet piloted one of the flights. Do you think it's possible NASA would let us control the reentry? Or use Vachet to fly the *Phoenix*?"

"No, they'll probably go with Post," Rosen answered. "However, your mission control staff has had experience with actual landings at Rota. We'll tell Houston your operations center would be the best choice to control the reentry. Considering the bad feelings which still exist between NASA management and my command, we'd work better with you. And when the *Phoenix* does make its reentry, my F-15s will have to pull a maximum effort to ride shotgun for it."

"I understand, my friend. We have worked well together. I hope we can cooperate well enough to bring our countrymen down. Do you think they really have a chance of landing at Rota?"

"Events can change, and we don't know about this new generation of Soviet ASATs. My staff is continuing their evaluation, in the event the reentry has to be aborted. Nothing will be certain until the *Phoenix* is safely on the ground."

"Would you mind if my staff added some data to your ongoing evaluation?" Daurat asked. "We have several ideas for alternate landing sites, ones that do not appear on NASA's list. Ones the Russians may have not considered when they wove their anti-satellite web."

Chapter Sixteen

"Is that the last? Are there any others?" Nikolai Grachenko asked, turning to the room's chief video technician after the screen in front of him, Nagorny, and Fedarenko had gone blank.

"No, comrade Foreign Minister," said the Technician. "Those are all the tapes the Americans sent us."

"They're quite enough," said Fedarenko, glancing at the sheet full of notes he had taken. "They prove conclusively the Americans and French were only interested in rescuing our men. It was magnificent to watch them."

"Yes, they're conclusive and magnificent," Nagorny agreed, a peaceful smile on his face and the glimmer of tears in his eyes. "As a military man I can appreciate professionals carrying out a difficult and dangerous task."

"It's more than what you say. What we saw represents all that is noble in mankind. That crew is nobility personified."

"Are you two having another argument?" said Grachenko with a sly grin. "Is it who can outdo the other in superlatives? I take it we can agree what we saw here was a humanitarian act?"

"Of course it was," said Fedarenko, lifting the notes off his clipboard. "I took these numbers from the footage readouts on the screen. They can help us extract what we need to show the premier."

"Yes, most useful. You can stay here and direct the technicians in creating a tape we'll show to Gussarov and the other members of the Politburo."

"What will you and Nagorny be doing?"

"Pietr will contact the Premier," said Grachenko. "I will contact our allies in the Politburo. Despite the conclusiveness of our evidence, we'll need all the help we can rally. With France and America placing their strategic forces on alert, this crisis has become a confrontation."

"You're referring to what the American President told his country?" said Fedarenko, his elation disappearing and his mood growing somber. "That we want to destroy their shuttle simply because it rescued our cosmonauts without our permission?"

"American politicians always want to make things simple," Nagorny complained, his mood also changing. "This helps President Bush with, what do you call them? Primaries?"

"American politicians may be simple," said Grachenko. "But American politics is not. And what Bush said was a lot less inflammatory than what the French Premier accused us of."

"Had they only kept quiet about this, we could've simply destroyed the weapons and allowed their spacecraft to land wherever they wanted it. Now, with this confrontation, we're forced to take other actions."

"What actions?" asked Fedarenko. "Why can't we just say that both sides made mistakes and correct them?"

"For you, in the Academy of Sciences, it's so easy to admit mistakes," said Nagorny, a sharp tone to his voice. "But for us, it is not. Do you remember five years ago? When the German teenager landed a plane in Red Square? Both Defence Minister Ustinov and the air defence chief were removed from their posts. Something similar will have to happen here."

"You mean you'll be forced out in disgrace?"

"Not likely, Doctor," Grachenko answered. "Blame can be laid on Marshal Suvorov. It was he who mounted the death watch and it was he who went to Gussarov with the request to launch the Hydras."

"If he leaves, I say fine," said Fedarenko. "He should've been removed the moment he started his watch."

"It was his duty to defend our country," said Nagorny.

"By trying to kill our cosmonauts and those who

saved them?"

"I didn't agree with it either!" Nagorny's rage exploded, though fortunately it was short-lived and he quickly cooled down. "Look, that's not important. We will stop the weapons. What we may not stop is Suvorov. We push him into a corner, and I can't say what he'll do. He has friends throughout the army."

"What about the Hydra weapons, Pietr?" said Grachenko. "How long will it take to destroy them?"

"A matter of minutes once we have the self-destruct codes. Of course we must work out an agreement with the Americans. I hope they attempt nothing before then."

"Arkady, where . . . Where are we?" Kostilev finally asked weakly. "Who are these people?"

"You are aboard the United States spacecraft *Phoenix*," Grachenko said, slowly and carefully. "And these are the men and women who rescued you."

"Major Kostilev, how do you feel in there?" said Ripley, standing beside Grachenko.

"Tight, but not tight. When will you allow me out of here?"

"Not any time soon. We're going to try for a reentry, I'll let your commander fill you in on what's happened. Let's finish with these seats. Harrison, your station is topside."

While the mission specialist seat had been unstowed, they had yet to be anchored to the middle deck. As Ripley and the others turned to grab them, Harrison pushed off the floor and sailed through the roof hatch. On the flight deck she found the mission specialist seats already anchored, the cargo bay doors closed, and Vachet helping Post with his anti-gravity suit.

"Here, you're set," Vachet advised, handing Post his suit's air lines. "Would you care for your flight helmet?"

"No, not until after I'm back in my seat," said Post. "It's time we had a real pilot fly this ship."

Both Cochran and Post were now wearing bulky orange suits ribbed with air bladders around their stomachs and legs. Once in his seat, Post connected his air lines to the ports at the base of the cockpit's center pedestal. The anti-gravity suits would help him and Cochran ride through the reentry without blacking out; the suits would stop blood from pooling in their lower bodies by inflating the bladders.

"Julie, check the aft crew station and make sure it's secured," said Cochran, moments after she arrived on the flight deck. "Then check the payload sensors."

"Ed, any other duties for me?" Vachet asked.

"Yes, we're coming up on T minus sixty minutes to reentry. This is the best time for our Gatorade."

Vachet turned to one of the smaller lockers on the flight deck and opened it. Inside were four containers of Gatorade which Vachet distributed to the other crew members before drinking his own.

"Drink up, or you won't be able to walk off the orbiter," said Cochran, finishing his. "Here, Paul. After you collect the rest, go below and check on our friends."

Cochran sailed his empty container to Vachet, as did the others. He grabbed them out of the air and was holding them in one hand when he dropped through the hatch to the middle deck.

"Ed, the aft station is secure," Harrison reported. "The cargo bay doors are locked and the payloads are stable."

"Thanks, Julie. Take your seat, we're going to transfer to our reentry orbit," said Cochran, tapping the controls on his communications panel. "Commander to crew, T minus thirty seconds to OMS burn. Walt, what's the status of the flight programs?"

"GPC and BFS program load completed," said Post. "Gimbaling OMS nozzles full up. OMS and RCS thrusters under GPC control."

"Good, let's let the lady do the flying for us."

Seconds later, when both the OMS engines and

thrusters fired, there wasn't the usual sensations of either acceleration or deceleration. Instead everyone on the flight deck was lifted out of their seats; only their restraint belts kept them from drifting to the ceiling.

On the middle deck, everyone who wasn't resting inside a bunk felt the floor drop away from their feet and watched the ceiling bear down on them. Most grabbed something anchored to the deck's floor or walls so they could stay in position. A few, however, decided to drift free and ended up pressed against the ceiling.

"I always wanted to know what it was like to be a fly," said Ripley, resting comfortably above the others.

"Jack, Renée, get down from there," Vachet ordered. "We have a lot of work to do."

"You should know by now we can't do much during an engine burn. You might as well hang on and enjoy the ride."

Both the OMS engines and thrusters were fired by the general purpose computer. Though the *Phoenix* maintained a relatively level attitude, it had dropped precipitously from the altitude it had maintained for the last one and a half orbits. Some of the activated thrusters were in the shuttle's nose module, and the glare from their exhaust jets blinded the flight deck team for the duration of the burn. Exactly three minutes later, the flames died out. The shuttle had lost fifty miles in altitude and was back in its proper reentry orbit.

"Switching GPC program load to Three-Zero-Two," said Post, tapping out the commands on his computer keyboard. "I'll let the ship fly itself through this maneuver as well."

"Commander to crew, we're going for attitude change and de-orbit burn," said Cochran. "Hold on, this ride isn't over yet."

Faster and more precisely than Post could attempt it, the GPC swung the shuttle around until it was flying backwards. The moment it achieved the proper attitude, both the OMS engines and aft-facing thrusters were fired. Objects and people had yet to stop swirling around the middle deck when the deceleration effects sent them all crashing against the front bulkhead.

"Jack, catch that!" Vachet shouted. "Don't let it open!"

A coffee container had slipped out of Grachenko's hand and was flying toward the bulkhead. Ripley extended both hands and caught the zero-G cup by its lid. Apart from some tiny spheres of coffee leaking through its mouthpiece, its contents remained inside.

"This gives a whole new meaning to the phrase 'coffee to go,'" said Ripley. "Don't touch those buttons, Stefan. If you do, the galley will spray the deck with hot water."

The shuttle's deceleration increased as the burn continued. What should have been done nearly half an hour earlier was now being attempted in an effort to get the *Phoenix* through a hole in the web of Hydra weapons. The spacecraft had spent only a brief time at its normal reentry altitude when its unusual de-orbit maneuvers were completed and it was at the beginning of a long, gentle descent into the Earth's atmosphere.

"Toulouse, this is *Phoenix*. OMS burn completed," Cochran reported. "Our altitude is 175 miles, and our velocity is 17,000 miles an hour."

"Roger, *Phoenix*. You are in atmospheric pre-entry coast," said Raquel Jordan. "Begin post-OMS burn checklist immediately."

"Roger, Toulouse. Commencing check." Cochran reached into the cockpit's flight data file and pulled out one of the reentry cue cards. "Walt, what's the APU status?"

"APUs one, two, and three have powered up and their hydraulic pressures read low green," said Post.

Unused since the *Phoenix* had achieved orbit, the auxiliary power units had been reactivated and were operating at their lowest levels. Later on in the landing cycle they would be used to work the flight control surfaces, landing gear, brake systems, and nose wheel steering. All three APUs were on, though only two would actually run the systems.

"Shutting down OMS engines," said Cochran, reaching for the center overhead panels. "Isolating all OMS systems."

"RCS thrusters to manual control," Post advised. "Loading program Three-Zero-Three into GPC and BFS. Ready to manuever orbiter into position shown on the CRTs."

"Let me warn the middle deck. Commander to crew. Prepare for attitude change. We're in pre-entry coast."

The shuttle was still flying backwards, but when Post started to work his joystick, it rotated gently to the left. Not as fast as the earlier, computer-guided maneuver, the attitude shift was easier for those on the middle deck to endure. Most of them gathered near its center and watched the deck swing around them.

"This type of movement still gives me an effect," said Grachenko, holding his head until the dizziness passed. "It also reminds me of how our *Mir* station would spin."

"Well you won't have to suffer it much longer," said Vachet. "Soon you'll have gravity to contend with. To prepare for it you'll have to drink this. It's called Gatorade."

"Gatorade?" Grachenko had a questioning look on his face as he accepted a container from Vachet. "Is it made from reptiles? What does it do?"

"It does what your salt and mineral pills do, only it tastes a little better. It will help prepare your body for its return to a gravity environment."

"Even with it, your medical crews will still have to carry us off this spacecraft," Grachenko warned before he unsealed the container and drank its contents. "What are we to do next?"

"You and Stefan will return to your bunks for the reentry," said Vachet. "We're recharging the portable oxygen systems for your use. They'll act as your personal egress air packs."

"Toulouse, this is *Phoenix*. We've completed our post-OMS checklist and the orbiter is in its normal attitude," Cochran reported. "Our velocity is still 17,000 miles an hour and our altitude is 165 miles."

"Roger, *Phoenix*," said Jordan. "Prepare to assume reentry attitude and do the entry switch-over checklist."

"Roger, Toulouse. Do you have any updates from Mount Cheyenne on the Hydras?"

"Not yet, but if anything dangerous develops we'll let you know immediately. Toulouse, out."

The shuttle was now at its lowest altitude since its launch. It had completed the first phase of its reentry cycle and was just under five thousand miles from Rota, Spain, where it would be landing in exactly fifty minutes.

"This is Mount Cheyenne to CNES Mission Control, we've got a change in the tracks of Hydras nineteen and twenty," said Rosen. "Looks like our friends are in a little trouble."

"How dangerous is it, General?" Daurat responded. "Will the orbiter have to abort a reentry again?"

"No. We were expecting we'd have some trouble with this pair and we can take care of them. At least now we have a better idea of what the search cones for the radar-guided Hydras are like. Warn our friends, but tell them not to worry, we're already running interference for them."

"Your data on the Hydras and the F-15s is appearing on our main screen," said Daurat. "Inform us the moment the interception occurs, or if there's a change in any of the other ASATs. Toulouse, out."

"We will. Let us know if anything happens at your end. Mount Cheyenne, out," said Rosen. The moment he placed the telephone back on its cradle he was slipping his headset back onto his ears. "This is Command One to Intercept Control. Advise on status of Maverick Echo Three and Four."

"Command One, the fighters are now passing forty thousand feet," replied the Intercept Control Officer. "They will acquire their targets in the next twenty seconds."

Rosen looked up at the main screen and concentrated on two green squares over the Gulf of Mexico: Maverick Echo Three and Maverick Echo Four. The escalating numbers beside them were their airspeeds and altitudes. Once they started to slow, the fighters would be near the end of their zoom climbs, and the Vought ASATs would be released. Closing in on them from the west were two closely spaced orbital tracks—the Hydras, which were also overtaking the shuttle.

"Things are going to be close once again," said Rosen. "Damn, these weapons have capabilities that are absolutely amazing. Mary, are your orbital evaluations continuing?"

"Right up to the minute," Captain Widmark answered, glancing away from her computer screen. "These weapons seem to be varying their tracks from one orbit to the next. They must have some kind of artificial intelligence."

"Keep on it. Colonel, how's the *Phoenix* doing?"

"The crew just turned the shuttle around and they're preparing to do their entry switch-over checks," said Ericson.

"Good, start a commentary on what they're doing," Rosen ordered. "I want a running account of what's happening."

"This is Space Defence Operations to Maverick Echo Three. Move to the right. We want to center you in your vector."

"Roger, Space Defence. Moving starboard," said Captain Gene Larson. "You let me know when I've gone far enough."

Larson dipped the right wing of his F-15 and kicked in

269

a little left rudder. The aircraft slid sideways as it continued its zoom climb, increasing the distance between Larson and his wingman until they were more than eight miles apart. Except for the bright afterburner flames set against a darkening horizon, they were almost invisible to each other.

Unlike the earlier intercept over the North Pacific, the two F-15s from the Forty-Eighth Fighter Interceptor Squadron were climbing through a cloudless sky above the Gulf of Mexico. Behind and below them, the afternoon sun danced off the waters of the Gulf. Ahead lay the growing blackness of space, and soon it would be dark enough for them to see the stars. Above 50,000 feet, night fell so completely the pilots switched on their navigation and anti-collision lights.

"Space Defence Operations to Echo Three, you're approaching Armstrong's Line. You and your wingman should have the target satellites on your screens."

"Roger, Space Defence. I've acquired my target on my CRT. I'll have a lock on it soon. Maverick Three, out."

Though Larson's APG-63 radar already showed a target at extreme range, he knew there wasn't yet enough of a return signal to provide an adequate lock for his Vought. He waited until he had crossed the frontier to space before changing modes on his head-up display to long-range interception.

Against a background that went from deep blue, to violet, then to black, the green symbols and numbers on the HUD's glass plate became almost incandescent. Larson had to tone down their brightness in order to see the sky beyond them and catch a fleeting glimpse of space. Moments later, the green target blip and circle began flashing.

"Space Defence Operations to Echo Three, you and your wingman are cleared for weapons release."

The Vought slung under Larson's F-15 received its final data feed and ignition commands, and when the fighter reached 80,000 feet, the missile was kicked away, its main engine burning uncontrollably. For a moment it was in a free-fall until the thrust the engine was producing took effect.

The Vought arced away from the F-15 and began the second phase of the interception. Moments later, the wingman's ASAT joined it as the two fighters ended their zoom climbs. They looped and started to fall back toward the distant, glittering waters of the Gulf of Mexico. Several hundred miles in front of the missiles Larson and his wingman had launched were the targeted Hydras. Further out from them was the *Phoenix*.

"Toulouse, this is *Phoenix*. We're commencing entry switch-over checklist," said Cochran.

"Roger, *Phoenix*," Jordan answered. "You may proceed."

"Switch-over list in place," said Post, attaching another cue card to the board between the front windows. He glanced through it for a second, before starting to recite its procedures. "Cabin relief A and B. They're on your side, Ed."

"Cabin relief, enabled," said Cochran, hitting the toggles.

"Antiskid system?"

"Antiskid, on."

"Nose wheel steering?"

"Nose wheel steering, off."

"Entry roll mode?"

"Entry roll mode, off."

"Throttle and speed brake controls, full forward," said Post, grabbing the throttle lever on his side of the center pedestal and pushing it forward until it locked in place.

Cochran did the same with the lever on his lower cockpit side panel. In orbit they were unused and, with people moving repeatedly in and out of the cockpit seats, they had slipped from their original positions. The levers had been employed on ascent as throttles for the main engines and would be used in around twenty minutes to operate the shuttle's speed brake.

"ADI error and rate systems to medium," Post read off, hitting a row of toggle switches on the front instrument panel. "Air data system?"

"Switching air data system to navigation mode," said Cochran, hitting a switch on his front instrument panel.

"Hydraulic main pump pressure switches?"

"Pressure switches to normal operation."

"And the hydraulic pressure indicators show high green," said Post, before he pulled the cue card off the board. "The APUs are nominal. Switch-over check completed."

"Toulouse, this is *Phoenix*. Switch-over completed," Cochran repeated. "Do you have an update on the intercepts?"

"Affirmative, *Phoenix*. Your air force has launched the ASATs and reports that interception will take place in under three minutes. Proceed with HUD activation and test orbiter aero-surfaces. You are T minus forty-five minutes to landing."

"Roger, Toulouse. We're activating our HUDs."

Unused until now, the cockpit head-up displays lay folded above the front instrument panel glareshields. To activate them, Cochran and Post hit the Raise/Lower toggles on their respective HUD control panels. The double sets of combiner glass pivoted out of their wells until tilted in the angle at which the data shown on them could be seen with the view outside the cockpit. Next, Cochran and Post would test the HUDs before using them.

At 400,000 feet the first stages of the Voughts burned out, then separated a moment later. The second-stage Altairs ignited and pushed the intercept vehicles beyond what remained of the Earth's atmosphere and beyond the pull of its gravity.

A minute after ignition, the Altair engines were

jettisoned, along with the spin tables and motors. The furiously rotating vehicles continued on their sub-orbital trajectories, homing toward the rapidly approaching Hydra warheads. For the next two minutes, the momentum they had built up during their swift ascents would be enough to carry them to their interceptions.

In turn, as they closed in on the descending spaceplane, the Hydras increased the firing of their thruster quads. Though it made them easier targets, it also made them unstable, as they were constantly shifting position, slowing, then speeding up with each pulse of fire. The changes were minute, but at a closure rate of more than 30,000 miles per hour, any change could be important.

The first Hydra to be intercepted evaporated in a nuclear-like flash, the result of a direct hit from the lead Vought. Its cloud of glittering fragments had yet to blossom when the second Hydra was grazed by the remaining Vought. At the last instant the Hydra had moved a few inches to one side.

The smaller ASAT broke up immediately, while the Hydra lost one of its thruster quads and some of its external panels. Internally, its guidance system was knocked out and its infrared sensors destroyed; it started to tumble uncontrollably. It would be impossible for the Hydra to continue its interception of the *Phoenix*, and what was left of its control system knew it.

The Hydra self-destructed with the detonation of its warhead and fuel cells. Unlike that of its companion, its end wasn't an immediate disintegration. It was a fireball, an expanding mass of flames that lasted for several seconds until it had consumed the available fuels. It was a powerful thermal source in the cold vacuum of space, and it lasted long enough to attract attention.

Far to the south, a similar vehicle in a similar orbit detected the burst of heat. For more than three hours it had been wandering, ever since its radar-guided companion had destroyed a Japanese satellite. It was following no organized search pattern but was actively seeking infrared sources. The fireball attracted the lone Hydra immediately, and even after it died out, the ASAT continued to deviate from its orbit. Farther ahead it had detected a second, more permanent, source.

"General, we've got a problem," Mary Widmark warned, pushing her chair away from her computer console and turning to face Rosen. "That lone wolf is acting up."

"What? Sergeant, get Toulouse back on the line," said Rosen, pulling his headset off. "Show me what's going on."

Rosen had been relaxing after his command's second interception when Widmark's alert caused him to sit upright. He scrambled out of his chair and in moments was standing beside her.

"It started to leave its track right after we destroyed Hydras nineteen and twenty," said Widmark. "The explosions may have attracted it, and I think it's locked onto the *Phoenix*."

"Show me its predicted course," Rosen ordered. "Along with the shuttle's reentry track."

To comply, Widmark tapped a few of the command keys. The undulating lines which represented the *Phoenix* and the lone Hydra completed their journeys across the screen. With the stroke of another key, she presented the two tracks, and their intercept point, on an altitude and distance graph.

"If it continues reentry, the shuttle will be destroyed at 350,000 feet," said Widmark. "And roughly a thousand miles downrange from its current position."

"Command One to Operations," said Rosen. "Intercept Control Officer, are there any F-15s ready to assist the *Phoenix*?"

"I'm painting in the available fighters now," the officer replied, and on the room's main screen, pairs of green squares appeared in the area of the spaceplane's reentry track. There were three pairs, the closest of which was almost under the shuttle. "I have one element in position, but they're being refueled by a tanker and won't be ready for another six minutes."

"Thanks, Operations. I'm afraid they won't be able to help us. Mary, can our friends return to orbit?"

"They can return right up to the point of communications blackout," she said.

"Larry, what's the *Phoenix* doing now?" Rosen asked.

"Testing their flight surfaces," said Ericson. "Next they'll dump the fuels from the nose thrusters."

"My God, if they dump those fuels they'll never be able to maneuver while in orbit. Sergeant, hand me that phone. I hope Daurat is on the other end."

"Entering program Three-Nine," said Cochran. "RCS to GPC control. Changing joystick to flight control, activating rudder pedals. Unlocking aero surfaces. You first, Walt."

Post threw a switch on the joystick pedestal, changing it from thrusters to flight surface control, and eased his feet onto the rudder pedals. For the first time since the test prior to lift-off, the shuttle's ailerons, elevons, body flap, and rudder were operated. The rudder doubled as its speed brake and, after being swung from side to side, was split open to test all the hydraulics. After Post was finished, Cochran repeated the operation.

"Our guests are strapped into their bunks," said Vachet, rising through the floor hatch. "Ripley, Pellerin, and Simon are in their seats. The middle deck is secure for reentry."

"Good. You'd better take your seat," said Post. "We're coming up on atmospheric interface. We'll be in a gravity environment in a few minutes."

"I will miss weightlessness." Vachet pushed away from the cockpit seats and drifted back into his own.

Harrison helped him down, then handed him part of his restraint belt. "My body may never grow accustomed to it, but I think I could."

"Saint Ex, you were made for this realm," Cochran remarked. "Aero surface test completed. Locking surfaces in neutral positions. Returning RCS to manual operation. Walt, stand by to dump propellants from nose module. Toulouse, this is *Phoenix*. We're ready for RCS dump."

"Roger, *Phoenix*. Proceed with dump."

"Loading program Three-Six," said Post, tapping out the commands on his pedestal keyboard. "And the forward RCS system is armed."

"Enter dump commands," said Cochran. "Let's give the lady her proper center-of-gravity."

"*Phoenix*, this is Toulouse. Stop operations immediately!" The voice on the headsets and cockpit speakers was different. It was no longer Jordan but Daurat himself, and his sharp warning caused Post to jerk his hand away from the keyboard before he had even finished with the program number. "Kill propellant dump! We just received an advisement from Mount Cheyenne. A third Hydra is closing on you. Return to orbit immediately."

"Jesus, not again. Toulouse, if we continue reentry, when will we be intercepted? How much time do we have?"

"If you continue, you'll be destroyed at an altitude of sixty-six miles. You have seven minutes."

"No one's ever tried a return to orbit from this altitude," said Post. "None of our flight programs will work."

"I know they won't, but we've got to abort this reentry . . ." Cochran's words trailed off as he searched the instrument panel. "We'll use the abort system. Toulouse, we will try to regain orbit. Walt, reactivate the OMS engines."

"Can we use that system now? It's designed only to work during launches, when we have the main engine running."

"We don't need the main engines. We have near-orbital velocity; we just need altitude and a little more speed."

Cochran dumped the reentry program from the GPC and set it to take commands from the abort system. To activate the system, he pressed one of the buttons on his front panel, a far simpler procedure than what Post had to do.

"Propellant isolation switches one through eight, open," the pilot said, hitting row after row of toggles on the overhead panels. "OMS system ready for arming."

"OMS engines, armed," said Cochran, pressing a set of buttons on the center pedestal. "Keep the nose angle at thirty-eight degrees or better. Commander to crew, stand by for OMS burn. There's another ASAT after us, so we have to return to orbit."

"Status lights show engines ready. Time to return, Boss."

"We'll go with 'Abort to Orbit' mode. Once I set this we'll be committed. Let's hope it works."

Cochran already had his hand on the abort selector dial, and once he set it on the ATO position, both the OMS engines and aft-facing thrusters ignited. On the decelerating spaceplane the sudden thrust pushed everyone against their seats, or into their bunk bedding. The ship stopped its descent, stopped its deceleration, and began to climb.

Post maintained the shuttle's nose-high attitude which, while it had been perfect for reentry; was also perfect for its return to orbit. Somewhere over the Azores, where it should have been entering the blackout zone for its landing, the *Phoenix* had regained the speed needed for orbital insertion, and its climb rate jumped dramatically.

"Toulouse, this is *Phoenix*. Another two minutes of OMS burn and we'll be at minimum orbital altitude," said Cochran. "Advise Houston of our situation, and see if you can get an update on the Hydra from

Mount Cheyenne."

"Roger, *Phoenix*. We will advise Houston," said Raquel Jordan, back at her CAP COM post. "We suggest you secure all non-essential systems for orbit."

"Shit, she's right. We got a lot of things to shut down," Post remarked, taking a hand off his joystick grip and reaching for one of his side panels.

"No, Walt. You're to maintain our attitude. Julie, you're closest, you take care of the APUs. I'll do the rest."

Cochran dug into the flight data file for the auxiliary power unit shutdown cards, which he handed to Harrison. The rest of the cards he pulled were for himself. His task was to deactivate the navigation and flight systems the shuttle would've needed later in its reentry.

"Let me put these in the right order," said Harrison, shuffling the cards. "Be careful, Walt, I'm coming forward."

She unlocked her restraint belts and moved up to Post's seat. Of the two mission specialists seats on the flight deck, Harrison's was closest to the cockpit, and she only had to drift a few inches before she was directly behind Post. From her new position, she could reach the auxiliary power unit controls.

"Enabling APU auto shutdown," she reported, throwing a single switch and deactivating all three units. For all the associated systems, it was more complex. Harrison had to feel her way over the panels and hit the correct triplets of switches. "Check complete. Everything's dead, commander."

"Good, I've finished the shutdowns on my side," said Cochran, "Toulouse, this is *Phoenix*. Have you any updates for us?"

"Roger, *Phoenix*. Houston is working on new flight programs for you. Your air force advises that the warhead is still in pursuit and is slowly overtaking you. Both would like to have you turned over to them. The choice is yours."

"Tell Bernie we'll be getting in touch with him. Can you put Houston on hold for us?"

"Affirmative, we'll keep them away from you. Your friends are standing by. Good luck, *Phoenix*. This is Toulouse, out."

"Thanks, Toulouse. Walt, ten seconds to burn termination." said Cochran, reaching for his com panel. "I'm switching us to NORAD secure channels."

While Post ended the orbital reinsertion burn, Cochran switched the spaceplane to SDC control. After a few moments Rosen was informing him on the latest danger to the *Phoenix*.

"Ed, the lone wolf is chasing you. Somehow, destroying the other two Hydras drew it onto your track. Its velocity has increased, and if your speed remains constant, you'll be intercepted in forty-eight minutes."

"Does that give us enough time to reach the West Coast, where your F-15s can deal with the ASAT?" Cochran asked.

"I'm afraid not," said Rosen. "Current projections show you'll be three minutes short. You can either increase your speed or throw another decoy in its path."

"Increasing speed would require another OMS burn and I want to conserve our fuel. We'll try another decoy. Is the Hydra following us infrared or radar guided?"

"We can't be sure. Intercepting a Hydra results in instantaneous destruction, not a fireball. The debris creates a big, temporary, radar image, so this Hydra's probably radar guided."

"Thanks, Bernie. We'll start preparing a decoy. *Phoenix*, out," Cochran responded, then he looked over his shoulder at Vachet and Julie. "Looks like you two will be going to work. Paul, do you know the procedures for satellite activation?"

"Not as well as Simon, but I do," said Vachet, reaching for the lock on his restraint belt.

"She would be the best, but I don't think we can wait for her. Better get to work. Julie—"

"I know and I'm on my way," said Harrison, acknowledging her orders before they had been given.

Since she had already left her seat, all she had to do was turn and thread her way around the mission specialist chairs to reach the aft crew station. When she got to it, Harrison leaned against the back of Vachet's chair to steady herself instead of taking the time to slide her feet into the shoe attachments.

Vachet had to wait until Harrison slid by him before he could move to the payload control station. He used her seat instead of standing to get at the controls; it had been anchored so close to the station that it was virtually impossible for him to stand.

"Unlocking cargo door latches," Harrison reported.

"Good. Activate the remote arm as well," said Cochran. "Commander to crew, we're back in orbit. However, we still have the ASAT pursuing us. We're launching another decoy. If we need your help we'll let you know."

"Renée, he said he'd let us know if they need our help," Ripley admonished, grabbing her hand as she reached for her belts. "With the seats in place it's cramped up there."

"But I know satellite operations best," said Simon. "I can have it activated in minutes."

"So can Paul. All three of you were cross-trained on your satellites. He's your commander, he can do the job."

"I understand your desire to help," said Grachenko, fitted snugly into the middle bunk. "But we can't all be the rescuer. Sometimes, the hardest thing to do is sit back and wait. Believe me, I know."

"Good God, where's that coming from?" Post asked holding a hand over his eyes when a blinding light invaded the flight deck.

"Through the cargo bay," said Harrison, pulling her

280

sunglasses from one of her flightsuit pockets. "It's the sun. It's low enough that it streams directly through the cargo bay windows. It'll make my work more difficult."

"Is there anything we can do to help?" said Cochran.

"I think if you were to roll the orbiter on its back that would blot out most of the glare. The sun is sitting just above the OMS pods, and I can barely see the tail."

"Digital autopilot is coming up with the rotation rate," Post responded. "Commencing maneuver."

He briefly pushed the joystick to the left. The shuttle rolled onto its side, then its back, before stopping. For the first time since lift off, the *Phoenix* was flying in a head's-down attitude. The sun's glare was reduced to a harsh disc of light which silhouetted the spaceplane's angular tail section. While it remained difficult to look at, Harrison could at least work.

"Unlocking and activating RMS," she said. "Paul, how's the satellite coming along?"

"I'm afraid it's not. I didn't get the activation sequence right," Vachet admitted, punching a row of buttons until the flashing lights died out. "If I can make a suggestion, there's a simpler decoy we can use. Why not deploy the fuel tank? I wouldn't have to activate it, just unlock it."

"Well it's certainly big enough," said Cochran. "And we were supposed to dump the actual propellant tank after we emptied it. Julie, can the entire rig be pulled out of the bay?"

"Yes, and I do have an RMS program for it."

"All right, deploy the tank. We can get that out faster than the Fleet Com."

"Roger. Loading RMS program five," said Harrison, turning the program select knob. "Stand by for computer operation."

The moment she hit the auto sequence proceed toggle, the remote arm lifted off its catches and started to perform its complex ballet of computer-directed movements. It rotated and maneuvered until its end effector

281

was dropping over the grapple pin on the cargo bay fuel tank. When the control panel indicated it had a capture, Harrison halted it long enough for Vachet to unlock its pallet latches.

When she tapped the software stop button again, the arm resumed its operation, lifting the multi-ton payload from the bay. The program ended its run with the fuel tank sitting twenty feet below the inverted shuttle at the end of the partially extended arm.

"Mount Cheyenne, we're ready to position the decoy for release," Cochran reported. "And we need some help doing it."

"Switching RMS to manual control," said Harrison, activating her hand grips. "Standing by for instructions."

"*Phoenix*, this is Mount Cheyenne," said Rosen. "Reposition decoy to port side of orbiter and angle it twenty-five degrees past your vertical. That should clear your rudder."

"Instructions understood, I'm moving the rig."

Harrison activated the remote arm's elbow joint and, using the rotational hand grip, swung the raised portion of the arm until the tank had moved from over the open cargo bay to above the spaceplane's port wing.

"*Phoenix*, this is Mount Cheyenne. Depress decoy until it's parallel with the orbiter's x-axis. Move the arm's active section backwards by at least thirty degrees. When you release the decoy, move the section forward as you open the end effector."

With the wrist control, Harrison tilted the fuel tank rig from its vertical position until it was facing directly aft, along the shuttle's x-axis. She retracted the raised portion to the point where the rig could be seen through the skylights. In its release position, the remote arm formed a truncated Z.

"Mount Cheyenne, this is *Phoenix*," said Cochran. "We're ready for release. Do you have any further instructions?"

"Negative, *Phoenix*. Just stand by for a countdown.

282

The lone wolf is now 350 miles behind you and closing. What's your decoy? It certainly is big."

"The cargo bay tank and its refueling rig."

"That's going to make one hell of a flash when it goes up. Standby. T minus ten seconds. Nine. Eight. Seven . . ."

While the flight deck team repeated the countdown, Harrison was the only one to do any work. She grabbed the translation control grip and held her fingers over the "derigid" and "open" buttons. At two seconds she pushed the grip forward. At one second she tapped the "derigid" button and the tank's payload grapple was pushed to the front of the effector. At zero seconds she hit the "open" button. The capture wires sprang back from the payload grapple, freeing the tank.

The extra push it received from the remote arm sent the decoy sailing past the orbiter's tail. In moments it was no more than an oddly-shaped blip silhouetted by the sun's glare. With nothing left to do, Harrison returned the remote arm to its stowed position on the cargo bay's port side.

"I think I have this activation sequence correct," said Vachet, watching the status lights which had frustrated him earlier come on in the right sequence. "Not that it matters."

"*Phoenix*, this is Mount Cheyenne. Your decoy is tracking properly. It'll close to proximity range in fifteen minutes."

"Thanks, Bernie. Give us distance readings every minute until the last five minutes," Cochran requested. "Then give us the readings every thirty seconds."

"Will do, Ed. Keep the channel open."

As ordered, the minutes were marked off by Rosen giving the distances between the fuel tank and the closing ASAT. Most of those on the middle deck came topside to watch the interception, and even Grachenko joined them. At the five minute mark, tension started to rise as Rosen switched to giving the distance every thirty seconds. At the one minute mark, he decided on his own to change the reading intervals to every ten seconds.

"T minus twenty seconds and the distance to target is three miles," said Rosen.

"Jack, how much fuel was left in the rig?" Cochran asked.

"About a third," said Ripley. "Maybe thirty-five percent."

"Bernie's right. It's going to be one hell of a flash."

"T minus ten seconds and distance is one point six miles."

"Will we need to wear sunglasses?" Grachenko inquired.

"Not if you want a good view of the intercept," said Ripley. "It should happen right behind the tail fin."

"The countdown has ended," said Rosen. "And the decoy is within radar proximity fuse range."

The crew held their breath as they waited for both the explosion and confirmation of the Hydra's destruction by Space Defence Command. After several seconds, the response they finally got from Rosen was not what they had expected, or wanted.

"*Phoenix*, it didn't work," he warned, his voice suddenly grave. "Your decoy passed well within proximity fuse distance but didn't trigger the ASAT. Distance between you and the Hydra is down to 150 miles."

"Shit, what the hell went wrong?" Cochran demanded. "We did everything just like we did before. Have these weapons grown smarter since the last time?"

"Perhaps the Hydra isn't radar guided," said Grachenko. "Perhaps it's infrared. If it were, it would ignore your decoy. While large, it was a poor heat source."

"Bernie, could this weapon be infrared instead of radar guided? One of our guests just made the suggestion."

"That would explain things better," said Rosen. "But it ruins any evasion maneuvers. To change orbit or increase speed requires an engine burn, which only makes you a better target."

284

"Then it's back to plan one," said Cochran. "Julie, Renée, power up number four Fleet Com. Sorry, Paul, but I have to go with those who are most experienced."

"I understand. I would do the same in your position," Vachet explained. "We'll give the women room to work."

Moving over the floor hatch, Vachet led Pellerin, Ripley and Grachenko back to the mid deck. In moments Harrison and Simon had enough room on the flight deck to resume their procedures, which they ran through with an urgency more feverish than before.

"Main and auxiliary power on line," said Simon, running her hand down the same line of buttons which had frustrated Vachet. "Do I have enough time to test the systems?"

"Yes, but not much," said Cochran. "I want the interception to occur as far behind us as possible."

"Selecting program four," Harrison reported. "Returning RMS to computer operation."

Once again, the remote arm was gliding under GPC control. Its end effector dropped toward one of the last two payloads in the cargo bay. With the removal of the Fleet Com, only the Orbital Pharmaceutical Factory would be left. The space that had been filled to capacity on lift-off was now almost empty.

"Spin table detached from satellite body," said Simon, finishing her status board check. "All systems on line, we have no failures. Proceed with extraction, Julie."

This time Harrison didn't stop the programmed sequence either before or after the system recorded a successful capture. The remote arm itself halted for only a moment to allow its gearing and motors to reset themselves for reverse operations, then smoothly extracted the Fleet Com. The program ended with the satellite perched under a slender, fifty-foot tall pole.

"Changing RMS to manual control," said Harrison, taking hold of the hand controller grips. "How much time do we have left?"

"Ten or twelve minutes," Cochran answered. "Distance is down to 100 miles."

Harrison again performed the instructions Rosen had given earlier, rapidly switching from one RMS system to another and working the hand grips so hard she shifted against the mission specialist seat she'd been using to brace herself.

"Somebody catch me, I'm starting to slip," said Harrison as she felt herself beginning to float free.

This time it was Simon who turned and caught Harrison by her shoulder, pushing her back down while she kept her hands on the controller grips and continued to operate the remote arm. A minute later Harrison had the arm back in its Z-shaped release position and the Fleet Com facing directly aft.

"My God, I can see it," said Simon. "Julie, hurry up."

Just above the starboard OMS pod hung a tiny black disc, the Hydra, silhouetted by the sun's glare. Harrison looked at it for only a moment before she again activated the translation controller and held her fingers over the end effector buttons.

"Ed, advise Mount Cheyenne that decoy number two is away," Harrison ordered, pushing the controller forward.

Once more the remote arm pivoted towards the tail of the *Phoenix* and the Fleet Com was released. Simon let go of Harrison and returned to her station. Control of the decoy had passed to her, and she immediately ran into the same problem Harrison had faced. To work the satellite's joystick, Simon had to use both hands, but the moment she did she started to rise off the floor.

"I'm going to need help or I'll float away," she warned.

Simon felt a pair of hands grab her ankles and force her back onto the deck. When she turned she found Grachenko lying partway out of the floor hatch and holding her down.

"Hurry, please," he said. "Ripley is holding me from the other deck and it's very painful."

286

"Renée, Mount Cheyenne is tracking both the Hydra and the Fleet Com," said Cochran. "The Hydra is seventy-five miles and closing. The Fleet Com is at one point nine miles. At current closure rates, they'll meet in seven minutes."

"I'll give the decoy's speed a slight kick. Here goes."

Simon pushed one of the joysticks and the aft thrusters on the satellite fired, increasing its departure rate from the *Phoenix*. At the end of the burn, its speed had increased tenfold and it was attracting the attention of the pursuing ASAT.

"The Hydra is deviating and picking up velocity," said Rosen, moments after the burn had concluded. "It appears to be torn between going after the decoy and continuing after you."

"Sounds like it only goes for the decoy when the thrusters are firing," said Cochran.

"You got it, *Phoenix*. Can you keep firing them for the next six and a half minutes?"

"Tell your friend I have ways to keep the satellite hot," Simon answered. "I'm going to initiate rotation."

By working both joysticks, Simon fired the satellite's lateral thrusters to start it spinning. After it had built up a measurable level of centrifugal force, she flipped it and the Fleet Com was flying tail-first. All the while the Hydra kept deviating toward it, until the maneuvers ended, and the *Phoenix* once again drew the weapon's attention.

"Two minutes to interception," said Rosen, his countdown reports coming every fifteen seconds.

"Simon, how's the Fleet Com's fuel state?" asked Cochran.

"Down to twenty-three percent," she said. "But there's another way to keep it hot. Main engine ignition, enabled."

The moment the system indicated it was ready, Simon fired the satellite's main engine. Used to change the Fleet Com's orbit, it was fueled by a different set of propellant tanks than the thrusters. And the exhaust jet the main engine produced was far hotter than anything the thrusters could emit. It proved an irresistible attraction for the approaching Hydra.

"*Phoenix*, ASAT deviation and velocity are increasing," said Rosen. "It's taking the bait. Time to intercept, ten seconds."

The engine burn had slowed the Fleet Com to a halt and was beginning to accelerate it in the opposite direction when the conical-tipped anti-satellite weapon closed to proximity fuse range. It disappeared in a sharp flash which even illuminated the flight deck of the distant shuttle. Its expanding cloud of flames and shrapnel overtook the Fleet Com. A moment later a fireball erupted out of the sun's glare behind the *Phoenix*.

For the moment it was out of danger. But the shuttle was still no safer than when it had started its latest reentry attempt. And given the dwindling supplies of propellants, water, and oxygen, the *Phoenix* now faced yet another threat. Its remaining time in orbit was limited. The longer it stayed, the more it risked becoming the most expensive and tragic derelict in the history of voyaging.

"I just received your summons, Marshal. What news do you have?" said Jurkov, as he entered Suvorov's office.

"I had a phone call from one of my Politburo allies, perhaps my last ally," Suvorov replied. "He gave me some very unsettling news. It appears as though our enemies have succeeded in convincing the premier to reverse his launch orders."

"Which enemies? You mean the Americans?"

"No, Jurkov. Though they certainly helped. The appeasers, Foreign Minister Grachenko and Konstantin Fedarenko, have won, and it appears that Nagorny has joined their ranks."

"But Marshal, I thought he was your friend?" said Jurkov, taking a seat in front of Suvorov's desk.

"He has forgotten what it's like to be a soldier defending our motherland." The tone in Suvorov's voice was sour and the expression on his face was by turns angry and depressed. "He's become a political animal. And a traitor! I have no doubt that Nagorny and Premier Gussarov will remove me from my command. Before they do it, there's much for us to do."

"But what else can we do? Destroying the codes for the Hydras should be enough."

"I want to ensure that the American shuttle will never land, and I fear the Hydras will not be enough. The Americans are the perfect enemy, resourceful, deceptive, and I'm certain they will find a way to elude our weapons. Which means I must plan to destroy the shuttle when it's in the atmosphere."

"That would be easy to do, Marshal, if the vehicle were to land at Baikonur."

"Don't irritate me, Jurkov!" Suvorov said angrily. "Of course, I command one of the largest air forces in the world, but it's entirely based within the confines of the Soviet Union. Except in one area . . . Yes, I see you understand."

"The overseas military missions," said Jurkov. "How simple. Most of their air staffs are from our service, not the tactical air force. It's ingenious."

"I'm glad you think so. There are many people I must contact, General. For the time I have left in my command, I can't be concerned with my normal duties."

"I understand. I'll be honored to assume your watch. Whom will you be talking to?"

"I'll contact the air defence commanders of the overseas missions," Suvorov answered. "Especially of the missions in Cuba, Vietnam, and elsewhere. I have many friends there. They still understand what it means to be patriots, and they have the latitude to act without Moscow's approval."

Chapter Seventeen

"Command One to staff, we're at T minus ten minutes to ASAT destruction," Rosen told his operations center. "Keep monitoring your surveillance systems. Let me know if the condition of any of the Hydra warheads changes."

"I still can't believe it. The Soviets have admitted to their mistake and will destroy the remaining weapons," said Mary Widmark, as she watched the flashing tracks on the main screen.

"I'll believe it when I see it," Ericson countered. "This is only an agreement among gentlemen. Nothing's been signed or written down. We're just taking their word, and even after all these years of glasnost, I still don't trust the Russians."

"Larry, please. Even I think a little optimism is called for," said Rosen. "Ten years ago, what's happening would've been unthinkable. The Soviets have admitted they made a mistake and we haven't been forced to make any concessions. This has been remarkable, and it will culminate in just over eight minutes. Command One to Operations, give me an update on interceptor force status and availability."

Rosen turned his attention back to the main screen, where the pairs of airborne F-15s were encircled as the intercept control officer reported on their conditions. There were far fewer aircraft aloft than there had been earlier. Both planes and pilots were becoming worn out, and many had landed at air bases along the east and west coasts of North America. After advising on the status of the airborne fighters, their control officer described the condition of those on the ground.

"And the last pair to stand-down landed at Ramey Air Force Base in Puerto Rico twenty minutes ago," he concluded. "Are there any pairs you'd wish to order back into the air first?"

"No, just put them all on standby alert," said Rosen. "T minus three minutes to ASAT destruction. Command One to ELINT Control, has there been any increase in signals traffic from Voyska PVO headquarters to their relay satellites?"

"Not yet, sir," said the electronic intelligence officer.

"Strange. Ask Fort Mead if they're hearing anything. They've got more ELINT capability than we do and theirs are better."

"Something's beginning to smell here," Ericson grumbled. "There should be a buildup in traffic."

"Perhaps what you're smelling is yourself," said Widmark. "You haven't had a shower in the last three days."

"Watch it, Captain. Or your next assignment will be Elmendorf."

"All right you two, save it for later," Rosen finally ordered. "T minus two minutes to ASAT destruction. Command One to Communications, are all outside lines still clear?"

"Yes, General. We have lines to Houston, Toulouse, the Pentagon, and Omaha," said the communications officer.

"Good. Pipe anything from them straight to me. Command One to ELINT Control, any response from Fort Mead?"

"My team's just getting something from them now, sir," was the immediate reply. Then the line fell silent for several moments until the message from the National Security Agency had been completed. "The NSA says the secure uplink facilities at PVO headquarters haven't even been activated. There is considerable radio traffic between the headquarters and Moscow, all of it scrambled and most of it voice transmissions."

"Something's up, and I hope to God it's not what I think it is," said Rosen. "Stay on it, ELINT Control."

"What do you think could be happening?" Mary asked.

"Marshal Suvorov is a well-known hardliner, and he may be trying to sabotage the agreement. Command One to staff, T minus one minute to ASAT destruction. Let's look alive. If anything's going to happen it'll happen soon."

Briefly, the noise level in the center rose as the various teams advised the stations and bases they were tied to that less than a minute remained in the countdown. Afterwards it fell to near-normal levels, then dropped almost to silence as the final seconds ticked off. Above the hum and clacking of machinery the only human sound was a murmur from the personnel reciting the count. When it reached zero, the building tension did not evaporate as it normally would have, mostly because nothing happened on either the main screen or the side panels.

"Command One to staff. Report immediately on any changes to the ASATs," Rosen urged, before he turned to Ericson and Mary. "I'm glad I didn't take you up on your wager. It would be bad form for a general to be seen paying off a colonel."

"I suppose you're happy that something has gone wrong," said Widmark, turning to Ericson as well.

"No, I'm not," he said. "I would've had more fun if I could've just sat back and watched the fireworks."

"Command One, this is ELINT Control. We've got some activity at PVO headquarters. The uplink facilities are operating and there's a heavy data flow to the relay satellites."

"Thanks, ELINT Control," said Rosen. "Stay on it."

"But there's still no change in the Hydras, General," Widmark added, checking the main screen. "Spacetrack doesn't show it. Nor do the radar nets or the early-warning satellites."

"Command One, this is Communications. We have a priority call from the Pentagon."

"Put it on line two. Let's see if they're as much in the dark as we are," said Rosen as he picked up the telephone receiver and pressed one of the panel buttons. After identifying himself, he fell silent while the caller filled him in on the situation from Washington's end. Rosen kept his comments to a few affirmative noises and an occasional "I see." He glanced at the main screen repeatedly, hoping to see change in the orbiting Hydras, but there were none. At the end of the conversation, Rosen informed the caller of their current status and promised to keep his command on alert.

"Well, General, does somebody there know what's happening?" asked Ericson.

"No more than we do, and they've got NASA, the State Department, and the White House demanding answers. They think it's similar to what I said, some form of military dissension, or even a revolt. The hot line is heating up, and NASA will have to go back to finding an alternate landing site."

"And what are we supposed to do?" Widmark asked.

"We'll keep as many interceptors in the air as we can and help NASA find a landing site for the *Phoenix*. I hope they'll use the information we and Toulouse gave them."

"Reiss, this may be the one time I'm glad to see you in here," said Reynolds the moment the main doors opened and the director of Manned Flight Operations entered the astronauts' lounge. "Can you tell us why the Hydras haven't been destroyed?"

"How did you know about it so soon? The grapevine?" Reiss asked, caught off guard by the question.

"Not quite. There was a special report on TV a few minutes ago," said Harrison. "The reporter wasn't too specific, but she did say that the agreed deadline has passed and there has been no apparent resolution to the catastrophe in orbit."

"Well, they're right. For some reason the Soviets aren't living up to the agreement they proposed in the first place. The White House and State Department can argue with them about it, but what we've got to do is reestablish our advisory group. We have to bring the *Phoenix* down, and quickly. Remember what Life Sciences told us. With a forty percent increase in its crew size, the orbiter is consuming its oxygen at a faster-than-normal rate. It has only twenty-one hours of breathable atmosphere left. OMS and APU fuel states are low, and they're even running out of lithium hydroxide."

"What about the astronauts in Houston? Will they be working on the same problem as us?"

"No, they'll continue to work on reentry programs should the Russians actually destroy the Hydras," said Reiss as he started handing out folders of landing site information to the astronauts currently occupying the lounge. "We must work on the assumption that the Russians either cannot, or will not, destroy the Hydras. Now I want all of you to report back to the briefing room at the launch center. The rest of the advisory group will join us there."

"If you want the best alternate landing site we don't have to wade through this again," Reynolds observed, giving the folder he was handed a cursory glance. "We figured it out the first time. It's what the French told us. Kourou."

"Out of the question, Reynolds. I told you before: Kourou isn't acceptable. Its landing facilities are sparse and it has no qualified personnel. Ascension is a better choice. Wideawake Field has a longer runway."

"Just barely, and there's a rise in the middle of it. At least the one at Kourou is flat."

"Look, mister, this isn't the place to argue about it. We're all going back to the briefing room at the launch center."

"No, this is the place to argue about it," said Harrison, stepping forward and motioning to the rest of the astronauts in the lounge to join in. "This *is* the place to decide. As you just mentioned, the crew only has twenty-one hours left. We decide on the emergency site now, and the truth is Kourou's being rejected on political grounds, not for technical reasons."

"That's not true. Kourou would be dangerous for the orbiter to land at," Reiss insisted, his anger giving way to nervousness as the other astronauts gathered around Harrison and Reynolds. "Walter Post has never flown any simulations of it."

"Paul Vachet has flown computer simulations of Kourou," said Reynolds. "And you know it."

"You can't be serious. Would you trust him with the lives of your friends? It's out of the question. Bradford, would you trust some poet who fucks up a satellite launch with your wife?"

"Yes, I would," Harrison answered firmly. "Paul's trained to be a shuttle pilot, not a mission specialist. I trust him. He was his country's top test pilot."

"Well, it won't happen," said Reiss. "NASA won't let an amateur fly the *Phoenix* and it won't approve Kourou as the landing site."

"Well we're not going to rubber stamp the Ascension landing," spat Harrison. "You're forgetting something, Reiss. If NASA won't let an 'amateur' fly the *Phoenix* and land it at Kourou, there's another organization that will. The CNES controlled the rescue operation and they could just as easily land the orbiter. All we'd have to do is let my wife and our friends know and they'll do the rest. Face it, mister, you're outnumbered and there isn't a damn thing you can do to stop us."

Harrison motioned again as he spoke and the assembled astronauts formed a circle around Reiss. The director started to say something, but the threat caught in his throat as the circle was closed. Whatever defiance Reiss still had in him evaporated when the astronauts all took one step toward him; it was the only intimidating move they needed to make.

"As Cochran would say, the bullshit and politics ends right here and now," said Reynolds. "We'll do just what you ordered, George. We'll all go to the launch center's briefing room, and we'll make the formal decision on Kourou. We'll either make it with you or without you. Which will it be?"

"Nikolai Grigorivich, I see it's the three of us again," Nagorny remarked, when he entered Grachenko's office and found both the foreign minister and the director of Glavkosmos waiting for him. "I only wish the circumstances were better."

Nagorny didn't wait for his friend to offer him a seat but walked over to the office couch and dropped into it. He didn't take his greatcoat off, in spite of the fact that it was covered with melting snow. He merely removed his cap and tossed it wearily onto the table in front of him.

"Yes, have you noticed how this confrontation has taken on an ironic symmetry?" said Grachenko. "At first we didn't believe the Allies when their shuttle crew rescued our cosmonauts. Now they don't believe us. They don't believe we are unable to destroy the anti-satellite weapons still in orbit."

"When are the ambassadors due to arrive?" Fedarenko asked, checking his watch.

"The French and American ambassadors will be here in another forty minutes. And the British ambassador will also attend our meeting. It's likely the British will join the French and Americans in placing their strategic forces on alert."

"This is a nightmare," said Nagorny. "A nightmare all of us in the army hoped we would never face. The West can deploy its strategic nuclear weapons faster than we can. The latest intelligence shows the Americans are putting three more missile subs at sea, and only one French missile submarine was spotted remaining in port. Their bombers are dispersing; we cannot locate two-thirds of America's B-1s. If they and the French were to launch a strike, my staff estimates they could use seventy

296

percent of their warheads. By comparison, we'd be lucky to use half of ours."

"Would it really come to that?" Fedarenko asked, his voice hushed and the color draining from his face.

"It could, my friend," said Grachenko. "Remember, we fired our most sophisticated weapons at their shuttle, a spacecraft on the first rescue mission in history. We then agreed to destroy those weapons, but failed to live up to it. On the face of these matters, we've done everything reactionary American politics accuses us of: initiating provocative military actions, failing to abide by agreements and treaties, hiding behind a wall of propaganda when the truth is self-evident. When the ambassadors arrive, I expect we'll hear it all."

"Yes, and in spite of what they might accuse us of, it's imperative that we work constructively with them. Marshal, what are you doing to destroy the Hydras?"

"For the last hour and a half we've been transmitting both flight command codes and strategic weapon self-destruct codes," said Nagorny. "So far, the weapons have ignored them all. Suvorov knew what he was doing. Our central code files are criminally out-of-date. Somewhere in them are the correct codes, and what we have to do is transmit all of them."

"And how long will this take?" Grachenko requested.

"All will be sent in another thirty-four hours."

"I see. And, Doctor, how much time does the American shuttle have left in orbit?"

"According to the information NASA supplied me, the shuttle can remain in orbit for another twenty hours," said Fedarenko, checking his wristwatch again.

"The Americans are lying to you," said Nagorny. "The shuttle's original mission was to last for two more days."

"No, they're not. The original mission time was estimated for a crew of seven. They now have ten, and they've done more EVA work than was expected. I have no reason to doubt the NASA figures."

"This puts the Americans in a desperate situation,"

297

said Grachenko. "Perhaps they'll be willing to accept our proposal."

"What proposal is this? What have you two planned?" Nagorny asked, his interest stirring.

"When the ambassadors arrive, I will propose to have the *Phoenix* land at Baikonur." Fedarenko lifted his attaché case onto his lap and opened it. This time, he hadn't memorized all the reports and studies he carried with him. Most had only recently been transmitted from Baikonur, and it would have taken him hours to read them. "Our shuttle landing facilities are the only operational facilities in the world not rendered useless by the Hydras. These are the complete programs NASA will need to land their shuttle at Baikonur. The favorable reentry window will occur in thirteen hours. Here, look if you wish."

Nagorny struggled off the couch and walked over to Fedarenko, where he selected one of the folders from his attaché case. For a few moments Nagorny scanned the contents silently, before he started making remarks.

"You translated this to English," he said. "It's difficult for me to read. Some of this looks classified. Is it?"

"Of course it is," Grachenko answered. "The plan to land the shuttle requires that a lot of classified information be released. We must be willing to give it to the Americans if we're to be seen as sincere. What do you think of our offer?"

"It's too dangerous," said Nagorny. "I would not make it."

"Somehow, I knew that's what you would say," said Fedarenko, his bitterness starting to show yet again. "Above all other factors, state security comes first."

"Stop trying to guess what or how I think, Doctor. My reasons are more than just state security. I'm also thinking about the safety of the American shuttle, its international crew, and our cosmonauts. Before I came here, I learned something very disturbing. For more than two hours prior to his arrest, Suvorov was in his office making a series of phone calls. He used KGB lines, so we in the army can't trace where he called. But I have my suspicions as to whom he called and why."

"Even with his arrest, Suvorov is still dangerous," said Grachenko. "Tell us your thoughts, my friend."

"Suvorov had the second largest air force in the army at his command," Nagorny started. "More than 3,000 fighters, more than 10,000 missile launchers. And Suvorov had strong contacts with the district, army, and corps commanders in the Air Defence Forces. I suspect he may have told them to complete what he started, destroying the shuttle if at all possible. Should it land anywhere near our territory, Air Defence may have a reach long enough to intercept it. If it lands inside our territory, they will certainly be able to do so."

"This puts us in a considerable dilemma," said Grachenko. The smile had disappeared from his face and his sense of accomplishment over the offer he had worked on was gone. "If we make a humanitarian gesture, we could be sealing the fate of that spacecraft and everyone aboard it. Has Suvorov told your people anything about whom he talked to?"

"No, both he and his deputy have refused to say anything about his conversations," said Nagorny, handing the folder he had been studying back to Fedarenko. When it wasn't accepted, he let it drop into his attaché case.

"I'm sorry, Marshal," Fedarenko apologized when he realized he had not accepted the folder. "This destroys everything. If the Americans take our offer, and the shuttle is destroyed by our own aircraft, that could start the nuclear war you warned us about. What can we do now? What do we say to the ambassadors?"

"Whatever we say, or offer, we had better decide on it soon," said Grachenko. "We have less than a half hour before they arrive. We don't have enough time to consult the Politburo, or Gussarov. My friends, what do we decide?"

"*Phoenix*, this is Houston. Our studies have been completed, and the diplomatic meeting has ended in Moscow," Tom Selisky remarked. "We have several options for you. I suggest you get one of your guests topside. They'll want to hear this as well."

"Roger, CAP COM. Stand by on your landing advisory list until we get one here," said Cochran, who then looked over his right shoulder. "Saint Ex, find out which of the cosmonauts has finished eating. Especially if it's Arkady."

"I think he might be done," said Vachet. "Or will be."

After acknowledging his orders, Vachet briefly disappeared through the floor hatch. He ascended to the middle deck instead of descending to it; with the *Phoenix* still flying on its back, the middle deck was now the higher of the two compartments. In the zero gravity of space the reorientation meant little to the crew, except that they could now view the Earth through the skylight windows. A few seconds later, Vachet reappeared on the flight deck with Grachenko, eating the granola bars from his lunch, in tow. Once he had arrived, Cochran asked for the advisory list to be read.

"Wideawake Field on Ascension Island is favored by NASA management," said Selisky. "The CNES spaceport at Kourou, French Guiana isn't covered by the Hydra web and is another possibility. And so is Baikonur, which the Russians have offered. Ascension reentry will be coming up in seven hours. Baikonur will be in eleven and Kourou in sixteen."

"Good God, I never thought about Baikonur, or Kourou. Paul, what's the field like at Kourou?"

"It's a ten thousand foot runway with a paved, thousand foot overrun at either end," Vachet answered.

"It has all the normal air traffic control facilities. However, its microwave landing system isn't compatible with that of this ship, and it has none of the specialized equipment or facilities for post-flight handling of a shuttle. They would have to do a lot of improvising."

"There would be no need for improvising at Baikonur," said Grachenko. "The quality of our orbiter facilities is second only to yours. And since the reentry window is coming up sooner, Baikonur would be the best choice."

"As good as it is, I wouldn't take the offer, boss," Post warned, turning in his seat so he could see the men hovering behind him. "Remember, the astronaut return treaty wasn't renewed back in 1990. If we were to land at Baikonur, your country would be under no obligation to return either us or this ship."

"Yes, but it wouldn't be as tricky to land at as Ascension," said Cochran. "And it's five hours ahead of Kourou. Remember, Walt, we only have eighteen hours of oxygen left. And we're running low on propellants for the OMS and APU systems. Saint Ex, have you ever been to Kourou?"

"Yes, several times over the years," said Vachet. "Kourou is very similar to Canaveral. It's sited on tropical lowlands, near the ocean. The *Hermes* aerodynamic prototype is at Kourou, and is flying a series of test landings. Because of my preparations for this mission, I was unable to participate in it. However, I did fly computer simulations of Kourou."

"Excellent. Neither Walt or I have ever flown simulations of Kourou. You would make the best pilot, and I think Kourou is close enough to North America for Bernie's F-15s to cover us."

"But Commander, an earlier return would benefit all of us," Grachenko advised, making one last attempt to persuade Cochran. "Landing at Baikonur would especially benefit Vassili. His temperature is rising, probably the result of an infection arising from his broken arm."

"So we're back to 'commander' are we? Well, you're

right," said Cochran. "I am the commander, and more important, this is my lady. If I had to leave her behind somewhere, I wouldn't like it. You, Paul, NASA management, and everyone else can advise me, but I make the final decision. And right here and now I say it's Kourou, and Saint Ex will fly my lady."

"Looks like I'll be an observer this time," said Post, trying to cover his wounded pride. "You think NASA will go along with your decision? Ascension was management's choice."

"By now they should know better than to disagree with one of my decisions," Cochran replied, almost purring his response. "And if they want to be pricks about it, I'm sure we can convince Daurat to help us."

"It was probably he who originated the idea to use Kourou," said Vachet. "I'm honored that you have the confidence to elect me to pilot your ship. However, sixteen hours is a long time to wait, and Kostilev's condition is bad. Mr. Siprinoff thinks the infection is being caused by bone marrow leaking into Kostilev's bloodstream. It's a situation which only happens in zero gravity, and it's bound to get worse."

"Then increase his antibiotic doses. My decision remains firm, we're going for Kourou. Paul knows the field and he's pilot-qualified on this ship. Even if Baikonur were the better choice, your country's record over the last few days doesn't exactly encourage one's trust. I'm sorry, Arkady, but the decision stands. Kourou is the safest place on earth for my crew and my lady. CAP COM, this is *Phoenix*. The decision has been made. Get everything in gear for Kourou. Will you advise Toulouse and Mount Cheyenne or shall I?"

"Colonel Lobachev, you're late," said Major General Victor Khlabistov, when the doors to the briefing room opened and the Air Defence Force officer quickly slipped inside. "Had I not warned the guards about you, they

302

wouldn't have allowed you in."

"Sorry, General. But I was waiting for some last minute information," Lobachev apologized, taking the only empty seat at the room's main table. "General, why do I only see PVO and KGB officers present? I see no one from the naval staff, tactical air force, or army. Why is this so?"

"Because these are the only people we can trust. A few hours ago I received a call from Marshal Suvorov. He has entrusted to us, and to the PVO staffs in other overseas missions, an important operation. One that will resolve our disaster in space to our country's benefit. Its outline is in the report before you."

In front of everyone at the table was a plain folder, which Lobachev joined the others in reading as he took his seat. For the next several minutes, the briefing room was relatively silent as the KGB and PVO officers Khlabistov had ordered to the meeting read through their copies of the report and studied the maps and charts with it. One of the first to finish reading, and the first to speak, was the commanding general of the KGB staff in Havana.

"Marshal Suvorov is ordering us to do a very provocative act," he said. "He's fortunate the aircraft and missile batteries we may be using wear Cuban markings."

"Also Nicaraguan and Surinamese markings," Khlabistov added. "We don't know where the American shuttle will land, but if it attempts to land in Florida, the Panama Canal Zone, or French Guiana, we'll have the missiles and aircraft to destroy it. Colonel, since you were so concerned about obtaining the latest information, show us the status of your squadrons."

Lobachev rose and walked over to the wall map the general had motioned to. The island of Cuba was laid out in exacting detail, all its military bases shown and to what degree they were under Soviet control indicated. Though they had the largest armed forces in the Caribbean, the Cubans were not in sole command of a single base inside

303

their own country.

"Two flights from the First Squadron are quartered at San Julian," said Lobachev, pointing to the air base just outside of Havana. "And the third flight is on temporary duty at Cienfuegos Bay. All three flights of the Second Squadron are based at Mayari, at the opposite end of the island. However, they can be easily dispersed to other Air Defence fields. The remaining squadrons in our command are equipped with MIG-21s, useless for the long-range missions we'll be doing."

"Do you have enough pilots in both squadrons to man the planes?" asked another KGB official.

"Yes, we duplicate the Cuban staffs in the MIG-23 squadrons. It's not the same with the others. General, I believe it's possible for a few aircraft to penetrate American airspace as far north as Canaveral. But there's another way we can work to destroy the shuttle. We all watched the F-15s perform their satellite interceptions over the Gulf. By interfering with them, we can ensure that the Hydra weapons do their job."

"A good idea, Colonel. Look into it," said Khlabistov. "Colonel Chuykov, what's the distribution of forces in Nicaragua and Surinam?"

"We only have surface-to-air missiles in Nicaragua," said another Air Defence Force colonel. "However, some of them have enough range to destroy the shuttle if it attempts to land at the Canal Zone air bases. In Surinam, the missiles we have lack the range. But we do have a squadron of Hind gunship helicopters. As the KGB will confirm, its commander has been most cooperative with us."

"Excellent, Colonel. Gennadi, since we can't trust the rest of the military or the GRU, can we look to you for communications and security?" asked Khlabistov.

"No one dares question what we send on our communication channels," said the senior KGB official. "As for security, I can have teams at your bases within the hour."

"Thank you, Gennadi. The air bases Lobachev mentioned and our radar stations will need your protection. Comrades, if there are no further questions, I suggest we go to work. Lobachev, I know you'll want to be with your men at San Julian. The duties Marshal Suvorov tried to carry out have passed to us. With his arrest, we're the last patriots our country can rely on."

"The Americans turned our offer down, didn't they?" Ryumin asked, after Sakolov lowered the telephone receiver and dropped it back on its cradle. The long-awaited call from Fedarenko was at an end.

"You can order the field crews and other teams to stop working up for a landing," said Sakolov, nodding slowly in agreement. "After all these hours of sitting back helplessly, at last I thought we could get back in and help."

"Looking at it from their side, I can understand why they would turn down our offer. Our failure to destroy the Hydra weapons—our launching them in the first place—doesn't generate much trust. What did Fedarenko tell you?"

"Not only did both governments turn down the offer, so did the American and French astronauts. I can't understand what they could choose instead of us. All American fields that can take the shuttle are covered by our weapons."

"I know where they could land the *Phoenix*," said Ryumin, turning to his center's main screen, where the tracks of the shuttle and surviving Hydras crisscrossed the world map. "If you would only think beyond our country and the United States, you would see it. I saw it in the first study I did."

"Anatoly, please don't play mind games with me . . . France!" The realization made Sakolov stiffen. His dour expression brightened and he glanced at the main screen. "France, of course. They have runways at both Istres

305

and Kourou."

"Istres is too dangerous. Malyshev and I discovered that doing the studies. Kourou, however, would be perfect."

"When do you think the shuttle could reenter?"

"Our computers don't have the data base to make such projections," said Ryumin. "Though Malyshev thinks it can reenter in thirteen or fourteen hours."

"I see, I see. Anatoly, who else knows this?"

"Beyond my deputy, just the members of my command console team. Do you think we should tell Moscow about our discovery?"

"No," Sakolov ordered, after thinking out his decision. "If NASA and its astronauts have decided not to tell Moscow, then perhaps we shouldn't either. After all, the lives of our friends depend on what NASA does. Not even Fedarenko is to know what we've discovered."

Chapter Eighteen

"Houston, this is Mount Cheyenne. Our latest projections are ready," said Rosen, his console screen filling with the information Widmark was transferring from her computer. "The *Phoenix* will be out of danger for the rest of its time in orbit."

"Thanks, General. Looks like we were getting worried over nothing," Bill Corrigan answered, his sigh of relief as audible as his words.

"I understand why you'd be nervous. In the last few days, so much has gone wrong it seems a miracle when anything goes right. Bill, what's the current situation on the *Phoenix*?"

"Right now Post is relieving Harrison as orbiter watch officer. They're the only two people awake on the

306

Phoenix. We're carefully monitoring their fuel and life support; we hope they don't run out of either before we get them down."

"Your problems are getting more serious," said Rosen. "But we'll try to get rid of a few of them. My forces will begin their deception maneuvers soon, which should draw a little Soviet attention. Keep us informed, Bill. Mount Cheyenne, out."

Rosen placed the telephone receiver back on its cradle, then surveyed his staff. Since he had returned to his center they had been operating at a low level of activity. On the main screen, the same number of Hydra tracks still crossed the map, as did the shuttle's track. The number of airborne F-15s was down dramatically over the time of their initial deployment, but the seeming letup was deceptive. The center was waiting, quietly preparing for the coming rush of operations. A storm was brewing, and the countdown clock had already been started.

"General, I have the Soviet update ready," said Ericson, stepping up to the command console.

"Good, let's hear it," said Rosen. "Mary, coordinate display control with Larry's update."

It took a few moments for Widmark to contact display control and arrange for what Rosen had requested. Only after she had indicated that display control was ready did Ericson begin to read.

"In Cuba, the MIG-23 squadron at Mayari has dispersed," he said. "The Navy listening post at Guantànamo Bay says the fighters headed west, landing at Moròn, Santa Clara, and Varadero. The MIG-23s at San Julian and Cienfuegos Bay have remained in place, but they're on alert as well. There's no change with Cuba's air defence missile batteries, though their radar stations are quite busy. They're actively tracking even regular airline flights and our patrol planes.

"In Nicaragua, both radar stations and missile sites are on alert. The stations are tracking all aircraft going in

307

and out of Panama, and their SAM-4s could intercept the shuttle were it to land at the Canal Zone airfields. As for Surinam, the French report the MIG-21s based there haven't flown for at least ten hours. The only SAM batteries are around the capital, and their SAM-2s don't have the range or altitude to hit anything landing at Kourou."

As Ericson read from his update sheets, Widmark notified display control to illuminate the countries he mentioned. On the main screen, symbols for air bases, missile batteries, and radar stations appeared in each country.

"The most important country on the map, and he hardly knows anything about it," Rosen commented. "And if we were to start snooping around, we'd only draw attention to what's happening at Kourou. What's Soviet activity like in the rest of the world?"

"Those old TU-128 Fiddlers the Russians have in Vietnam were spotted airborne recently," said Ericson, as the air base symbol lit up in the lower left corner of the main screen's world map. "They were intercepted by F-14s from the *Eisenhower*. With their range, they could threaten Yarmouth Field in Australia."

"I see. Is the navy cooperating with our global watch?"

"Only for as long as the carrier's at sea. The *Eisenhower* is heading for Subic Bay. However, the Royal Australian Air Force will move a squadron of F-18s to protect Yarmouth. Someone should remind the navy that one of their own men is flying the *Phoenix*."

"True, but we don't have the time for such arguing," said Rosen. "Thanks, Larry. As of now you're off-duty. Go get something to eat and some rest, you deserve it. Good night, Larry, or rather, good afternoon."

Ericson handed Rosen his update sheets before dragging himself through the doors at the back of the main console. A few yards down the corridor was a cafeteria and next to it were sleeping quarters for the

308

center's staff. For the past several days this had been where most of the officers ate and slept. Only Rosen had his own, private quarters, and even he had not been to his real home since the rescue of the cosmonauts had begun.

"General, Operations is ready to advise you on the status of the forces assigned to them," said Widmark, as Rosen eased back into his command chair.

"Command One to Operations, proceed with the update," he said. "Let's find out how our plans are going."

"Roger, Command One," replied a new intercept control officer. "Currently, our ASAT interceptor force has three pairs of F-15s airborne, one over the Pacific, one over the Atlantic, and one over the Gulf of Mexico. We still have only twenty ASAT missiles on inventory; Vought hasn't yet been able to deliver any more weapons. Our NORAD-guided force now includes Air National Guard squadrons in Florida and Louisiana. Tactical Air Command has assigned NORAD two E-3s, one of which will shortly be airborne over Florida, and has promised to assign an F-16 squadron to protect Edwards."

"Tell NORAD to keep after them to live up to that promise," said Rosen. "TAC's so large it has a habit of losing things. How long before the commencement of our deceptions?"

"Three hours, forty-five minutes to initial interception. We'll destroy a pair of Hydras over the Gulf of Mexico."

"And how many Vought-armed F-15s are based in Puerto Rico?"

"We have four at Ramey, and two are flight-ready," said the intercept officer. "Do you want them up now?"

"No, that might give away the shuttle's destination," Rosen answered. "If we did anything to make Kourou safer, we'd give it all away. Keep on it, Operations. Much depends on how well we deceive the Soviets."

"It's a pity we can't just ask the Russians what they're doing in Cuba and the other countries," said Widmark, after the intercept control officer had ended his report.

"True, it could solve a lot of our problems. But the White House and the Pentagon have decided against any such communications. With the breaking of the agreement, I can hardly blame them. We took the Soviets at their word, and they failed the test. Diplomacy and negotiation won't end this confrontation; only the bravery of a handful of men and women will. Mary, get me Communications. Let's see what Toulouse has to say."

"All right, Lieutenant, you may lock the doors," ordered the highest-ranking officer in the briefing room. "Everyone who should be here has arrived."

"Sorry I was behind in my arrival, Colonel," said the last officer to enter the room, joining a tiny group of senior Air Force, Air Defence Force, and KGB officers. "But the new bases for my gunships are at the border, some distance away."

"Understood, my friend," Colonel Pietr Dunaev replied. "A MIL-24 isn't as fast as a MIG-21. The matter concerning which I've called you here is of grave importance to our country. If we're lucky, we will end this tragedy in space."

Except for the KGB officials, a murmur of surprise swept through the assembled officers. A look of satisfaction crossed Dunaev's face as he watched the reaction; it was the most enthusiasm he had seen his men evince in months.

"But how is this possible?" asked the late arrival, Major Vladimir Yurasov. "This is Surinam. It's a swamp-covered backwater. It's not even ranked with Nicaragua. Down here no one considers us much of a threat."

"That's the beauty of our position," said Dunaev. "Not even the French consider us a threat. Yet we're in striking range of their most important space facility, and General Khlabistov in Havana thinks Kourou the most

310

likely landing site for the American shuttle."

"If it is, it would explain a lot of recent activity at Kourou," said the deputy commander of Dunaev's squadron.

"I not only consider it possible, I think it would be a smart move on the Americans' part to use the French spaceport. Alexei, our KGB friends don't know what's happened at Kourou. Go to the map and explain it to them."

The deputy commander went to the briefing room's one map, which was placed on the wall behind Dunaev, and pointed to one of the three countries it showed. In particular he raised his hand to a rocket-like symbol near the country's coastline.

"This is Kourou," he specified. "One hundred and eighty miles from our location. In the last ten hours its Diane tracking station and the downrange stations at Cayenne and Royal Island have been activated. Civilian aircraft are restricted from its airspace and a flight of Mirage fighters has been sent from their base at Cayenne. All this activity is standard for an Ariane launch, but none is scheduled for this time."

"Couldn't this all be in response to another test drop of their *Hermes* shuttle?" asked one of the KGB officers.

"Not likely. The French have never used the downrange stations to track one of the *Hermes* flights," said Dunaev. "And the intelligence trawler *Tyumen* reports that an American Starlifter transport landed at Kourou some four hours ago. It flew right over them."

"What do you think this means, Pietr Vasilivich?"

"I believe it brought in equipment for the American shuttle to use. Such as, perhaps, a microwave landing system."

"Has the *Tyumen* told Moscow of these developments?" asked the senior KGB officer.

"As commander of our military mission in Surinam, all such reports have to go through me," Dunaev replied, and he began to smile. "No, Moscow doesn't know what's

311

happening in this corner of the world. They're preoccupied with events inside Russia, and calming down the Americans."

"Which means, you've been given a free hand," said Major Yurasov. "What do you intend to do, Pietr?"

"When we see the French preparing for a shuttle landing, we'll launch our forces. Alexei, explain what we've planned."

"After our maneuvers with the Surinamese People's Army ends tonight, our MIL-24s will remain at these airfields," said the deputy commander, pointing to bases along the Surinam-French Guiana border. "They'll prepare for a strike against Kourou. All our MIG-21s are being armed, and we'll attempt to intercept the shuttle when it begins reentry."

"That means engaging the French Air Force," Yurasov quickly added. "And since they're equipped with late model Mirage F-1s, they will easily outgun you."

"Which is where you come in, my friend," said Dunaev. "The French, of course, will engage us. But a flight or two of gunships approaching Kourou at jungletop height would go unnoticed until your anti-tank missiles had destroyed the shuttle."

"How would you use helicopters to destroy the shuttle? The Americans claim it's the fastest, most sophisticated aircraft in the world," said the senior KGB officer.

"Don't be blinded by American boasting, Yuri. In orbit, the shuttle is probably everything they claim it is, but on reentry, their technological wonder is a powerless glider with only one chance for a landing. If Major Yurasov were to arm his gunships with laser-guided, AT-6 missiles, the shuttle would be an easy target. Even for my aircraft it would be easy—the shuttle's glowing heat tiles will pull the infrared-guided Atolls off our wings. But those with the best chance are Vladimir's men. My friend, it all comes down to you."

"Somehow, I knew it would," said Yurasov, clearly uneasy that the decision was being forced on him. "I feel I should point out the obvious, you are Air Defence Force, I am Tactical Air Force. I don't have to obey you. Especially when it's apparent that your orders to intercept the shuttle did not originate with Moscow."

"Who then will you obey?" Dunaev asked, trying not to be critical. "The appeasers in the Politburo and Foreign Ministry, who capitulated to the Americans? Or are you a soldier, who swore an oath to defend Mother Russia? I know I may sound archaic, but nonetheless it's true. Fate may hand us the chance to end the tragedy that's overtaken our country."

"Of course you're right about the appeasers, and we do have the obligation to defend our country. I only wish our orders could be more official."

"Why should they be official when the aircraft we fly wear Surinam markings? Surinam has had territory disputes with the French for years. If anything does happen, we can blame our hosts."

"I see the logic, and the deception, in your plans," said Yurasov, starting to smile nervously. "All right, Colonel, my squadron will join. I hope fate will allow your plans to work the way you want them to."

"It will, my friend, it will. If fate works for us, the *Phoenix* will not rise from its ashes."

"There, how do you feel, Saint Ex?" Post asked, straightening up after making the final adjustments to the anti-gravity suit which Vachet was now wearing.

Vachet hovered above the flight deck and flexed his arms and legs. The orange suit did not fit him properly and its ribbed air bladders squeaked as they rubbed together. However, its straps had been readjusted and the suit didn't pinch or attempt to slide off him, as it had in the last attempts.

"It's comfortable enough," Vachet said eventually. "I

only wish I were taller, I would fit it better."

"If we were to stay longer in orbit, you would be taller," said Grachenko. "Cosmonauts on long-duration flights have grown by as much as four centimeters, nearly two inches."

"Unfortunately, we don't have the time to allow our pilot to grow into his suit," Cochran answered. "It's more important for him to fit the chair and the role. Well, Saint Ex, I guess it's time for you to take your position. Watch his air lines."

As Post grabbed the hoses floating from his side, Vachet raised his legs and easily sailed into the pilot's seat feet first. While he locked his restraint belts, Post attached the hoses to the oxygen supply ports at the base of the cockpit's center pedestal. Vachet adjusted his seat and headrest, then the rudder pedals, until it all felt comfortable to him.

"Houston, this is *Phoenix*. I have a new driver," Cochran reported. "Paul Vachet is now orbiter pilot."

"Roger, *Phoenix*. We read you," said Caroline Ross. "Does Paul have anything he'd like to say?"

"Roger, Houston. I have a request," said Vachet, with his headset plugged in and his com panel activated. "For my first order as pilot, I would like an update on Kourou's status."

"Roger, *Phoenix*, we have one ready. The air force has delivered a portable microwave landing system and it should be operating in another ninety minutes. The Kourou landing strip and available orbiter facilities have been prepared for you and additional orbiter service equipment is en route. Weather advisory is for thirty percent cloud cover for today and tonight. Winds are out of the northeast at seven knots, and there's a twenty percent chance of rain. Except for the fact that you're reentering at night, your landing conditions are excellent."

"What are political conditions like, Houston? Pellerin has reminded me we've had territorial disputes with

314

Surinam and that its Marxist government has made strident accusations about our operations out of Kourou, calling them examples of space-age imperialist exploitation."

"I only know about the political confrontation between us and the Russians," said Ross. "Our space disaster has become a superpower crisis. As for local political problems in French Guiana, I don't know. We'll ask Mount Cheyenne if they've heard anything from Toulouse."

"So you guys still aren't talking to each other," Cochran observed, activating his com panel. "I smell George Reiss behind this. He always hated allowing the French in."

"No, this is from Johnson Center management. Reiss has been strangely quiet. We haven't heard much at all from him."

"Well, I'm not going to worry about it. Houston, how long do we have to our de-orbit burn?"

"*Phoenix*, you are T minus two hours, fifty-seven minutes, and counting to OMS burn," said Ross. "FIDO advises you can begin reentry preparations."

"Roger, CAP COM. Paul, activate your flight controls. We'll reorientate the lady for OMS burn."

Vachet unlocked his joystick and began tapping out commands on his GPC keyboard. Almost a day after its last reentry attempt, the *Phoenix* was still flying upside down. Its basic flight attitude had been left unchanged to conserve the dwindling supplies of hydrazine and nitrogen tetroxide. Now, it had to be maneuvered for the upcoming de-orbit engine firing.

"The digital autopilot has selected the optimum pitch rate," said Vachet, watching the data appear on his display screen. "Switching RCS system from GPC to manual control."

"*Phoenix*, this is Houston. Did he say 'pitch rate'?" Ross asked, skepticism audible in her voice.

"Yes, we're not going to roll the orbiter," said

315

Cochran. "We've got more fuel in the nose module and we're going to make use of it. Stand by, Houston. Commander to crew, prepare for radical attitude change. Okay, Paul, go ahead."

Vachet pushed his joystick forward with one hand, shielding his eyes with the other. The computer-selected thrusters in the module ahead of the cockpit emitted blinding jets of flame, which caused the rest of the crew on the flight deck to either shield their eyes or pull out their sunglasses. Moments after the RCS engines had fired up, the airliner-sized spaceplane began to move, its nose pitching away from the Earth.

Cochran and Vachet felt themselves being pulled out of their seats by the centrifugal force the maneuver generated. Glancing over his shoulder, Cochran saw Grachenko and Post drift toward the cabin ceiling; eventually they stopped by putting their hands against the skylight windows. Vachet eased pressure off the joystick when his display screen showed the *Phoenix* approaching the maneuver rate established by the digital autopilot.

After twenty seconds, the shuttle was flying perpendicular to the Earth. Cochran and Vachet could no longer see the planet's rim, just the star field of space. After thirty seconds the *Phoenix* began taking on an oblique angle and was starting to fly backwards. Vachet pulled back on his joystick, activating thrusters in the OMS pods at the tail.

"Commander to crew, we're almost at the end of the attitude maneuver," Cochran advised. "Once it's over, help our guests back into their bunks and break out the seats."

The shuttle's pitch rate slowed the moment the tail thrusters fired. Instead of being pulled out of their seats, Cochran and Vachet felt the centrifugal force abate, and gradually they returned to them. The Earth's rim returned to their view, appearing at the bottom of the cockpit windows instead of at the top, where it had been for most of the last twenty-four hours.

The *Phoenix*, once again upright, was now flying tail first. In two orbits it would be over northern Australia, firing its OMS engines to end its mission for a third time. Low on fuel, low on oxygen, and still pursued by anti-satellite weapons, this would be the last chance the *Phoenix* and her crew would have to return to Earth safely.

"Maverick Echo Three, this is Space Defence Operations. What's your weapon status?"

"Space Defence, my Vought is full green," said Gene Larson.

"Roger, Echo Three. Separate and come to heading zero-zero-five. Stand by to intercept. Prepare to drop external tanks."

Unlike their first operation, when they had flown due west, Larson and his wingman swung around until they were flying only a few degrees off true north. As the F-15s came out of their turns, they broke away from each other, separating by more than five miles in preparation for the coming interceptions.

"Echo Three, we have an advisement from Dragon Lance on area traffic. Switch to channel Delta-Five-One."

"Roger, Space Defence. Switching to Tac Com channel," said Larson. "Echo Three, out. Echo Four, change to Delta-Five-One."

Larson reached for the controls under his head-up display's combiner glass, and changed over to the tactical communications channel used by the E-3 AWACS jet orbiting at a discreet distance from the F-15s. Moments later, Larson was talking to one of the operators on the warning and control platform.

"Echo Three, this is Dragon Lance. We have two high-speed targets closing on your position. Distance, thirty miles relative your position and closing from the southeast. They're MIG-23s and radar cross section shows them to be armed."

"Roger, Dragon Lance. Looks like we have a problem. Get us some help. Echo Four, reform and turn starboard."

The fighters dipped their wings and slid toward each other, remaking their element before swinging steeply to the right and turning to face the intruders. They had just barely come around when a pair of specks were sighted in the distance.

The APG radars on the F-15s instantly presented the MIGs on the cockpit CRT screens, while the ECM systems warned that they, in turn, were being scanned by fire-control radar. The MIG-23s quickly grew large enough to be identified by Larson and his wingman, then flashed past the F-15s at a closure rate of more than fourteen hundred miles an hour. While a thousand feet higher than the Eagles, they rocked them with their shockwaves as they shot by.

"Dragon Lance, this is Echo Three. Our visitors have said hello. They're using their weapon radars on us."

"Roger, Echo Three. Your visitors have split and are coming around. They're slowing and changing their configuration. We're detecting their chatter on the aviation distress frequency."

"Roger, Dragon Lance. Echo Four will take over communications with you. I'll handle the Cubans, or whoever they are."

Larson changed his radio once again while his wingman stayed on the secure channel used by the E-3. The moment he made the switch, Larson could hear the MIG pilots speaking in Spanish with curious, heavy accents. As he glanced over his left shoulder he caught sight of a MIG-23 closing in on him.

From its original, supersonic velocity it had slowed until it was only marginally faster than the F-15s. The swing-wing fighter had pivoted its wings out from their fully swept position to an intermediate position of forty-five degrees, and the set of petal-like speed brakes around its tail were still deployed. What had been a multi-colored blur could now be seen as a mottled green and sand-colored fighter with light blue undersides.

"This is Captain Gene Larson, United States Air Force, to unidentified Cuban aircraft. You are interfering with a legitimate military operation in international airspace."

"It is quite true you are in international airspace," Lobachev replied, with intentionally broken English. "Whether you are flying a legitimate operation is another. We are here to see if you are a threat to Cuba or not."

"We're more than three hundred miles north of your country, if that is your country."

Larson gave a hard look to the fighter sitting on his left wing tip. It was close enough for him to read the warning stencils, close enough for him to see the man in the cockpit. With his oxygen mask on and his helmet visor down, he was as faceless as Larson decided he should be.

"We are Soviet-trained Cuban pilots," said Lobachev. "We were sent to investigate your suspicious activities and to decide if they pose a threat to Cuba. If they do, we reserve the right to stop them."

Larson glanced again at the MIG-23. As the E-3 had warned, it was armed, with pairs of air-to-air missiles on its fuselage and glove wing pylons. The fuselage pylons held Aphid infrared-guided missiles, while the pylons below the fixed sections of the wings, the "gloves," held radar-homing Apex missiles. By comparison, the only weapon Larson was carrying was the Vought. His F-15's normal armament of four Sidewinder and four Sparrow missiles had never been installed. In their place were external fuel tanks and FAST packs. Not even the ammunition for his Vulcan cannon was in place; it had been considered superfluous for a satellite intercept mission.

"Echo Three, this is Echo Four. My friend's deployed his laser ranger-finder."

The warning from his wingman made Larson concentrate on the MIG's nose instead of its weapons. And just ahead of the nose gear doors, a bulge the size and shape of a shoe had appeared. Its front end was a V-like glass plate, behind which a laser would scan for short-range, air-to-air weapons ranging. Larson's immediate response was to activate his only remaining weapon, his tactical electronic warfare system.

"Your wingman is correct," said Lobachev. "We will observe your activities, but we will also defend ourselves."

Rather than change channels and talk with his wingman, Larson raised his right hand and signalled him. What a million-dollar communications set would've been unable to do, a few quick hand gestures did: the wingman had been given his instructions without the escorting MIGs' knowledge.

"All right, comrade amigo, observe this!" Larson shouted, pushing his throttles forward and gesturing to his wingman to begin.

The F-15s surged ahead of the MIG-23s, then swung in front of them. Larson glanced in the mirrors in the canopy frame to make sure Lobachev's MIG-23 was directly astern, then hit the external stores jettison button. And the six-hundred-gallon wing tanks slid off their pylons and fell toward the MIG.

At first Lobachev could not believe the target he was being given; if only he had permission to fire, the Eagle would be his. Then he realized that the external tanks had detached and were tumbling at him. He instantly rolled his fighter to the left, away from his wingman. Lobachev was inverted by the time he realized the tanks had missed him, yet he continued the roll, righting his MIG a few hundred feet below his original altitude. As he did so, he caught sight of his wingman levelling off after having climbed to avoid the tanks released in his path.

"Get them!" Lobachev ordered. "Don't bother with permission from Havana. We have the right to defend ourselves."

The F-15s rolled away from each other and dove as the MIG-23s were recovering. Freed from the drag of the huge tanks, Larson could feel his aircraft accelerating faster and responding with more agility, even though it was still carrying a 2,000-pound anti-satellite missile. He quickly passed Mach 1. When he looked again at his opponent, the MIG was just sweeping its wings back for combat.

"Echo Three to Echo Four, take 'em on," said Larson. "Show 'em we still have a few tricks up our sleeves."

Larson could feel his pressure suit constrict as he pulled his F-15 through a tight, steeply banked turn. His nose pointed skyward, and the MIG-23 appeared in the sights of his HUD, which he realized would have to be switched from its long-range interception mode if his tactics were to work.

Lobachev didn't have to look at his instruments to see what his opponent was doing. He glanced down past his left shoulder and caught sight of the ascending F-15. He didn't have time to worry about his wingman, he would have to care for himself. All Lobachev wanted was the man who had nearly killed him.

With the HUD mode changed to air-to-air override, the symbols on the combiner glass indicated the MIG's speed, altitude, weapons status, radar mode, ECM conditions, and whether the aircraft was climbing or diving. Larson glanced at the stats while he watched the MIG-23 turn toward him, then checked the panel to his Northrop ALQ jammer. As he had expected, his opponent was using his radar for a weapons lock. The ALQ identified the frequency used and the strength of the pulses. Quickly, Larson matched the frequency with his APG set and stepped up the power.

Lobachev only needed a few more seconds to complete a lock for his Apex missiles when his radarscope was snowed out and the Christmas tree lights on his fire control panel went back to red. The APG set on the F-15 had overpowered and disrupted the High Lark radar, ending the attempt for a target lock.

"Bastard!" Lobachev shouted, though he kept his anger under control and changed tactics. He switched to his infrared weapons, and activated his laser range finder.

A shrill alarm sounded in Larson's cockpit the moment a sensor net detected a laser beam scanning his aircraft. Originally installed as part of a combat training system, the net had since taken on an operation role with the use of laser range finders on Soviet fighters. Larson had expected the change and was ready for it; he slammed his throttles to the firewall and pulled the joystick back until it touched the edge of his seat. The F-15 responded by standing on its tail and climbing vertically on twin columns of white shock diamonds.

For a second Lobachev had a range on his opponent, then it disappeared. When the reading in the lower right corner of his head-up display went to zero, he glanced through the combiner glass and found the F-15 had vanished as well. His heart started skipping beats until he found the Eagle, its afterburner plumes glowing brightly, already half a mile above him.

"Echo Four to Echo Three, I got 'im! I'm glued into my friend's six o'clock and he's not getting rid of me."

"Good, stay on him till the cavalry arrives," said Larson.

He could not see his wingman or the second MIG-23 on his radar screen or sight them visually, but he knew their contest was over. His wingman would remain on the MIG's tail until whatever help Dragon Lance was vectoring in had reached them.

The contest which had yet to be decided was between Larson and the lead MIG, and Larson had climbed so high it was impossible for him to see his opponent. For a moment he feared the MIGs would concentrate on his wingman and shoot him down. Then his tail warning radar started to beep.

Lobachev now had both a radar lock and a laser range

fix on his opponent. And yet, it was all useless to him. The F-15 was just a little too distant for either cannon fire or Aphid missiles, and while it was well within Apex range, launching those missiles required that they fall some distance before their motors generated full thrust—far too dangerous in a vertical climb.

Initially, at full afterburner, his MIG-23 matched the F-15's climb rate. But above 40,000 feet, the rapidly thinning air caused the MIG to lose both thrust and lift. Lobachev knew he would stall soon and, without the pressure suit he saw his opponent wearing, knew he couldn't survive the high altitudes the F-15 would reach. He tempered his anger and made the decision Larson had feared earlier.

Larson's tail warning radar gave him a range and bearing on the MIG-23 behind him. When the readings began to change, he knew his opponent was giving up the chase. In his canopy frame mirrors Larson caught a streak of fire arcing behind him, disappearing under his tail. He pulled the joystick back to his stomach and ended his climb with a loop.

At the top of the loop Larson spotted his wingman, still chasing the second MIG-23, and his opponent driving to overtake them. When his Eagle's nose pointed back to earth he reversed his controls and put his aircraft in a vertical dive. The F-15 picked up speed rapidly, even with its afterburners off. Soon it had passed Mach 1 and was closing in on the lead MIG.

Lobachev again had a target lock on an F-15, though once more there was little he could do with it. The second F-15 was too close to his own wingman for a missile launch and too distant for his cannon. Lobachev would have to wait until he had closed to effective gun range. He could already taste his victory, and could hear Radio Havana announcing how Cuban craft had responded to American aggression over the Gulf of Mexico.

Not even the growl of tail warning radar would distract him. He knew it was the lead F-15 coming to the rescue of its wingman, but nothing would stop Lobachev. Captain Gene Larson could try all the tricks he had. Regardless, his wingman would be destroyed, and then it would be his turn.

Levelled off and streaking in behind his opponent, Larson waited until his HUD indicated he was half a mile away before hitting his afterburners and priming the flare dispensers on his FAST packs. For a moment Larson considered ramming his opponent or shearing away his rudder. However, the updates from Dragon Lance indicated that such actions were unnecessary.

"Game over, Yankee," Lobachev said to himself, his HUD's aiming circle floating over his latest target. "You're mine."

A dark blur flashed over his canopy just an instant before the shockwave rippled through his fighter. It felt as though it were coming apart, and the sonic boom sounded like an explosion even through Lobachev's helmet. The MIG swayed drunkenly in the blur's wake. It was several seconds before Lobachev realized the identity of the blur, and then he was forced to start jinxing instead of trying to shoot down his opponent.

As he roared over the lead MIG, Larson toggled a salvo of flares from the chutes on his FAST packs. Half a dozen of them, burning at different temperatures, spread in front of the MIG-23. Designed to decoy infrared guided missiles, they also caused the Soviet fighter to dodge frantically, lest one of the flares be sucked in by the plane's intakes.

"Bastard, you've done this to me for the last time!" Lobachev railed, switching his HUD to missile engagement mode. "If you're listening to me, good-bye, Captain Larson."

By raising the nose of his fighter, Lobachev got an immediate target lock. The shrill tones on his headset told him that he not only had a lock but that one of his Apex missiles was ready. He pressed the button atop his joystick grip and felt the Apex under his right wing glove fall away.

Its solid-fuel engine had already ignited, and by the time it had dropped ten feet, it was burning at full thrust. The slender, multiple-finned missile surged away from the MIG, its set of nose fins picking up target return signals and its tail fins maneuvering to pitch it after the ascending F-15.

Trailing a thick plume of smoke, the Apex ignored the much closer F-15 and MIG-23 pair and climbed steeply in pursuit of Larson's fighter. Now at maximum speed, the missile was more than seven hundred miles an hour faster than the Eagle. It would overtake and destroy the aircraft in twenty-five seconds.

Lobachev reduced his speed to watch the intercept. The other F-15 could wait; he wanted to savor his first kill. So intent upon the F-15 was he that it was several moments before he realized his tail warning radar had been reactivated. And a second plume of smoke had entered his field of view.

As rapidly as the Apex was overtaking Larson's F-15, the second plume had been closing in on the missile. When the two intersected miles above Lobachev's MIG there was a flash of light followed by a shower of fragments. When at last Lobachev had noticed his tail warning radar, it showed two targets.

"This is Cajun Lead to unidentified Cuban aircraft. Break engagement immediately and jettison your external weapons."

Lobachev touched the main power buttons on the High Lark panel, shutting down his radar and effectively ending the dogfight. Then he looked up at his rearview mirror. To his left he spotted what appeared to be another F-15. A movement to his right caught his attention, and he discovered a fourth Eagle overtaking the one which tailed his wingman.

"Unidentified Cuban aircraft, you have not jettisoned your weapons. Comply at once."

"Cajun Lead, this is not the Wild West," said

Lobachev. "You're not the sheriff and I will not drop my six-guns."

"You've committed a hostile act against an American aircraft flying in international airspace. Jettison your weapons."

"You're not Cleet Eastwood, and your orders are insulting."

"That's *Clint* Eastwood, pal, and I still have seven missiles on my ship with your name on them. So go ahead, make my day."

The F-15 disappeared from the rearview mirror and crept into sight on Lobachev's port side. He could see that one of its Sparrows was missing, but the wing pylons still retained their Sidewinder pairs. It angered Lobachev that he had lost his chance at victory, and what infuriated him even more was the unit identification on the side of the F-15: Louisiana Air National Guard.

No matter how he hated it, he knew his MIG-23 was no match for a heavily armed F-15. He reached for the armament switches on his front instrument panel and hit the jettison toggles. The remaining Apex and the two Aphids fell away from their pylons. Initially the slipstream carried them backwards, but as their speed dropped off they fell into ballistic arcs, spiralling toward the waters of the Gulf, some six miles below.

"Glad you're finally seeing things my way," said Cajun Lead, his Southern drawl becoming more noticeable as tension abated. "Echo Three, you and your wingman can continue your intercept."

"I'm afraid not," said Larson, bringing his aircraft down to the same level as his opponent and Cajun Lead. "Space Defence Operations says we've missed our launch window. My wingman and I are to return to Eglin immediately. So even without shooting us down, our friend here has succeeded in stopping our intercept of those ASATs. But only until the next orbit."

Larson saluted both Cajun Lead and his opponent, then broke away to join his wingman, who had given over the pursuit of the second MIG-23 to Cajun Two. They regrouped and banked gently to the northeast. In just over an hour they would be landing at Eglin Air Force Base on Florida's panhandle. There, the Vought anti-satellite weapons would be checked for damage while another pair of ASAT-armed F-15s would be called in to destroy the Hydras on their next orbit.

While Larson and his wingman flew north, Lobachev and his backup headed south. To add insult to his defeat, his fuel state was so low he would have trouble returning to Cuba. Once he was on his new heading, Lobachev reduced speed and swept his wings full forward. Unarmed and slow, he and his wingman were now of little threat to anyone. Even so, the Louisiana Air Guard F-15s continued to escort them, until Dragon Lance warned of a massive takeoff of fighters from Cuban airfields.

"General, the second American transport is on final," reported Colonel Alain Bresson as he walked across the Kourou tarmac to a group of French army and air force officers. As he entered the group, he saluted its highest-ranking officer, General Charles LaFont, commander of all military forces in French Guiana. "In fact, you can see it land."

The group turned in the direction of the distant buzzing and watched a camouflaged C-130 dive at the end of Kourou's orbiter landing strip, flare out, and touch down. When it rolled to a stop it still had half a mile of runway to cover before it reached a taxiway and could swing in for the tarmac. Waiting for it was a C-141 Starlifter, a flight of Mirage F-1C fighters, a few CNES aircraft, and most of the helicopters of the French Army Light Aviation Detachment based in the colony.

"What are they bringing in, Colonel?" LaFont asked, watching the *Hercules* roll up the taxiway.

"Service equipment for the *Phoenix*," said Bresson. "A special boarding ramp and a power supply vehicle."

"I see. Isn't our equipment good enough for them? It supported this machine well enough for the last month."

LaFont pointed to the most prominent civilian aircraft on the flightline, the *Hermes Prototypon de L'épreuve Aerodynamique*. The size of a large business jet, the *Hermes* aerodynamic test prototype was of a similar design to the American shuttle. The main differences were that it had wing tip fins in place of a tail fin and no main engines, only thrusters and orbital engines.

"The *Phoenix* is much larger than the *Hermes*," Bresson answered. "Remember, it's an operational spacecraft. Ours is merely a test vehicle. General, I would like to report that my entire squadron will be operational in a matter of hours. The spare parts the Americans brought in will allow the F-1s here and at Cayenne to be flight-ready by this evening."

"Good, we need to show our socialist neighbors a maximum effort," said LaFont. "Especially after their recent border maneuvers. Captain, please continue your report."

"Yes, General," said an army intelligence captain. "There have been no flights by Surinam's MIG-21s based at Paramaribo since yesterday. Also, there have been no flights by the Hind attack helicopters from their border airfields for the last five hours. Since the border maneuvers are continuing, this is very unusual."

"Have any tactical sorties been flown today in support of the maneuvers?" Bresson asked.

"Apart from flights by liaison aircraft and transport helicopters, none. The only conclusions I can draw are that either the Russian 'advisers' have left, or all available aircraft are being prepared for a mission."

"Has there been any unusual activity?" asked LaFont. "Unusual radio traffic or reports from our agents?"

"Our ELINT capabilities in this command are very limited," the intelligence captain admitted. "I can't tell you if their radio traffic with Havana or Moscow has been unusual or not. The navy has the best intelligence

328

gathering capabilities."

"And the one warship they've based here, the *Drogou*, is watching the spy trawler *Tyumen*," added LaFont. "Since we have little intelligence, we must prepare for the worst case scenario. Colonel Bresson will stop the MIGs, the Navy will prevent the *Tyumen* from interfering, and to stop the Hind gunships, we have Major Mayer's detachment. Major, I think you should explain your strategy."

"Thank you, General," said Major Henri Mayer, commanding officer of the French Army's Light Aviation Detachment. Of all the officers present, he was the only one wearing a flightsuit, having just disembarked from one of the Pumas on the tarmac. "As with Alain's squadron, all available aircraft in my units will be used. The Gazelles have been armed with HOT missiles, the Alouette 3s with rocket pods, and the Pumas are dispersing Mistrale teams to locations around the countryside."

As Mayer spoke, he swept his hand down the line of helicopters. Those nearest the group were Gazelles, whose sleek lines, narrow fuselages and ducted-fan tail rotors gave the impression of speed even though they were just sitting on the tarmac. Attached to their sides by stub pylons were pairs of launch tubes for HOT anti-tank missiles, their only armament. Next to them, from an earlier age, were the Alouette 3s.

These had wider fuselages, sat higher off the ground than the Gazelles, and had a less warlike appearance than the later machines. The most fearsome things on them were their weapons: light machine guns mounted in the side hatches and conical-tipped rocket pods farther back on the fuselage sides.

Last came the Pumas. The largest helicopters on the Kourou flightline and the largest in French Guiana, they were almost the same size as the Hind gunships the Gazelles and Alouettes would face. They, however, carried no weapons. Only three could be seen on the tarmac; the fourth was delivering two-man Mistral teams to locations in the surrounding savannah and western foothills.

"How many of your machines will you have available Major?" asked LaFont.

"All the Gazelles and Alouettes, and four out of the five Pumas," said Mayer. "The fifth is down at Cayenne for a major overhaul. Four Gazelles you don't see here are already forward-based at the border, near Saint Laurent. The remaining six will depart for the border once they're armed. Our best will be our first line of defence against the gunships. But even they aren't as fast or as heavily armed as the MIL-24s. I doubt we can stop them all, so the Alouettes will remain in the Kourou area as our second line. Lastly, we are having the Mistral teams and the Crotale systems flown in from Cayenne."

"Thank you, Major. Did I hear you say 'we'?"

"Yes, sir. I'll command the anti-tank squadron personally. My deputy will command the Alouettes and the Pumas."

"Good, I like your initiative. Captain, can you tell me the condition of your missile battery?"

"General, it's nearly operational," said the air force officer LaFont had turned to. "The acquisition vehicle is at the western end of the landing strip. The missile firing vehicles are being positioned. Once we've laid the data cables, my battery will be ready. What about the second battery?"

"If everything's on time, the Transall will arrive with it in forty minutes," LaFont answered. "I take it you'll place the other battery at the runway's eastern end?"

"Yes, we'll just taxi the aircraft down and roll the vehicles out."

"Excellent. Now it's time for us to see the reporters."

LaFont motioned to a lieutenant to bring over the other group of people standing on the tarmac. They were civilians, reporters, and camera crews from French television and the major newspapers. They were at

Kourou to cover the test flights of the *Hermes* prototype, and until now had been kept in the dark about the military activity at the spaceport.

"Good afternoon, ladies, gentlemen. I trust you've been entertained by our operations?" said LaFont, as the group was brought within earshot.

"Enraged would be a better word," said one of the reporters. "I've been appointed by my colleagues to be our spokesman. The blackout you've forced on us has been intolerable. We have not been told why the American planes are here, or what they have flown in. Your orders have denied us access to overseas cables and satellite channels. European Space Agency and CNES personnel won't talk to us about what they're doing or what you're doing. But we can guess. The *Hermes* isn't due for a test flight and there's no activity at the Ariane pads or the assembly building. You're not sending anything up, you're preparing to receive something—"

"In fact, we are." LaFont decided to cut off the reporter before he got to his conclusion. "In a few hours you will be covering the most important story of the year. The American shuttle *Phoenix* will be landing here."

Even though they had suspected it, a gasp still spread through the assembled journalists. The newspaper reporters immediately took out their note pads and tape recorders while the television crews shouldered their video cameras.

"Could you repeat what you just said, General?" the group's spokesman requested.

"You heard me well enough the first time," said LaFont, smiling slightly. "I have no intent of turning this into an interview. An hour before the shuttle lands you'll be notified. You're the only reporters in the world to know this, and that's the way it will remain. All of you will be kept at the spaceport. You won't be allowed to contact anyone outside of it, and this includes your editors and producers."

"But they have to be told," said one of the television

reporters, while the rest of her colleagues groaned and swore. "We can't keep the people we work for in the dark. You can trust our superiors as much as you trust us."

"That's just the point, my dear. I don't trust you, and will make no exceptions. You will scoop the Americans, the British, the Germans, everyone. And if that isn't enough for you, and you attempt to break security, just remember this. There's a certain, notorious penal colony just off our coast. If any of you break security on our operation, I'll see to it Devil's Island is reopened just for you."

"I knew you'd think of coming here," said Reynolds after he had left his car and started walking toward the memorial. The bronze statues were golden in the late afternoon sun and cast long shadows out to the beach. Almost hidden in the shadows was Brad Harrison. He stood near the end of the memorial's arc of statues, almost in front of that of Christa McAuliffe.

"I just had to have a little solitude before I went in," Harrison admitted, turning to Reynolds. "And like you said before, here you can be with people who understand you."

"Yes, soon enough we'll be busy. Right now we need a little peace. In a few hours it'll all be over and we'll either have heroes, or a reason to put ten more statues out here."

"Ten? Oh yes, the cosmonauts the *Phoenix* rescued. I see what you mean. If they're together in death, they should be remembered that way. Did we do the right thing, Clayton? What Reiss said to us here is really haunting me."

"Forget what the prick said and remember what you said," Reynolds advised. "We take a thousand risks every time we go into space. What's one more where rescuing people is concerned? We did the right thing, and your wife and our friends did the right thing. The only ones who should feel ashamed are the Russians and our chicken shit management. Because of them, the end to this crisis rests on the bravery of a handful of men and women."

Chapter Nineteen

"Jack, how's everything down here?" Post asked, dropping through the roof hatch and coming to a stop before touching the floor of the middle deck.

"We're in our seats and our guests are in their bunks," said Ripley, locking his restraint belts. "We've got our flight helmets out, our personal air packs ready to activate, and we've given our portable oxygen systems to our guests."

Ripley nodded to the bunks, where Post could see the POS backpacks strapped to the tier. These would provide emergency oxygen to the cosmonauts should the *Phoenix* depressurize during reentry. The face masks to the backpacks floated like balloons at the ends of their air hoses; the Russians would not have to wear them until the rest of the crew donned their helmets.

"Arkady, how are your people doing?" Post asked next.

"We're comfortable," said Grachenko, looking up from a sheaf of papers he was reading. "Vassili got more injections half an hour ago. They should last him until we land."

"Good. Does Paul know you're reading his manuscript?"

"Not to worry, I have his permission."

"Okay, what you've got should keep you busy until reentry," said Post. "Stand by, we're going to adjust our orbit."

To steady himself while he floated on the middle deck, Post had kept a hand on the hatch rim. When he had finished his check, all he had to do was pull himself up and he was back on the flight deck.

"How's it going on the middle deck?" Cochran asked, glancing over his shoulder.

"Everyone's ready for de-orbit maneuvers," said Post.

"And everyone here is secure for maneuvers except you. Better strap in. You ready, Saint Ex?"

"RCS thrusters changed to manual control," Vachet said nervously, as he checked his instrument panels. "And my CRT is showing both current and proposed orbital tracks."

"Take her easy, Paul. We'll begin as soon as Walt's finished," Cochran ordered. "I'll advise Houston."

The moment Post locked his belts, Vachet pressed his joystick to the left, initiating a burn on the right lateral thrusters. The *Phoenix* was still flying backwards, which forced Vachet to reverse most of his flight commands. Moments after doing so, the airliner-sized spaceplane began sliding to the right, leaving its original track and aligning itself perfectly for the Kourou reentry window.

Vachet watched the change on his display screen, ending the thruster burn as the shuttle blip moved from one undulating line to the other. To halt the slide, he briefly pressed the joystick in the opposite direction. The *Phoenix* was in its new track, and in half an hour its OMS engines would be fired to reduce its velocity to sub-orbital speed.

"*Phoenix*, this is Houston. We confirm your new track," Selisky reported. "You are T minus one hour, thirty-one minutes, thirty-seven seconds to landing. Do you want any updates?"

"Roger, CAP COM," said Cochran. "We'd like an update on the ASATs from Space Defence and on Kourou from the French."

"Nothing new from Mount Cheyenne, but here's what

334

we got from Toulouse. The microwave landing system delivered to Kourou is operational. All its available facilities are prepared for your arrival. French military forces in Guiana report that they're at one hundred percent readiness, but we have no reports concerning any military activity in Surinam. The French are afraid that if they investigate, they'll tip off their neighbor to what's happening at the spaceport. *Phoenix*, please update your condition, over."

"Go ahead, Paul. That's the pilot's responsibility."

"Oh yes. Sorry," Vachet apologized, quickly scanning his panels. "Houston, life suport advisory as follows. We have approximately three hours, twenty minutes of oxygen remaining. If we don't make this reentry, we won't have enough to make the next Kourou window. APU fuel state is low, we can only put two units on line. We have sufficient OMS fuel for de-orbit maneuvers, but it's doubtful beyond them."

"If all goes well, you won't have to worry about it," said Selisky. "*Phoenix*, we now have an update from Mount Cheyenne. One of the Hydra pairs in equitorial orbit is changing course. You're going to be chased home, but your friends are preparing for it. They've stopped all decoy intercepts and will conserve their limited supply of ASATs for your reentry."

"Looks like everyone is dealing with shortages," said Cochran. "CAP COM, we're T minus one hour, twenty-six minutes to landing. Are you ready for a Go No Go decision?"

"Roger, *Phoenix*. We're ready," said Selisky. "FIDO says we're go for de-orbit burn."

"Roger, CAP COM. Saint Ex, you take care of the APUs, I'll do the GPC load."

Cochran handed Vachet a cue card from the flight data file before running his hand over his general purpose computer keyboard. Vachet moved down the rows of auxiliary power unit controls, hitting the first two switches in each triplet. Instead of activating all three

APUs, as was normal, he would use only two because of the limited fuel supply.

As Cochran hit the GPC "Proceed" key, the program monitoring the shuttle during its preparations for de-orbit burn was dumped and replaced with one to run it through the burn and the pre-entry coast afterwards. The *Phoenix* was almost ready for its return, and in a half hour it would be irrevocably committed.

"Maverick Zulu One, this is Space Defence Operations. We're recalling the backup F-15 to Ramey."

"Roger, Operations," said Major Anthony Ikeda as he touched a pair of switches on his armament panel. "It sounds like we're finally going to be a part of this action."

"Roger, Zulu One. The shuttle will retro-fire in twenty minutes. Come to course Two-Zero-Zero and jettison tanks."

"Roger, Two-Zero-Zero degrees. Well, Brian, it looks like getting this backwater assignment is going to pay off."

With Ikeda leading the way, the two F-15s banked to the right and quickly settled onto the south-southwesterly heading. The moment they levelled out, the bulky wing tanks slid off their inboard pylons. With the exception of their Vought ASATs, the Eagles were stripped clean and ready for interception.

"Zulu One, we confirm your course change. Accelerate to seven hundred knots and activate your IFF systems. We need to track you as accurately as possible."

"Roger, Operations. We'll trip our IFF," said Ikeda, tapping his identification transmitter. "Now we'll see if we're as good as the rest of our squadron."

After Ikeda triggered his IFF system, he opened up his throttles and had his wingman do the same. From cruise speed, the F-15s rapidly accelerated past Mach 1 without using their afterburners. In just over a minute they had left Puerto Rico behind and were hurtling into the eastern Caribbean at 800 miles per hour. By the time the *Phoenix* had completed its de-orbit burn they would be approaching the Venezuelan coast, in position to begin their intercept climbs.

"They're on track for Kourou. I hope you people are satisfied," Reiss sniped, as the launch center's main screen revised the orbit of the *Phoenix*.

"Yes, as a matter of fact, we are," said Reynolds, speaking for the astronauts clustered around Reiss and the center's command console. "In an hour and a half, it'll all be over."

"More than just this mission will be over. When word gets back to Houston and Washington about what you people have done, this mutiny will mean the end of all your careers."

"Reiss, will you give it up?" said Harrison, growing tired of listening to the threat. "Firing us would mean doing away with half the astronaut corps."

"Maybe he wants to put an ad on late-night TV?" suggested one of the other astronauts. "Are you interested in travel, exotic locations, and risking your life because of congressional budget cuts? If so, then you too can become a NASA astronaut."

"You can find it funny, but there are people in this agency who'd love to cut the astronaut corps," said Reiss. "And they'll remember your mutiny. And should something happen to the *Phoenix*, they won't wait until afterwards to hang you. They'll do it by tonight. Take a look and see your future . . ."

Reiss pointed to the main screen, where the orbital tracks of all vehicles were being updated. It took a few moments for the astronauts to see what he had noticed. One of the double tracks for the Hydra pairs had changed, matching the new orbit of the *Phoenix*. Though a considerable distance behind the shuttle, they appeared to be rapidly overtaking it.

"Do you feel the noose tightening around your necks?"

"Don't try scaring us, mister," Reynolds argued. "We know Mount Cheyenne's watching the orbiter. They know about those ASATs and they're vectoring F-15s to stop them. If the *Phoenix* were to have tried for Ascension, several ASAT pairs would be after it and NORAD's F-15s couldn't protect it."

"We didn't know that for certain," said Reiss. "You were the ones who made the prediction, not me."

"And our friends and my wife chose to believe it," Harrison added. "They made the final decision, and if they're brave enough to live with the consequences, then so must we be. From what the screen's showing, those Hydras should be in visual range by the time the *Phoenix* makes its de-orbit burn. Space Defence Command is sure cutting the interception fine."

"I wish we could get something on their F-15s," said Reynolds. "It would ease our fears, and stop the threats."

"Colonel! I'm sorry I wasn't able to attend your pilots' briefing!" LaFont shouted so Bresson could hear him above the clatter of the departing Alouettes. "I just learned we're to broadcast the shuttle landing live, to the Soviets."

When the last of the army helicopters lifted off the Kourou tarmac, the noise level fell back to a more normal state. The spaceport's flightline was now almost empty; only the Pumas, the U.S. Air Force transports, and Bresson's Mirage F-1Cs remained. Those that had not departed had been returned to their hangars for the night. Soon the F-1s would be gone.

Each of the gray and white fighters had a GAMO support truck parked next to it and a ground crew completing their pre-flight procedures. LaFont had found Bresson doing the walk-around of his aircraft and signing the release forms.

"Let's hope this goodwill gesture is more successful than the rescue of their cosmonauts," Bresson finally said, signing the last forms on his clipboard. "Thank you, Victor. General, have you heard anything from Mayer since he left?"

"Yes, his anti-tank helicopters have dispersed to landing areas along the Maroni River as planned. They'll begin patrolling in the next half hour. When will you leave?"

"As soon as the Alouettes finish their departure. Once we're up, the other flights at Cayenne will join us at the border. Each flight will patrol its own sector, and together with Mayer's squadron, we'll effectively seal border airspace."

"Colonel, one of your pilots is carrying a pair of field glasses," LaFont observed. "Is that normal equipment?"

"Oh yes, Duprée," said Bresson, smiling slightly. "He wants to be the first one to actually see the shuttle. He thinks the binoculars will help. I think he'll find it difficult to use them with the canopy frame. However, he's welcome to try."

"Since I wasn't at your briefing, do you have any last questions for me?"

"I have only one question for you. What should I do if any Surinam Air Force aircraft violate our airspace?"

"If it's so much as a dove with a green and red flag in its beak, blow it out of the sky," said LaFont, before he shook Bresson's hand. "We can't allow a petty border dispute to incinerate the world. More important, we've been entrusted with the safety of this shuttle. French honor is at stake. Good luck, Colonel, and bring us back a spaceship."

LaFont and Bresson saluted as they parted company, LaFont moving to the tarmac's safety perimeter and Bresson to the ladder on the port side of his Mirage. He climbed up to the cockpit with his crew chief and, working together, they had Bresson strapped into his fighter in less than a minute. The crew chief also wished

339

him luck, then climbed down and removed the ladder.

"Kourou Tower, this is Skyguard Lead," Bresson advised. "My flight is ready to start engines."

"Roger, Skyguard. Proceed with engine start. Tell us when you're set to taxi."

Bresson signalled to his ground crew as his hand glided over the fuel tank switches and opened one. In moments, while he activated the fuel pumps and pushed the throttle to its first setting, the ground crew finished clearing the area around the Mirage. When they were done, only the umbilicals connecting the aircraft to the GAMO support truck remained.

A deep rumble shook the jet as its Atar engine ignited and spooled up. The alternators began operating, supplying electric power to the rest of the systems. One by one, the umbilicals were disconnected. External power, cooling fluid, data relay and heating lines were all removed from their fuselage jacks.

"Kourou Tower, this is Skyguard Lead. My flight is ready to taxi," said Bresson, glancing at the other fighters.

"Roger, Skyguard. You are cleared to proceed. Use taxiway C-One to reach the orbiter strip. The Alouettes have departed. Please advise when you're ready for takeoff."

The F-1s were now on their own power, filling the tarmac with low screams. As the support trucks pulled back, only the plane handlers remained standing in front of the jets. Bresson acknowledged the signals from his handler before he switched on his landing light and closed his canopy.

The nose lamp threw an arc of harsh light across the tarmac, illuminating what had been cloaked by the rapidly growing darkness. Bresson had to readjust the brightness of his cockpit displays before he released his brakes and obeyed the signals of his plane handler.

Bresson's wingman followed him out to the taxiway, the rest of the fighters swinging into line behind him. With their departure, the tarmac's population was down to the Starlifter, the Hercules, and the Pumas.

"Kourou Tower, this is Skyguard Lead," said Bresson. "We've completed our final checks and are ready for takeoff."

"Roger, Skyguard. You may proceed. Contact Kourou Traffic Control on your departure. Good luck, Skyguard."

"Thanks. We'll be back with our guests soon."

The orbiter runway was large enough to accommodate all four F-1s. They arrayed themselves in staggered pairs at its eastern end, with Bresson and his wingman forward of the other pair. When they got their clearance, they opened their throttles, leaving the others to wait until they had cleared the field.

They had almost two miles of concrete in front of them, yet Bresson and his wingman needed scarcely more than a quarter of it to get airborne. At two thousand feet, and an airspeed of 120 miles per hour, the F-1s raised their noses. A few hundred feet later they bounced off their double sets of main wheels and rose into the darkness.

By the time Bresson and his wingman reached the opposite end of the runway they were almost a mile above Kourou, with the second pair accelerating after them. The jets became clusters of flashing lights, moving through the night like formations of high-speed fireflies. Once they had formed up, the Mirage F-1s flew west to the border with Surinam, where they'd wait for the rendezvous that would end the crisis.

"Edward, look. I think it's the Hydras," said Vachet, poiting at the cockpit's forward windows.

Cochran glanced up from his instrument panels in time to catch the distant glimmerings of thrusters being fired. Though the Hydras themselves were too far away to be seen, the attitude control jets were faintly visible.

"Don't worry about them," Cochran ordered. "The F-15s will kill them. Concentrate on your OMS and APU checks."

"System checks completed," said Vachet. "Orbital engines armed and under GPC control. Number One and Two APUs are running. Their hydraulic pressure gages read low green. T minus thirty-seven seconds to OMS burn."

"Good. Advise Houston we're ready and I'll warn the middle deck. Commander to crew, prepare for de-orbit maneuvers."

"Houston, this is *Phoenix*. We're go for de-orbit burn."

Houston's reply had barely been given when the OMS engines and aft-facing thrusters were ignited. With the OMS exhaust nozzles pointing up as far as they could, the *Phoenix* not only decelerated but descended as well. For the last fifteen hours it had skirted above normal reentry altitude, remaining in a neutral track to avoid attracting the ASATs. Now, with its track altered and its altitude dropping, the shuttle was a better target for the pursuing Hydras.

On the middle deck and flight deck, the effects of the reentry maneuver were soon apparent. Those who were seated felt the deceleration push them against their chairs. Then, as the descent rate increased, they started to slide up until the restraint belts dug into their shoulders. Those in the sleeping bunks had their heads pressed against the backboards and were starting to rise off the pallet mats. Again, there were restraint belts to hold them, though the pressure of the straps digging in made everyone feel uncomfortable.

Four minutes after the engines ignited, one-third longer than a normal de-orbit burn, the firing ceased. The *Phoenix* had entered pre-entry coast, a long, gentle descent back to Earth. It was committed to reentry; most of its fuel had been used, and there would be just barely enough to control the shuttle's attitude for the remainder of its time in space.

"*Phoenix*, this is Houston. You are T minus fifty-five minutes to landing. Begin post-OMS burn activities."

"Roger, CAP COM," said Cochran. "Paul, check the APUs. Shutting down OMS system. RCS cross-feed switches, open."

The remaining fuel in the OMS tanks was pumped into the RCS cells in each pod. Cochran monitored the operation through the overhead pressure gages. When the ones for the OMS tanks were reading almost zero, he closed the cross-feed lines and the tanks, and shut down the helium pressure and vapor isolation systems.

"The APUs are nominal, ready for operation," said Vachet.

"We'll put them on line soon. But first we reorientate the lady. Activating RCS and DAP. Commander to crew, prepare for radical attitude change."

"RCS thrusters on manual control," Vachet informed, taking hold of his joystick grip. "I'll roll the *Phoenix* on her back first. It's the least fuel-consuming of maneuvers."

Vachet waited until the DAP showed the correct numbers on his screen before squeezing the grip. An array of thrusters in the OMS pods fired, beginning a starboard roll. The maneuver went slowly, creating few effects apart from changing the positions of Earth and space for the flight deck team. At the end, the shuttle was once again in a head's-down attitude.

"DAP is selecting pitch rate," said Vachet. "Better shield your eyes in some way. This is going to be bright."

The flight deck team put their sunglasses on as the nose module emitted jets of flame. Again Cochran and Vachet could feel themselves being pulled out of their seats as the *Phoenix* started to pitch up. Only the nose module thrusters had to be fired to start the maneuver; they would save the fuel in the OMS pods to end it later.

After twenty seconds of firing the airliner-sized spaceplane was standing on its tail. The nose module engines were shut down, and inertia would complete the reorientation. For a few moments, Harrison and Post could see the Hydra pair through the skylight windows. Then they were gone, swept from view as the shuttle finished pitching over to an oblique angle.

For the first time in almost a day the *Phoenix* was flying nose first and right side up. A selection of tail thrusters were fired to halt the maneuver. The spaceplane slowed, then stopped with its nose sitting thirty degrees above the horizon. The *Phoenix* was in its proper reentry attitude. Now all Vachet had to do was hold it there for the next thirty-eight minutes.

"*Phoenix*, this is Houston. You are T minus fifty minutes to landing," said Selisky. "FIDO advises you bring the APUs on line and commence entry switch over checklist."

"Tell Bill the APUs are ready for normal operation," Cochran answered. "I'll get out the checklist. Walt, it's Gatorade time. Get enough for us and the middle deck team."

"Zulu One, this is Space Defence Operations. We confirm your course change to Two-Seven-Five degrees. Separate to launch distance and complete ASAT activation."

"Roger, Operations," said Ikeda. "Okay, Zulu Two, you heard the man. Time to split and get ready for the high blue."

At 35,000 feet, night had not yet fallen over the Caribbean. There was still enough light for Ikeda and his wingman to see each other and to do the separation visually. They banked away until the distance had opened from a few hundred feet to five miles. In the dying light they became shadows to each other, except for the flash of their strobing anti-collision beacons.

"Operations, this is Zulu One. Our ASATs read full green. We're ready to begin interception."

"Roger, Zulu One. Stand by for countdown to initiate

zoom climb. T minus twenty-five seconds. Twenty-four . . ."

"Check your pressure suit one more time, Brian," Ikeda ordered. "The high blue is no place to find a problem."

"And it's also no place to be Luke Skywalker," said the wingman. "Remember what Colonel Hall told us, and especially you. This isn't supposed to be a high-tech Banzai charge."

"Now would I do something like that?"

"Tony, even from this distance I can see you grinning. Will you promise me you won't do anything crazy?"

"Two seconds. One. Initiate zoom climb."

"Sorry, Brian. I'm gone," said Ikeda. "Talk to me later."

Ikeda rammed his joystick forward, and the fraction of a second he gained allowed him to plunge ahead of his wingman. Soon the F-15s were pushing a thousand miles an hour as they dove to build up momentum. In twenty seconds they dropped to 25,000 feet and Ikeda began his pull out.

Two miles below his starting altitude, he dipped briefly into night as he levelled off and pointed his nose skyward. The moment he started gaining altitude, Ikeda hit his afterburners. The F-15 emitted twin plumes of blue-white flame as it leaped for the glittering star field above it. Climbing rapidly, it soon passed Mach 2. When Ikeda looked back, he could see his wingman just lighting his own afterburners.

Only then did he realize how far ahead he had gone. There was little he could do about it: Ikeda was at maximum speed and committed to his zoom climb, and his wingman soon would be. There was no way the gap between them could be closed.

To deal with the Hydra pairs, Space Defence Command wanted the Voughts to be launched simultaneously by the leader and wingman. Now the launch times would be different and could not be changed—for Ikeda to slow and allow his wingman to catch up would mean losing the momentum necessary to finish his zoom climb. The F-15s were set on their ballistic ascents; events would not allow them to be restarted. From now until the shuttle landed, everyone would have to go with what they had.

"How do they feel?" Cochran asked, as he watched the indicator needles for the flight surfaces move in sync with Vachet's working of his rudder pedal and joystick.

"They're perfect," said Vachet, his earlier nervousness abating. "It almost feels like I'm flying an aircraft."

"Good. Lock aero surfaces and return your joystick to RCS operation. CAP COM, this is *Phoenix*. Entry switch-over checklist completed. Head-up displays activated. Aero surfaces check finished."

"Roger, *Phoenix*. Proceed with RCS dump," said Selisky.

"Roger, Houston," Vachet answered. "Entering program Three-Six. The forward module is armed."

"Hold it for a moment," said Cochran. "CAP COM, do you have any updates from Space Defence Command?"

"Roger, SDC reports the ASAT pair behind you is closing the gap," said Selisky. "But the F-15s are nearing their launch altitude. Expect an intercept in six minutes."

"Thanks, Houston. We're proceeding with RCS dump," Cochran replied. "*Phoenix*, out. Okay, Paul, enter the next command."

"Program Three-Seven, loaded," said Vachet, hitting the right sequence of buttons on his GPC keyboard. "And executed."

Brief plumes of mist curled out from either side of the nose section ahead of the cockpit. The propellant tanks for the nose module had been opened and were venting what was left of their fuels to space. Apart from the plumes, the only other indication of the dump was the drastically falling pressure gauge for the module. Though currently it had little effect on the shuttle, shortly it would.

In ten minutes the *Phoenix* had hit atmospheric interface, reentering a gravity environment. The retention of the nose module's fuel had thrown off the spaceplane's center of gravity. Jettisoning most of it had eliminated the problem. What was left of the fuel would be used to maintain flight attitude until the control surfaces became effective. Fifty seconds after starting the dump, Vachet commanded it to end.

"CAP COM, RCS venting is complete," said Cochran.

"Roger, *Phoenix*. Prepare your G-suits for operation. You are T minus forty minutes to landing. Houston, out."

"Zulu One, this is Space Defence Operations. You've crossed Armstrong's Line. Do you have target locks on the Hydras?"

"Roger, Operations. I have a lock," said Ikeda, watching the blip and aiming circle on his HUD start to flash. "My wingman has acquired his target and should have a lock soon."

"Roger, Zulu One. You and Zulu Two are cleared for weapons release. Your wingman is to fire as soon as he has a lock."

"Brian, did you hear that?"

"Affirmative. I'll fire when my HUD begins flashing."

"Good, see you below," Ikeda responded, hitting the missile button on his joystick grip.

His Vought ASAT received its final burst of target data and commenced its ignition cycle. By the time the F-15 reached 80,000 feet, the pylon's support pins were pushing against the Vought. Ikeda felt his aircraft rock as it was kicked away. He slapped down his helmet's visor, saving his eyesight as a harsh glow filled his cockpit. His view was obscured by the missile's tail fire until he pulled his joystick all the way back.

347

He ended his ballistic-like ascent with a loop, using up what remained of his fighter's momentum. At the top of the loop he retracted his visor and looked down. Ikeda caught sight of his wingman, easy to do with the glow of a missile launch silhouetting the F-15. Nearly a minute after his, the other Vought was away and climbing toward its distant target. The last shots in history's first space war had just been made.

"White Fox Lead, this is Paramaribo Tower. Radar is tracking high-speed, high-altitude targets in Guiana airspace. They appear to be Mirage F-1s in squadron strength."

"This is a surprise," said Colonel Dunaev. "But we can handle them. What does Major Yurasov have to report?"

"All available gunships are ready for takeoff and are awaiting your orders," said the tower's senior operator.

"Tell the major to proceed and enter hostile airspace. Do we have clearance for takeoff?"

"Affirmative, Colonel. You are cleared for departure."

"Roger, Paramaribo Tower. White Fox Lead to flight. Proceed as drilled. Maintain minimal radio traffic and remain at the flight level I select until we reach the border."

On a signal from Dunaev, the other MIGs released their brakes and opened their throttles. The four aircraft accelerated down Paramaribo's main runway in unison. Though they had all been equipped with a fuel tank and a quartet of Atoll missiles, the MIG-21s were only moderately loaded and had reached rotation speed after using just a third of the runway's length.

First Dunaev, then the other three pilots raised their nose wheels. It was Dunaev who first broke free and leaped into the air. The rest of the MIG-21s followed, regrouping their formation by the time they reached the runway's opposite end. They did a shallow climb-out and circled the base as the rest of the squadron's available jets moved to the runway.

When the second flight began its takeoff roll, Dunaev swung his flight away and headed east. The remaining flights in his squadron followed the same procedure: climb to a thousand feet, orbit the airfield briefly, and depart for the border. The MIGs didn't regroup into a larger formation; in the growing darkness it was easier to maneuver as separate flights and they wanted to create the best diversion they could. Once they reached the border it would all begin.

"Saint Laurent Control, this is Skyguard Lead. We're at 60,000 feet and approaching the border," said Bresson, as he watched the cursor on his HUD's altitude graph stop moving. "Can you give us a report on border activity?"

"Roger, Skyguard Lead. All anti-tank helicopters are now in their patrol areas. We have no activity along the border, but there are aircraft over Surinam's capital. They're too distant for us to tell what they are, but if they come east they'll be in effective radar coverage in a few minutes."

"For us it'll be quicker," said Bresson, reaching for the radar mode buttons above the main scope. "Skyguard Lead to squadron, switch your IVMs to track-while-scanning mode. Watch for low-altitude targets."

With the press of a button, Bresson changed the operating modes of his IVM radar from air-to-ground mapping to the more powerful track-while-scanning mode. The scope's image of the Guiana-Surinam border and the Maroni River which marked it changed little. What was new was the appearance of airborne targets, most of them on the French Guiana side. They were Gazelle anti-tank helicopters, moving slowly on their patrol routes and occasionally disappearing into the ground clutter.

"Skyguard Lead to flight, spread out for maximum radar effectiveness. Warn me the moment any of you

349

spot anything unusual. Arm your Magics and your 5-30s."

Since leaving Kourou, Bresson's Mirage F-1s had maintained a neat, closely spaced formation. At 60,000 feet the air was cold and clear, and the moon had risen early. They had more than enough light, and the pilots' visibility was excellent.

When Bresson gave his orders, the slim, high-winged fighters spread out gracefully, until their formation was more than two miles across. The other order had each pilot in the flight hit the arming switches on his weapons panel. The wing-tip-mounted pairs of infrared-guided Magics were activated, along with the much larger, radar-homing Super 5-30 D missiles attached to their underwing pylons.

Bresson repeated the same orders for the other two flights in his squadron. As they approached the border, they armed their weapons and began a passive search for hostiles. After less than a minute, he ordered the squadron to commence a gentle port turn. They would circle near the border until they made their rendezvous with the *Phoenix*.

"*Phoenix*, this is Houston. We have an update from Mount Cheyenne. One of the Hydras is moving ahead of its mate. General Rosen believes it's the infrared Hydra."

"He's probably right," said Cochran. "Harrison reports that the thermal tile sensors are already showing a temperature increase. Houston, how long before interception takes place?"

"First interception will be in two minutes, nine seconds. The second will be in two minutes, twenty-seven seconds."

"We'll be able to sweat that out. We've completed our entry attitude check and we're ready to inflate our G-suits."

"Roger, *Phoenix*. You're cleared to proceed."

350

"Stand-by, Paul. There'll be a real surge of pressure into the bladders," Cochran observed, reaching for a set of controls at the base of the center pedestal. "Activating system."

Cochran pressed the rocker switches for both his and Vachet's anti-gravity suits. The hoses running from the pedestal base to their suits became taut, as did the air bladders around their stomachs and legs. These were being filled with oxygen tapped from the life support system and would compensate for the G-force of gravity the commander and pilot would experience.

"Suit pressure levels are nominal," said Cochran. "Paul, how does yours feel?"

"It's pinching my groin," said Vachet, shifting uncomfortably in his seat. "But I think I can live with it."

"Good. Entering flight program Three-Zero-Four into GPC. CAP COM, this is *Phoenix*. Software transfer for atmospheric entry, completed."

"Roger, *Phoenix*. You are T minus thirty-five minutes to landing," Selisky advised. "Your velocity is 17,000 miles per hour, your altitude is 110 miles. Activate personal egress air packs. First interception will take place in one minute, twenty-eight seconds."

At 400,000 feet, the lead Vought was ejecting its first stage and igniting its second-stage Altair. The engine boosted the intercept vehicle through the last remnants of the atmosphere. It had escaped gravity, and for the next minute would increase velocity to maintain its sub-orbital track.

Thirty-five miles above the Vought, and nearly a hundred miles in front of it, was the *Phoenix*. Already the black tiles covering its undersides were heating up, and soon they would begin to glow. Even now they provided an excellent thermal target, but the infrared telescopes on the Vought ignored the shuttle. Their guidance system

351

had been programmed to track a much smaller target, one more than fifty miles behind it.

As the Vought passed under the shuttle its Altair burned out and was ejected. The intercept vehicle had achieved maximum velocity. It was only seconds away from the infrared-guided Hydra, which in turn was overtaking the *Phoenix*. The Hydra's thruster quads were firing almost continually, keeping the ASAT on course though the faint wisps of atmosphere slowed it and dragged it slightly off track.

The minute changes in speed and position made the Hydra a less than perfect target: they came so quickly and were so numerous that the Vought couldn't compensate for them all. It struck the Soviet ASAT a glancing blow instead of making a direct hit, and broke up instantly. The Hydra survived only a moment longer.

With one of its thruster quads obliterated, it started to tumble wildly; what remained of the guidance system knew it had no hope of regaining flight stability. It ordered a self-destruct, evaporating the Hydra in a blossom of flame and debris. The fireball burned for several seconds, long enough to attract the second Vought. When it died, the interceptor started to swing back to its original track, entering the debris cloud.

Most of the Hydra's remnants were tiny fragments of metal, plastic, and silicon chips. They were small, even when compared to the coffee-can-sized intercept vehicle, and they had no mass. They were like snowflakes, and bounced off the vehicle without causing damage. However, the Hydra's self-destruction had also created larger, denser fragments, and moments after entering the cloud, the Vought was hit by the remains of a lithium battery.

The jarring collision knocked it into a tumble, throwing the infrared telescopes off their target. Some of the jets in its thruster ring were damaged, and those still intact couldn't stabilize it in the final seconds before its programmed interception of the radar-guided Hydra. The

Vought flashed by its target, missing by several hundred yards. The people tracking the ASATs needed only a few moments to comprehend the failure—and their complete inability to do anything about it.

"My God, what the hell can we do now?" Ericson asked, watching the two lines on the main screen move past each other. "What about the reserve pair of F-15s?"

"They're sitting on the ground at Ramey," said Rosen. "I ordered them to stand down after the first pair had checked out. We have to tell Houston. Mary, how fast can you do one of your computer projections?"

"I'm on it," Widmark replied, breaking out of her shock and turning to her station's keyboard. "What do you want?"

"A projection on when the remaining Hydra will overtake the *Phoenix* and another on when the Hydra will burn up. It doesn't have a heat shield. Perhaps the *Phoenix* can outrun it."

"Your last request may give me some trouble. I don't think I have the data base to make an accurate projection."

"Anything is better than nothing, Captain," said Rosen, as he switched his headset to an outside line. "I'll let Houston know we've got big trouble."

Chapter Twenty

"*Phoenix*, this is Houston. Mount Cheyenne reports first interception successful. We're awaiting confirmation of the second. You are T minus thirty-one minutes to landing. Your altitude is eighty miles. Stand by for atmospheric interface."

"Roger, CAP COM. We've deployed our personal air packs and helmets," said Cochran, connecting the line from the air pack behind his seat to the helmet he was wearing. "The middle deck is ready and we're seeing reentry effects on the flight deck."

Visible in the lower corners of the cockpit windows was a dull red glow. The *Phoenix* had yet to hit the boundary layer between space and atmosphere, but already it was subject to the effects of atmospheric friction. Because of its nose-high attitude, the view out the cockpit was of space; the glow was only visible in the lower portion of the windows. In minutes the glow would become bright orange and fill the windows. The triple-paned windows themselves would become hot, almost too hot to touch, and the air temperature in the crew compartment would reach ninety degrees.

"Pilot to crew, thirty seconds to interface," Vachet advised, while Cochran was busy with Houston. "Julie, what's the readings on the tile sensors?"

"Readings go from 900 degrees on the nose and wing-leading edges to 400 degrees on the aft fuselage," said Julie, reading from a panel of LED displays to her right. "We have full thermal protection system integrity."

"Ten seconds to interface," said Cochran. For the moment the stream of commands from Selisky had abated. "You're handling this better. Any last thoughts, Saint Ex?"

"As I said before, I will miss this realm, this harsh and beckoning frontier," Vachet replied. "When I look at it from the safety of our cradle, it will be through different eyes."

"Here we go, interface."

Apart from Cochran's warning, the only immediate sign of the shuttle's entry into the atmosphere was the sudden dropping of the G-suit and personal air pack hoses. Soon, however, everyone could feel the return of gravity as a sudden increase in pressure. For the first few moments it made them feel uncomfortable, especially the

354

cosmonauts. Then, their bodies started to accept the natural force, though it would be some time before the passengers and crew of the *Phoenix* had readjusted both physically and psychologically to gravity.

"Remember, don't make any rapid head movements or you'll get dizzy," Cochran warned Vachet. "And concentrate on your instruments, don't listen to your inner perceptions."

"*Phoenix*, this is Houston. We've got a problem," said Selisky, his announcement breaking the long silence from mission control. "Mount Cheyenne reports the second interception did not take place. Its ASAT failed to make contact with the second Hydra."

"You mean it's still behind us?"

"It's still closing on you, Ed. We've got big problems."

"Don't give me this 'we' shit," Cochran snapped. "You're not up here, only my crew and my ship are. You're supposed to be coming up with ideas for us. Do you have any?"

"FIDO thinks you may have enough fuel in your OMS pods to attempt a return to orbit," Selisky advised.

"Out of the question, Houston. We're below atmospheric interface, and if we got back into orbit, what would we do for fuel and oxygen? You guys better have another idea."

"Mount Cheyenne thinks you can outrun the Hydra. Since it doesn't have a heat shield, it can't survive reentry."

"Your friend's right," said Vachet. "Reentry heating will eventually explode the Hydra's warhead. If we can stay ahead of it, we can escape it."

"FIDO, what's the minimum pitch angle an orbiter can take on reentry?" Cochran asked, after thinking for a moment.

"The range is thirty-eight to twenty-eight degrees," said Corrigan, sharing the CAP COM channel with Selisky.

"No, Bill. What's the *minimum* reentry attitude angle

355

my lady can take before she melts?"

"Twenty-four degrees. Wind tunnel tests have established that as the minimum reentry angle. But those were done with models, not attempted with full-scale vehicles. I can't predict what will happen. The decision is yours."

"Funny, I think you told me something similar at the start of this mission," said Cochran. "You're right, this is my decision. Thanks for the information, Bill. Paul, decrease reentry attitude to twenty-four degrees. CAP COM, I want constant updates on the Hydra, starting now."

"White Fox Five to White Fox Lead, one of my aircraft is reporting low thrust and high engine temperature. He requests permission to abort."

"Permission granted. Tell him to return immediately to Paramaribo," Dunaev ordered. "And he's not to declare an emergency until he's over the field. White Fox Lead, out."

Dunaev glanced to his right in an effort to see the fighter abort from the distant flight. Away from the lights of Paramaribo, the jungle and tropical savannah took on a velvety blackness. The terrain below was featureless. A broken cloud cover obscured the moon, resulting in little ambient light. For Dunaev, the brightest lights outside of his cockpit were the formation and anti-collision beacons on the other MIGs in his flight. Even though the second flight was twenty miles away, he still caught sight of an ascending cluster of lights and a spurt of flame; the stricken MIG-21 was using its afterburner to get the thrust its engine itself could not produce.

"Fox Three to White Fox Lead, the abort has probably cost us our cover," said the commander of the lead flight's other element. "The French must be seeing it."

"If they're not watching, they must be listening to us," Dunaev replied. "But it does not matter. We're almost to the border, and our gunships are deep inside French airspace. We'll begin climbing in moments. Keep the formation loose until then."

"General, I have a projection on when the ASAT will overtake the *Phoenix*," Widmark advised. "It's coming up on your monitor. The *Phoenix* may just have a chance."

"What chance? This shows it being destroyed just before it hits the blackout zone," said Rosen, studying the graph which appeared on his console monitor. It showed the reentry track of the Hydra overtaking that of the shuttle at 320,000 feet.

"That's if the closure and deceleration rates remain the same. If you'll check the main screen, you'll see that they're not."

Rosen glanced at the multi-story screen, where the changing numbers beside the shuttle and Hydra symbols indicated that their closure rate had slowed. The shuttle's velocity was holding steady at 16,800 miles per hour.

"The orbiter's reentry attitude is down to twenty-four degrees," said Rosen. "If it can maintain that without melting, our friends may just outrun the Hydra. How's the second projection coming, Mary?"

"I'm still working on it," she replied. "It'll be a couple of minutes yet."

"I'm afraid we don't have that time. Bill Corrigan needs the information to pass to the *Phoenix*. As Ed would say, right here and now we need an answer, any kind of an answer."

"God, what a difference a few degrees make," said Cochran, noticing the increase in turbulence the *Phoenix* was being subjected to. "Julie, what's the latest temperature readings?"

357

"Nose and leading edges are at fifteen hundred degrees," Julie answered. "The rest of the readings are cooler."

"We haven't even hit the LOS blackout layer yet, and already the carbon composites are halfway to their maximum heating level. How's the lady handling, Paul?"

"Like a Mirage 2000 in light turbulence," said Vachet, watching the pitch angle readout on his display screen. "One of my few advantages over Walt as pilot is that I'm very familiar with delta-winged aircraft."

"*Phoenix*, this is Houston. Mount Cheyenne reports the Hydra is now thirteen miles and closing. The rate has slowed, but you're still in danger. You are three minutes, forty-three seconds to loss of signal, and at the new rate the Hydra will overtake you in three minutes, twenty-seven seconds."

"I hope reentry heating will destroy it before then," Cochran noted. "You guys have any idea when it will happen? Our own temperature readings are far higher than normal."

"Mount Cheyenne says the ASAT is almost hot enough to glow," said Selisky. "However, they're still doing projections on when it will self-destruct."

"It looks like it's time for some seat-of-the-pants flying." As Cochran spoke, he glanced out the cockpit windows. The reentry glow, almost halfway up the windows, was changing to orange. Outside temperature was growing hot enough to ionize the surrounding air into an enveloping sheath of plasma. The sheath would develop at a predicted rate, the factors of which Cochran knew. In a few moments the information had raced through his mind and he had made his decision. "Paul, take her to twenty degrees."

"Ed, this is FIDO. You're taking her below mini-mums," said Corrigan, sharing the CAP COM channel with Selisky again.

"I know, but NASA engineers build safety limits even

358

into the minimums. I always said this ship was the best damn flying machine in the world, even when everyone else was calling her a white elephant. Now we're going to see who is right."

"Here they come, just where I expected they would," Bresson remarked, as groups of airborne targets flashed onto his radar scope. The flights of MIG-21s had finally climbed high enough to be separated from the ground clutter. "Skyguard Lead to Skyguard Three, switch your IVM to automatic tracking. Skyguard Two and Four, switch to high-altitude search and start watching for the shuttle."

"Skyguard Five to Skyguard Lead, my flight has detected hostile aircraft inside our airspace. We show a formation of three aircraft flying up one of the tributaries to the Maroni River. We believe they're helicopter gunships."

"Roger, Skyguard Five. Report your discovery to Saint Laurent Control immediately. Don't attempt to track the hostiles or contact the Gazelle flights on your own. Let Saint Laurent handle it. When you turn back for the border, switch your IVMs to automatic tracking."

"Skyguard Three to Skyguard Lead, my ECM is detecting Spin Scan emissions," said the commander of the lead flight's second element. "Though far too distant for an Atoll launch."

"They know where we are, and we know where they are," said Bresson, checking his own electronic counter-measures panel. "Let's hope they don't take it any further than this. I don't think our astronaut friends would like to descend into a dogfight."

"If not here, we might have one over Kourou. Are you sure one of our flights shouldn't intercept those gunships?"

"No, let the army handle them. If we don't put up a

formidable appearance to those MIGs, they might try t
take a chance, and the *Phoenix* will never make it t
Kourou."

From its pronounced, nose-high attitude the space
plane had pitched forward until it was almost level. Like
flat stone skipping across a lake, it skimmed through th
upper layers of the atmosphere, hardly losing any speed
The high temperatures had continued to build—alread
the shuttle's undersides were glowing, from dull red t
orange, and it hadn't even reached the blackout zone. A
envelope of plasma was slowly covering the *Phoenix*, an
trailing out behind it.

Moving inside the trail was the Hydra, its blunt nos
and the lower half of its body also glowing, even melting
But in spite of the incinerator-like temperatures, it
thrusters continued to operate, pushing it closer to th
descending spaceplane.

"*Phoenix*, the ASAT is four miles behind you an
you're one minute to loss of signal," Selisky reported.

"Thanks, CAP COM," said Cochran. "What the hell'
that thing made out of? Titanium? Our thermal reading
are still higher than normal, but we have full TP
integrity."

"This is like flying inside a neon tube," said Vachet. "
can hardly see anything of space."

"When the glow reaches the top of the windows, we'l
be inside the blackout layer. And then, we'll be on ou
own."

"*Phoenix*, you are forty seconds to loss of signal. The
ASAT is two point four miles behind you and still closing
Mount Cheyenne reports it is inside your ionization
trail."

"This is it. Right here and now we're going to find
out just how great this lady is," said Cochran, reaching
down with his left hand and stroking a section of the
cockpit's bulkhead by his seat. "C'mon, honey, don't

disappoint me."

A muffled thunderclap rumbled through the *Phoenix*, and Cochran felt the shuttle shudder unnaturally. It was unlike anything he had ever felt in an orbiter before. Barely two miles behind it, reentry heating had finally consumed the Hydra. Its warhead had reached ignition temperature, and the robot evaporated in a brief shower of flames, the violent reentry slipstream immediately quenching them.

"Boss, I think that was—" Post started to say.

"Yes, that was the ASAT," said Cochran. "Everyone, check your systems."

"Ed, we have a problem," Vachet warned, pointing to his cockpit side window. "Its outer pane is beginning to melt."

"So's mine." Cochran glanced to his left and found the outer pane softening and starting to wrinkle near the center. "Ease off, Paul. Return us to normal attitude. Houston, the Hydra has exploded and we're returning to a normal attitude."

A burst of fire from the vertical thrusters in the OMS pods pitched the shuttle's nose up, almost doubling its angle, returning it to its original reentry attitude.

"CAP COM, this is *Phoenix*. Do you read me? Tom . . . Oh shit," Cochran uttered, when he looked up and found the glow of the plasma envelope completely filling both the cockpit windows and the overhead skylights. "God, we're in it. The blackout layer. I can only wonder when the transmissions were cut, and what Houston heard before it happened."

"You can ask Houston in twelve minutes," said Vachet. "We should prepare to deactivate the RCS roll thrusters."

"Well, Harrison, where would you like the statue of your wife placed?" Reiss asked with a mixture of taunting and menace.

"Shut up, dickhead, leave him alone!" Reynolds shouted. "We don't know what kind of problem Vachet was talking about when we lost the feed. The *Phoenix* is still on track, it hasn't tumbled out of control. We'll find out in twelve minutes."

"We can't tell if anything's happened, mister. The ionization envelope has rendered our radar and infrared images of the orbiter fuzzy. We can't tell if we're tracking an intact vehicle or a close-flying formation of debris. Not until velocity slows and aerodynamic pressure is reduced will we know."

"Yes, and until then we're going to spend the longest twelve minutes of our lives," Harrison said, speaking for the first time since the blackout began.

"If we've lost the *Phoenix*, this will only be a foretaste of what the rest of your lives will be like," said Reiss, as he turned to face the astronauts in the launch center. "This is what you helped your friends to do. Now you can live with it."

"There, to the left," said Mayer, stopping his slow scans of the horizon with his night vision binoculars. "You see them?"

"Yes, I do," the gunner replied, turning his periscope sight in the direction Mayer had indicated.

"Then target the middle ship and fire. Piranha One to Piranha Two, Hinds to the left and climbing. We're taking the middle ship."

The two Gazelles rose slightly to clear the treetops and banked to the left. They advanced to full throttle, overtaking the trio of Hind gunships as they climbed out of a densely overgrown river valley. The ponderously large helicopters flew in a line-astern formation and without lights. Moving against a jungle background, they were invisible except to the night-vision binoculars and light-enhancement sights Mayer and his gunner used.

"I have a lock. Firing one," said the gunner, a flash of

362

light illuminating the Gazelle's cabin.

A blunt-tipped missile exploded from one of the tubes mounted on the helicopter's side. Trailing behind it was a set of wires through which its guidance commands were sent. All the gunner had to do was keep his cross hairs on target; the HOT system would do the rest.

"Pilot to gunner, keep scanning," Major Yurasov ordered, when he noticed the image on his television monitor had stopped moving. "We know the French have their tank killers up, Vitali."

"Flight engineer to pilot, missile launch to port!"

"Scorpion Lead to flight, we're under attack to port!"

The Hinds had just started responding to Yurasov's warning when the HOT missile slammed into the middle ship. Its hollow charge warhead detonated in the cabin behind the pilot and gunner's cockpits, first killing the flight engineer, then the other two crew members as a fireball consumed the gunship. The munitions and fuel it was carrying were still exploding when the Hind crashed into the jungle. Its leader climbed steeply and the other wingman swung to the left.

"Piranha Two, watch their chin turrets," Mayer warned. "Stay behind them if you can."

"Scorpion Three, guns and rockets only," said Yurasov. "Save the spirals for the shuttle."

The second Gazelle fired on the tail-end Hind while it was still turning. The burst of flame was the first warning to its crew that they were under attack. Before the pilot completed the turn, the gunner trained his sights on the French helicopter and squeezed the triggers. Located in the MIL-24's nose turret, the multi-barrelled machine gun sprayed a line of tracers at the Gazelle, forcing it to break off its attack.

For as long as he could, the Gazelle's gunner held his cross hairs on the Hind, and in spite of the launch aircraft's frantic maneuvering, the HOT missile kept on track. However, when the sight reached the travel limits of its mount, the lock was broken and the Soviet helicopter easily evaded the missile.

"He's turning! Fire if you've got a lock!" Mayer shouted.

In the first moments of the intercept, Yurasov's gunship had climbed almost a thousand feet before he swung it around. Without tail warning radar, he had no idea what he would discover behind him. He began launching rockets before he had a target in his sights, the pods under the sharply drooping wings ripple-firing their weapons at the rate of one per second.

The barrage surprised Mayer just as his gunner unleashed his second missile. For a few seconds it tracked straight for the Hind, until the stream of unguided rockets started flashing around the Gazelle. None of them came close, but they forced Mayer to gyrate his helicopter violently to avoid being hit, and the anti-tank missile shot under Yurasov's machine.

"Piranha One, this is Piranha Two! We're in trouble!"

Mayer ceased his wild maneuvers and levelled his ship; immediately catching sight of his wingman and the other MIL-24. It too was firing rockets and its chin turret in pursuit of the weaving Gazelle. The river the Hinds had climbed out of was now being used by Piranha Two to escape destruction.

"Target and fire!" Mayer told his gunner. "I'll watch for the other gunship."

He had barely swung his helicopter in the direction of the river when another burst of light illuminated its cockpit. A third blunt-tipped missile exploded out of its tube and dove into the river channel, rapidly overtaking the third MIL-24.

"Scorpion One to Scorpion Three, watch behind you!"

As Yurasov issued his warning he pulled his gunship out of its dive, then turned due east.

"Major, we must stay and help him," said the gunner. "In a few seconds we could have the Frenchman in range again."

"We don't have the time or the fuel for a protracted

364

dogfight," said Yurasov, giving his helicopter full throttle. "We have twenty minutes before the shuttle lands, and only one chance at it. Veshkin can handle the French by himself."

"Piranha One, I've been hit! I'm losing lateral control!"

A burst of gunfire from the Hind's chin turret had caught the wingman in his tail boom, damaging the control linkages and drive train for the tail rotor. Without its thrust to stabilize flight, the Gazelle slowed and began to spin. The Hind slowed as well, though not to watch its kill.

Yurasov's warning had just ended, and the gunship was turning to meet its new adversary, when the HOT missile from Mayer's Gazelle struck it above its starboard wing. The helicopter's fuselage was torn in two, the tail boom landing in the river an instant before the rest crashed down beside it.

The MIL-24 continued to burn even after it had landed in the water, and its funeral pyre was only a few hundred yards away from where the damaged Gazelle had spiralled in. Mayer swept over the wreckage of both and spun his machine around to face the remaining Hind only to discover it had vanished.

"Where the hell did it go?" Mayer asked, putting his Gazelle into a hover. "It can't be behind us, and it's not above us."

"I have it," said the gunner. "The 24 is disappearing into the foothills. Distance, seven kilometers."

"He's won. We'll never be able to overtake him. I'll let Kourou know that one got through. Stand by on the winch. Let's see if we can rescue our friends."

"Yes, thank you for the information," said Rosen, using one of the outside lines. "Houston is in touch with Kourou, but they're telling us little of what's happening there."

"I understand, my friend," Daurat replied. "We're linked to Kourou as well, but we're hearing little on the orbiter's condition. I was hoping you could tell us something."

"Of course. The *Phoenix* has passed its period of maximum heating. It's still on track, its altitude is thirty-eight miles, and its speed is 11,000 miles per hour. It will exit the blackout in less than three minutes."

"Thank you, General. We'll be talking again soon."

"So, you didn't tell the French either," said Ericson, when Rosen put the line to Toulouse on hold and hung up the receiver.

"Why bother? We'll find out soon enough if what we're seeing is the shuttle breaking up or not," said Rosen. "In all likelihood, the reentry track is growing indistinct because the *Phoenix* is moving beyond the effective range of our PAVE PAWS radar. Still, we can't be sure . . . None of us can be sure until we either hear Cochran's voice, or the pilots of those Mirage jets see something."

"Skyguard Lead, this is Kourou. At Houston's request we're patching your conversations through to them," said LaFont, temporarily overriding Saint Laurent control. "They claim you should be seeing the *Phoenix*."

"We have a high-altitude radar track," said Bresson. "Nothing visual, yet. All aircraft in my flight have switched to high-altitude search. The other flights will watch the MIGs."

Bresson glanced again at his ECM panel, where the alert light for Spin Scan, MIG-21 radar, was still flashing. Even though he was no longer tracking the MIGs, he knew they were out there, still flying on their side of the border and just outside radar-guided missile range.

"Houston can listen," LaFont continued. "But they can't talk to you."

"Good. The CNES people at your base have already

interrupted us enough times."

"I understand, Colonel. Civilians always ask too many questions. Kourou, out."

"Skyguard Four to Skyguard Lead, I still haven't spotted anything definite."

"All right, Duprée," said Bresson. "When we swing around you'll get a better view."

As the flight wheeled gently toward the border again, a target blip reappeared on Bresson's scope. It was the shuttle, still on course and still hundreds of miles away. It would be several minutes before the *Phoenix* dropped far enough to be seen visually. At night, without exterior lights, even Duprée would need the shuttle to come closer before sighting it.

"Skyguard Lead, I have it!" Duprée shouted soon after, pressing his binoculars against the top of his canopy bubble. "It's the shuttle, I can see it! It's glowing like a hot iron!"

Though it had passed its period of maximum heating eight minutes earlier, the entire underside of the *Phoenix* was still glowing a dull cherry red. There was no need for navigation or anti-collision lights.

"CAP COM, this is *Phoenix*. Sorry for the delay," said Cochran. "We're exiting the blackout layer. We've deactivated the RCS pitch and roll thrusters."

"Roger, *Phoenix*. We copy," Selisky managed to say calmly, while everyone around him broke into a wild cheer the shuttle crew could hear. "Your altitude is 180,000 feet. Your speed is 8,300 miles per hour, and you're 500 miles from Kourou."

"Roger, Houston. While you guys finish celebrating, we'll commence the roll reversal."

Vachet pressed his joystick grip to the right and the *Phoenix* responded by sliding into a gentle starboard turn. The maneuver was the first in a series of roll reversals designed to bleed off the shuttle's velocity without using much distance. Though it had just crossed the Venezuelan-Guiana border, in less than three minutes it would be at the Surinam-French Guiana border, and by then it would have to reduce its airspeed to approximately 2,000 miles per hour.

"Skyguard Lead to flight, stand by to jettison tanks," Bresson ordered. "Prepare to go to afterburner. Skyguard Lead to Skyguard Five, what's happening with our friends?"

"They're still patrolling in separate flights at 50,000 feet," said the leader of the second Mirage flight. "But there's heavy radio traffic between them and Paramaribo."

"They must be talking about the shuttle. Skyguard Five, you're now responsible for border defence. If our friends create any trouble, destroy them at once. Don't wait for permission to fire from Saint Laurent. Skyguard Lead, out."

"Preparing for second roll reversal," said Vachet. "Move speed brake to one hundred percent."

"Roger, moving speed brake," Cochran repeated, grabbing hold of his throttle lever.

The spaceplane's rudder split open and spread forward, jarring the ship as it extended into the slipstream. Coupled with Vachet swinging the *Phoenix* over to port, the speed brake cut velocity drastically. By the time it was over the middle of Surinam, the shuttle was down to less than half its former airspeed.

"How long before the spaceship lands?" LaFont asked, looking over the shoulder of a radar technician.

"Six minutes, forty-one seconds, and counting," said the CNES operations officer. "Everything looks nominal."

"Then it's time to let the Russians know officially what we're doing. Advise teleciné center to begin transmissions to Paris. They'll relay it to Moscow. It's already morning there, so someone in authority must be awake to see this crisis end."

*   *   *

"Skyguard Lead to flight. Jettison tanks, and execute turn."

The belly tank each Mirage carried fell from their pylons as they swung to the right. After patrolling the border for half an hour, they were now heading away from it.

"Skyguard Lead to flight, go to afterburner."

At Bresson's command, the four F-1s dumped fuel into the chambers behind their Atar engines. The plumes of fire they emitted would push them to supersonic speed in less than a minute. They were also visible for miles, to the MIG-21s on the other side of the border, and even to the *Phoenix.*

"Moving speed brake to sixty-five percent," said Cochran, chopping back his throttle. "Deploying air data probes."

"Ed, I think I've spotted our escorts," Vachet advised. "To the right and down."

"Oh yes, I see them. How fast are those jets?"

"The Mirage F-1 can sustain Mach 2.2."

"Then they won't remain in front of us for long," said Cochran, checking the probe readings. "Our speed is still in the region of Mach 3.8. Prepare for last roll reversal, and follow the descent trajectory on your CRT. We have to hit the heading alignment cylinders perfectly."

The *Phoenix* crossed the border at 90,000 feet, half the altitude from the point where it left the blackout layer. Most of the reentry heat had dissipated and its undersides no longer glowed, though they were still too hot to touch. The shuttle was down to a third of its former velocity; even so it was still flying more than a thousand miles an hour faster than an artillery shell. In less than a minute, it would overtake the jets six miles below it, then enter the landing pattern for the spaceport.

"Kourou Approach Control, this is Houston. The orbiter is approaching Waypoint One," said Selisky.

"We're handing control for the final reentry phase over to you. Good luck."

"Thank you, NASA. We'll contact them immediately," said the operations officer. "General, I need not tell you that these next few minutes . . ."

"I understand completely," LaFont replied. "I'll notify airfield defences. They'll be on full alert."

"Skyguard Four to Skyguard Lead, I've reacquired the shuttle. It must be doing at least Mach 3."

"Yes, I have it as well," said Bresson, glancing at his radarscope. "Don't worry, by the time it reaches our altitude it'll be slow enough for us to catch."

The *Phoenix*, now more than forty miles ahead of its escorting fighters, was S-turning one last time before reaching the heading alignment cylinders, two side-by-side columns 18,000 feet in diameter which were positioned at the end of Kourou's .main runway. The shuttle would spiral down one of them, reducing its velocity until it had the proper approach speed and was ready to intercept the auto land glideslope.

"*Phoenix*, this is Kourou Approach Control. You're at Waypoint One, are you ready to make cylinder selection?"

"Roger, Kourou. We're selecting the starboard cylinder," Cochran answered, as Vachet pushed his joystick to the right. "We're beginning terminal area energy management interface."

For the last few minutes of its reentry, the shuttle would receive information from Kourou's microwave landing system. The data was shown on both the cockpit's CRT display screens and the head-up displays. It allowed Cochran and Vachet to use the speed brake and other flight surfaces to carefully bleed off airspeed and keep the *Phoenix* on its ideal trajectory.

"Deactivating RCS yaw thrusters," said Cochran. "Rudder is now active. Where are these escorts of ours, Saint Ex? We're below 60,000 feet and below Mach 2."

370

"They'll be here, I saw them when we entered the cylinder," said Vachet, glancing through his side window. "In fact, you'll hear from them at any moment."

"*Phoenix*, this is Skyguard Lead. My flight is overtaking you. I'm approaching you on your port side," Bresson informed them. "Welcome to Kourou."

With the *Phoenix* travelling under Mach 2, the Mirage F-1s no longer needed their afterburners and shut them down. The flight split into its elements and coasted into position on the shuttle's wing tips. By craning his neck as far to the left as he could, Cochran finally spotted the two high-winged fighters. Their cockpit lighting was at maximum brightness and he could see their pilots, even noticed them waving.

"Kourou, this is *Phoenix*. We've just received the official welcome from your escorts," said Cochran. "We're in the cylinder and we're nominal to profile. Five by five."

"Roger, *Phoenix*. We copy. Your airspeed is now Mach 1, your altitude 45,000 feet. You are T minus two minutes, fifty seconds to landing."

Seconds later, and for the first time since the initial moments of its lift-off, the *Phoenix* was moving at subsonic speed. It continued its rapid, spiralling descent toward Kourou, a bright ganglia of light set against a black background. The orbiter runway was a ribbon of illumination, its rows of beacons flashing at either end. Around the spaceport moved tiny clusters of red and white lights, the Alouette 3 helicopters on patrol. All aircraft in the Kourou area had been ordered to fly with the exterior lights on, and all obeyed. Except one.

"Damn, I can't raise any aircraft from the other flights," said Yurasov, switching his radio back to "receive only" mode. "They must have turned back, or been intercepted."

"Then we must be it," said the gunner. "And we're in the perfect position. I've armed the Spirals, but I have

371

trouble following the shuttle. The escorts are brighter than it is."

"Switch to infrared. The shuttle will still be hot from its reentry. Advise when it's in missile range."

Flying slowly, at less than thirty miles an hour, the Hind maneuvered out of the foothills and across the Kourou savannah, carefully following the terrain and staying low. It was below radar, flying so close to the jungle canopy that the treetops swayed in its rotorwash.

"Kourou, this is *Phoenix*. We're approaching runway entry point," Cochran reported. "We've acquired auto land guidance."

"Roger, *Phoenix*. You are T minus two minutes to landing. You need not acknowledge any further transmissions."

"Just like the simulations," said Vachet, watching the auto land data appear on his HUD. "But I wish I had flown this for real, just once. It would make it feel more normal."

The *Phoenix* left the heading alignment cylinder at just over 13,000 feet, hitting the runway entry point perfectly. Seven and a half miles ahead of it lay the orbiter landing strip. Vachet pitched the shuttle into the glideslope angle indicated by his HUD for his approach to it.

As the shuttle's speed fell below 400 miles per hour, the wingmen of the escort flight pulled ahead. They would overfly the strip before the *Phoenix* reached it, while Bresson and the other element leader stayed with the spaceplane.

"I'm tracking the shuttle on infrared," said the gunner. "And laser ranging has locked onto it."

"I'll put us in the proper firing attitude," said Yurasov. "Put all Spirals on line. This is our only chance."

Yurasov raised the gunship above the treetops and slowed it to a hover. He pitched its nose up to give the laser designator the widest possible tracking field, and

372

could see from his cockpit displays that his gunner did indeed have a lock. All four anti-tank missiles would be fired. He was already making plans for his escape when the MIL-24 shuddered violently.

Its nose pitched farther up, and then the machine was spun to the left, battered by more explosions. Flashes of light filled the cockpits. The explosions and a boiling surge of heat were the last things Yurasov experienced before his aircraft disintegrated around him. Detonation of its weapons and fuel completed the Hind's destruction. Its furiously burning remains took only moments to crash into the jungle below. Even so, debris was still falling when an Alouette 3 arrived on the scene, its sixty-eight millimeter rocket pods empty.

"*Phoenix*, you are T minus thirty seconds to landing. Begin preflare."

"Adjusting glideslope to one point five degrees," said Vachet, trying to smoothly work his joystick and rudder pedals in coordinated movements. "I want full speed brake."

"You got it," Cochran replied, pulling the throttle lever to its backstops. "Altitude, 1,900 feet."

Vachet reduced the shuttle's glideslope angle by ninety percent, and for the last half minute of its flight it sank gently toward the landing strip. The remaining Mirage F-1s were still sitting on its wing tips, though they had opened their own speed brakes in order to maintain formation.

"Landing gear, armed and ready," said Cochran. "Altitude, 135 feet."

"*Phoenix*, you are T minus fourteen seconds to landing."

"Deploy landing gear," said Vachet, pulling the joystick back to raise the spaceplane's nose.

"Altitude, ninety feet. Landing gear, down."

Cochran lifted a guard plate beside the arming control and pressed the button under it. As the *Phoenix* whistled over the approach beacons, its nose gear and sets of main gear snapped out of their wells and locked in place. The additional drag they created dropped the shuttle's speed below 300 miles an hour. It was losing lift rapidly and, in seconds, would stall if it didn't land first.

"*Phoenix*, your main gear is at ten feet. Nine feet . . ."

Vachet held the shuttle in a perfect, nose-high attitude and held his breath until he felt a solid jolt ripple through the airframe. Barely 1,000 feet down the runway the main gear touched the concrete, releasing tiny clouds of smoke which almost glowed in the perimeter lights. Vachet kept the nose up for a few seconds longer allowing deceleration to lower it.

"*Phoenix*, your nose gear is at three feet. Two feet. Contact. *Phoenix*, you are down."

"Roger, Kourou. We copy," said Cochran, finally breaking the silence with the spaceport. "Go easy on the brakes, Paul. We have a mile and a half of runway to use."

At the same moment the nose wheels made contact, the Mirage escorts retracted their speed brakes and leading edge flaps. They surged ahead of the *Phoenix*, climbing to join their wing men and form a Combat Air Patrol over Kourou. From the tarmac a pair of Puma helicopters lifted off, while a convoy of French and American vehicles proceeded down one of the taxiways. Both formations had a common destination: the *Phoenix*, which had now passed the runway's midpoint.

With each application of its brakes, the shuttle's landing gear emitted puffs of smoke, and the ship itself had started tracking to one side. A combination of rudder and nose wheel steering brought it back on the centerline, in time for the brakes to be applied again. For the last few hundred feet, Cochran and Vachet let the *Phoenix* roll to a halt on her own momentum. Even so, the main landing gear wheels still let off smoke as they continued to burn from the heat the brakes had built up.

For a few moments the spaceplane sat alone on the vast ribbon of concrete, until the Pumas arrived. They

374

hovered a few dozen feet over it and churned the air with their rotorwash to dissipate any stray leaks of hydrazine or tetroxide from the OMS pods. In a minute they would be joined by the convoy. But first there were procedures the shuttle crew had to perform.

"Harrison, do a complete check on our payload," Cochran ordered. "Walt, I can hear them cheering, but go see what else they're doing on the middle deck."

"Clearing ET and SRB separation systems," said Vachet, pressing the buttons on the external tank and solid rocket booster control panels. "APU auto shutdown, enabled."

"G-suit pressure system, off." Cochran tapped the rocker switches at the base of the center pedestal, releasing the air in the anti-gravity suits he and Vachet wore. For the first time in almost an hour, they could move comfortably.

While the cockpit team finished the deactivation of the orbiter's systems, Post and Harrison climbed out of their seats. After standing up, they needed a moment to make their initial readjustment to moving around in gravity. Harrison easily turned and bent over the satellite control panels, but Post had to quite deliberately step over to the floor hatch, then remember to use the ladder to reach the middle deck.

"Well, Saint Ex, we're home," said Cochran, when he was finished with all his shutdown procedures.

"No, we're back where we feel safe and comfortable," Vachet answered. "We've returned to the cradle. And I must admit that even I feel less nervous here."

"Somehow I knew you'd say that."

"Commander, the Orbital Pharmaceutical Factory is still stable," Harisson reported. "Internal power will keep it so for about an hour."

"Boss, the convoy's arrived," said Post, reappearing in the floor hatch. "We'll get external power soon. There's a staff car in the convoy and Pellerin says a general's in it."

"Sounds like we're getting the official welcome," said Cochran. "Thanks, Julie. Let's go and see what awaits us."

Cautiously at first, Cochran and Vachet unstrapped and eased out of their seats. They followed Harrison through the hatch, climbing down the ladder attached to the airlock chamber instead of floating from one deck to the other. On the middle deck, they were greeted by Grachenko and the other cosmonauts; even Kostilev wrapped his one good arm around them.

"My friends, we have made history," said Grachenko, emotion cracking his voice.

"Yes, and now we're going to find out how everyone else has judged our actions," Cochran replied. "George, open the hatch."

Pellerin stepped back from the shuttle's main hatch, where he'd been using the observation window to watch the convoy's arrival, and pulled with him the sealing lever. A loud hiss filled the middle deck as he broke the pressure seal. Ripley helped Pellerin with the locking latches, then together they pushed out the 300-pound hatch and gently lowered it.

There was a slight, inward rush of air when it first opened. Unlike the scrubbed, temperature and humidity controlled atmosphere inside the shuttle, this was hot, damp, air with the strong scent of the nearby ocean. To the *Phoenix* crew, and especially the cosmonauts, it was the most wonderful thing they had smelled in a long time.

"Commander Cochran? I am General Charles LaFont," said the officer standing below the hatch. "As military commander I welcome you, your passengers and crew to Kourou, French Guiana."

"Thank you, General. You don't know how happy we are for this crisis to be over," said Cochran. "Where are the CNES people? Why aren't they with you?"

"Because this crisis isn't quite over. They're in a long-distance conference with NASA officials. They're trying to come up with an explanation of your actions, one you're to read to the television cameras. Your landing was broadcast live to Europe, North America, and even Moscow. NASA, CNES, and most especially Washington and Paris, want to put out the official version of your rescue mission. But if you hurry, you can tell the truth before the meeting ends."

"What exactly do you mean?"

"The cameras are still transmitting, Commander," LaFont explained. "I'm told the arrangement with Moscow is that they'll continue to transmit until your passengers leave your ship. How long would it take for it to be towed in?"

"Normally, post flight takes twenty-seven minutes," said Cochran. "Though it has been done in as little as fifteen."

"Then I suggest you hurry the procedures, and decide among you who'll be your spokesman. No matter how well intentioned, a bureaucracy will not have an individual's wishes in mind. While it's not official policy, I believe those who risked their lives know best why they did it. Good luck."

"Moscow wants to make sure all three of us are alive and that no deceptions are tried," said Siprinoff, after LaFont had left and Cochran had stepped back from the main hatch.

"Yes, and we can use that to our advantage," Cochran observed. "What LaFont said is true. NASA, and almost everyone else, will try to stage manage us. But if we act fast, we can explain what we did in our own words. Not read from a prepared script, or have what we say reinterpreted by officials, or questioned by reporters."

"And there's not likely to be many here," Pellerin added. "Only a few staff reporters to cover the *Hermes* tests."

"So, we've got an opportunity we can't pass up. And I think I know who should be our spokesman."

"You mean the man who wrote this?" Grachenko asked, returning to his bunk and pulling out of it a sheaf of papers. "I believe you may be right."

"Now just wait. I would need hours to write a speech explaining what we did and why we did it," said Vachet, defensively. "We only have minutes. Ed, you saw how long it took me to write what I read at our press conference. And besides, I'm not the one who should read it."

"But everything you need is already in here. All you need do is select and adapt."

"Yes, I could do what you say." Vachet accepted the overstuffed folder from Grachenko, and began looking through it. "But I'm still not the one who should be our spokesman."

"You're the most eloquent speaker on this ship," said Cochran. "If not you, then who?"

"You're the *commander* of this ship," said Vachet. "It's your responsibility to be our spokesman."

"Me? How can I do it?" Now it was Cochran's turn to be defensive. "I don't like reporters. And why is it my responsibility?"

"Because it is. Throughout this mission, you've managed to spread the responsibility for it among us. Now, as our commander, you must step forward and represent all of us."

"As a fellow spacecraft commander, I believe what he's saying is true," Grachenko added. "From what your crew told me, you originated the plan to rescue us. You are the best one to explain it to what may be a harsh and critical world."

"All right, we're wasting time," said Cochran. "Since you're all in agreement, I'll do it. But I want you to write my speech, Paul. I know you need solitude, so the flight deck is yours. We'll do the post-flight procedures from here. When you come back, I want the Gettysburg Address of space exploration."

"Doctor, the shuttle is moving. I thought you claimed

378

it wouldn't be towed in for several more minutes?" Nagorny questioned, when the bank of monitor screens he was watching showed the *Phoenix* being swung onto a taxiway.

"The Americans and French must be changing their operation," said Fedarenko, briefly interrupting his telephone conversation. "Baikonur has also noticed it. They think the operation's being rushed because American television finds this wait boring."

"Whatever the reason, it throws our schedule off," said Grachenko, glancing at the television center's wall clock. "The premier is still en route. It's likely our men will appear before he arrives. And Gussarov did want to see it live."

"I'm afraid he will have to view a playback of it, Nikolai," Nagorny remarked. "Like the rest of our countrymen."

"Then someone will have to tell him."

"Since you called him last, I guess it's my turn." Nagorny turned and started to scan the center for an unused telephone. "Even at the end of this crisis, I'm still the one who calls Gussarov with the bad news."

With a tug attached to its nose gear, and the auxiliary power truck hooked to its tail, the *Phoenix* rolled off the orbiter landing strip and onto the nearest taxiway. While a Puma helicopter remained over it, CNES support vehicles and French Army armored cars rounded out the convoy escorting the shuttle to the spot on the tarmac where the boarding ramp and TV cameras awaited it.

Except to occasionally use the radios, or check the OPF satellite, none of the crew came onto the spaceplane's flight deck. They gave Vachet as much solitude as was possible, and in fact, he did not know that the *Phoenix* had arrived until he felt the boarding ramp being pushed against its side.

"Your Gettysburg Address," said Vachet, handing

379

Cochran a slim folder as he stepped off the ladder to the flight deck. "I hope you can read it as well as my directions."

"Yes, I should be able to," Cochran finally replied, after he looked through the different sheets of paper, and the notes printed on them. "Thanks, Saint Ex. It looks like Pellerin was right, there aren't many reporters. That should make it easier for me. LaFont is having wheelchairs brought up for the Russians. We'll bring them off first, then we'll go before the cameras."

Cochran and Vachet stepped onto the boarding ramp when the medical teams appeared and helped carry the Russians down to the wheelchairs. Except for the clicking of still cameras and the whir of video ones, the press group remained silent. Not a question was asked, not even when Cochran walked up to the podium and adjusted the microphones.

"I am Edward Alger Cochran, commander of the United States spacecraft *Phoenix* and leader of the rescue mission that saved the men you see behind me," he began, laying the folder on the podium and opening it. "Tonight, we commemorate both tragedy and triumph. We bear witness to the disasters our technology can create, and the miracles it can achieve. In the midst of our success in saving these men, we remember the one we could not save. In earlier ages of voyaging, during burial ceremonies they would say, 'We look forward to the day of resurrection, when the sea will give up its dead.' On that day I don't know if space will give up its dead but if it does, the name of Colonel Frederick Andreivich Poplavsky will be first on the list.

"We will not forget his courage, or the ideals he lived for, but he didn't die for them, or for his country. He's not a martyr, nor will he be remembered that way. He was a professional who knew that for every advance, there's a risk of failure. His crew mates knew it as well. And when we looked at them, we saw them not as Soviets, but as

380

fellow professionals. On the shores of the final frontier, whether we are called star voyagers or sailors of the cosmos, we are in essence the same.

"We know what we did was illegal, against the express orders of both countries. But we couldn't just sit and watch fellow professionals die because of national paranoia, and national pride. My crew and I chose not to remain in the pit of man's fear and ignorance, but to reach for the summit of his courage and vision. Beyond the rescue of three men, we hope what we've done is seen as something greater. We know it will not change the way our nations look at each other; no single act can do that. But in the face of tragedy, we hope what we've done shows humanity can still triumph, if we continue.

"Six years ago, in the wake of a greater space disaster, my country's former president told us that 'nothing ends here.' Tonight, in both tragedy and triumph, we remember those words, remember their eloquence, and repeat them. Nothing ends here. We must remember that man achieves nothing by being timid, that to continue is not folly but a reaffirmation of our true spirit. Man, the builder. Man, the explorer. Man, the challenger. We betray our callings, all that we are, if we accept failure and give up.

"After more than thirty years of voyaging beyond the thin blue veil which surrounds our world, we are still only beginning, still only testing the shores of the final frontier. When and where the voyaging will end, I cannot tell you. But it will not end tomorrow, or even after a thousand tomorrows. When we touch the first planet outside of our own, we will still be beginning. When we reach the first star beyond our sun, we will still be beginning. And even when we've learned all the mysteries of time and space and all that space contains, we will still be only beginning. It is for this future, as much as any other reason, that we did what we did. We can only hope you understand. Man's destiny is greater than the confines of this cradle we call Earth. Our home is where our courage and vision leads us—man's destiny is the stars."

"NASA Nine-Zero-Five, this is Kennedy Traffic Control. You're cleared for final approach. You need only acknowledge when you're down and report to Ground Control. We've got one hell of a reception waiting for you, and Director Cochran advises you're a little late for it."

Piggybacked on a 747 carrier aircraft, the *Phoenix* returned to Cape Canaveral the same way it had landed at Kourou, in an enveloping blanket of darkness. The shuttle-carrier combination touched down on the space center's orbiter landing strip, not far from where the voyage had begun. Halfway down, the strip rows of floodlights were snapped on, washing away the night. Most illuminated the *Phoenix* and its carrier, while others swept the massive crowds which had gathered for its return.

As the two aircraft swung onto the end taxiway, the fireworks were started. At first they exploded in the distance, providing the *Phoenix* with a glittering backdrop to its arrival. Later, when it had reached the arena formed by the VIP grandstands and the 747's engines were safely shutdown, the fireworks would burst overhead.

For his first official act as NASA's director of manned flight operations, Cochran presided over the return of his lady. Vachet and the rest of her crew were also there to greet her, as were the leaders of France and the United States, together with representatives from the Soviet Union. All the speeches they made, and all the awards they handed out made the same acknowledgment: the ordeal was over. All those who had flown on her had returned safely, her voyage was at last a triumph. The stain of her unfortunate baptism had been washed away. The *Phoenix* was a jinxed ship no more.

382

STOCKHOLM, Sweden   October 26, 1992

Today, the Royal Swedish Academy of Sciences has announced that the Nobel Peace Prize has been awarded to the following people: Director and Shuttle Commander Edward A. Cochran, Pilot Walter Post, Mission Specialist Julie Harrison, Mission Specialist Jack Ripley, Senior Pilot Paul Vachet, Mission Specialist George Pellerin, and Mission Specialist Renée Simon, the crew of Mission 81L, the *Phoenix*, and to Spacecraft Commander Arkady Grachenko, Major Vassili Kostilev, and Major Stefan Siprinoff, the crew of the *Soyuz 71*.

NASA, CNES, and Glavkosmos have already advised the Nobel Committee that their personnel will attend the award ceremony early next year. Because his latest work has not been published in time for consideration, Paul Vachet wasn't nominated for this year's literature prize. However, it is expected that he will be nominated in 1993 for his book, *Future Flight, Future Man*.

THE CHALLENGER'S LAST TRANSMISSION
by Paul Vachet
(From his book, *Future Flight, Future Man*)

Give us this endless sky,
This endless night,
And ships worthy enough to sail it,
And we will unlock mysteries
That are beyond your comprehension.
Understand that the dreams and visions we shared,
Are the visions of Future Man.
Do not mourn our loss,
For we have touched the future.
And we know
That what we have dreamed
Will one day come to be.